Pocket Books

Books by Kasey Michaels

The Legacy of the Rose
The Bride of the Unicorn
A Masquerade in the Moonlight
The Illusions of Love
The Secrets of the Heart

Published by POCKET BOOKS

KASEY MICHAELS

the SECRETS of THE HEART

POCKET BOOKS

New York   London   Toronto   Sydney   Tokyo   Singapore

An *Original* Publication of POCKET BOOKS

POCKET BOOKS, a division of Simon & Schuster Inc.
1230 Avenue of the Americas, New York, NY 10020

Copyright © 1995 by Kathryn Seidick

ISBN: 0-671-79341-1

First Pocket Books printing February 1995

10 9 8 7 6 5 4 3 2 1

POCKET and colophon are registered trademarks of
Simon & Schuster Inc.

Cover art by Mitzura Salgian

Printed in the U.S.A.

To Frank Shipman,
a true Renaissance man!

I never could believe that Providence had sent a few men into the world, ready booted and spurred to ride, and millions ready saddled and bridled to be ridden.

Richard Rumbold
(on the scaffold, England, 1685)

PROLOGUE

A SIMPLE VOLLEY

─ ∼ ─

I vow, I love the game, for this is the finest sport I have yet encountered. Hair-breadth escapes . . . the devil's own risks! Tally ho — and away we go!

Baroness Orczy

Once more into the breach,
dear friends, once more!

William Shakespeare

Just shortly before ten of the clock, Herbert Symington bade his host and hostess a pleasant good night and rather drunkenly tripped down the stairs toward the impressively designed if a tad overly ornate coach and four that was his latest acquisition and one of which he was enormously proud.

It was a grand time to be alive, Herbert Symington truly believed. An Englishman with his wits about him could make a tidy profit from the cheap labor filtering in to Little Pillington. Independent weavers put out of business by the big new mills had lost their livings and would work from before dawn to past dusk for a few shillings a week in order to feed their families.

"Take me home, coachie," Symington commanded, giving a sweeping wave to his driver and a drunken kick to the groom, who didn't move fast enough in lowering the steps to the coach to suit his master.

"Lazy jackanapes, I ought to sack you," he muttered under his liquor-sour breath, pulling himself into the coach and collapsing heavily against the velvet squabs as the coachman prematurely gave the horses their office to start.

"Stupid oafs, the lot of them," Symington grumbled into his gravy-stained cravat as he adjusted his considerable girth more comfortably.

And then he blinked—twice, just to be certain—and peered inquiringly into the semidarkness. "Who's there?" he asked, leaning forward to address the vague shape he believed he saw sitting cross-legged on the facing seat. "God's eyebrows, am I in the wrong coach? That'll teach me to steer clear of the daffy. Speak up, man—say something!"

The click and scrape of a small tinderbox answered him, followed by the sight of the growing, disembodied glow of the business end of a cheroot.

"Good evening, Herbert, you're looking well," a low, well-modulated voice answered him at last. "And how charitable of you to share your coach with me. Well sprung, I must say, and doubtless cost you a pretty penny. Enjoy yourself at the trough tonight?"

Symington swallowed down hard at the sudden lump of fear that had lodged in his throat. "What the devil? Who are you? *Coachie!*" he bellowed. "Stop at once!"

"Please, good sir, lower your voice," the unknown intruder pleaded as the coach raced on through the night, bypassing the turn to the right that would have led to Symington's house and rapidly leaving the dark streets of Little Pillington behind. "The confines of this coach preclude such full-throated volume. Besides, as your coachman and groom have seen fit to leave your employ and join mine—no loyalty in today's topsy-turvy times, is there, Herbert?—I fear I must point out the fruitlessness of further protest. And, to be sporting, I should also advise you that I am armed, my pistol cocked and aimed directly at your ample stomach. Therefore, as any sudden movement might cause the nasty thing to go off, you most probably would be well advised to remain quietly in your seat."

"The devil you say!" Symington's gin-bleared eyes were fairly popping from his head now as a fragrant, blue-tinged cloud of cigar smoke wreathed the shadowy figure from chest to curly-brimmed beaver. "You —*your* coachie, you say? Am I being kidnapped, then?"

An amused chuckle emanated from the shadowy figure. "Hardly, Herbert. Kidnapping you would indicate that I believed you had some sort of intrinsic worth. I am here this evening merely to request a boon of you."

"A—a *boon?*" Symington repeated, automatically holding out his hand to take the neatly rolled and tied sheet of paper the stranger was now offering him. "And what is this?" he asked, holding the paper gingerly, as if it might somehow turn on him and bite his fingers.

Another blue cloud of smoke issued from between the stranger's lips, blowing across the coach to accost Symington's nostrils. "Yes, it is dark in here for reading, isn't it? You do read, don't you, Herbert? Very well, I shall attempt to recall the salient points. Let's see. First, you are to immediately cease and desist employing persons under the age of ten in your mills."

"What?"

"Hush, Herbert, as it is not your turn to speak.

5

Second, you will oblige me in setting up schools for these children, keeping them occupied while their mothers are at work. You will also feed these children one meal a day—even on Sunday, when henceforth no one will work the Symington mills—with meat served to the children twice weekly."

Symington's ample belly shook as he began to laugh. He laughed so heartily, and with such enjoyment, that soon tears streamed from his eyes. "Are you daft?" he choked out between bouts of mirth. "Why would I do that?"

"I do not believe I had finished, Herbert," the stranger said quietly once Symington's hilarity subsided, which it did when he remembered the cocked pistol. "You will roll back the laborers' shifts from fifteen to fourteen hours and present every worker with a mug of beer at the end of each shift. You will employ a doctor for your workers. You will also increase all wages by ten percent, beginning tomorrow. I think that's it—for now."

The cocked pistol was no longer of any importance, for this man, this arrogant stranger, was talking of dipping into Herbert Symington's pockets, the depth of which were more important to him than his own soul, let alone his corpulent corporeal body. "The devil I will! Coddle the bastards? Fill their bellies? *And* cut their hours? How am I supposed to make a profit?"

"Ah, Herbert, but you do make a profit. A tidy profit. Enough profit to afford this coach, and that most lovely new domicile you have been building for yourself this past year. You're to move into it early next month, I believe, and have even gone so far as to invite a few of the *ton* to join you in a party to celebrate your skewed belief that fortune and breeding

6

are synonymous. I'm delighted for you, truly. Although I would not have chosen to use so much gilt in the foyer. Such ostentation smacks of the climbing cit which, alas, you are. You know, Herbert, I believe I detest you more for your mistreatment of your workers because you were one of them not so long ago."

"Who are you to judge me?" Symington bellowed, not caring that his voice echoed inside the coach. This man had seen his house, been inside his house? How? But if he had been, then he should know how far Herbert Symington had come since his long-ago years in the Midlands. "Yes, I was one of them, never so bad as the worst of them, better than the best of them. Smarter. More willing to see what I needed and take it!"

"Yes, Herbert. You did. But you chose to make that steep climb on the broken backs of your fellow workers, screwing down their wages, damning them to damp hovels, disease, and crippling injuries," his accuser broke in neatly. "And now you call them the swinish multitude and keep your heel on their throats so that no one else might have the opportunity for betterment that you had. Do you have any idea of the hatred you are fomenting with your tactics? You, and all those like you, are creating a separate society, a generation of brutalized workers turned savage in their fear, their hunger, their—but enough of sermonizing. We are nearly at our destination, Herbert, as your monument to your greed lies just around this corner, I believe. Observe. Soon you will be toasting your toes by your own fireside."

As the stranger used the barrel of his pistol to push back the ornate lace curtain covering the nearest window of the now slowing coach, Herbert Symington looked out to see his nearly completed house, his pride, his proof of affluence, engulfed in flames from portico to rooftops.

"No," he whispered, shaking his head, unable to believe the horror he saw. His house. His beautiful house! "Oh, sweet Christ! *No!*"

"The paper, Herbert," the stranger said, coldly interrupting Symington's anguish. "Don't crush it so, or you might not be able to read my demands, for shock has a way of erasing recently learned specifics from one's mind. What I have offered you tonight is in the way of a small exercise in consequences. In addition to the home you still inhabit in Little Pillington, I believe you have recently acquired a townhouse in London. Not in Mayfair, of course, but amid its increasingly fashionable fringes. And we must not forget those three lovely mills. So many possessions. So much to lose. Tonight's lesson would prove enough for an intelligent man. Are you an intelligent man, Herbert? Or are you willing to risk disobeying me?"

"You bastard!" Symington growled, clenching his hamlike hands into impotent fists as the glow from the fire glinted on the barrel of the pistol. "Oh, I know who you are now! I've heard the stories. I know what you've done to other mill owners. So now you're after me, are you? Well, I won't bow down to you like the others have. You'll hang for this, you miserable scoundrel—and I'll be there to watch you dance!"

"That's the spirit, Herbert. Down but not out!" the man said encouragingly as the door to the coach opened and the groom reached in to let down the steps. "You take that thought with you. Take it and hold it close to your heart, along with my list of demands. And, oh yes, thank you for the coach. It will bring a considerable sum, I'm convinced, proceeds which will doubtless fill many a stomach these next months. Once again, Herbert, good evening to you. I sincerely wish I will not find it necessary we should meet again."

"Oh, I'll see you again, you heartless bastard. See you and more!" Symington tried desperately to make out the facial features of his tormentor in the glow from the fire, but it was useless. He felt himself being pulled unceremoniously from his beloved coach before a well-placed kick from his former employee nearly sent him sprawling onto the gravel drive in front of the inferno that was once his house.

The coach drove away, the sound of delighted laughter floating back to mock him, and Symington angrily yanked off the ribbon holding the list of demands, bent on ripping the paper into a thousand pieces.

As he unrolled the single sheet, something long and soft fluttered to the ground and he picked it up. He held it to the light from the blaze before cursing roundly, flinging the thing from him, and turning to slowly walk the three miles back into Little Pillington.

Behind him, lying abandoned on the drive, a single peacock feather winked blue and green in the light from the blazing fire.

BOOK ONE

THE GAME BEGINS

＊

The world is full of fools, and he who would not see it should live alone and smash his mirror.

attributed to Claude Le Petit

CHAPTER 1

~

Society is now one polished horde,
formed of two mighty tribes,
the Bores, and Bored.

Lord Byron

Lady Undercliff had been sadly out of sorts for a month, or so she informed anyone who applied to her for the reason behind her perpetual pout.

She was incensed because her thoroughly thoughtless husband had adamantly refused to return from his hunting box in Scotland until the second week of the Season, thus delaying the annual Undercliff Ball, which, as everyone was aware, had been held the *first* week of the Season these past sixteen years.

Not that she could not have pressed on with her plans for the ball without Charles, for heaven only knew the man had never lifted a finger for any but his own pleasure in all his life. But her ladyship was very conscious of appearances, and opening the ball without her husband at her side would only cause speculative gossip, especially since that sad interlude the man

13

had indulged in most publicly three years past with that absurd Covent Garden warbler.

Besides, Lady Undercliff considered herself to be a perfect wretch at recollecting names, and she had grown to rely on his lordship's guidance during those tedious hours spent in the receiving line, complimenting friends on the birth of another grandchild or remembering to inquire as to the welfare of another acquaintance's old-as-God Great-aunt Imogene.

And Charles knew she counted on his memory, damn his hunt-mad, philandering hide to perdition!

In the end, there had been nothing else for it but to live with the consequences of her mate's selfishness, and Lady Undercliff had been forced to take her pleasure where she found it, which is the same as to say that the tradesmen's bills her dearest husband Charles would find falling like snow upon his study desk in the next weeks would much resemble a blizzard.

Lady Undercliff had always taken great pride in her ability to delight both her guests' eyes and stomachs with her lavish entertainments, but she had definitely outdone herself in her preparations for this particular ball.

The delicately draped bunting that hung everywhere, the dozens and dozens of ceiling-high plants, the hothouse bouquets, the rented gilt-back chairs, the painted cherubs and other statuary, the hiring of a score of servers, the presence of musicians in three drawing rooms in addition to those in the ballroom, the luscious sliced salmon, the dazzling variety of Gunther ices, indeed, even the silver-on-silk gown and flashing diamonds worn by the lady herself—all had been ordered with a glib "And have all bills forwarded directly to my husband, the earl."

And yet, with the hour relentlessly creeping toward midnight on the evening of the ball, and with the compliments of the happy partygoers still ringing in her ears as she remained adamantly at the top of the stairs, Lady Undercliff continued to pout.

"This is entirely your fault, Charles," she sniped at her husband, who was most probably wishing himself away from the receiving line and safely ensconced in the card room, a drink at his elbow, although she'd not give him that satisfaction. "He isn't coming."

"Prinny?" Lord Undercliff asked, frowning. "Who wants him here anyway, Gert? We'd have the servants scraping rotted eggs from the windows for a week if the populace caught sight of him rolling his carcass in here. Ain't the least in good odor with the masses, you know—or you would, if you weren't always worrying about all the wrong things."

"Not his royal highness, Charles," Lady Undercliff gritted out quietly from between clenched teeth, "as if I'd want that terrible old man lumbering in here with his fat mistress and shoveling all that lovely salmon down his greedy gullet. And don't call me 'Gert'! The man I am speaking of is St. Clair."

Lord Undercliff looked at his wife down the length of his considerable nose. "St. Clair? That pranked-out mummer? Thunder an' turf, now you've gone and slipped your moorings, Gert. What is he to anything? He ain't but a baron. You've got three marquesses, a half dozen earls, and two dukes cluttering up the place already. What do you need with St. Clair?"

"You don't understand," Lady Undercliff spat. "But then, you never do. He must be here!"

"Yes, yes. He's amusing enough, I'll grant you that, but I can't say I like what he's done to our young men. Everything poor Beau has taught them about proper dress seems to have flown out the window thanks to St. Clair and his colored satins. Soon he'll have us all powdering up our heads, Gert, and if he does that I just might have to call him out myself. Demmed nuisance, that powder, not to mention the tax. Besides, didn't we turn the powder closet into a water closet just a few years past?"

Lady Undercliff gripped her kid-encased hands together tightly in front of her, knowing that if she did not win this struggle to control her overset emotions she would soon plant her beloved but woefully obtuse husband a wisty facer straight on his mouth.

"Charles, I don't care a fig if St. Clair has all you gentlemen shaving your heads and painting your pates purple. No party is a success unless he attends. No hostess worth her salt would dare show her face in public again if Christian St. Clair deigned to ignore her invitation. *Now* do you understand, Charles? And it's all your fault—you and your stupid hunting box. I'll never forgive you for this, Charles. Never!"

"Females!" Lord Undercliff exploded, slapping his thigh in exasperation at his wife's outburst. The single life was much preferable, he had often been heard to remark, if only there existed some way of setting up one's nursery without having to shackle oneself with a bride who was never the sweet young beauty you thought she'd be but only a female like any other, with contrary ways no man could ever fathom, shrewish voices, and feathers for brains.

He peered past his wife and into the crowded, overheated ballroom. "You've got Lord Buxley, Gert. He's popular enough. And that Tredway chit as well. Wasn't she the toast of London last Season?"

"Yes, Charles—*last* Season," Lady Undercliff informed her husband tersely. "Lady Ariana Tredway lends the party some cachet, as does Lord Buxley, but my primary coup for this evening seems to be the presence of Gabrielle Laurence, although I cannot for the life of me understand the attraction. *Red* hair, Charles. I mean, really! It's not at all *à la mode*."

Peering around his wife once more, Lord Undercliff caught sight of a slim, tallish girl waltzing by in the arms of the thrice-widowed Duke of Glynnon. He could not help but remember the chit, for he had bowed so long over her hand during his introduction to her in the receiving line that his wife had brought the heel of her evening slipper down hard on his instep to bring him back to attention.

Miss Laurence's lovely face, he saw now, was wreathed in an animated smile as she spoke to the duke, her smooth white complexion framed by a mass of lovely curls the color of fire that blazed almost golden as the movements of the dance brought her beneath one of the brightly lit chandeliers. He grinned, remembering her dark, winglike brows, her shining green eyes, and, most especially, the small round mole he'd noticed sitting just to the left of her upper lip. Ah, what a fetching piece!

"Your judgment doesn't seem to be bothering the duke overmuch, Gert," Lord Undercliff remarked in an unwise attack of frankness, sparing a moment to catch a glimpse of Miss Laurence's remarkably perfect bosom, which was modestly yet enticingly covered by an ivory silk gown. "As a matter of fact, I believe old Harry is drooling."

"Oh, go back to Scotland, Charles, until you can learn to control yourself," Lady Undercliff spat out, then broke into her first genuine smile in a month.

"He's here! Charles, darling, he's here! Stand up straight, and for goodness sake don't say anything stupid."

Lord Undercliff, once a military man and therefore accustomed to taking orders, obeyed his wife's command instinctively, squaring his shoulders and pulling in his stomach as he turned to greet their tardy guest and his small entourage of hangers-on, a wide, welcoming smile pasted on his lordship's pudding face.

"Lady Undercliff! Look at you! *Voyons!* This is too much! Your beauty never ceases to astound me! I vow I cannot bear it!" Lord Christian St. Clair exclaimed a moment later, having successfully navigated the long, curving marble staircase to halt in front of the woman and execute an exquisitely elegant bow, while gifting her hand with a fleeting touch of his lips.

Lord Undercliff's own lips curled in distaste as he watched this ridiculous display, taking in the baron's outrageous costume of robin's-egg-blue satin swallow-tail coat and knee breeches, the elaborate lace-edged cuffs of his shirt, the foaming jabot at his tanned throat, the high collar that by rights should have sliced off the fellow's ears by now.

The man was a menace, that's what he was, bringing back into fashion a fashion that hadn't been *fashionable* in years. And the young males of Society were following him like stunned sheep, more and more of them each day sauntering down Bond Street in clocked stockings, huge buckles on their shoes, and wearing enough lace to curtain a cathedral.

"I throw myself at your feet, beseeching mercy. A thousand pardons for my unforgivable tardiness, dear lady, please, I beg you," Lord St. Clair pleaded, rising to his full six foot three of sartorial splendor to gaze adoringly into Lady Undercliff's rapidly widening eyes.

"I had been dressed and ready beforetimes, eager to mount these heavenly stairs to your presence," he lamented sadly, "but then dearest Grumble here observantly pointed out that the lace on my handkerchief"—he brandished an oversized, ornate lace handkerchief as proof—"did not in the slightest complement that of the rest of my ensemble. Imagine my dismay! There was nothing else for it but that I strip to the buff and begin again." He sighed eloquently, looking to Lord Undercliff as if for understanding.

He didn't receive any. "Could have just changed handkerchiefs, St. Clair," his lordship countered, he believed, reasonably. "Or left off altogether trailing one around with you everywhere like some paper-skulled, die-away miss with a perpetual fit of the vapors."

St. Clair's broad shoulders shook slightly as he gave a small gulp of laughter that soon grew to an appreciative if somewhat high-pitched giggle. *"Sans doute.* Ah, Undercliff, what I would not give to find life so simple. Grumble," he said, turning to George Trumble, one of his trio of constant companions, "how naughty of you not to point out that alternative to me. No, don't say anything," he continued, holding up a hand to silence his friend, who hadn't appeared willing or able to answer. "I remember now. My affections lay more deeply with the handkerchief than the remainder of my costume. Forgive me, Grumble. Ah, well, no hour spent in dressing is ever wasted."

"Only a single hour—for evening clothes?" Lord Undercliff spluttered, giving the baron's rig-out another look, this time appreciating the cut of the coat, which was not quite that of the past century but more modern, with less buckram padding, flattering St. Clair's slim frame that boasted surprisingly wide shoulders and a trim waist. And the man's long, straight legs were nearly obscene in their beauty, the thighs muscular, the calves obviously not aided by the careful stuffing of sawdust to make up for any lack in that area.

"Used to take Brummell a whole morning just to do up his cravat," his lordship continued consideringly, wondering if sky-blue satin would be flattering to his own figure. "Just pin that lace thing-o-ma-bob around your neck and be done with it, don't you? And the ladies seem to like it. Maybe you have something here, St. Clair. Thought satins would take longer, but if they don't—well, mayhap I'll give them a try m'self. Rather weary of Brummell's midnight blue and black, you know."

"Charles," Lady Undercliff interrupted, her smile of pleasure and triumph at having snagged St. Clair for her ball rapidly freezing in place as she listened to her bull of a husband making a cake of himself, "you are neglecting our other guests. Lord Osgood, Sir Gladwin, Mr. Trumble—we are so pleased you've agreed to grace our small party this evening."

Lord St. Clair stood back to allow his friends to move forward and greet their host and hostess, which they did in order of their social prominence.

Lord Osmond Osgood, a tall though rather portly young gentleman known to his cronies as Ozzie, was first to approach, winking at the earl before clumsily bowing over her ladyship's hand and backing away once more, nearly tripping over his own feet.

Sir Gladwin Penley, his usual uninspired gray rig-out brightened by his trademark yellow waistcoat, simultaneously apologized for his tardiness and grabbed hold of Lord Osgood's forearm, saving that man from an ignominious tumble back down the staircase. "My delight in the evening knows no bounds, my lady," he intoned solemnly, giving no hint to the fact that he'd been dragged to the Portman Square mansion under threat of having St. Clair in charge of the dressing of him for a fortnight if he cried off in favor of the new farce at Covent Garden.

George Trumble was the last to bow over Lady Undercliff's pudgy hand, keeping his comments brief and hardly heartfelt, for everyone was aware the only reason an invitation had been delivered to his door was the usual one: If George Trumble were not one of the party, then the hostess could go cry for St. Clair's presence. "How good of you to invite me, your ladyship," he said quietly, then turned his back on the woman before she could be sure she'd seen cold disdain in his eyes.

But if George Trumble knew he was here on sufferance, and Sir Gladwin Penley may have already been wishing himself elsewhere, and Lord Osmond Osgood might be wondering how soon they could leave without causing a stir, Baron Christian St. Clair's posture showed him to be in his element.

He turned back to Lady Undercliff and offered her his arm, telling her without words that it was no longer necessary for her to stand at the top of the stairs now that the premier guest had arrived.

And if the Prince Regent did dare venture out of Carleton House under cover of darkness to attend, well then, he could just find his own way into the ballroom.

With her ladyship at his side, and Lord Undercliff

following along behind with the remainder of St. Clair's entourage, the baron entered the ballroom just as the clocks all struck twelve, stopping just inside the archway to gift the other occupants of the room with a long, appreciative look at the magnificence—indeed, the splendor—that was Baron Christian St. Clair.

Miss Gabrielle Laurence was enjoying herself immensely, as befitted both her hopes for her debut and the reality of the past ten days that had found all her most earnest wishes coming true. For her instant success within the rarefied confines of Mayfair and the select members of the *ton* was not the result of mere happenstance.

Gabrielle had planned for it—indeed, *trained* for it—and if her smile was brighter than most, her manner more ingratiating, her conversation more scintillating, her behavior, her gowns, her air of vibrancy more interesting than was the case for any of the other hopeful debutantes, those young ladies who were not enjoying a similar success had only themselves to blame.

The Undercliff Ball had proven to be another feather in Gabrielle's figurative cap of social success, the evening thus far a never-ending whirl of waltzes with dukes, cups of lemonade brought to her by adoring swains, effusive compliments on her "ravishing" gown, her "glorious" hair, her "rosebud" lips, and even a single stolen kiss on the balcony, especially when she considered that the "thief" had been no less than Lord Edgar Wexter, heir to one of the premier estates in Sussex.

All in all, Gabrielle Laurence was at this moment a very happy young woman, which explained her sudden chagrin when she belatedly realized that the young viscount she had been regaling with the latest gossip about Princess Caroline was no longer listening to her but instead staring in the general direction of the doorway, his usually vacant blue eyes glazed over with slavish admiration.

Gabrielle sighed, snapping open her fan to furiously beat at the air beneath her softly dimpled chin. "I'd look," she said to herself—for the viscount certainly didn't hear her, and probably wouldn't if she screamed the words at him—"but I already know what I would see. It's that overdressed ape St. Clair, isn't it?"

No matter where she was, Gabrielle knew she could not for long escape hearing about Baron Christian St. Clair, arbiter of fashion, purveyor of inane wit, and the single man who held the power of social life or death over the members of the *ton.*

No matter what she was doing, her enjoyment of the moment could be instantly reduced to ashes by his entrance onto the scene, where he immediately became the cynosure of all eyes, the center of the social universe.

The man wielded more power than the Prince Regent, held more social consequence than Beau Brummell had ever commanded, and was more sought after than the Duke of Wellington, hero of the late war against Bonaparte.

It was indecent the way Society fawned over the man, adopting his ridiculous fashions, aping his effeminate ways, shunning green peas on Tuesdays because he did, strolling rather than riding in the park because he abhorred horses, eagerly hopping through each foolish hoop he set up for them as if his every drawled inanity were gospel, his every soulful sigh to be worried over, his every smile to be cherished as if a gift from the gods.

It was enough to make Gabrielle Laurence wish she could dare turning her back on the man.

Which, of course, she couldn't, not without risking social disaster.

But that did not mean she would fawn over him the moment he entered a room the way those giggling debutantes and their hovering mamas were doing now as St. Clair leisurely made his way down the long ballroom, his loyal trio of dull wrens undoubtedly freed to go their own way now that their leader was in his glory.

Counting slowly to ten, and waiting until the last possible moment, until she could absolutely *feel* the man's presence behind her, Gabrielle blinked rapidly to put a sparkle in her wide, tip-tilted green eyes, spread her mouth in a welcoming smile, and turned, her hand extended gracefully as she trilled, "La, St. Clair, I would know you were approaching even if I were to be suddenly struck deaf. The visible stir your presence makes in a room is almost akin to that of a Second Coming. All in blue this evening, I see. I believe the viscount is nearing tears, so overcome is he by your exquisite presence."

"Miss Laurence, I vow you bid fair to unman me with your sweet compliments," St. Clair intoned, bowing over her hand, the touch of his firm, dry lips searing her skin, a shiver of awareness, of stubborn, defensive dislike skipping down her spine as his blue-green gaze lifted and met hers, holding her in thrall for several heartbeats. "Zounds, but I can yet again feel my puny attempts at brilliance fading into nothingness, faced with your overwhelming beauty."

"Which you have so very kindly served to bring into fashion, my lord," Gabrielle replied sweetly, inwardly gritting her teeth at the infuriating knowledge that she was speaking the truth. If St. Clair had used his seemingly bubbleheaded yet razor-sharp wit to comment disparagingly on her red hair she might as well have retired to the country and taken the veil for all her chances of ever becoming a success in Mayfair.

For despite Gabrielle's planning, all her careful preparation to take London by storm, she knew she owed the man considerable thanks for his unexpected championing of her, and it galled her no end to admit it.

Yet admit it she did, tonight and every time she was in his company, for if she was young and somewhat sure of herself, she was not stupid. Her ritual obsequiousness was the unspoken price she nightly had to pay for St. Clair's continued public favor. Shylock, in comparison, could not have been more insidiously demanding than Baron Christian St. Clair when he had called for his "pound of flesh."

"I've visited your tailor just this afternoon, my lord," the young viscount piped up after nervously clearing his throat, for he had been hovering around Gabrielle for the past quarter hour, partly because it did him no harm to be seen with her, but mostly in the hope St. Clair would appear, for everyone already knew St. Clair had been making it a point to single out Miss Laurence first at any engagement he favored. "I've commissioned an entire wardrobe from the man, paying him double if he has half of it complete next week," the young man ended, clearly proud of himself.

"Indeed." St. Clair inclined his head apologetically to Gabrielle for having to desert her to speak with the viscount, then turned to the young man, inspecting him through the stemmed, gilt-edged quizzing glass he leisurely lifted to his left eye. "How commendable of you, my lord, and how woefully overdue. Ah, that was too bad of me. Please, my lord, forgive my naughty tongue. However, if I may be so bold as to inquire," he drawled, allowing the quizzing glass to fall to mid-chest, for the piece was suspended from his neck by a thin ivory silk band, "would you tell me what colors you selected?"

The viscount swallowed down hard, making it painfully clear to everyone that his throat had gone desert dry. "Green, Clarence blue—and dove gray, I believe. Did I choose correctly?" he asked dully, as if already sorrowfully convinced he had erred in his choices.

St. Clair allowed time for the silence to grow and for their near neighbors to lean closer to hear his pronouncement when it came. *"Bien.* Excellent choices, my lord," he exclaimed at last, beaming at the young viscount. And then he frowned. "Oh dear, how do I put this delicately? I fear you will have to shed a few pounds in order to do credit to the cut of the jacket, my lord, not that anything I say is of the slightest consequence. Still, may I suggest you stable your mount and walk yourself briskly through the park each day for the promenade? That should rid you of your, um, *bulges* in no time. Don't you think so, Miss Laurence?"

Longing to tell him that she thought it would be lovely if the visibly wilting viscount were to quickly search out his backbone and summarily stuff St. Clair's quizzing glass down the baron's gullet, Gabrielle smiled and said, "I have always believed judicious exercise to be healthful, sir."

"Ah, *exactement,* Miss Laurence," St. Clair responded just as Lady Undercliff's overpaid musicians struck up yet another waltz. "And, so saying, perhaps you would honor me with your participation in the dance, another highly desirable form of healthful exercise?"

As social suicide was not on Gabrielle's agenda for this or any evening, she dropped into a graceful curtsy and then allowed St. Clair to guide her onto the dance floor even as other couples joined them, the floor rapidly becoming crowded with persons eager to prove their agreement with the baron's prescription for "healthful exercise."

At last they were alone—or as alone as any two people could be on the dance floor—and now their private war could recommence. St. Clair lightly cupped Gabrielle's slim waist with his right hand while she rested hers in his left, their bodies precisely two and one half feet apart. A slight pressure from St. Clair's hand moved Gabrielle into the first sweeping turn of the waltz, and she smiled up at him, saying, "I do so loathe you, St. Clair."

His smile was equally bright as he appeared to enjoy her opening salvo of the evening, for they had been throwing verbal brickbats at each other from their first meeting, exchanges Gabrielle could not remember which one of them had begun and which she still could not decide if she enjoyed or dreaded.

"Encroaching mushrooms, my dear," he answered smoothly, sweeping her into another graceful turn, "usually do dislike their betters. Tell me, please—as I am all agog to know—do you lie awake nights, Miss Laurence, planning sundry vile terminations to my existence?"

"I wouldn't care to waste my precious time thinking

27

of you in any way at all, my lord," Gabrielle countered, nodding a greeting to a female passerby, who was looking at her in undisguised envy for having snagged St. Clair yet again for his first waltz of the evening.

"Too true, Miss Laurence, too true," St. Clair said, his hand on her waist gripping just a hair tighter than it had before, causing another unwelcome, disturbing frisson of awareness to sing through her blood. "You are much too occupied in forwarding yourself to think of others. Fame is fleeting, dear girl, and you are clever to enjoy the pinnacle of popularity upon which I have placed you while you can. Consider this: I may deign to cut you tomorrow, and all your fine success would come crashing down around your ears. Wouldn't that be dreadful? Perhaps you should encourage our fuzzy-cheeked viscount to offer for you while you still bask in the sunshine of my approval."

"I am visiting this fair city only to enjoy the Season, my lord. I am not on the hunt for a wealthy husband, not in the least," Gabrielle bit out from between clenched teeth, still maintaining her smile, but with an effort, for she knew she was lying. Lying, and desperate, not that she could ever allow St. Clair to know.

"You don't wish to marry? Gad, there's a shocker! Feel free to perceive me as astonished!" St. Clair countered. "Then I was wrong to take one look at your meticulously constructed façade of gentility and see an empty-headed, fortune-mad beauty out to snare a deep-in-the-pockets title? Forgive me, Miss Laurence. I should have realized that you are in hopes of setting up an intellectual salon, or perhaps intent upon conquering Society in order to gain their cooperation with some private agenda you have yet to reveal—a series of good works, perhaps?"

Gabrielle opened her mouth to argue with him, but he cut her off.

"But, no. That isn't it. Why, do you know what I think? I think you loathe and detest men. Don't you, Miss Laurence? You hate us and wish to have us all fall in love with your beauty so that you might, one by one, grind our broken hearts in the dust. Why didn't I see it before? How deep you are, Miss Laurence. How very deep."

"Oh, cut line, St. Clair!" Gabrielle declared hotly as, the waltz over, he took hold of her elbow and guided her toward the balcony. "I may as well admit it, for it is obvious to me that you will keep mouthing inanities until I do. *Yes,* like every other unattached young lady here this evening, I am on the hunt for a rich, titled husband. The deeper his pockets and the loftier his title the better. I am mercenary, hardheaded, strong-willed, and so depraved by my ambition as to be capable of debasing myself by being polite to you in order to advance my standing in Society. Fortunately for my plans, in general I enjoy the company of gentlemen. It is only *you* I despise. There! Are you happy now?"

"Ecstatic, my dear," St. Clair answered genially, drawing her toward a small stone bench and motioning for her to be seated. He then spread his lace-edged handkerchief beside her and, carefully splitting his coattails, sat down himself. "I had begun to wonder if you were to be content merely trading barbs as we have done this past fortnight. But we have progressed. We are becoming, at long last, entirely open with each other. You despise me, and I return the compliment."

"Which in no way explains why you have deigned to bring me into fashion," Gabrielle said, studying Lord St. Clair out of the corner of her eye, taking in the sight of his expressive winged eyebrows above eyes that turned from blue to lightest green with his moods, the straight, aquiline nose he looked down to such effect, the shape of his generous mouth, the marvelous way his longish, light, golden mane was tied back in a small queue.

The man wasn't simply handsome, drat him. He was beautiful! What a pity the Fates, which had gifted him with such beauty, had somehow neglected to stuff his handsome skull with a brain. Or was she as wrong in assuming that as she was in her protestations that she couldn't abide him?

"So, as we are being honest this evening—why have you chosen to bring me into favor, my lord?" she dared to ask outright, wearying of their constant fencing.

St. Clair produced a small enameled box from his waistcoat and went about the business of taking snuff, his expertise in the movements of the procedure marred only at the last, when he screwed up his handsome face most comically, pinched two fingers against the bridge of his nose, and then gave out with a prodigious sneeze.

She giggled, unable to help herself, for he looked so silly. Almost adorably silly.

"Ah, please forgive me, Miss Laurence," he said, drawing a more serviceable handkerchief from his sleeve and wiping delicately at his nose. "Deuced evil habit, snuff. I've seen men with half their noses eaten away from the stuff."

He gave a horrified shiver, then smiled. "Do you know what, Miss Laurence? I believe I will forswear the nasty habit beginning this very evening, if only by way of a public service, as no one will dare take snuff if St. Clair does not. Am I not wonderful to use my elevated stature for the betterment of mankind? Indeed, I am confident I am, especially when I consider my vast and most costly collection of snuffboxes. Too small to make into posy pots, I imagine I shall just have to give them all away to needy snuff takers in Piccadilly. And then I believe I shall reward myself with a new waistcoat. I saw the most interesting fabric the other day—silver, with mauve roses. Now, dear girl, what were you saying?"

"Never mind, my lord." Gabrielle rolled her eyes, giving up any notion that she would ever understand this man, and telling herself that she didn't want to understand him. He was probably only what she saw before her: a paper-skulled, imbecilic clotheshorse with more hair than wit, more self-consequence than a strutting cock, and all the mental acumen of a cracked walnut. She would be the world's greatest fool to believe otherwise, no matter how pretty he was, no matter how many times his smiling face had invaded her dreams these past two weeks.

Besides, she believed she already knew why he had undertaken to champion her. He had done it simply to prove that he could take what he considered to be an unknown, fire-headed country bumpkin and raise her to the level of a Lady Ariana Tredway. The only thing she couldn't understand was why he allowed her to speak so uncivilly to him—and why he found it so necessary to be mean to her whenever no one was about to overhear them.

And one more thing bothered her, unnerved her, haunted her in the night long after she should have found her rest. Her reaction to each touch of his hand, each penetrating look of his oddly intelligent, impossible-to-read eyes. Why, she could almost think herself attracted to him, if she didn't believe herself above such nonsense.

"Yes, well then," St. Clair said as the silence between them lengthened, rising and holding out his hand to her after retrieving his lace handkerchief, "as we seem to have run out of cutting things to say to each other, may I suggest we return to the ballroom? We have been absent for a sufficient length of time for those who are inclined to low thoughts to have taken it into their heads that we have been indulging in a romantic assignation. Why I continue to be so kind to you I do not know, but once again I have served to raise your consequence. Now, I fear, I must reward myself by twirling a less unwieldy partner around the floor and then take my leave. I wouldn't wish for Lady Undercliff to preen overmuch at having snagged me for an *entire* evening."

"Unwieldy?" Gabrielle angrily snatched her hand from his, stung by this latest in a string of insults even as she relaxed in her resurgence of anger, which was much easier to deal with than any softening of her feelings toward the inane dandy. "I'll have you know I am considered to be a wonderful dancer. Why, the viscount has only this evening vowed to pen an ode to my grace in going down the dance."

"That unpolished cub? Odds fish, m'dear, what is that to the point?" St. Clair responded as they reentered the ballroom. "The sallow-faced twit also seriously believes he will cut a dash in dove gray. He'll probably insist upon a pink waistcoat as well, a thought that nearly propels me to tears! Ah, look, the gods have smiled! I do believe my poor trammeled-upon feet are saved. Lady Ariana approaches, smiling a greeting to me, her dear friend. You would be wise to observe her, Miss Laurence. Lady Ariana is a veritable gazelle on the dance floor. To quote the illustrious Suckling, 'Her feet beneath her petticoat, like little mice, stole in and out as if they feared the light. And oh! she dances such a way, no sun upon an Easter day is half so fine a sight.'"

"You quote so often, St. Clair," Gabrielle shot back, inwardly seething. "It is so sad that you never have an original thought."

"Oh, I am mortally wounded by your sharp tongue," he responded theatrically, "and needs must retire the field at once." He gave a subtle signal to the viscount, who had been hovering nearby, painfully conspicuous in his hopes for another moment's notice from the popular baron, and that man hopped forward sprightly to take Miss Laurence off St. Clair's hands.

"How exceedingly amicable of you, my lord," St. Clair intoned, bowing slightly in thanks. "It is the true sign of a Christian to be willing to graciously take back a young lady who has just recently deserted him for the better man. Miss Laurence, I leave you in good company. If you will excuse me?"

Gabrielle's smile beamed brighter than the chandelier hanging above their ballroom, the chandelier she secretly wished would slip its moorings to come crashing down on St. Clair's arrogant head.

"Will we be seeing you at Richmond tomorrow, for her ladyship's garden party?" she asked, praying for a drenching rain on the morrow so that the baron would not dare attend and chance ruining one of his exquisite ensembles. If the painted popinjay refused to ride because he considered hacking jackets too barbaric for words, he most certainly would not deign to appear at a picnic in anything less than his usual outlandish satins.

"Point du tout, Miss Laurence. I fear you all shall simply have to make do without me," he replied, lifting the lace handkerchief to his lips. "I abhor picnics, and can think of nothing more uncivilized. If I wished to be crudely rustic I should never have fled the countryside for London in the first place, which I did the moment I realized there existed an entire lovely segment of the populace that did not believe the pinnacle of their existence to be an afternoon spent lying on their backs in the fields, chewing hay. Why, just think, Miss Laurence: Can you really imagine me pushed into a tent with the milling crowd, or forced to sit on a blanket spread on the grass?"

"And pray why not, my lord?" Gabrielle could not resist asking. "After all, I hear most idling, wastrel grasshoppers flit about in the grass quite happily without benefit of a blanket at all."

St. Clair gave a small, trilling laugh just as the viscount winced, evidently convinced Miss Laurence had said something dreadful and wondering why he had thought being in her company would do his own reputation any good.

"C'est merveilleux! But you are so droll, my dear girl," the baron continued, smiling broadly. "You almost make me believe you have some sort of sense for amusing repartee. I shall leave you now, my heart light that you have said something brilliant. Good evening all," he said, bowing once again, this time lifting Gabrielle's hand to his lips before turning to Lady Ariana and leading her onto the floor, at which time the musicians immediately halted in the midst of the Scottish air they were playing and broke into another waltz.

"Isn't he magnificent, Miss Laurence?" the viscount gushed, his tone filled with awe, earning himself a speaking look from Gabrielle as she excused herself, wishing her skin didn't still tingle from the touch of St. Clair's lips, and, mumbling something about having a crushing headache, asked to be returned to her chaperone.

CHAPTER 2

There was a general whisper, toss, and wriggle,
But etiquette forbade them all to giggle.

Lord Byron

Lady Ariana Tredway did her best to put a bright face on her position of Baron St. Clair's second choice as he whirled her around the dance floor, listening to his inane but amusingly risqué chatter concerning a certain peer recently winged in the buttocks by his pistol-waving wife, the silly man having been discovered *in flagrante delicto* in his own library with a certain fast matron.

St. Clair was such a fool, but a powerful fool, and Lady Ariana hated him for his slight defection from her side in this, her second Season, as greatly as she adored him for having deigned to speak with her at all.

It was silly to have such a brainless popinjay as the arbiter of every step Society took, every stitch they wore, as all of Society was silly, but it was the way of the world, and Lady Ariana accepted it as thoroughly as she accepted the fact that she was the most beautiful woman to grace Mayfair in decades.

And Lady Ariana was not entirely conceited in her determination of that beauty. Her hair was soft blond, a most necessary color for a young lady wishing to be thought of as a true English beauty, and her china-blue eyes were the envy of two Seasons of hopeful debutantes. Her petite form provided an added fillip, as did her softly rounded curves, straight white teeth, and a sulky mouth that owed none of its deep pink color to the paint pots many misses were forced to use.

She was known all through Mayfair as the young lady who had in the past year turned away the suits of no less than two marquises, a truly lovestruck earl, and one Honorable whose fortune was favorably compared with that of Golden Ball himself.

She was pampered and petted by her powerful Tory father, indulged by her rather plain mama who in these past twenty years had still not quite moved beyond her gratitude that the Fates had blessed her with such a comely daughter, and sought after by all who would be invited to the best parties.

Indeed, in the insular, almost incestuous twelve hundred or so souls that made up the *crème de la crème* of English Society, Lady Ariana Tredway had, just this past Season, shared the premier social pivot with only Baron Christian St. Clair.

Until this *new* Season, that is, when that same socially powerful Baron St. Clair had taken it into his silly head to champion Gabrielle Laurence. No wonder Lady Ariana despised the chit without having spoken more than a half dozen words to her.

"Christian?" Lady Ariana chirped, hoping to gain his full attention. She addressed the baron informally, as their acquaintance had progressed to that point, if no further—for everyone knew the young lady was hanging out for a duke and was written up in the betting book at White's as being certain to snag one this Season.

Besides, as everyone also knew, Baron Christian St. Clair remained uninterested in females other than to squire them on the dance floor, and Lady Ariana Tredway was much too intrigued with herself and her ambitions to care overmuch for anyone else. "Must you persist in teasing that poor Laurence girl so horribly? You've been at it for nearly a fortnight, and it's thoroughly embarrassing to watch."

St. Clair raised one eloquent eyebrow and stared at her just as if he hadn't understood her. "Teasing, Ariana? *Sacré tonnerre!* Whatever do you mean?"

"Oh, stop it, Christian. You know very well what I mean," she said, pulling away from him so that he had no choice but to follow her off the dance floor or remain standing there, abandoned. "You are only puffing her up in order to prick her soundly, deflating her consequence in an instant. I believe you to be very mean in this, which is not at all like you. Usually you are droll and amusing, not brutal."

"Mon dieu, has it come to this?" St. Clair clucked his tongue as he stepped in front of her, halting her progress. "You've gone and had a thought, haven't you, Ariana? How very bad of you. And it will cause lines in that lovely forehead if you are not careful. Can't get a duke with wrinkles. Of course, as I understand the duke of Glynnon was seen waltzing with Miss Laurence earlier this evening, you might be worrying yourself needlessly, your hopes already dashed."

"Don't avoid my question, Christian," Lady Ariana

countered, bristling at the baron's deliberate dig and pointedly looking past him, yet only vaguely noticing a commotion to her left, at the doorway to the ballroom. "You took one peep at that dowerless girl—her father gambles, or so Papa says—and immediately decided you could not like her. I agree she is presumptuous, believing she could sweep into Mayfair and conquer us all, but is it really necessary to humiliate her?"

"*Au contraire,* my dear. You couldn't care less that I have the power to destroy the fair Laurence. What you are really asking, I fear, is *when* I will bring her down," St. Clair responded amicably, lifting his handkerchief to the corner of his smiling mouth. "Leaving you, I presume, free to once more reign as the toast of London. I may be dim, but I can see where this conversation is heading and want no part of it. If you dislike Miss Laurence, cut her yourself, and see if your consequence is up to the challenge. But please, save me from these female machinations. I am only a simple man acting out of charity, totally devoid of intrigue, and I dislike your insinuations intensely. Why, if you two beautiful young ladies were to descend into a catfight I would doubtless be forced to cut you *both* and take up another cause, another delightful creature whom I would then instantly catapult to social success."

Lady Ariana was stung into replying without first measuring her words. "I believe I might be better served to join forces with Miss Laurence and see if we couldn't discover some way to put *you* out of favor, Christian."

St. Clair's shrug was entirely French, for if he was every drop the Englishman, he had spent the years following Waterloo enjoying Parisian society, obviously taking on some of their more eloquent manner-isms, even to the point of sprinkling his conversation with snippets of not necessarily germane French.

"If you must, my dear," he returned affably. "I am naught but a momentary whim, like poor Brummell before me, and exist merely at the pleasure of Society. But, then, as I recall, it took both Prinny and a year's long disastrous run at the tables to bring Beau down. Do you believe you and Miss Laurence to be capable of a similar feat?"

Lady Ariana looked closely into St. Clair's now deeply blue eyes and wished herself out of this poten-tially dangerous conversation, which she had only entered into because she was upset at the man's attention to the Laurence chit. She was within a heartbeat of going too far with the usually affable baron, and she decided to pull back.

"Forgive me, Christian," she said, smiling apologet-ically. "I have barely eaten all day in order to be certain the line of my gown would be as you desire it. I am all out of sorts tonight, I suppose."

Then she turned toward the doorway and the sound of raised voices that had momentarily ceased but had now begun again. "Christian? Do you think some-thing is wrong?" she asked, gesturing toward the doorway with her fan.

St. Clair turned and lifted his stemmed quizzing glass to his eye. "How fatiguing. I've heard less ruckus in a fish market. Not that I've ever visited any such establishment, but I have heard stories, you under-stand. *Comment*—do you suppose the place has caught on fire? That is what will come of layering the place with bunting. Come, we will make our escape."

St. Clair offered Lady Ariana his arm and they made their way toward the main doorway, becoming part of the throng of partygoers now congregating there. He stopped just beside the equally tall but darkly handsome Lord Anthony Buxley, who, Lady Ariana was depressed to see, had the opportunistic Miss Gabrielle Laurence hanging from his sober midnight-blue sleeve.

Almost immediately, seeing that the four purest diamonds of society were in their midst, several people politely gave way, until the quartet of exquisites had a clear view of what was transpiring in the hallway just outside the ballroom.

"And I'm telling you, Undercliff," a red-faced, corpulent man of at least fifty was informing their host, "I don't give a bloody damn if you've got the bleeding king inside. I swear it, the Peacock's come to Little Pillington. We have to talk, Undercliff! *Now!*"

"Good Lord, Miss Laurence," Lord Buxley declared clearly above the sly titterings of the onlookers, trying to draw his companion from the scene, "it's naught but some importuning tradesman. Come away and we'll go down to dinner before all the best tables are taken. There's nothing here of interest."

Miss Laurence, however, appeared to have no intention of removing herself from the inquisitive throng. "What would his lordship have to do with a tradesman? And didn't the man say something about the Peacock?" she asked Lord Buxley, whose good manners obviously forbade him from deserting the scene in favor of the supper rooms, a bolt hole that seemed to appeal to him very much more than continuing to be in such close proximity to Lord Undercliff and his loud, crude, uninvited guest.

"Please, Miss Laurence," Lord Buxley repeated quietly, looking to Lady Ariana, who believed she interpreted his glance correctly, and he wanted nothing more than to be shed of the situation. She felt much the same herself. No wonder her papa spoke so highly of the man. Pity he wasn't a duke, for she had set her cap for a duke and would not settle for less.

"Why, my lord?" Miss Laurence persisted with, to Lady's Ariana's mind, no more intelligence than she expected of the young woman. After all, hair that red was bound to have singed the girl's brain. "All I asked was what the man might have to do with Lord Undercliff."

"What would his high-and-mighty lordship have to do with me?" Herbert Symington all but shouted, having heard Gabrielle's artless question in the silence that had immediately followed St. Clair's polite, suggestive clearing of his throat.

Symington took two steps forward, showing all intentions of not stopping until he was nose to nose with the curious beauty, and said, "We're partners in business, Undercliff and me, little missy, even if he don't want anyone to know it. Partners in the Symington weaving mills, in Little Pillington."

A ripple of excitement, of disgust, of amused understanding, ran through the crowd of peers who considered any endeavor even vaguely related to trade to be a sin on a par with treason or even incest—although those two transgressions could be excused if there existed ample motive for either profit or personal satisfaction.

But to descend to trade! It was the outside of enough, completely beyond the pale, as poor Lady Undercliff immediately proved by fainting dead away in Lord Buxley's reluctant arms.

Lady Ariana, sensing a golden opportunity to show Miss Laurence in an ill light, snapped open her ivory-sticked fan and began waving it as she pronounced clearly, "I should hope you're happy now, Miss Laurence. Thanks to your unseemly curiosity, poor Lady Undercliff has swooned in embarrassment. St. Clair, be a dear and assist me in extricating myself from this sad crush of titillation-seeking nosey-parkers."

Now, she then thought, inwardly preening as she looked to the frowning baron. *You have no choice, St. Clair, but to cut her now!*

Lady Ariana held her breath. She could feel the hesitancy and indecision that held the remainder of the partygoers frozen in place, awaiting St. Clair's decision as to the correctness of their presence at Lord Undercliff's social destruction. By simply turning his back the baron could destroy the Undercliffs, and Miss Gabrielle Laurence as well.

St. Clair lifted his quizzing glass once more, leisurely surveying the multitude, hesitating as his gaze took in the puce-faced Herbert Symington, the visibly quavering Lord Undercliff, and the obviously unconscious Lady Undercliff.

"Tiens! Do I detect a want of steadiness in our small group, an unwillingness to act? Very well," he then drawled affably, "as it would appear it is left to me to take charge, I will. Lord Buxley, I commend you on your timely capture of our dearest hostess in her time of need. Perhaps you will now retire and give her over to the servants—with Lady Ariana's assistance, as she considers herself too angelically pure for such goings-on as we are witnessing—while we vile, despicable souls remain riveted here at gossip's head table, ravenous for sensation and unabashedly avid to lap up any drop of scandal. After all," he continued, allowing the quizzing glass to drop, "as some observant wit has written, 'Society in shipwreck is a solace to us all.'"

Lady Ariana winced as the shaft of St. Clair's verbal arrow unexpectedly sank home in *her* chest. He had not cut Gabrielle Laurence. He had turned the weapon of his tongue on her instead, damning her with faint praise, calling her angelic when what he'd really meant was that she was a stiff-backed prude who had not insulted just Miss Laurence but all these several dozen milling people who were eager to witness Lord Undercliff's very public embarrassment.

"Christian," she began, squeezing his arm as she looked up at him, "please—"

"Tut, tut, my dear," he broke in as two footmen came to Lord Buxley's aid, taking the slowly recovering but still unsteady-on-her-feet Lady Undercliff away, "don't say another word. We are all human, and therefore we all understand. Of course you may remain—you and Lord Buxley both. I know I could not leave now, even if I shall most sincerely hate myself in the morning—as we shall *all* most sincerely berate ourselves for our eagerness to hear what Mr. Simons here has to say."

"That's *Symington,* my lord," Herbert Symington broke in rather rudely even as Lord Buxley, known far and wide as a true stickler for the conventions, sharply turned on his heel and strode away.

Lady Ariana didn't know which of the two gentlemen she disliked more at that moment: Christian St. Clair for forgiving her, or Lord Anthony Buxley for having the courage to defy the man. Lord Buxley, probably, for now the smiling Miss Laurence and her most annoying, vulgar beauty mark were standing directly beside the baron, basking in the glow of his approval.

"Symington, you say?" St. Clair inquired casually, again employing his quizzing glass to great effect as he inspected the mill owner from head to toe, but quickly, as if the sight of the man's poorly cut brown jacket and too-tight breeches were offensive to his sensibilities.

"La, sir," the baron continued, "I can't imagine why you have taken it into your head to believe I care either way what name you give to yourself. But, please, we *are* most avidly interested in what you have to say, as it is obvious you are operating under some sort of strain. You look, to be frank, as if you have just recently been ridden hard, and then put away wet. Not that such things matter in light of other, more interesting gossip. Miss Laurence here, for one, appears to be eager for news of the Peacock. Whatever has that terrible, terribly *exciting* creature done this time?"

And now, at last, Lady Ariana understood. How could she have been so stupid? The baron was attempting to protect Lord Undercliff, his inquiry deliberately bypassing Undercliff's association with Symington to concentrate on the much more provocative subject of the Peacock.

And the rest of the evening's guests also understood and would not speak publicly of Lord Undercliff's acute embarrassment, knowing St. Clair would not be best pleased if they did so. Oh, he was clever, Christian St. Clair was, earning himself the powerful Lord Undercliff's undying gratitude while still indulging Society's appetite for scandal. Everyone was happy. Everyone save Lady Ariana, and Herbert Symington.

"What did he do?" Symington bellowed, causing Lady Ariana to bring herself back to attention after indulging herself in a lesson on how St. Clair's mind worked. "I'll tell you what the Peacock did. *Just tonight he robbed me of my new coach and then burned my new house straight down to the ground!*"

"'Tare an' hounds! Another house? That's the second this month," someone behind Lady Ariana exclaimed.

"And the sixth—no, the seventh—this year," another gentleman added, before both subsided, probably realizing that such intimate knowledge of the Peacock's activities might urge the others present to look at them and wonder if they, like Lord Undercliff, might owe some part of their fortunes to secretly dabbling in trade.

"Now that you mention it, there is the air of burnt wood about you, Simons," St. Clair said, lifting his scented handkerchief to his nostrils. "How lamentable."

"Why did he burn down your house, Mr. Symington? Are you like the mill owners the Peacock has written about in the newspapers?" Miss Laurence asked, proving to Lady Ariana once again that the girl didn't have a smidgen of sense in her head. A wise young lady, a prudent debutante, would never speak directly to someone as obviously common as the mill owner.

Mr. Symington opened his mouth, ready to answer, when St. Clair cut him off by waving his hand, the one holding the lace handkerchief—an object the mill owner stared at almost greedily. "Please, please, don't subject us to a recitation of your virtues and the disaster of your poor, burned house, Mr. Simons, as I am convinced you were about to do. Likewise, we all are already quite familiar with sundry uplifting tales of the Peacock's mission to punish the wicked for the wretched despair of the poor. Why, I have been so very affected by the man's anonymous treatises to the newspapers concerning underfed children and injured workers that I have had to raise my servants' quarterly wages, out of pure guilt. Haven't we all reacted similarly?"

A murmuring chorus of "Of course!" and "Raised 'em all just last week! Can you even ask?" and "Those letters! So affecting!" trilled through the throng, all of them sounding very self-satisfied at having done their part to boost the Peacock's mission.

"Did you see him—see the Peacock?" one plump-armed matron dared ask, poking Symington with her fan. "We hear he is magnificent!"

"And so daring," another, younger woman put in. "I heard that just last week he and his brave band rode directly into Spitalfields to rescue a poor wretch about to be taken to Newgate for nothing more than picking up an apple that fell from a grocer's cart."

"He's very tall, isn't he?" a dark-haired debutante asked, her kid-encased hands pressed to her breast. "Tall, so very, very handsome, and gallant and prodigiously well-spoken, or so I've heard. He's no common highwayman, everyone says. He must be one of us—but who?"

"Ladies, please," St. Clair interrupted at last, just as a few of the gentlemen began to grumble that this Peacock fellow was becoming much too much the sensation with the females to be anything but an out-and-out rotter. "We are all enthralled with the Peacock's romantic exploits, but the man is just that—a man, and one who chooses to keep his identity a secret, which cannot be considered commendable. We shouldn't be raising him onto a pedestal."

"Heavens no," Miss Laurence slid in quietly, so that Lady Ariana and the baron were most probably the only ones who heard her amid the general murmurings of the crowd. "That would mean we first

47

would have to topple *you* off, wouldn't it? Unless you are already tottering? How does it feel to know you have competition?"

"I don't believe this!" Symington exclaimed, spreading his arms wide, which he could do with ease, for no one in the small crowd appeared willing to be within ten feet of him. "You blockheads care for nothing but adventure! The bounder's burning up houses to make honest mill owners like me bow down to his demands. And they're *doing* it, curse their timid hides. Well, he's not going to best me! I'm going to fight him, and I'm not going to rest for a moment until I see his pretty hide turned off from the gallows outside Newgate prison."

"Mon Dieu! Such enthusiasm, Simons," St. Clair remarked, shaking his head. "I commend you for your determination to bring the crusading scoundrel to justice. However, what is much more to the point than your swaggering braggadocio—did you say his 'pretty' hide? That would mean you have seen him, wouldn't it? Dear man, if for just a moment—indulge the ladies. How does he appear, this Peacock person? Is he all they say?"

"How should I know?" Symington asked, breathing heavily now as the two footmen returned and, at Lord Undercliff's easily interpreted gesture, placed themselves on either side of the mill owner. "He was waiting for me inside my coach just as I came from m'dinner, sitting in the corner smoking a cheroot and hiding his face in the dark. Couldn't see him worth a damn except to know he's most likely tall, like you, and he speaks like a gentleman. Then he took off with my brand-new coach and left me to walk three miles back to Little Pillington," he ended, seemingly close to tears.

"He did? Why, I do believe I must begin to admire this Peacock fellow. Obviously he saw your crying need for exercise, Simons." St. Clair's high-pitched, musical laugh was the signal for everyone to indulge their own amusement even as the footmen firmly took hold of Symington's arms at each elbow and all but dragged him into a small anteroom at the head of the stairs, Lord Undercliff hastening after with nary a backward glance for his guests.

"And that, good friends, concludes this evening's farce, I believe. Come, my dear ladies," St. Clair said after a moment, holding out his crooked arms so that both Miss Laurence and Lady Ariana might avail themselves of his escort as he led them back to the alcove where their chaperones waited.

"What now, Christian?" Lady Ariana inquired, honestly intrigued as to what he would do next.

"What now? Why, first, I believe Lord Undercliff is to be commended for his originality," he commented loudly, "don't you? This has been quite the most stimulating entertainment any host has offered this Season. Yes, yes, I must remember in the morning to join his lordship's other guests in sending round my compliments."

"You may have been amused, but I think the entire episode was distasteful in the extreme," Lady Ariana said feelingly, knowing now for certain that Lord Undercliff would be safe from social disaster, thanks to St. Clair. "In fact, Christian, much as it pains me to agree with that crude man, the best thing that could happen is for that absurd Peacock and his band of marauding brigands to be captured and dealt with as rapidly as possible. Did you hear those silly women? They seem to believe the man is to be admired, when everyone knows he is little more than a thief, a ruffian.

You'd think they didn't know the price of goods will rise twice for every penny the mill owners are forced to raise wages. Why, Papa says—"

"Ah, dearest child, you aren't about to tell me what your papa says again, are you?" St. Clair interrupted wearily. "The man," he explained, looking at Gabrielle, "like our suspicious home secretary, Lord Sidmouth, sees insurrection lurking around every corner."

"But it's true, Christian," Lady Ariana persisted, sure she could show up the country miss with her knowledge of government. "The Peacock is inciting the populace to illegal acts. Why, he's even worse than that odious Orator Hunt, telling the common people that they deserve better. Why? We are *all* suffering now that the war is over. It isn't only the ungrateful peasantry that has had to live with deprivation, but to have to maintain iron gates on our townhouses in order to keep the rioting rabble away is preposterous. Or do you wish to see a copy of the late French Revolution brought to our own doors?"

"Tiens! Why would I care a snap about such far-fetched nonsense? What I do wish, dear girl, is for you to desist in being such a staunch little Tory and remember that bluestockings tend to frighten off suitors, most especially dukes. Or do you believe I shall be amused to champion you when you are in your *fifth* Season, long in the tooth and still prosing on and on about insurrection?"

"If you're still powerful enough five years hence to wield any influence at all over Society," Miss Laurence piped up, causing Lady Ariana to draw in her breath in surprise at the girl's daring in defending her. "I would say the Peacock has already begun to make inroads on your consequence. After all, breathlessly awaiting your entrance in order to admire the cut of your latest new coat barely compares with hearing of the daring exploits of the Peacock. Are you jealous, St. Clair?"

"Hardly, Miss Laurence," St. Clair replied with a smile, so that Lady Ariana longed to box his ears. Didn't the man know when he was being insulted? Then he went on, renewing Lady Ariana's faith in him: "But you must tell me, my dear: Are you to be numbered in the growing multitude of eager ladies wishful of having the Peacock kidnap you as he did Mr. Symington, not to punish you, but to whisk you away for a night of unbridled passion?"

His words were a slap in Gabrielle Laurence's face, reducing her to a witless child who not only couldn't see the danger in the Peacock's provoking exploits but also one who was so infantile as to indulge in romantic musings about the man. Lady Ariana found herself almost feeling sorry for the senseless chit who had thought she might get the better of St. Clair.

Except that Gabrielle did not seem to take offense at St. Clair's words. "You're nearly correct, my lord," she answered as she moved away from him and toward Lord Buxley, who had reappeared in the ballroom and was even now heading in her direction. "I *am* quite taken with the Peacock. It would, after all, be such a social coup to be the one who unmasks him. Oh, and by the bye, St. Clair, I believe I should point out that you slipped just now and referred to Lord Undercliff's uninvited guest by his correct name, proving that even *you* have not been unaffected by the Peacock. Either that, or you are not as witless as you would have us all suppose. Interesting thought, isn't it?"

St. Clair stuck his quizzing glass to his eye as he

watched her go. "Odds fish, Ariana, I begin to believe I have petted our little country kitten just so she could hiss and scratch at me. I vow there is no gratitude left in this world. No gratitude at all, although I imagine Undercliff will be trailing after me soon, wearying me with his thanks. Ah, the tribulations of social consequence. Sometimes, dear lady, I question whether the prize is truly worth the trouble."

"Anything is worth it to people like us, Christian, as social consequence remains the be-all and end-all of our existence," Lady Ariana said quietly, watching Miss Laurence and Lord Buxley move off toward the supper rooms, mentally restructuring her earlier opinion of the young lady and wondering if it would not be possible to become friends with her, if just to bedevil St. Clair, who seemed to derive great pleasure from setting the two beauties at each other's throats.

CHAPTER 3

Men are but children of a larger growth.

John Dryden

The small private study situated on the second floor and to the rear of the St. Clair mansion in Hanover Square was crowded with long-legged men slouched at their ease in burgundy leather chairs ringing the blazing fireplace, their discarded jackets draped behind their heads, cravats hanging loose, snowy white shirts undone at the neck, their hands gripping glasses of warmed brandy, for the April day had gone damp and chilly.

Lord Osmond Osgood, who had stayed so long at the Undercliff Ball card tables the previous evening that his usually indifferent luck at gaming had finally turned in his favor sometime just before dawn, stretched and yawned widely as he languidly waved away Sir Gladwin Penley's offer of a cheroot.

"Haven't the energy, Winnie, thanks just the same," he said. "Suckin' in, blowin' out, tappin' the ashes. And there's the singein' of m'cravats, and fishin' pieces of tobacco off m'tongue—and for what?

Like the smell, can't abide the taste. I'll just breathe in whenever you blow a cloud if it's all right with you. I say, did I tell you how much I won?" he ended, winking.

"That you did, Ozzie—twice," Sir Gladwin answered dully, the rarely animated features of his long face assembled in their usual passionless expression. "And if you were to give me half the winnings to apply toward your outstanding bills, I would appreciate it. Having duns at our door is beginning to lose its novelty."

"Warned you not to move in with Winnie, Ozzie. It's like being married, but with no bedding privileges." George Trumble, who had been eyeing the dish of comfits on the table beside him, rose, picked up the dish, and placed it out of harm's way. He was beginning to see his stomach before he could catch sight of his toes and did not wish to end like his late father, who'd entirely let himself go until he had to be winched up onto his favorite horse.

"Kit," George continued after seating himself once more, Lord Osgood's description of the ennui to be found in smoking having interrupted his conversation with St. Clair, "are you convinced he didn't recognize you? I can't believe you dared to look him straight in the face, allowed him to hear your voice. That's taking daring too far."

"Now, Grumble, don't fret like an old hen over her single pullet," St. Clair answered, crossing one long, booted leg over the other. "Symington was much too dazzled by my glorious rig-out last night to connect me with his newfound nemesis. I told you that handkerchief was just the correct touch. Besides, I enjoyed myself thoroughly, which made the unexpected interlude worth any risk."

"You know, Kit, at times I wonder if you can tell anymore where the play-acting ends and the truth begins, for I truly don't understand you sometimes."

"Ah, then I am become an enigma to you, Grumble?" St. Clair teased. "Would it help if we were to work out some sort of private signal which would alert you whether you were addressing Kit or London's darling?"

George looked at his friend of more than twenty years, a man's man who at least for this moment barely resembled the simpering, lace-edged-handkerchief-waving, overdressed fop who reigned supreme amongst the *ton*.

Christian's buckskins were comfortably old and slightly shabby, his black, knee-high boots thoroughly polished but bare of tassels, his open-throated, full-sleeved white muslin shirt a far cry from the starched splendor of his evening clothes.

Even his chin-length blond hair, swept back severely and anchored with a satin ribbon whenever he was in Society, hung freely around his youthful, handsome face from a haphazard center part, giving the man the air of a swashbuckling pirate.

How George loved his friend, and how he worried for him.

"Look, Kit," George began earnestly, hating the tone of pleading in his voice, "we've had a jolly good time these past months, and done a world of good, to my way of thinking, but perhaps we should draw back for a while. I mean, having Symington smack in front of us at Undercliff's ball? That's cutting it a slice too fine for my mind."

"Spittin' mad, wasn't he?" Lord Osgood piped up, winking at George, who could only roll his eyes and look away. "Aw, come on, Grumble, don't be such a sober prig. Consider it. Symington has issued us a challenge. We can't back off now. It wouldn't be sportin'."

"True enough, Ozzie," St. Clair agreed, pushing his spread fingers through his hair, allowing the heavy blond mane to fall toward his face once more. "Neither sporting nor honorable, in a skewed sort of way. As a matter of fact, I have already decided the Peacock should make Mr. Herbert Symington a return visit tomorrow evening, just to see if he has introduced the new rules to his mills."

"And what about Undercliff?" Sir Gladwin asked, shifting slightly in his chair. "Symington isn't in this alone. I still can't picture it—Undercliff dabbling in trade."

"Neither can I," St. Clair agreed. "I'd have given a hefty sum to have been present when dear Gertie recovered sufficiently from her indelicate swoon to begin ripping strips off his lordship's hide."

"Yes, it must have been a jolly good ruckus," Lord Osgood chimed in.

"But, be that as it may, my friends," Sir Gladwin persisted mournfully, "we're now left in the uncomfortable position of knowing we are attacking a fellow peer when we attack the Symington mills. The Peacock's reputation as a rascal to be admired might suffer an irreparable dent if Society were to understand that, besides tweaking the mill owners and our dear nemesis, Sidmouth, he is also dipping a hand into the pockets of one of their own."

George tried to hide a wince as he saw a steely look come into Christian's eyes, and he hastened into speech. "Now, Winnie, you know the Peacock doesn't exist for the titillation of Society. We have a mission, a serious mission. People are suffering untold horrors, and it is our duty to bring their plight to Society's attention. Isn't that right, Ozzie?"

"Never said it couldn't be fun," Lord Osgood grumbled into his glass, avoiding everyone's eyes. "Besides, Kit tried it the other way, being hangdog serious and all in his single speech to the Lords, and look what it got him. Roasted the fella to a turn. Ain't that right, Kit?"

St. Clair smiled at his friend. "Please, Ozzie, it isn't polite to remind me of my debacle. That was so long ago, and the incident has luckily faded from most minds. Disappearing back into the countryside was the best thing I could do at the time, and my years in Paris proved a boon. No one remembers the Johnny Raw I was when they are being dazzled by the exquisite I have become."

"And there's not a man jack of them who wouldn't fall to the floor, convulsed in hysterics, if anyone was to say you was the Peacock," Sir Gladwin added. "Still, with everyone in town so hot to discover the Peacock's identity, I can't help but worry."

"Good, Winnie," St. Clair said, grinning. "You worry. Both you and Grumble do it very well." Then, sobering, he turned to George to ask, "What did we get for Symington's coach?"

George allowed himself to relax for a moment, happy to act in his role of St. Clair's loyal "lieutenant" of sorts. He saw himself as the man who managed all the details of heroism or, as he was wont to think, played the part of crossing sweep, clearing Christian's path of the mundane, and then going a step further, following after him with a sturdy broom, managing the consequences of his friend's grandiose schemes.

It had been thus since their childhood: Kit dreaming up mad adventures and George making sure they had meat pies tucked up in their pockets before they ventured out for an afternoon of dragon slaying.

"Sufficient to buy twenty dozen pairs of clogs for the children in and around Little Pillington," he told St. Clair, "and with enough left over to have weekly deliveries of bread to the town square for three months, deliveries I've already arranged. I didn't sell the horses, though. They're being ridden north by Symington's coachman and groom, to the Midlands, where they can be of use to some of the few farmers still left on their land. All in all, Kit, a good night's work, even if we didn't have sufficient time to salvage much from that grotesque castle before we heard you coming and had to torch the place. It's a shame Symington couldn't stay later at his party."

"I doubt Symington makes a pleasant guest. His host must have intelligently called for evening prayers an hour early, then quite happily waved dear Herbert on his way," St. Clair commented, reaching into his pocket to draw out a scrap of paper. "Good work, George, as usual. I commend you. However, I received rather disconcerting news a few hours ago from our connection in Little Pillington."

"What is it?" Lord Osgood asked, leaning forward as if to read the note himself.

"A hapless mill worker by the name of Slow Dickie was apprehended last night, lurking about somewhere in the area of Symington's burnt mansion," Christian told them, crushing the note into a ball and flinging it into the fire. "No one could say he was stealing, as they found nothing on him save a rather bedraggled peacock feather. So sad. I had imagined Symington saving the thing and perhaps having it preserved beneath a glass dome on his mantel. But that is beside the point. This Slow Dickie fellow is to be publicly whipped for trespass. We can't have that, gentlemen."

"Any suggestions?" George asked quickly, looking to the two other men, hoping to see some sign that either of them shared his growing unease. Or was he, George Trumble, the only one among them who saw what was happening?

More than a year before, Christian had brought his three oldest friends into his scheme to tweak both Lord Sidmouth's and the communal Tory nose while bringing aid and comfort to the downtrodden at the same time. But what had been initiated for all the best intentions had begun to turn dangerous these past six months, not only for themselves, but for those downtrodden masses as well. Poor, hopeless, hopeful men like this Slow Dickie person, for one. Perhaps such insight was beyond Ozzie and Winnie. But didn't Christian see what was happening?

Or was the proud Christian too consumed with avenging old grudges, with getting some of his own back from those who had scorned him, to recognize when enough was enough?

Although, in the beginning, Christian had been brilliant. If St. Clair's fire-breathing, well-intentioned speech to the House of Lords all those years before had done little else, it had proven to him that the comfortable few were not about to put themselves out for the masses. George could still recall that inglorious day and the Member who had called out jeeringly, "Regulate the mill owners? Did you hear that? Next he'll be taking up the Irish cause! Shout him down, my lords. Shout the seditious rascal down!"

St. Clair, George remembered, had been devastated by his first real defeat. A young man of means, with both wealth and privilege carved out by his forefathers and given to him as his birthright, St. Clair, who had helplessly watched Lord Sidmouth's actions from the sidelines for several years, was convinced that he had been gifted with the money, the talent, and the courage to right the wrongs done the displaced farmers, turned-off soldiers, and exploited mill workers.

From the time they had been children together in Kent, George had known that Christian would always be a man with a mission, a man imbued with his father's courage and his mother's soft, caring heart. All Christian lacked was the power to convince his fellow peers of the folly of keeping their collective government heel on the peasantry's collective neck. Taking his fight against exploitative mill owners, repressive Corn Laws, and other inequities to Parliament after Wellington's soldiers returned to England to be met with high prices and no source of employment had been just the sort of thing the hotheaded St. Clair had deemed "reasonable."

But, after his speech, the younger Christian had immediately been branded persona non grata in a society that did not appreciate having a mirror held up to its shortcomings. As he had told George when the two old friends had gotten woefully drunk that same night to commemorate Christian's political debacle, he now knew that his would be a lone voice in the wilderness if he continued to be a firebrand for his unpopular causes.

But what could Christian do? He could, of course, give away his vast fortune to those less fortunate and earn himself the mantle of martyr, but he could do that only once, and the problem would not be solved.

As Christian had seen it, there was nothing else for

it than that he should change his strategy. He had retired to Kent for a space to lick his wounds and anonymously set up charities George agreed to administer for him.

He had then departed alone for the glittering court of postwar France, stopping first in Calais to visit with a bitter but still brilliant Beau Brummell, trading dinners and gifts of wine for tidbits of helpful information on the exploitable weaknesses of Society from the acknowledged master of manipulation.

Once in Paris, that centuries-old hotbed of intrigue, Christian learned how even a young, brash, somewhat abrasive lad from the country could use the arts and cultured airs of the sophisticated gentleman to succeed where determination and belligerent indignation had failed.

The Baron Christian St. Clair who had finally returned to London was barely recognizable as being the same angry young fellow who had been in Society's orbit for scarcely a sennight two Seasons earlier, for this Baron Christian St. Clair was exquisitely dressed, beautifully mannered, and a constant source of delight to both the gentlemen and their ladies.

To those he now enchanted, the baron was an elegant fop whose presence at any party was to be considered a social coup, a deep-in-the-pockets dandy with delicious notions as to fashion, an amusing dinner companion, and a clear favorite with the eligible debutantes and their doting mamas.

In short, George thought now with a wry smile, within the space of the first few weeks of his triumphant return to the city of his great embarrassment, Christian had wrought a veritable miracle, replacing the departed Beau Brummell as the most dazzling light in the glittering world of a *ton* eager to discover and then worship at the shrine of another dashing figure of manners and fashion.

Never giving up his private charitable contributions on behalf of the mill workers and other poor souls, Christian had begun to implement his influence with Society through wit and humor and his immense social consequence, tweaking them into awareness of the terrible problems that plagued England without them ever knowing he was doing it.

And the method of his enlightenment bordered on pure genius.

Letters to the London newspapers, eloquent, beautifully written letters, told of the terrible injustices of Sidmouth's government, informing, educating, but without preaching. Each missive arrived at the newspaper offices accompanied by a single peacock feather, causing the interested but not very original publishers to dub their unknown contributor the Peacock.

While enjoying the social round, St. Clair made it a point to comment favorably on the concerned soul who was penning the letters. From that moment on it became *de rigueur* for all those in the *ton* to read these letters, even to commit the most affecting passages to memory in order to recite them at parties.

Every week another communication was published. Each related a sad tale of a despondent mother forced to sell her young son to a chimney sweep, or spoke of an old woman found starved to death in an alleyway, or profiled a father of ten incarcerated for debt and denied *habeas corpus* because he could not afford £25 for a lawyer.

The Peacock's story of the plight of a crippled

soldier—a man once seen fighting by the side of the Iron Duke at Salamanca—who had been caught stealing the piddling amount of five shillings' worth of bacon, then sentenced to death because he was "undermining the whole structure of a free society and was not fit to live," had been rumored to have reduced the Queen herself to tears.

One other particular column had caused quite a stir throughout Mayfair, with a rich and pampered Society lining up on either side of the issue as to whether or not a hapless youth should be hanged for chipping the balustrade of Westminster Bridge!

These letters, that gave the poor names and made them real, alive, and no longer faceless multitudes, had proven to be an inspiration. Soon the *ton* had been agog with delicious titillation, all the lords and their ladies certain that this mysterious, eloquent Peacock was one of them, but not knowing his true identity.

But, over time, it hadn't been enough for Christian to make his peers aware of the problems. He needed the laws changed, and he lived for the day Lord Sidmouth and his hidebound Tory cronies were removed from power. Christian was impatient for change, too impatient to content himself with working entirely behind the scenes.

And that, George remembered now half joyfully, half worriedly, was when the Peacock's further adventures had been conceived. Christian understood the *ton* now, had correctly deduced how their minds worked. He saw how they adored being amused, knew they universally despised ambitious mill owners and other tradesmen who believed their newfound wealth had earned them a higher rung on the social ladder, and cleverly surmised how they would rally behind a romantic figure who dashed about righting wrongs and causing Lord Sidmouth and all authority fits.

The first mill owner had bowed to the Peacock's demands within a week—not twenty-four hours after his vacant country house had mysteriously burned to the ground. The victory was heady, delicious, and soon to be repeated, even enlarged to missions designed to rescue individuals from Lord Sidmouth's zealous laws—with all of it reported to the populace every week in the Peacock's entertaining letters.

George had seen this week's letter before Christian had sent it on to the newspapers, and his comic depiction of the boorish, bombastic Herbert Symington was sure to send Society into convulsions of mirth at that ignorant, greedy man's expense.

And so it was that Christian, who had carefully set himself up as the last possible person who could be the daring Peacock, was now free to listen to the growing discontent for Lord Sidmouth's laws within Society, help the peasantry, feel as if he were living out his convictions, and have a jolly good time while he was about it.

Which, George had decided some weeks ago, was precisely the problem.

To George's mind, since the advent of the Peacock's adventures throughout the countryside several months ago, Christian had begun to lose sight of his initial mission. He—indeed, all of them—had been caught up in the thrill of the thing, the hairbreadth escapes from Sidmouth's spies, the purposeful hoodwinking of Society, the power to bend mill owners to their demands.

And at what cost? Lord Sidmouth was drawing down on the masses more cruelly each day, punishing them with ever more oppressive edicts and deeper penalties, taking his revenge on them because he was thus far unable to capture the Peacock.

Now Symington—backed by Lord Undercliff's fortune—had openly declared that he would not buckle under pressure from the Peacock's threats. Would Symington hire his own private army of brigands to seek out Christian and the rest of them? It wasn't inconceivable. And how many more men, poor wretches like this Slow Dickie person, would be made to suffer for Christian's ideals?

George felt ashamed of himself, hated himself for what he was thinking. He was close to seeing himself as Christian's Judas, a disciple who loved him dearly, admired him for his good works and high ideals, yet feared for what his friend was doing in the name of goodness. Judas had turned his friend over to his persecutors in the conviction he was helping him, helping those who blindly followed, believing in salvation. Would it come to that? Dear God, don't let it come to that!

"Grumble? Grumble!" St. Clair called out, laughing. "For the love of heaven, man, pay attention. You're staring at that candy dish as if it contained golden nuggets. Why not just throw some into your mouth and have done with it? God's teeth, but that's revolting. Port and sugarplums," he said, shuddering. "Now listen for a moment. Winnie has concocted an idea as to what to do about the problem of Slow Dickie. You must hear what he has to say. It's priceless, Grumble, I promise. Absolutely priceless!"

George looked up, shaking his head to clear it, happy to avoid Christian's gaze by pretending to concentrate on Sir Gladwin's scheme. "I know I'm going to regret this, but—what sort of idea, Winnie?"

Sir Gladwin pulled a face, slicing a look at St. Clair. "I don't know as how I want to repeat it, seeing as how Kit is grinning like a bear."

"Well, it *is* different, old friend," Lord Osmond piped up, winking at George. "Especially that part about dressin' up poor Grumble here as a washerwoman and settin' him down in the village square as lookout. Grumble—you think you could manage a wriggle when you walk?"

George rolled his eyes, sighing. How could he have been so stupid? Kit was no Christlike figure, and he, George Trumble, was no traitorous disciple. To think so would be nothing short of blasphemous. They were, all four of them, nothing more than overgrown children, perhaps a little more caring than some, and definitely more foolishly adventuresome than most— but still fairly ordinary, in their own twisted way. Unfortunately, they had placed themselves in extraordinary positions.

George reached for the candy dish. No wonder he ate so much, he thought, sighing again. If he didn't, he shouldn't have the strength to *worry* so much. "Never mind, Winnie. You're right. I *don't* want to hear it."

Christian stood up, then leaned one arm negligently against the mantelpiece. "Very well, Grumble. You're aptly named, I'll grant you that. I suppose we should move on. After all, I have promised to grace the theater this evening and must soon begin considering my rig-out. Do you suppose the peach would suit? I shouldn't wish to clash with the draperies."

Sir Gladwin frowned, obviously considering St. Clair's question as if it really mattered, which everyone else knew it didn't. "I don't know, Kit. Refresh my memory: What color are the draperies?"

George chewed another sugarplum, then quickly swallowed both the confection and his guilt. "Leave it, Winnie," he said. "Kit's only trying to muddle our minds so we'll be confused enough to accept his plan to rescue this poor Slow Dickie fellow. You do have a plan bubbling inside that clever head of yours, don't you, my friend?"

St. Clair nodded, then flashed his closest friend a bright smile as he took his seat once more, perched just at the edge of the chair, obviously eager to lay his plan out for his friends. "I never could fool you, could I, Grumble? Yes, I have a plan; one that will serve us in two ways. Grumble, Winnie's notions of you as a washerwoman to one side, tell me: Are you up for a bit of play-acting?"

George stopped his hand inches from his mouth, the sugarplum hanging suspended in air as he narrowed his eyes, looking at St. Clair. "Why?" he asked, already sure he didn't wish to hear his friend's answer.

St. Clair leaned back in his chair, still smiling. "No real reason. Let's just say there is a certain beautiful young lady whose keen intelligence I have never doubted but whose shallow priorities disgusted me. Let us also say that this certain young lady has now shown not only the usual hysterical female interest in the Peacock's identity but also an unnerving acuity which must be deflected. In other words—"

"Don't play the dandy with me, Kit. In *plain* words," George interrupted, sensing danger, "Gabrielle Laurence is beginning to pierce your disguise—or thinks she is. Damn and blast, Kit, I told you to stay away from her. She's not brick-stupid like Lady Ariana and the rest. And Miss Laurence is also not at all grateful to you for bringing her into fashion when she was determined to accomplish that feat on her own. I doubt she appreciates going to her bed each night wondering if the great St. Clair is going to cut her the next day, destroying her."

"True enough, Kit," Sir Gladwin added. "She don't like you above half, and anyone with a clear eye can see it. And, the way Grumble tells it, I don't know as how I can blame her. We all warned you not to tease the chit."

"Ah, gentlemen," St. Clair said, pressing his hands to his chest and raising his pitch a notch as he deftly employed the affected tones he used to such advantage in Society, "but I do *so delight* in her dislike."

"Well, there's always that, I suppose," Lord Osgood said, winking as he snatched the candy dish from George, obviously not bothered that he too would be abusing his palate by mixing fine port with the sugary confections. "Though I never thought I'd live to see you tumble into love, Kit."

"Love?" George exploded, taken totally off-guard. "Ozzie, however did you come up with such a ridiculous notion?"

"I didn't," Lord Osgood answered simply as George looked up at St. Clair in an assessing manner from beneath hooded eyes. "I just now remembered my Aunt Cora once tellin' me I was top over tail in love with m'cousin Abigail because I was always pinchin' her. Of course, we were both little more than infants at the time, and when Abby up and married that Dutchman last year I didn't turn a hair. Never mind, Kit. Sorry I mentioned it."

"Think nothing of it, Ozzie," St. Clair answered, but, George noticed uneasily, for once his friend's smile did not quite reach his eyes.

CHAPTER 4

*La! Did you ever see such an unpleasant person?
I hope when I grow old I shan't look like that.*

Baroness Orczy

Frapple, I'm so damnably tired. All that dashing about from here to there last night, and no less than three different parties this evening, with everyone demanding my presence . . ." Christian trailed off wearily, collapsing into a chair in his dressing room. "I seem to remember hearing of some equally exhausted man putting a period to his existence some years ago because he had been so defeated by this constant dressing and undressing."

"I shall have the kitchen staff sequester all the knives at once, my lord," Frapple answered calmly, continuing to lay out his master's apple-green velvet evening clothes. "And don't muss your breeches by slouching, if you please. Meg had the devil's own time pressing them."

"How good of you to worry so for Meg. Do I scent a romance in the air, Frapple?"

"Hardly, my lord. Riding herd on you at all hours,

when would I find the time?" A tall, still ramrod-straight man of two and fifty, Frapple had been Christian's trusted adviser and man-of-all-work since his lordship had been in short coats, and he did not frazzle easily. Indeed, as he was rumored to be the by-blow of the baron's great-uncle Clarence St. Clair, he may have come by his flippant nonchalance quite naturally, just as he had come by his slowly graying blond hair and thin, aquiline nose. If it weren't for the man's mustache, and his more advanced years, in a dim light Frapple might even be taken for an older Christian.

In any event, Christian loved him as he would have the older brother he'd never had, and Frapple returned this affection, although he refused to allow his lordship to forget their very disparate stations in life.

Christian smiled now at the man he privately considered to be the best of his relatives, then yawned widely. "I won't be returning home this evening, Frapple, if you wish to spare a moment for romance," he said, raising his legs in front of him so that he could admire his new evening shoes. "I need to travel to Little Pillington to remind Herbert Symington of my existence. Thank God I'm known not to tarry too long at any one party, and won't be missed. If I'm lucky, I should be in Little Pillington at least two hours before dawn."

"You won't allow yourself to be caught, will you?" Frapple asked, intent on examining his lordship's chosen lace neckpiece for wrinkles before sighing, roughly stuffing the offending thing into his pocket, and removing its twin from the cabinet.

"Frapple!" Christian exclaimed. "Don't tell me you're worried about me."

"Not in the slightest, my lord," the servant answered, already heading for the door to the hallway, the apple-green velvet jacket in his hand. "It's only that I'm much too long in the tooth to have to begin again with a new employer. Why, the man might even think I'd kowtow to him. Now, I'm just going to have Meg do something with this left sleeve. It's rather crushed. Please, my lord, as I may be detained for some minutes, I must beg that you do *not* change your mind about your rig-out for the evening and endeavor to dress yourself. We both, I hope, remember the disaster that befell the ecru satin."

Christian nodded and waved Frapple on his way, not wishing to revisit the subject of the form-fitting ecru satin jacket and the seam he had split in attempting to don it without aid, or even to think of any of his Society clothing.

If he had his druthers, which he of course did not, he would step back in time and attempt to bring into vogue a more comfortable, less constricting fashion than he had done in reinventing flamboyant Georgian dress. Thank God he'd stopped short of powdering his hair.

He rose from his chair and drifted into the adjoining bedchamber, seating himself at the desk he used when composing his weekly letters to the London newspapers. What would be his subject for next week? Would he tell of the mill workers he had seen who'd been crippled by faulty machinery, their thumbs mashed into useless lumps of nothingness? No. That might unduly upset the ladies, who did not appreciate detailed descriptions of gore served up with their morning chocolate.

Starving babies were more to the ladies' tastes, Christian had already learned. The ladies could delicately weep into their handkerchiefs between helpings of coddled eggs and bemoan the fate of the "poor, wretched darlings" without having to do more than send off a bank draft to one of the local orphanages. It was so morally uplifting, this generosity that soothed their shallow consciences and that cost them nothing but money.

Christian propped his elbows on the desktop and rested his head on his hands. He was tired. So tired. And it had little to do with the endless social whirl, his private missions, or even the strain of keeping his two identities separate from each other.

He was tired of the poverty, the heartache, the sad, hollow eyes and the crying mothers. He was tired of hearing about men such as Slow Dickie, being beaten merely because he could not defend himself against being beaten.

He was exhausted by the futility of saving a few while the many still suffered. He was weary of this back-door subterfuge meant to waken his peers to the desperate plight of those they would call the "solid English citizenry."

But mostly, Christian was angry. How could his fellow peers be so blind, so damnably selfish, so fearful of the masses that they would be foolish enough to incite them to insurrection?

His peers. Idiots! Jackals! The whole bloody lot of them! Christian slammed a fist against the tabletop, jarring the small lidded crystal bowl holding his supply of ink. All they cared about was the cut of their coats, the latest gossip, and clinging to their supposed superiority with all their might.

When Christian went into Society he did it to hold up a looking glass to their foibles, showing them with his own overdressed, overly impressed-with-himself posture the folly of worshiping such cultivated shallowness and hoping they would somehow summon up the brainpower to compare their pampered, wasteful, wasted lives with the majority of their countrymen who had to scrabble for their daily bread.

Yes, he had pricked their consciences. Yes, a few of them now interested themselves in good works. Yes, they slyly ridiculed Lord Sidmouth as they went down the dance, tsk-tsking at his insistence upon championing the master over the servant. But they did it only to mimic the popular Baron St. Clair, to show their wit, and to prove their "humanity." Not a man jack of them had yet dared to stand up in Parliament to say a word against either Lord Sidmouth or his oppressive edicts.

Christian balled his hands into fists, feeling wave after wave of angry impotence wash over him. Setting himself up as the leading influence in Society had not been enough. The letters had not been enough. Only when the Peacock had begun to ride had any real changes come to places like "Mud City" and other squalid manufacturing villages in the Midlands.

Only when Christian had escalated his mission from cajoling, to eloquence, to *violence*, had most of the *ton* even acknowledged that there might be some real injustice to be found in the oppressive Corn Laws and the working conditions in the mills.

And still they didn't really understand. Instead of emulating the Peacock, Society had decided to be dazzled by him, and to set themselves the project of discovering his true identity.

What a waste. What a damnable, damning waste! And for what? A few dozen pairs of clogs? One more crust of bread for the sad-eyed, stick-thin children of the mill workers? One less hour of near slavery in an already interminable workday?

Christian could see the growing disillusionment in George Trumble's eyes, sense the unspoken questions, the quiet censure. Their mission, begun with such enthusiasm, such purity of purpose, had grown almost beyond their control, the tail now beginning to wag the dog, their ever-increasingly dangerous exploits demanded by an easily distracted Society's hunger for more adventure, more excitement, more titillation, more, more, *more*.

And now Herbert Symington and his partner, the powerful if obtuse Lord Undercliff, had dared to challenge the Peacock's one great success. Turning fire-starter had not been pleasant for Christian, but what had been an impulsive ploy had immediately proved effective. Mill owners were beginning to ease their stranglehold on their workers on their own, in the hope the Peacock would then spare their houses, their possessions.

However, if Christian were to allow Symington to best him, the work of these last six months—indeed, the success of the past year and more—would all vanish in the twinkling of an eye.

For Christian knew Society now, had learned all about it at the knee of the disenchanted Brummell, and he recognized that English Society loved only one thing more than raising a person onto a pedestal.

That one thing, as Brummell's disgrace had shown so clearly, was to topple him off again.

And if Christian St. Clair were to fall, if the Peacock were to fail, then the poor would have no champion left to them. Men like Slow Dickie would have put themselves in jeopardy for nothing.

Was it any wonder Christian was so tired? Tired, and disillusioned, and thoroughly disgusted with his fellow man. Was he the only person in London with the intelligence to understand that, unless something were done to alleviate the suffering of the many, it was inevitable that the privileged few would eventually become equal victims of their degenerating civilization?

England was stunting the physical and spiritual growth of an entire generation, a generation of children uprooted from their farms and villages and forced into slums, away from sunlight and open fields.

An entire generation was being raised without mothers close by to teach them, without seeing the inside of either church or school, watching their mothers and sisters turning slattern with poverty, their fathers and brothers either beaten down in the mills or becoming hard, cruel, reckless men whose only ease came either in a pint of cheap gin or in bashing one of their fellows senseless for no other reason than that violence brought with it a modicum of power.

Yet in London the chandeliers still glittered, the supper-room tables groaned beneath piles of exotic foodstuffs, the sound of music, and laughter, and the rustling of silken skirts, echoed throughout ballrooms from one end of Mayfair to the other.

Lords still drove to Newmarket for the races, their ladies still spent lavishly on dinner parties and routs and soirees, young men lived for the turf and table, and silly debutantes still whispered behind their fans, their minds filled with nothing but the anticipation of securing themselves wealthy husbands who drove to Newmarket for the races so that they could stay home and spend lavishly on dinner parties and routs and soirees.

Christian leaned back in his chair, all this deep thought giving him the beginnings of a headache.

Foolish gentlemen. Spendthrift ladies. Posturing, preening young lords. And feather-brained, mercenary young debutantes. All of them not worth one Slow Dickie and his fight for survival. The devil with all of them!

"And the devil with Gabrielle Laurence," Christian said out loud, startling himself with his vehemence.

Gabrielle Laurence. So startlingly beautiful, so unusual. So very intelligent—or at least he believed she could be as he'd watched her shift her brilliant green gaze around the ballroom, obviously mentally measuring everyone she saw. But even Gabrielle, whom Christian had discovered the very first night of the Season, had quickly shown herself to be no more than another pretty shell washed up on the glittering beach of the *ton,* with nothing of substance, of worth, inside her.

Oh, yes, she was bright, even witty. But her aspirations rose no higher than making herself the Sensation of the Season and then snaring a brilliant match with some wealthy, titled gentleman. Still, Christian could not quite lose his fascination with her, could not cease wondering how it would feel to hold her, how she would taste if he kissed her, how those lovely green eyes would open wide as he introduced her to ecstasy.

And so he'd employed his social consequence to give the fiery-haired Original what she wanted, just to find himself despised for his helpful intervention—which fascinated him ever more.

George had been correct to say that Gabrielle did not appreciate being in Christian's debt. Gabrielle, whose dowerless state had made social success nearly impossible on her own, must have recognized the very real possibility that the powerful St. Clair's favor could be withdrawn at any time, leaving her just another hopeful debutante. Or even less in fashion than the other young ladies making their debut, as she would then be plagued with two problems: her unusual and unfashionable red hair, and St. Clair's defection, which would cause others to shun her.

Gabrielle's quick understanding of her precarious position, that of having her continued success depend upon the whim of a man she so obviously loathed, had served to reinforce Christian's conclusion that beneath that beautiful shell there was at least the possibility of intelligence.

Over these past two weeks he had become convinced of it. Her daring when they were alone, her deliberate baiting of him in ways that no other person save the inimitable Frapple had dared since his ascension to the pinnacle of social power, had shown him that Gabrielle Laurence was his match in many ways. Which had served to make him even more angry with her.

She, a young woman who was not poor but yet not nearly as wealthy as most debutantes, should know that the social whirl was a hollow world. She, of anyone he had met, possessed the intelligence to thoroughly disdain this same social whirl and apply her great resolve and determination to more substantive matters.

Of course, there was also this business of how she disliked *him*—never failing to describe him as a brainless dandy more worried over the cut of his coat than anything else.

Did she loathe all men?

She said she didn't, reserving her disdain exclusively for him. But there was something—some negligible *something*—that told him that she knew this was all a game, that Society itself was a pawn in that game, and she played at it only because she was a woman, and if it was the only game she was allowed to play she was determined to be the clear victor.

Unfortunately for Christian, he was beginning to believe Gabrielle had discovered another game, and she was out to win that one as well. That game? To discover the identity of the Peacock. It wasn't as if everyone else hadn't already figuratively signed on for a turn at this contest, everyone in Society agog to know the Peacock's identity. But everyone else only toyed with the game, contenting themselves with wild guesses and the "romance" of the thing.

Gabrielle Laurence was playing the game in earnest, whether in order to cement her position in Society without having to worry about continuing to curry Christian's favor or because reigning over Society had been too easy a success and she was now looking for another challenge, Christian did not know.

He knew only that she had come dangerously close to seeing beneath the veneer of his social pose, to catching his verbal slip the other night and immediately pouncing on it. Lady Ariana hadn't noticed. Christian doubted that anyone of his acquaintance save George would have noticed. But Gabrielle had.

"Which either proves that she is as intelligent as I thought, causing me to dislike her more for choosing to expend that intelligence so wastefully," Christian mused aloud, "or makes me a wishful fool, looking for more than is there and hoping against hope that the beautiful Miss Laurence fits the image of a woman I could love."

"Or," Frapple said from behind him as he entered the room, holding the apple-green velvet jacket in front of him as if it were the Holy Grail, "you are a lustful rutting dog like your Uncle Clarence, hot to bed a lovely lady, but trying to tell yourself you are different from him, and above such animal urges."

"That too." Christian turned slowly on his chair, one side of his mouth rising in a rueful smile. "Educating you may have been a mistake on my part, Frapple," he observed quietly. "Not only do you insult me, but you do it with great articulation. I should sack you for insubordination, you know."

"True, but then who would dress you, my lord?" Frapple motioned for Christian to follow him into the dressing room. "We must hurry," he told his employer. "Lord Buxley is below, asking to see you."

"Lord Buxley?" Christian repeated questioningly as the servant helped him shrug into the tight-fitting jacket. What did that sober Tory prig want with him? Or had the incident at Lord Undercliff's caused suspicion in someone other than Gabrielle Laurence?

Damn and blast! He didn't need this now. He was to visit Little Pillington tonight, not have one of Sidmouth's staunchest supporters tagging at his heels so that he could not chance leaving Mayfair. "Deny me, Frapple."

"I do, my lord, as often as possible. St. Peter in all his disgrace could not deny his master more," Frapple replied flippantly, giving Christian a sharp tap on each slightly padded shoulder as if to be sure the coat fit securely. "However, in this instance, his lordship will not retire. He says he is on the King's business."

Christian chuckled low in his throat, laughing in reaction to both Frapple's irreverent wit and the thought that Lord Anthony Buxley would stoop to using the King's name to gain access to the mansion.

"And what service would Lord Buxley have Baron St. Clair perform in the King's name, do you suppose?" he ventured, slipping his distinctive dull silver ring on the middle finger of his right hand. "Would he have Society's premier dandy bring Prinny back into favor with the *ton*? I fear that particular herculean feat, Frapple, would be beyond even me."

Frapple stepped behind Christian to secure the carefully constructed foaming lace neckgear around his master's throat, a much less time-consuming exercise than the starched-to-perfection neckcloths with which Brummell had tortured the gentlemen of the *ton* in his time. "In that case, I'll just have Meg chase his lordship out of the square with her broom."

"That will not be necessary, although it's a sight I'd pay dearly to witness. I'll see him, for my curiosity is piqued. A moment, Frapple, whilst this country bumpkin transforms himself."

Christian took a last, assessing look at himself in the glass over his dressing table, picked up his lace handkerchief, and turned to Frapple, a rather high-pitched giggle escaping him as he deliberately struck an elegant pose, flourishing that same handkerchief. "Impossible to bring the Prince Regent back into a good odor, you say? *Quelle absurdité!* That *I*, Baron Christian St. Clair, should be believed incapable of anything? Bruise me if I should countenance such arrant nonsense for even an instant. Frapple!"

"Yes, my lord!" the servant replied sharply, bowing as his eyes twinkled in amusement.

"My quizzing glass, man!" Christian commanded, lifting his chin. "Would you have me go naked to meet my guest?"

A few moments later, Frapple having satisfied

himself that his lordship was complete to a shade, Christian sauntered leisurely down the wide, curving staircase on his way to the drawing room, his agile mind busy behind the blank handsomeness of his face.

Lord Buxley had never visited him here in Hanover Square. Indeed, the man barely nodded to him when their paths chanced to cross in public. They were both gentlemen, so they were civil to each other, but they were at opposite ends of the same rung of the social ladder.

Lord Anthony Buxley was a staunch Tory, a backer of Lord Sidmouth's government and proud of the fact. Baron St. Clair, Christian thought with a small smile as he deliberately halted in front of a large mirror in the foyer and adjusted his sleeves, was a staunch nothing, backing only himself, and everyone was aware of *that* fact.

Lord Buxley, a good dozen years senior to the six-and-twenty Christian, was known as a Corinthian; a bruising rider, handy with his fives at Gentleman Jackson's, and a man who dressed well but was not overly obsessed with fashion.

Christian, in comparison, was the Compleat Dandy; he shunned horseflesh except to cowhandedly tool his high-perch phaeton in the promenade at five each afternoon, decried physical exertion other than brisk walking as brutish and prone to produce unwanted perspiration, and lived only to dress and undress and dress himself yet again.

They had little in common, Christian St. Clair and Lord Anthony Buxley, except perhaps their physical attractiveness, their pedigrees, both of them being descendants of illustrious families, and their prominence in Society. But if locked up together in a room, they would have nothing to say to each other. Nothing.

So why had Lord Buxley come here this evening?

"Yoo-hoo! Lord Buxley! Halloo!" Christian exclaimed as he entered the immense drawing room decorated in the elegant Empire fashion, taking his lordship's hand in his as that man stood up and approached him. Christian limply shook the older man's fingers before meticulously arranging his tall frame on a small, armless chair and motioning for his guest to seat himself once more.

"Voyons, Buxley," he began quickly when his lordship didn't speak, "but this is an unexpected delight. And don't you look exquisite this evening, my lord? The cut of your coat is to weep for, truly it is! *C'est merveilleux!* What is that shade—funereal black? And we must each have some champagne to celebrate your presence in my humble abode. I shall summon Frapple at once."

Christian watched as Lord Buxley bit down on his anger and distaste, pleased to see that the man was here very much against his wishes. Something was afoot, but whatever mission had brought his lordship to Hanover Square had clearly not been his idea.

"Can we get directly to the point, St. Clair?" Lord Buxley asked, obviously uncomfortable in the role of supplicant. "You witnessed that embarrassment at Lord Undercliff's the other evening?"

"Witnessed it?" Christian repeated, lifting one eyebrow. "My dear man, in all modesty I must remind you that I *salvaged* the moment. Why, if it were not for me, dearest Undercliff would even now be repairing to his country estate in abject disgrace, unable to show his head in the metropolis for years. *Tiens!* Don't tell me you are here to thank me, my lord? I assure you, thanks are not in the least necessary. I was only doing"—he giggled at his own wit—"the *Christian* thing."

Lord Buxley hopped to his feet. "You vacuous twit!" he exploded, his hands balled into fists as if only his fine breeding kept him from beating the baron into a bloody pulp. "Everything is a bloody game to you, isn't it? A test of your social power. Well, St. Clair, let me tell you a thing or two!"

Christian spread his hands, palms upward, as if to show he had nothing to hide, and nothing to fear. "Feel free to tell me anything you wish, my lord," he said soothingly. "I only ask you, do not exert yourself in such a way, as it is so wearying to see a man in your high state of agitation. Why, if I were to so exercise my nerves, I should then have to retire to my bed for a week. Have you tried taking a brisk walk, my lord? I owe all my good health and calmness of spirit to such excursions. I vow, it does wonders for the temperament, and the spleen as well, or so I'm told."

"Damn your brisk walks, and damn you!" Lord Buxley turned his back on St. Clair for a moment, then wheeled about, his black-as-raisins-in-a-pudding eyes flashing fire. "I'd rather drink flaming pitch than come to you for help, St. Clair, but I have no choice. You saw how the herd followed your lead the other night. I don't know how you do it, or why any of them gives a fig for your good opinion, but that's the way it is. I need you, Lord Sidmouth needs you. God help us all—*England* needs you!"

"Moi? Such an infinite honor, I'm sure." Christian pressed his fingers to his lips even as a girlish giggle

escaped him. This was just too good! "Dear Lord Buxley, how disturbingly serious you are. A veritable old sobersides, I've no doubt, and deuced earnest. And how you do *flatter* me."

Lord Buxley strode toward Christian as if intent on throttling him, stopping only a foot in front of him. "We want the Peacock," he intoned earnestly. "He has made fools of us long enough. The newspapers refuse to stop publishing his letters because their circulations have doubled since the Peacock became a contributor. The caricaturists are making a public circus of our efforts to capture the man—"

"Yes, yes, say no more," Christian interrupted, giggling yet again as he raised his lace-edged handkerchief to the corners of his mouth. "I have seen them. None of the artists has quite captured dearest Lord Sidmouth well, have they? I mean, to see his lordship depicted mounted on a jackass, racing about the countryside while blindfolded as a large peacock snickers at him from behind a tree—or drawn on his knees, his rump facing skyward, searching beneath octogenarian ladies' beds for the elusive Peacock— well, what can I say?"

"I would like you to say nothing, St. Clair," Lord Buxley countered, walking away once more, to begin pacing the small oriental carpet that lay against the highly polished wooden floor. "That is, I would like you—our government would like you—to stop quoting from the Peacock's letters. We would like you to say once and for all that the Peacock is a menace to all loyal Englishmen. In short, we would like Society to see this Peacock debacle for what it is: an assault against the government and all in the law which we hold sacred."

Christian looked up at Lord Buxley owlishly, wondering what the man would think if he knew he had just asked St. Clair to condemn himself. "Is that all, my lord? You simply wish the creature out of fashion? Wouldn't you desire for me to capture him as well? Oh yes, oh yes!" he exclaimed, as if caught up in the moment. "I must be in on the capture of this vile man who has for so long tweaked at our esteemed government. I hadn't realized the government was in danger. I must come to the rescue! Again, my lord, I am so *honored.* My head is veritably swimming—my senses are gone!"

"You? Capture the Peacock?" Lord Buxley's eyes narrowed as he turned to Christian, pointing a finger at him, clearly not similarly caught up in his lordship's enthusiasm. Not that he was amused by Christian's fevered declaration—or at least Christian didn't think so. But then, remembering that he had never seen the man smile, Christian decided only that he couldn't be sure.

"We will handle the ultimate capture, St. Clair," Lord Buxley said coldly, "and without your help. As if the painted ninny could catch a drop of rain in a downpour," he ended only half beneath his breath.

Christian clapped his hands in delight. *"You* will capture the Peacock, my lord? You, *personally?* Death and fiends, how above everything wonderful! Conceive me before you now, awestruck! Tell me: How do you propose to go about it? You must have been inspired by some brilliant new plan, for you have been so woefully unsuccessful in discovering him this past year and more."

Lord Buxley furtively looked to his left and right, Christian thought in some amusement, as if he expected the Peacock's spies to be lurking in the corners of the St. Clair drawing room, waiting with bated breath for word of this new "plan." Which, Christian considered further, discreetly coughing into his fist, would not be far off the mark.

"Lord Buxley?" he prompted as his lordship continued to hesitate. After all, Christian thought, this was too good a moment to let slip away.

Lord Buxley shrugged his broad shoulders. Really, Christian thought, his lordship would be an exceedingly handsome, well-set-up man, if he weren't so unpleasant. How would he look in emerald-green satin, a fall of ivory lace tied around his strong neck? *E-gad!* Christian mentally yelped. Were the fop and the adventurer beginning to meld together? Perhaps he had been working too hard at this play-acting and it *was* time to bring the farce to an end before he no longer recognized his true self.

"All right, St. Clair," Lord Buxley said at last. "It isn't as if you'd know what to do with the information, is it?" He bent slightly forward, somehow still maintaining his ramrod posture, and intoned quietly, "We have succeeded in infiltrating his latest wretched gang of malcontents—in Little Pillington."

Christian's blood ran cold, but the only indication of interest he showed was to tip his head to one side and giggle inanely. *"Mille diables!* Little Pillington, you say? Isn't that where that horrid man, Simons, has his factories? What genius, my lord! But so dangerous. Mingling with desperate cutthroats? I feel nearby to expiring at the mere thought of it! However did you manage this coup?"

"It was simple enough, and all my idea. Groups of seditious laborers have been meeting in secret all over the country, including Little Pillington, where the Peacock is currently operating. We've had men— agent provocateurs, if you will—introduced into nearly every group, so that there is little we don't know or can't learn with a few well-placed questions. We knew the Peacock was in Little Pillington a full hour before he struck at Herbert Symington. It's only a matter of time before we have him within our grasp! Then we will make short work of punishing all those miserable malcontents and lazy wastrels who would meet to bring down their own government!" he ended proudly.

"And all *your* idea, you said? Gad, sir, how very proud you must be," Christian complimented effusively, rising to escort Lord Buxley to the door. "However, exhilarating as this conversation is, I fear I am going to be late to Lady Skiffington's select soiree before the theater if I am not on my way within the minute. You don't mind, do you?"

"You'll do as I've asked, St. Clair?" Lord Buxley inquired, as Frapple stepped forward smartly to present him with his hat and cane.

"I'll sleep on the matter, if you don't mind, dear fellow," Christian told him, personally opening the door to the square for the man. "I confess to being malicious enough to enjoy my power, but I hesitate to use it in this instance. After all, my lord, when we think of the starving children, the desperate mothers . . ." He allowed his voice to trail off, shrugging eloquently.

"The Peacock must be stopped, St. Clair," Lord Buxley reminded him from between clenched teeth. "You owe your service to your King."

"Odds bobs, my lord," Christian responded, drawing himself up to his full height and screwing his face into a comically belligerent scowl, "I know that. But do I owe my service to Lord Sidmouth? That, dear man, remains the question. And you refuse to allow me to be in on the Peacock's capture. That is disappointing. But I will think on it, you have my word as a gentleman."

"I'd rather have your words spoken in the ballrooms of Mayfair. At least there they carry some weight. Good evening to you, St. Clair," Lord Buxley said, jamming his hat down on his head and rigidly descending the stone steps to the flagway, halting at the bottom to turn and add, "I should have known I'd get no help from you."

"Nonsense, old fellow," St. Clair called after him. "You could apply to me at any time for my assistance in selecting your wardrobe. To each man his *forte,* I say. Have a good evening, Lord Buxley. I know I shall."

Christian stood in the light from the chandelier, still smiling and waving at his lordship with his handkerchief until Frapple closed the door, at which time his inane grin evaporated. "Not a word, Frapple," he warned softly, knowing the servant had overheard everything Lord Buxley had said. "Not a single word of this to anyone—most especially Grumble. Do you understand?"

"What wouldn't I understand, my lord?" Frapple countered, handing Christian his hat and walking stick. "If your friends were to know how the noose tightens, they'd refuse to ride again. Why confuse the issue with common sense?"

Christian patted his servant and friend on the shoulder as he motioned for him to open the door once more. "I've no thought of running my head into a noose, Frapple," he assured the man. "And now, as my carriage awaits, I fear I must be going."

"Will you still visit Little Pillington tonight?" Frapple asked.

Christian winked, already planning his next meeting with Herbert Symington. "Frapple, how you wound me. Was there ever any doubt?"

CHAPTER 5

~

*She was . . . the darling of a brilliant throng,
adored, fêted, petted, cherished.*

Baroness Orczy

The same weak, fading, late-afternoon sun that
lighted St. Clair on his way to his first social engagement of the evening stole timidly through the front
windows and into the small drawing room of the
narrow Percy Street townhouse, falling on the furnishings some might find elegantly simple and others
might condemn as rather sparse. There were four
chairs scattered about the room, two of them clustered near the fireplace, a few tables uncluttered by
much in the way of vases or figurines, two paintings of
little merit, a gilt-edged mirror, and a single couch.

Gabrielle Laurence lay most inelegantly stretched
out on this green-and-white flowered couch, pouting.
In less than ten minutes she would have to begin
dressing for another evening of smiling and flirting
and dancing with twits with more hair than wit but,
luckily, also more money than brains. It was a de-

pressing thought, but such was the life of a diligent fortune hunter.

She wiggled her bare toes, just now propped on one arm of the couch, and complained, "If I have to go through one more evening of having that silly, fuzzy-cheeked viscount trampling all over my feet like a clumping camel, Lizzie, I swear to you I shall simply give up this entire charade and return home. The only thing worse than his lordship's clumping is his breath, which is also camel-like, and prodigiously odious."

Elizabeth Fletcher, Gabrielle's longtime friend who had graciously consented to serving as her companion for the Season, looked up from her knitting to remark, "And how would you know that a camel's breath is odious, Gaby? You've never even seen a camel."

Gabrielle sat up slightly, grinning at Elizabeth as she repositioned the embroidered pillow that was behind her head into a more comfortable spot, then threw herself prone once more, her unbound hair falling like liquid fire over the pillow. "I've read about them, silly," she responded reasonably. "Think of what they eat, Lizzie. Their breath couldn't possibly be fragrant. But that's nothing to the point. The viscount is entirely too smitten with me to make a complacent husband. No, he is definitely off our list. *Definitely.*"

"Very well, Gaby. His lordship, being summarily found guilty of possible slavish adoration, is *out*," Elizabeth said, laying down her knitting and pushing her gold-rimmed spectacles a smidgen higher on her nose, up past the slight bump she had long ago declared was a gift from the gods meant to make the wearing of spectacles easier for her, as it had long ago proven a perfect resting place for the dratted things.

She then shifted in her chair in order to slide a hand

into the pocket of her gown and pull out a much creased and abused sheet of paper containing the list of wealthy, eligible bachelors Gabrielle was considering as future husbands. Employing a knitting needle for her purpose, she then poked a hole through the paper next to the viscount's name. "Ta-ta, your lordship," she said, then frowned as she ran the point of the knitting needle down the list of names, counting the number of holes in the paper. "Only a little more than a fortnight, Gaby, and more than half of your prospects are gone. Is the crop of eligible gentlemen that shabby, or are you simply too particular?"

"I could always take a dead set at St. Clair, I suppose," Gabrielle offered, flinching inwardly. "He's deep-in-the-pocket enough, God knows, and much too involved with self-worship to pest me much as a husband. If only I didn't loathe him so. Otherwise he could be amusing, for I do enjoy arguing with him. It constantly amazes me that anyone so brick-stupid can be so witty. But he's shallow as a spring puddle."

"He's also handsome, and young, and eminently well received in society," Elizabeth said comfortingly. "And he has championed you, which relieves us from probing questions concerning your nonexistent dowry. To be dowerless is bad enough, but to be desperate for funds is unforgivable. Ah, well. You are now in the enviable position of being sought after for your beauty and social consequence rather than for any money you might bring to a marriage. We had worried about that, if you recall. Yes, St. Clair has been most helpful. Are you quite sure you don't wish to reconsider him?"

Gabrielle stared upward, in her mind's eye seeing Christian St. Clair's vacantly grinning face suspended above her, hating herself for even inwardly acknowledging that he was still quite the most handsome man she had ever seen, hating herself for the frissons of awareness, of excitement, that persisted in coursing through her whenever he touched her hand or said her name.

Set her cap at Christian St. Clair? She would have to be truly desperate to do any such thing, for if he were ever to learn about her true circumstances he would drop her like a stone, and she would be destroyed, both socially and in some part of her heart she refused to think about with any seriousness.

At last Gabrielle gave up searching the freshly painted ceiling for some sort of heavenly sign that might serve as an answer to her dilemma and turned onto her side on the comfortable couch, grinning at her friend. "What a perfect wretch I am, Lizzie. I'm in no position to be particular, am I? Being dowerless is bad enough, yet acceptable. Being within Ames's ace of debtors' prison is unforgivable."

Elizabeth made a great business of smoothing her pink muslin skirts as she rose and walked to the window overlooking the street. A woman easing closer to thirty than she would like, widowed too long to be wearing black yet too old to be sporting pink muslin, she had only three small vices in her life: the already mentioned affection for pink, a seldom indulged love for licorice candy, and her compliance in her bosom chum Gabrielle's mad scheme to marry a wealthy man, thus saving her beloved Rose Hill Farm.

"I shouldn't wish to see you throw yourself away on a man with camel's breath, if that eases your mind," she said at last, turning to smile at her friend. "However, we are rapidly running short of funds, and your father has sent yet another urgent missive requesting you immediately sell this supposedly vacant house and forward the proceeds to him in Italy—"

"—so that he can gamble it away within a heart-beat," Gabrielle ended wearily, "leaving my beloved Rose Hill Farm totally unprotected and our few remaining staff without their next quarter's wages. The income we received renting out this townhouse is nearly all the money I have, Lizzie. No, there's nothing else for it than that I have to find myself a husband within the month or else locate another tenant and return to the country, where we can all continue to starve in genteel poverty. Until Papa finds his way home to sell both places to finance his gambling, that is. Then we shan't have to worry about new thatch or the apple crop, for we'll all be living under the hedgerows."

"It is depressing, isn't it?" Elizabeth asked rhetorically, turning to look out the window once more. "Oh, fiddle! A coach has stopped in front of the house. Gaby—surely you didn't invite anyone here? We've discussed this and discussed this, and with no servants—and precious little food for any mouths but ours—it would be the height of folly to allow anyone to—"

"I didn't invite anyone, Lizzie," Gabrielle cut in as she swung to a sitting position and struggled to locate her shoes with one frantically searching toe while quickly running her fingers through her hair in a helpless attempt to smooth it into something resembling an evenly remotely civilized style. "Has the carriage door opened yet, Lizzie? Can you see who it is?"

"The footman is just now climbing down from the box," Elizabeth told Gabrielle as she prudently stepped to the right of the window in order that the person soon to alight from the carriage could not chance to look up and see her standing there, staring like some ill-bred looby. "Well, we'll just have to tell whomever it is that we're not receiving this afternoon."

Gabrielle chuckled softly. "That's brilliant, Lizzie. There's only one problem with that idea: How do we relay that message, considering that we are the only two people in the house and one of us must answer the knocker? Or perhaps we should simply fling ourselves to the floor and lie quite still until whoever it is goes away?"

"Yes, that might serve the purpose," Elizabeth said quickly, then shook her head. "Throw ourselves to the floor? Hide? What am I thinking! We are ladies, and above such foolery."

Gabrielle nodded in agreement. "Besides, Lizzie, they'd only come back again, and we can't spend our lives either crawling on our bellies to remain out of sight of the windows or living with lamps unlit of an evening for fear someone should realize we're at home."

"The footman has opened the door and put down the steps and—oh, my stars!" Elizabeth drew her breath in sharply and turned, wide-eyed, to goggle at Gabrielle. "I don't believe it! It's Lady Ariana Tredway! Your most pressing competition for Belle of the Season! What on earth could she want?"

"What indeed, Lizzie?" Gabrielle raised one expressive dark eyebrow as she considered her friend's question. What could Lady Ariana want with her? Surely not a friendly coze and a few girlish giggles over cups of tea while they verbally dissected various members of the *ton*. Not Lady Ariana, a young woman who'd already made it excruciatingly clear that she did not like Gabrielle above half and considered her an entirely *outré* female of little breeding, less sense, and entirely too much ambition.

The footman laid on the knocker with a will, the sound of brass hitting oak resounding through the narrow townhouse as if imperiously summoning its inhabitants to open the door to the Queen.

As the sound echoed into the second story, then died, Elizabeth looked to Gabrielle, who looked back to her, grinning, and then the older woman sighed, shrugged, and headed for the tiny entrance hall while Gabrielle arranged herself primly on the edge of the couch, her mind flying in a dozen directions at once.

If she served tea and cakes, would Lady Ariana recognize the cakes as being identical to the iced confections served at Lady Undercliff's ball? She doubted it. People of Lady Ariana's ilk never noticed things like that. They were much too occupied looking after their own consequence. Still, it might be fun to offer a plate, trilling sweetly: "Pilfered cakes, my lady?"

"How lovely to catch you at home, Mrs. Fletcher," Gabrielle could hear Lady Ariana saying as the door closed and the two ladies made their way back to the small drawing room. "And what a crushing pity it is that your butler has come down with the quinsy and your housekeeper refuses to answer the door. Servants today are so woefully independent, aren't they?"

Sparing a moment to silently congratulate Elizabeth on her heretofore unknown talent for invention, Gabrielle tilted her head and pasted an inviting smile on her face as Lady Ariana swept gracefully into the room. Elizabeth trailed in the woman's wake, her ladyship's light shawl and gloves clutched to her bosom as she pulled a face at the woman's slim back.

"Lady Ariana," Gabrielle exclaimed, holding out a hand to the young woman, "how terribly sweet of you to call! I am honored beyond measure by your visit, and must apologize for our sad situation. Our household is all at sixes and sevens thanks to Soames's illness," she added, believing that if Elizabeth could invent a butler, she, in turn, could have the pleasure of christening the fellow.

"I must apologize for dropping in this late in the afternoon, Miss Laurence," Lady Ariana said as she sat herself down in Elizabeth's chair, spreading her skirts delicately, "but I was in this neighborhood visiting an old retainer—taking her a quantity of once-brewed tea leaves and a few old blankets, as we can never be too forgetful of those who serve us."

Gabrielle batted her long eyelashes at her ladyship, saying, "Too true, too true. Once-brewed, you say? How—um, how *thrifty* of you, Lady Ariana."

"Yes, yes. At any rate, I decided to give in to impulse and asked my driver to see if you were at home. I cannot remember the last time I visited any of the *ton* residing this far afield from Grosvenor Square. These narrow houses have always fascinated me. So small— but you will do wonders with it when you have the time, no doubt. Have you no invitations for this evening, my dear? I see you're not yet dressed, not that the bucolic look is not quaintly flattering, I suppose."

Gabrielle bit the inside of her cheek at the veiled insult. Three insults, actually. Hinting that she lived in a hovel with an unfashionable address and that she had no invitations was bad enough, but the criticism of her ensemble was too much to be borne. After all, Gabrielle had worked long and hard on stitching her gowns after patterning them on designs shown in the very latest fashion plates, and none of them was in the least countrified! But she was in no position to argue with the woman who, thankfully, had not yet asked if one of the maids might be serving her some refreshments any time soon.

"La, Lady Ariana," Gabrielle trilled, touching her fingertips to the skirt of her gown, "I fear you have discovered me in disarray, for I have been occupied most of the day in answering invitations at my desk and will soon have to all but *dive* into my gown in time for the theater. You are to be one of the duke of Glynnon's party at Covent Garden this evening?"

"The—the Duke of Glynnon?" Lady Ariana stammered, her lovely pink cheeks flushing a shade deeper than was attractive. But she recovered quickly. "I haven't decided if I wish to be crowded into his grace's box on what may prove to be a horridly humid evening. It's such a trial, isn't it, picking and choosing from so many demands for our appearance? I live in constant horror of offending someone by not lending my consequence to their little affairs, at least for a moment."

"How true, how true," Gabrielle agreed commiseratingly, deliberately avoiding Elizabeth's eyes as that woman stood behind her ladyship's chair and pantomimed drinking tea, obviously in an attempt to boost Gabrielle into offering their guest refreshments. "And you have *so* much more experience than I in the matter, this being your *second* Season as an unmarried woman."

That verbal dart definitely hit home, Gabrielle decided, as she watched Lady Ariana twist her hands in her lap. *Show up on my doorstep unannounced, would she? Doesn't the woman know I already have enough on my plate without having to deal with her petty jealousies? And she can just go cry for tea and cakes!*

"Would you care for some tea, Lady Ariana?" Elizabeth, obviously more fearful of being considered a poor hostess than her friend, broke in as Gabrielle and her ladyship exchanged smiling glares, their personal battle lines already drawn and each of them mentally positioning her soldiers for the next verbal encounter. "Um—or perhaps you'd rather a glass of sherry, even though it does seem suddenly *warm* in here, doesn't it?"

Lady Ariana blinked her china-blue eyes and gave a slight toss to her head, as if bringing her mind back from her private contemplations—probably formulating some sort of attack that would end with Gabrielle being figuratively split in two by a cannonball—and smiled up at Elizabeth. "How belatedly gracious, but thank you, no. I have but a moment to spare, and wished to speak with Miss Laurence on a *private* matter. You wouldn't mind leaving us alone for a moment, would you?"

Again, Gabrielle avoided Elizabeth's eyes, concentrating instead on gathering her own thoughts, for she had a strange, niggling feeling that something momentous was about to occur, something that had precious little to do with two beauties struggling to trump the other's latest insult. As Elizabeth quit the room and Lady Ariana began to speak, Gabrielle knew she had believed correctly.

"A dear woman, your companion, but so unfortunately plain. Ah well, on to more important things. It has come to my attention that you are not best pleased with Baron St. Clair, Miss Laurence."

"'Best pleased,' my lady?" Gabrielle repeated, frowning deliberately and wishing she could box the woman's ears for her insult of Elizabeth. But she couldn't, at least not until she learned the real reason for her ladyship's visit. "Whatever would give you that idea? The baron has boosted me to the forefront of Society. I am forever in his debt, as I understand you were last Season. Why, the baron is the most delightful, generous, well-meaning—"

"He is impossible!" Lady Ariana cut in, her eyes glowing, her features animated, so that she gave the impression of leaning forward eagerly even as her posture remained ramrod straight. "He toys with us as he would jab a stick at a baited bear, teasing us with his condescension, threatening us with a withdrawal of his favor if any imp of mischief should make him decide to champion another hopeful debutante. And that inane *giggle!* Miss Laurence—Gabrielle—admit it: You loathe the creature as much as I do."

Gabrielle sat back, momentarily nonplussed by Lady Ariana's impassioned outburst. It hadn't occurred to her that anyone save herself had been laboring beneath St. Clair's possibly quixotic favor. "Well, your ladyship"—she hesitated, then smiled and added—*"Ariana.* Now that you mention it . . ."

Lady Ariana clapped her small hands together a single time, as if calling a meeting to order. "Just as I had supposed. Perhaps you didn't realize that I noticed your disdain for Christian while at Lord Undercliff's. Not that you said anything too cutting, for you are much too much the country miss, and still too attached to your milk teeth, to say anything totally biting. But I did detect a certain disenchantment with the baron."

"I hadn't realized I was quite so obvious," Gabrielle admitted, secretly surprised that the woman sitting before her, a creature she had dismissed as vain and fairly stupid, could be so discerning. She decided to pass over the woman's insult about her youth and inexperience and lead her on some more, just to see where Lady Ariana's odd conversation was going.

"I had only meant to tease him about his affected, annoying way of calling that man, Symington, by another name," she said, praying her smile appeared innocent, even stupid. "It was so patently patronizing of him when it was perfectly clear that he knew the man's name. In my opinion, the baron is not only overweening but unbearably rude and cruel."

"And impervious to insult, or else he is allowing you your head only to bring you crashing toward disgrace in some very public way in the not-too-distant future," Lady Ariana said, beginning to look around the drawing room curiously, as if mentally toting up the amount of furnishings and putting a price to each piece. Then she turned back to Gabrielle once more and skewered her with her innocent blue gaze. "I should like to bring the rotter down, Gabrielle. Are you willing to help me?"

Gabrielle coughed delicately into her hand, or as delicately as she could while attempting to hide a delighted giggle. "Bring the mighty Christian St. Clair *down,* Ariana? Turn the tables on him? Be so ungrateful as to use the social consequence he has bestowed upon us in order to destroy him? What a highly unique notion. What a singularly wonderful idea. And vastly diverting, I must say." She sobered, realizing she was about to throw her lot in with a woman she barely knew, did not like, and had no reason to trust. And all to destroy a man she did not like because she was frightened she could grow to like him too much. "But how are we going to bell our cat?"

"Ah, you are a droll little creature, aren't you?" Lady Ariana said kindly, causing Gabrielle's teeth to set themselves on edge. "I have no idea as to how—

not yet. But now that I know I can count on your assistance, your support, I am sure that we can discover some way to throw the baron into disgrace. Not that we will enjoy ourselves, of course, for we are above everything else ladies. But Christian has called the tune for too long, and it is time he paid the piper."

Gabrielle, although confused to notice that Lady Ariana's casual use of St. Clair's name had shot a slim arrow into her heart, was struck with a sudden inspiration. "The baron has threatened to cut you, hasn't he?"

Lady Ariana stood up, bending to retrieve the shawl and gloves Elizabeth had deposited on a small table before leaving the room. "He has alluded to the fact that he has the power to raise whomever he wishes to the height of popularity—and to bring them crashing down again as well. I don't believe he would ever be so horridly mean, but I have tired of living beneath his veiled threats. As have you, my dear new friend," she ended, smiling at Gabrielle, "or else you would not have been so eager to fall in with my scheme."

"A scheme with no solid plan behind it but merely a goal," Gabrielle reminded her, taking the woman's elbow as she led her to the door and wincing inwardly as she smelled Lady Ariana's expensive French scent. All Gabrielle had to her name was simple rosewater, a most "bucolic" perfume. "A commendable goal, I admit, but unless we are assured of success—and if St. Clair should catch wind of our intention . . ." She let her words trail off, hoping to discommode her ladyship.

The ploy worked. Lady Ariana turned and took hold of Gabrielle's two hands, squeezing her fingers with an astonishingly strong grip—most probably the result of her mad passion for tooling her own specially constructed curricle in the promenade. "You aren't planning to cry off from helping me, are you, dear friend? You wouldn't run hot-foot to Christian and apprise him of my plans? You couldn't—not when he has placed you in the same odiously precarious position as he has me."

Gabrielle hesitated for precisely five seconds before speaking, watching the pupils of Lady Ariana's lovely blue eyes widen in shock and dismay. "Such a disloyal thought never entered my head, dearest Ariana, my new and valued *friend*. I am merely saying that I do not wish to move against the baron until we are assured of success. You, I am assured, being the elder and ever so much more the clever miss, will be the one to discover the best plan. Then I shall join into your scheme with the greatest pleasure in life."

Lady Ariana visibly relaxed and even leaned forward to drop a quick kiss on Gabrielle's cheek, an insincere gift of affection Gabrielle could have existed without quite nicely. "You won't regret this, Gabrielle, I promise. But now I fear I must dash. We cannot be late for our evening engagements, now can we? Fortunately, *my* hair is always on its best behavior, giving me not a moment of trouble. Perhaps my French dresser, Marie, can suggest a woman who is handy with the curling stick, as your maid is so obviously lacking in that area. We friends must aid each other, after all. Well, ta-ta, my dear. Perhaps we can meet again in a few days and put our heads together to see what sort of schemes each of us has come up with to deal with St. Clair. I'm convinced yours will be most amusing."

"Yes, Ariana, we must do that," Gabrielle agreed, wondering why she was still smiling when she wanted nothing more than to push her ladyship down the three steps leading to the flagway and watch while the insulting woman landed facedown in a heap. "But I shall come to you next, so that we do not arouse suspicion." *And so that I won't have to worry about your all-seeing eyes and lively suspicions when I still cannot produce my devoted butler, Soames.*

Lady Ariana sighed, pulling her shawl close around her shoulders, as the sun had at last given up its fight with the dying day and dusk had fallen, bringing with it a damp chill. "I do adore Christian, you know. He is so endlessly amusing. But even if it weren't for having to rely on him for social success, it is imperative that he lose his position of power." She lowered her voice as she continued: "Unlike Lord Buxley, he champions that dangerous, seditious Peacock, you know. And *that* is unforgivable!"

"Your papa disapproves," Gabrielle said, remembering Lady Ariana's tirade of the previous evening. It was difficult to believe that the woman was seriously interested in politics, but easy to believe she was parroting her father's views, well-known views that were enough to have any young woman used to luxury fearful of losing her comfortable station to a horde of hungry peasants armed with pikes and a courage gained from the Peacock's championing of their sad cause. "I wonder why St. Clair is so eager to push forward the Peacock's words when he is also so plainly jealous of the impact the outlaw has on the ladies and gentlemen the baron believes to be his adoring subjects?"

Lady Ariana smiled indulgently. "Pure love of mischief, my dear girl," she said knowingly. "Christian enjoys tweaking authority nearly as much as he revels in watching all our young gentlemen falling over themselves to ape his dress and manner. He is not intelligent, not in the way of someone like Lord Buxley, who will reign in Society long after St. Clair is forgotten, but he is clever and vastly entertaining. Ah, don't frown. You are too young, too green, to understand the ins and outs of *ton* intrigue. Just promise you will follow my lead when the time comes, when a suitable plan presents itself, and together we will send Christian packing—leaving Mayfair open to conquest."

"A conquest you are willing to share with me—this year's sensation, or at least St. Clair has deemed me thus," Gabrielle pointed out, still confused by Lady Ariana's willingness to not only include her in her scheme to destroy the baron but also open the door to making the two of them the twin queens of Society. "You are much too generous, Ariana."

"Not really, dear friend," Lady Ariana admitted, surprising Gabrielle yet again with her candor—or was it her overweening confidence? "Perhaps I shouldn't say this, but I believe Christian has taken a *personal* interest in you, if you understand my meaning. I never would have believed him capable of feeling affection for anyone other than himself, or perhaps his tailor, but I think Cupid has nipped at dear Christian at last! And if the great St. Clair is on the verge of losing his heart he will be less liable to scent a conspiracy. You see," she concluded, her self-satisfied smirk momentarily robbing her of some of her pink-and-white beauty, "I am not *entirely* without a plan, even this early in the game. Just continue to smile in his presence and allow him to court you, never suspecting that the woman he might love is about to play a part in bringing him down."

"St. Clair?" Gabrielle questioned, her voice cracking, her heart skipping a beat. "Falling in love with me?"

Lady Ariana visibly shivered in delight. "Oh, it's delicious—just *delicious!* Good afternoon to you, dear Gabrielle. Papa has told me never to keep my horses standing above a quarter hour."

"And you mustn't disobey Papa," Gabrielle trilled, remaining in the open doorway, an insincere smile still cramping her cheeks as she watched Lady Ariana being handed up into her carriage, not turning away until she heard Elizabeth approaching behind her.

"You should have pitched her headfirst down the steps, Gaby," Elizabeth said as she stepped forward sprightly to shut the door.

"The thought had crossed my mind, Lizzie," Gabrielle said, pressing her hands together as she struggled to bring a niggling thought out of the dark recesses of her mind and into the daylight, where she might examine it.

Elizabeth sniffed. " 'Unfortunately plain'! And she utters her poison with such sweet sympathy dripping from her pointed tongue. You aren't going to throw your lot in with her, are you? That isn't why we came to London."

Gabrielle walked back into the drawing room, her mind awhirl with questions. Could she and Lady Ariana really bring St. Clair down? Did she want to see the man toppled from his social perch? Did he really have a "personal" interest in her? Was she, ordinary Gabrielle Laurence, really someone St. Clair "might love"?

And what did she care if she was?

She turned to Elizabeth to seek her opinion, surprising Elizabeth no more than she did herself when that dark thought stepped into the light and she opened her mouth to ask instead, "It's so odd: Why do you think St. Clair is so eager to champion the Peacock's causes? Does he do it, as Lady Ariana supposes, merely to infuriate Lord Sidmouth and all the Tories? The baron doesn't seem the least political—not a man who spends the majority of his time dressing and undressing and inventing new ways to make all of Society jump through hoops he has set up for them."

Elizabeth plumped the seat cushion so lately sat upon by Lady Ariana, then sat down, taking up her knitting once more, although she just placed it in her lap, clutching the needles. "You know, Gaby, I wondered about that myself. Of course, I've been wondering about the baron this entire fortnight, ever since we came to London and I first saw him going down the dance in those colorful satins." She shook her head. "He certainly isn't the man dearest Roger described to me."

Gabrielle curled up on the couch, disposing of her shoes once more and tucking her feet up under her skirt as Elizabeth shifted on her own chair, running her fingers along the edges of the cushion as if searching for something. "Your husband knew St. Clair? When?"

"Oh, eons ago. They were little more than boys in school together," Elizabeth said vaguely, beginning to search inside her knitting bag, first idly, then in earnest. "I remember Roger writing to me about the baron, telling me how hotheaded he was over the Irish question and other matters of a political nature."

"St. Clair? Are you sure?"

"Yes, quite sure. For a while, the baron supposedly even spoke in open admiration of the revolution in France. That's when his father, who was known to be most liberal in his own thoughts, must have had enough and grabbed him by the ear and dragged him home, hiring tutors to complete his education. But the years must have cooled his fire, for I've heard nothing about him except what we all can see—and that is his love for fripperies and social silliness." Her head jerked up, her eyes wide behind her spectacles as she exclaimed fearfully: "Gaby—it's gone!"

"Good Lord, Lizzie, you're white as any ghost! Gone? What's gone?" Gabrielle asked, grabbing up the tapestry bag and beginning to search its contents, not knowing what she should be attempting to locate, all thoughts of the Baron St. Clair leaving her head as Elizabeth dropped to her knees on the floor and began searching beneath the chair.

"The *list,* Gaby. Lady Ariana took the list!" Elizabeth sat back on her haunches and pushed at her glasses as she looked up at Gabrielle. "Now why on earth would anyone do such a thing? Oh, my *stars!*" she exclaimed, beginning to tug at Gabrielle's skirt. "Gaby, do you know what the list *says?*"

"No, Lizzie, I don't," Gabrielle answered honestly, helping her friend to her feet. "And, being already painfully aware of your penchant to label and list everything pertaining to our lives, I most probably don't *want* to know, do I?" she asked, gazing anxiously into Elizabeth's rapidly blinking eyes.

"I—I titled it 'Gaby's Glittering Grooms,'" Elizabeth blurted, collapsing into her chair. "Roger always said I was too attached to romantic nonsense."

"Roger was right," Gabrielle said, groaning as she rolled her eyes, knowing the jig was up, that Lady Ariana would immediately recognize Elizabeth's list for what it was. "She's got me now, Lizzie. I have no choice but to go along with any scheme she might have to bring St. Clair down. If I don't, that damning little list of yours will see more of Society than I would if I attended three functions a night for the month."

"Oh, Gaby," Elizabeth wailed, "I'm *so* sorry!"

Gabrielle shook her head and waved away her friend's apology. "There's no harm done, Lizzie, not as long as I keep dearest Lady Ariana happy—or discover some secret to hold over *her* head. Ah, Lizzie, I have so much to learn about these London hothouse flowers. As is the case with St. Clair, I believe we have tripped over another one of those lovely posies that is not overly intelligent but most definitely clever. And willing to do anything to be the most admired, sought-after bloom in the whole decadent bouquet! I hadn't thought snagging myself a fortune would be so difficult."

Elizabeth's chin was collapsed on her thin breast. "I believe I am beginning to harbor a distinct fondness for our worshipful viscount of the offensive camel's breath," she muttered quietly, most probably speaking only for her own benefit.

"Shh, Lizzie," Gabrielle said suddenly, feeling herself being struck with an idea. "I think I have something—*yes!* That would do it! It's brilliant! Well, possibly not brilliant—but good, quite good. No, I'm wrong. It's *brilliant!*"

Elizabeth sat up straight, instantly at attention. "Gaby? I don't think I like that look in your eyes. The last time I saw it, when your former tenant vacated, I found myself being transported here to Percy Street to run a rig on Society in order to save Rose Hill Farm. I vow, my head is still spinning! I don't think I could take another brilliant idea just now, truly I don't."

Gabrielle ignored her friend, already beginning to pace the one area of the carpet that was not threadbare (the furniture in the room had been cleverly arranged to hide the worst spots). "St. Clair, Lady Ariana, *Lord Buxley,* and the Peacock," she recited, touching her fingertips as she counted off each name. "A powerful nincompoop, a Tory debutante, another Tory—but with social *and* political consequence—and the mysterious, popular archenemy of that odious Lord Sidmouth."

She whirled about to face the frowning Elizabeth, explaining, "You see, I can't forget Lord Buxley, for he is vastly popular with the starchier crowd who bow to St. Clair but can't quite like him. So that makes four—five if I am so full of self-consequence as to include myself. St. Clair, Lady Ariana, Buxley, the Peacock, and me. That's entirely too many with which to share the pinnacle of Society, don't you think, Lizzie?"

Elizabeth, clearly confused, only shrugged and shook her head.

Gabrielle held out her right hand, pointing her index finger at her friend. *"But,* if St. Clair were to be toppled, and if Lady Ariana and Lord Buxley were to find themselves drawn to each other by their political leanings, that would take three of the five out of the running."

"Leaving only you and the Peacock to crow over Society," Elizabeth inserted, then asked, "Do peacocks crow? I think they screech, Gaby."

Gabrielle waved the question away, for she could feel a most delicious idea bubbling up inside her. "But what if the Peacock were exposed? The person who identified him would instantly become the sensation of the Season—especially if the Peacock turned out to be none other than St. Clair!"

She frowned, unable even in her excitement to

believe such nonsense. "Or Lord Buxley," she added, feeling even more stupid for suggesting that his lordship, such a dedicated Tory, could possibly be the Peacock. "No, it has to be St. Clair."

"But—but he's not the Peacock," Elizabeth pointed out reasonably.

"I know that, silly," Gabrielle countered, shifting her eyes back and forth as she cudgeled her brain for one last inspiration. "But if we could raise the *suspicion* that he is the Peacock, it would be enough to have him on the defensive, and enough to blot his social copybook long enough for me to appease Lady Ariana —the new owner of your note—leaving me free to find a way to throw her into Lord Buxley's lap so that she forgets about the note."

"You forgot to mention that your plan would also leave you to queen over Society, have your pick of wealthy suitors, and make a quick, brilliant marriage before anyone realizes what has happened or your papa can come home and stir up a hornet's nest by showing his pockets-to-let self at his club," Elizabeth ended, picking up her knitting once more. "It's a highly ambitious plan, Gaby, and it won't work," she ended shortly. "Not in a thousand years."

"No, it won't," Gabrielle agreed, collapsing onto the couch once more. "So we are back to 'glittering groom' hunting, sans your clever, revealing list and with an even more limited time to pull off our scheme, now that Lady Ariana has thrown a fly into the ointment. E-gad, Lizzie, do you suppose Lady Ariana's right, and St. Clair has fallen a little in love with me? I'd hate to believe that he is the best of my prospects."

"There's always the viscount," Elizabeth observed, stifling a laugh.

"Oh, *fiddle!*" Gabrielle exclaimed, deliberately aping her friend's frequent expression as she lifted her feet and, like a rag doll, slipped sideways onto the cushions, to flop upon her back and stare up at the ceiling once more, searching for answers.

All she saw was St. Clair's laughing, blue-green eyes looking back at her, reminding her that she faced another evening trading compliments and barbs with that infuriating, overdressed, self-absorbed man. Christian St. Clair as the Peacock? What a laughably ludicrous idea!

Almost as laughable as Lady Ariana's suggestion that the man might be falling in love with his latest *protégée.*

Almost as ludicrous as any thought that she might like the dratted man much more than she was willing to admit.

BOOK TWO

ADVANTAGE, PEACOCK?

He who will not reason, is a bigot;
he who cannot, is a fool;
and he who dares not, is a slave.

Lord Byron

CHAPTER 6

Love and War are the same thing, and stratagems and policy are as allowable in the one as in the other.

Cervantes

Quelle absurdité! A damned sordid tale, Grumble, wouldn't you say?" Baron Christian St. Clair pronounced in a carrying voice, immediately drawing all attention to his small party as he, George Trumble, Lord Osgood, and Sir Gladwin Penley stepped out from the baron's private box at the first intermission and took up positions in the crowded hallway of the theater.

St. Clair raised his stemmed quizzing glass to his eye and surveyed the assembled members of the *ton* (just lately absorbed by the play but now his captive audience). Then, with a flick of his wrist meant to show the flowing lace peeking from his satin cuff to advantage—in the end he had offended Frapple and chosen to be a vision in saffron this evening—he allowed the glass to drop, sighed languidly, and continued: "Yes, yet another tired tale of innocence debauched. Odds fish, gentlemen, and the hopeful scribbler has the effrontery to call this drama? I call it maudlin drivel, with the evildoers to be vanquished and sweet innocence to triumph in the end. How vastly conventional. Surely we are not going to expend more of our valuable time sipping warm wine out here and then return to our box to be bored to flinders by the second act?"

Having voiced his criticism of the hopeful playwright's effort, dooming the man to failure before the climactic final act, Christian hid a smile as he bowed to the company and turned for the stairway, wishing to lead rather than follow as everyone within earshot —and those to whom his condemnation had been whispered—exited the theater *en masse.*

It was growing heady, this influence he wielded over Society with such laughable ease. No wonder the Beau had lingered past his prime, unwilling to give up his premier position. He, Christian, would have to be careful not to make the same mistake—not that he shared Brummell's fatal flaw of gaming for deep stakes.

Lord Osgood, always a slow starter, hastened to keep up with his friend's long strides, nearly tripping over George as he leaped forward and grabbed at Christian's sleeve. "I say, Kit," he said, throwing an apologetic wink back at George, "I rather liked the play. Made me all but weep to see Isolde being tossed about a cold, heartless world that way, without a friend to call her own."

Christian smiled down fondly at the slightly shorter, definitely rounder man. "Touched your soft heart, did she, Ozzie?" he teased, surreptitiously removing Lord Osgood's hand from his sleeve before the material was crushed. "Or was it the actress herself who opened your tender sensibilities to assault? A fetching enough piece of fluff, I'll admit, if a bit long in the tooth and round in the heel to play the innocent."

"No more than five and twenty, Winnie says," Lord Osgood protested as Sir Gladwin Penley, never one to dawdle, brushed by them and down the stairs. "Not that I was thinking of setting her up anywhere or anything of that sort. Already have one filly in traces, if you'll recall. Two would cut yards too wide into my allowance."

George Trumble fell into step on Christian's left side as they approached the broad stairway, whispering into his friends's ear, "Winnie's gone ahead to secure your carriage, Kit. Are you still bent on traveling to Little Pillington tonight?"

"You're suggesting I might have grown fearful and changed my mind, Grumble?" Kit asked as his long legs made short work of three flights of blood-red carpeted stairs leading down to the high-ceilinged foyer. "Or could it be that you are the one who is turning womanish at this late date?"

Christian halted at the base of the staircase, immediately sorry for what he had said, for the brown wren who was his best friend was frowning. "Grumble— George—forgive me. That was uncalled for. I know you're worried, and I thank you for your concern."

Lord Osgood's round face split in a grin even as he wiped his perspiration-sheened forehead with a large handkerchief. "Wasn't that nice, Grumble? Ain't often Kit says he's sorry. Ain't often he's wrong, come to think of it. But you're wrong now, Kit," he added with a wink. "You shouldn't be within fifty miles of Little Pillington for at least another week."

Christian looked at each of his friends in turn, sighing as he prepared to refight a battle he'd believed already won. "Winnie is of a like mind, I suppose," he said, motioning for all three of them to step out of the way of the departing theatergoers who had politely refrained from brushing past them and were therefore stuck balancing themselves on the staircase like so many lemmings patiently awaiting their turn to leap into the sea.

He gifted the tottering, overheated, but still easily flattered company with an elegant, sweeping bow before turning back to face his companions.

"It's enough that we're committed to rescuing this Slow Dickie fellow," Lord Osgood whispered out of the corner of his mouth, making him look about as inconspicuous as a giraffe in a glass jar. "Besides, Kit, you're promised to Lady Blakestone for at least an hour."

"Damn," Christian swore quietly, having forgotten about Lady Blakestone's party. How could he have forgotten? Gabrielle Laurence would be there, most probably still hanging on the duke of Glynnon's arm, as she'd been when he had seen her entering the theater an hour earlier. "I'll have to make an appearance, I suppose. Her ladyship is always kind, if not always intelligent."

"If you're searching for intelligence, Kit," George said acidly, "I suggest you take up a lantern and go hunting on some island other than ours. Look at these fools—deserting the theater as if it were a sinking ship, fearful of being thought to like anything the great St. Clair has deemed inferior." He tipped his head and looked searchingly at his friend. "You're enjoying this power, aren't you? Maybe too much."

"I'll plead guilty to being at least mildly flattered," Christian admitted, slipping an arm through George's and steering him toward the door, intent on showing his face at Lady Blakestone's just long enough for people to remember that he had been there, then leaving for Little Pillington before he was tempted to tell his friends about his visit from Lord Buxley and the information that at least one agent provocateur had been active in the area.

The carriage Sir Gladwin had quickly summoned was one of only three that had thus far been pulled up in front of the theater, and within the space of a quarter hour Christian and his entourage were stepping out onto the wide flagway in front of Lady Blakestone's Portman Square mansion.

Only another ten minutes had passed before Christian had bowed over the liver-spotted hand of his flattered hostess, exchanged pleasantries with her illustrious and eminently henpecked husband, been served a chilled glass of his favorite champagne, and was free to mingle with the other guests, always keeping one eye on the doorway.

It wasn't long before he was rewarded by the sight of Gabrielle Laurence as she entered the ballroom on the arm of the Duke of Glynnon, old deaf-as-a-post Harry looking pleased as Jack Horner at having secured the popular plum as his companion for the evening. *Ariana must be beside herself with jealousy,* Christian mused, secretly pleased at Gabrielle's social success, even as that success made the competition for her favor that much more intense.

Not that he wanted her.

Excusing himself from the company of debutantes and dowagers he had been regaling with a retelling of that night's woeful production at Covent Garden— *"Alors,* ladies, but it was enough to make anyone of any smattering of sensibility weep in righteous chagrin for such foolishness"—Christian leisurely made his way toward Gabrielle, any but the most astute of observers unable to guess that his heart was pounding in anticipation of hearing her sweet voice as she condemned him.

"Your grace! Miss Laurence!" Christian called out loudly as he approached, his right hand extended so that his grace had no choice but to return the greeting, the duke's handshake more forceful than welcoming. "How wonderfully titillating to see you two together again this evening. Such an excruciatingly lovely couple. Beauty and the bank. If only you would please me, dear sir, by taking more pains in the selection of your evening attire, but I suppose that is too much to ask."

He leaned forward, delicately sniffing the air. "Do I scent a romance in the early stages of bloom? Let me be the first to congratulate you, your grace. And you too, Miss Laurence. My best good wishes on your lucky—um, that is, your well-deserved success. Wed him quickly, as I fear one of his creaking legs is already dangling over the grave."

His grace cupped a hand to his ear and leaned toward Gabrielle inquiringly. "What is this demned fool prattling on about, Miss Laurence? His mouth is always running, ain't it? Something about flowers, was it? Looks like a flower himself, don't he? All trouped out in blues and pinks and what'all. Yellow tonight, or sort of. Can't say as I see what all the blessed fuss is about."

Christian kept his features composed with a great effort, succeeding, he observed, much better than did Gabrielle, who could not hide her amusement at his expense. "No, no, your grace," she corrected, "St. Clair wasn't speaking of flowers. He was speaking of nonsense—something he does quite often, I might say."

"Touché, Miss Laurence," Christian responded as Sir Gladwin, acting on Christian's earlier request, came up to his grace and most deliberately launched into a loud conversation centering on the duke's greatest love, horse racing. "However, as old Harry is now otherwise engaged, may I be so daring as to open myself to further insult by asking that you accompany me on a stroll around the ballroom?"

"If I must, my lord," Gabrielle said, taking Christian's arm. "After all, having set this pattern each time we meet, it wouldn't do my reputation a dollop of good to have any alterations in our behavior. Will we also, I wonder, step outside onto the balcony to throw brickbats at each other before our waltz, or do you prefer to dance and then quarrel? Either way, I am amenable. Heaven knows I wouldn't wish to do anything that would upset the powerful Baron St. Clair."

"Ah, a blow to the heart! You are in rare form tonight. How you wound me, Miss Laurence," Christian said, his tone exaggeratedly horrified as he deliberately ignored the intoxicating scent of her innocently seductive rosewater perfume and studiously guided her through an open set of doors and out onto the night-dark balcony. "I have always endeavored to treat all ladies with the delicacy they deserve."

"In which case," Gabrielle countered, breaking away from him and seating herself on the stone bench that sat to one side of the small balcony, "you, sir, have just admitted that you do not think of me as being a lady. Otherwise you wouldn't make it your mission in life to insult me at every turn."

Christian, seating himself beside her, let his voice drop nearly an octave and his usual, social, and rather inane grin to disappear as he said, "Then how may I serve you? I too am nothing, you understand, if not amenable. Perhaps you'd rather I penned a sonnet to your immeasurable charms, Miss Laurence, or that I dog your steps day and night, bleating out my undying devotion to you. I could do that, you know. But I have chosen to treat you as an equal, a woman with a mind—not that I can greatly admire your stubborn refusal to use your intelligence for anything more weighty than securing yourself the most lucrative matrimonial catch you can lure to the hook."

"Ah, yes," Gabrielle countered sweetly, although she avoided his eyes as she spoke. "I can see where you are the more discerning in the use of *your* brainpower —as we all know the British empire rises or falls on the width of a buttonhole on the Baron St. Clair's waistcoat. Speak of the pot terming the kettle black!"

Christian's response was to laugh in true amusement, an expression of merriment he broke off quickly as he realized he had somehow forgone his usual high-pitched giggle. But he recovered before any harm was done, he assured himself, saying, "Speaking of clothing, Miss Laurence—although if you wish to speak of cooking utensils I suppose we could address that subject anon—don't I recognize that gown?"

"I—I beg your pardon?"

"Yes, I think you should. Although I believe the last time I saw this lovely creation—at Lord Hawkhurst's, as I remember—the flowers decorating the bodice were pink, not yellow, as they are this evening. How distressing. I must protest, dear girl. Although a thrifty wife is to be commended, a miserly debutante does not make a pretty picture. Besides, it is an insult to my consequence to champion a young lady who is so tight-fisted as to repeat her wardrobe within the space of a single fortnight."

Gabrielle's expressive green eyes narrowed menacingly as she looked at him as if he had just that moment chanced to crawl out from beneath a nearby stone and she'd enjoy nothing more than beating his slimy, reptilian self into a jelly with it.

Christian knew she was undowered, knew she might have sprung from an impeccable lineage but that she was not the daughter of a wealthy man. How could he have been so mean to her? So cruel? How low had he sunk? Why did this young, beautiful, innocent woman bring out the worst in him? He wanted to throw himself at her feet and beg her forgiveness for his boorish behavior, but he only returned her gaze, still maintaining his foppish pose.

"You know, St. Clair," Gabrielle said quietly, "I have tried and tried to discover something—some one thing—redeeming about you. Your loyalty to George Trumble that allows him to travel in the first circles—although whether he is pleased by his acceptance is still an open question. Your willingness to ease Lord Undercliff away from a potentially disastrous moment the other evening. Even your rather twisted championing of me this past fortnight, since I entered Society."

Christian deliberately raised his lace handkerchief to dab at the corners of his eyes. How delightful she looked when she was hating him. Lady Ariana wasn't well enough stuffed in her brain-box to more than dislike the fashionable darling he pretended to be. The majority of the *ton* fawned over him. But Gabrielle, dearest Gabrielle, had the brilliance, the intelligence, to hate him. "How affecting, Miss Laurence," he said, sniffing. "Forgive me, but I am overcome! I hadn't realized that you held me in such high affection."

"I don't, you vacuous twit!" she responded shortly, turning her back on him, her outburst telling him that not even the thought of her rash words putting a period to her elevated social stature was enough to keep a civil tongue in her head, so angry was she with her "benefactor."

"Zut alors! I don't understand!" he chirped, deliberately urging her on to further indiscretions. *This* was the woman he had thought she was—a woman blessed not only with fine looks but spirit! Daring!

He wasn't disappointed as she rounded on him, her cheeks flaming, to exclaim, "Would you *please* stop butchering the French language with that absurd accent? Others may find it amusing, but I do not. Furthermore, if you had been listening to me with more than half an ear you would have heard me say that I have *tried* to find something in you which I could like. I haven't succeeded. You are vain, silly, nasty as a young boy pulling wings from butterflies, and totally useless."

Suddenly, and without any warning, Christian felt any amusement he may have felt disappearing as his temper unexpectedly climbed toward the boiling point. He didn't know what inflamed him more: Gabrielle's taunting words or the way her eyes flashed and her breasts heaved in her agitation. What he did know was that he had taken just about as much verbal abuse at her hands as he was willing to endure, even if he had purposely incited it. Had he ever really thought it pleased him to spar with her night after night? How could he have been so dimwitted?

He didn't want her dislike, even though he openly courted it. He wanted her to—what *did* he want from her? Really? Her love? Dear God, did he really want her to love him?

Gabrielle, her denunciation of him having finished, or else she had grown too angry to say more, attempted to rise from the bench and storm back into the ballroom. But before she could escape, Christian put out his hands and took hold of her bare shoulders, pressing her back down. "You're wrong. I'm not entirely useless, Gabrielle," he said quietly, for—as George Trumble could have told her—the more angry Christian grew the more soft-spokenly sarcastic he became. "I do possess some talents."

Gabrielle stiffened beneath his hands. "Don't," she whispered, slowly shaking her head, clearly understanding what would happen next. "I apologize, truly I do. You don't want to do this. Don't do this, St. Clair."

"So sorry, dear lady," Christian drawled, inching her closer as the heat of his anger flamed his passions, "but I have decided to emulate your escort of the evening. I cannot hear a word you are saying."

Gabrielle began to struggle beneath his light grip, her eyes wide with fear—with anticipation?—but he ignored any niggling warnings his conscience might be uttering as he concentrated on her slightly parted lips, the delicious, intriguing mole just to the left of her mouth, the feel of her skin against his palms, the scent of fully blown roses emanating from her glorious hair.

His anger replaced now entirely by passion, still he didn't just roughly take her mouth. Instead, he anointed it with his own, sweetly, gently, careful not to frighten her more, controlling himself with an effort as her never strong struggles dimmed, then ceased entirely.

Only then, when she remained still in his embrace,

did he move his arms entirely around her, melding their bodies together from hip to chest as he deepened the kiss, teasing her with the tip of his tongue, sampling her sweetness, exulting as she drew her breath in sharply, then slipped her arms around his waist.

His irrational desire for her, never far from the surface since he had first seen her, exploded at her submission. She was fire, she was ice, she was all soft white skin and vibrant red hair, and he wanted to see all of her, kiss all of her, possess all of her—here, now, and the devil take the hindmost!

She wanted a wealthy husband? He was rich beyond her wildest imaginings.

She wanted social position? She could aim no higher than the Baron Christian St. Clair.

She had demonstrated a native if selfish intelligence. He could teach her to employ it more wisely.

She must have a heart. He would find it.

And if you are found out, dear, idealistic Peacock? If you should be unmasked, captured? What happens then to your beloved but not necessarily loving wife? Does she tumble with you, or does she run from you and your recklessly professed love? If you win her hand, and not her mind and heart, haven't you opened yourself to the greatest defeat, the worst loss?

Christian broke off the kiss abruptly, removing his hand from the soft warmth of the breast he had captured without a struggle, and pushed Gabrielle's head against his chest, silently cursing his inconvenient conscience for speaking up just when sweet reason was the last interruption he'd desired.

He pressed one last kiss against Gabrielle's flaming curls as he struggled to control his breathing, then set her away from him, deliberately ignoring the jewel-like glitter in her green eyes, the dozens of unspoken questions sparkling in those lovely eyes.

"*Voyons, mignonne!* How very shattering!" he exclaimed in patently mock horror, employing his lace handkerchief yet again, this time dabbing at his mouth as if to remove any trace of lip rouge, although it was obvious Gabrielle's beauty had no need of any such artifice. "But I believe I have proved my point. I am many things, but I am not useless. A talent for lovemaking is not to be sneered at, don't you agree? Just apply to all the unhappy wives in our midst tonight if you are pressed for an answer. Although I will say that all that exertion is vastly injurious to a well-pressed coat."

"Wh-what?" Gabrielle stammered, proving to him that he had not been mistaken. She had been as shaken as he by their embrace.

He raised his quizzing glass and inspected her gown, refusing to see the way her taut nipples pressed against the sheer fabric. "And I believe the next time I see that gown you will have changed silk flowers yet again. Those are sadly crushed, I fear, and not at all suitable for one who wishes to set trends and command the respect of other, lesser debutantes. But, alas, that is what comes of being a slave to passion."

Christian's quizzing glass flew from his hand as Gabrielle surprised him by slapping his face, the blow fierce enough to send his head snapping sideways on his neck as his right ear began to ring from the blow. "You miserable, loathsome, malicious, opportunistic *twit!* How I detest you! If I were a man I would call you out!"

Christian raised his handkerchief to his stinging

cheek. "If you were a man, Miss Laurence," he said, giggling in his practiced way, "the occasion should never have arisen in the first place."

It seemed to be Gabrielle's turn to sniff, and she did so with great disdain, quickly turning from physical assault to verbal punishment. "Is that all you can state? The obvious? Such a ripping riposte, my lord," she said, sneering. "I should have thought hours and hours before coming up with such an *original,* cutting rejoinder. Why, you almost make me believe you spend the day rehearsing what you will be saying of an evening, and any deviation in routine forces you to speak without preparation, causing you to utter drivel such as your last statement. And Lady Ariana says I am no match for your cutting wit? Ha!"

She hugged her upper arms close to her, quite deliberately feigning a chill as she openly savored the moment and her apparent verbal victory. "Oh-h-h, how I shiver in fear at your next words."

Christian didn't know whether to spank Gabrielle or kiss her yet again. What admirable pluck she had! What singular spirit! Another woman would be swooning, or at the least sobbing. She had been compromised, not only by his kiss but by her reaction to it. She had allowed his advances after only a token resistance, allowed his touch, budded and bloomed beneath his mouth, his hands. And yet she appeared neither frightened nor embarrassed by her actions. That took courage.

But she loathed him. Or so she'd repeatedly told him.

She thought him vain, and quite possibly stupid. Or so she said.

She could never like him, let alone love him. Or so he was sure she believed.

And he desired her while wishing in his heart of hearts that she could somehow be the perfect woman of his fantasies, and not just a beautiful woman whose ambitions lay with those of other beautiful women: a successful Season, marriage to a title and a fortune, and a life spent indulging every whim that entered her shallow, selfish head.

"What's the matter, my lord?" Gabrielle questioned as Christian remained silent, still wondering how he could be so enamored of a pair of melting green eyes and a smile that squeezed at his heart. "Have you run out of amusing things to say? Perhaps you should carry a list of diverting *bon mots* with you, and then you could refer to it whenever you find yourself stymied? Why, you haven't even fallen to quoting someone else's words, which you do so often. Oh, very well, if you are totally at a loss, I shall suggest something. Now, repeat after me, my lord: I apologize most profusely, Miss Laurence, for my dastardly assault on your person, and vow most assiduously that the events of this evening shall never be repeated."

Christian hid a smile behind his handkerchief as he noticed, not for the first time, that Gabrielle Laurence had a commanding way about her that spoke more of a life of responsibility than a dilatory existence cushioned on every side by wealth and her respectable lineage.

He had known her for little more than the space of two weeks. Had he judged her too quickly? What did he really know about her, other than the fact that he wanted her and disliked wanting her when duty was calling him in other directions?

Perhaps it was time he looked more closely into her background.

Perhaps it was time he got to know Gabrielle

Laurence, and not just rely upon his own opinion of who and what she must be.

But not right now. Right now he needed to be shed of her.

Christian stood up, then held out a hand to assist her in rising from the bench. "How uniquely fascinating you are, Miss Laurence," he said, bending to kiss the back of her gloved hand. "Except for a momentary lapse into physical abuse, you have maintained your composure and handled yourself as a woman of the world. Or perhaps you have experience in this area unknown to most innocent young ladies?"

"Be careful, St. Clair," Gabrielle warned him as she withdrew her hand. "You may still be the all-powerful social lion, but having gone so far as to have slapped your silly, grinning face, I no longer have anything to lose. Recovering your wit by attempting to attack me could prove deadly. Why, I just might believe myself justified in ripping the bodice of my gown and then running, screaming, into the ballroom to tell everyone that you have assaulted me. I would become an object of pity for a time, of course, but I would be able to surmount that problem, I'm sure. After all, I am the Belle of the Season."

She tipped her head to one side, the moonlight sending sparks of fire dancing in her hair. "I wonder, St. Clair: Would your consequence be enough to save you, or would the powerful baron be immediately shunned by the *ton* as a lecherous beast not worthy of their attention? What would happen to you if you no longer could strut about Mayfair like some all-powerful rooster, crowing and scratching and secure in your position?"

She stopped, biting her lip for a moment as her eyes

sparkled. "Why, now that I think about it, this might be easier than I had supposed."

"What might be easier than you had supposed?" Christian asked, wondering something himself. He was wondering why he had kissed this dangerous woman when he knew she disliked him, wondering how he could have forgotten how penetrating she could be, looking at him as if she could see the Christian St. Clair he hid so well.

Not that he could not live without his reputation and his consequence. He could retire to the country without so much as a backward look and not miss London for a moment—if it weren't that he needed to stay in Society in order to keep at a fever pitch interest in the Peacock and his exploits on behalf of the lower classes.

Couldn't he? Would it be that easy to give up the power he had found by becoming the latest arbiter of fashion, the most sought-after, feared, and admired man in the kingdom—including the Prince Regent?

Or was Grumble right, and he was losing sight of their main mission, flattered by his popularity and growing careless in his quest for universal acclaim? Was the Peacock out to save a downtrodden peasantry, or was he merely out for the greater glory of himself at the expense of those who had laughed at him when he'd tried reason rather than derring-do to gain their attention?

Damn! Should he be looking into Gabrielle's life for more hints to the real woman, or searching his own heart, his own motives, his own depths?

Christian belatedly realized that Gabrielle hadn't answered his question, instead walking to the edge of the balcony and looking out over the darkened gardens to ask quietly, "Why did you kiss me, St. Clair?" She turned, defensively bracing her slim body against the balusters, her hands to either side of her, gripping the stone railing. "And why do you detest me so?"

Christian forgot that she had said something intriguing as he felt himself being prodded back onto more familiar ground, grateful to leave any self-searching behind him for the moment. He could still best this green girl verbally without really trying, even if, curiously, his heart was no longer in the project.

He made a great business out of pleating his lace handkerchief "just so" and repositioning it in his left hand so that it trailed elegantly as he took the three short steps that placed him directly in front of Gabrielle.

"Why do I dislike you, Miss Laurence?" he repeated, his tone more serious than he had intended it to be. "Perhaps," he went on, refusing to look into her eyes but choosing instead to strike a pose—chin raised, shoulders back, left arm bent at the elbow in order to flourish his handkerchief—"perhaps I see in you a mirror of myself. Oh, to be like the Peacock, and dare everything for justice. I dare nothing, for fear I should lose face with those who simultaneously adore me and wish nothing more than to see my destruction."

He gave up his pose and looked down into her eyes, her suddenly dull, clouded eyes. "I've seen the spark of intelligence in your eyes, heard it in your voice. Yet you are vain and shallow, Miss Laurence, as am I. Pretty enough flowers, but with only stems, and totally lacking in roots. Good for little save putting in a vase and being admired until we wilt. Did you ever wish to be more?"

"Would you like me to be more, my lord?" she

asked, placing her gloved hand on his sleeve. "Would *you* like to be more? I have at times thought—"

"Want to be more than I am?" Christian threw back his head and giggled inanely, for he had her now. Had her at least momentary pity. She was vulnerable now to his sharp tongue, so that he could insult her, and divert her from what had rapidly descended into a too-revealing interlude. "What? And give up all that I have? Heigh-o! Have I ever heard such nonsense? Come, Miss Laurence, we must adjourn to the ball-room before tongues begin to wag. Straighten your bodice first, though, my dear girl: You are showing just a smidgen too much of your charms than is consid-ered proper."

Gabrielle opened her mouth as if to blight him with yet another of her simple yet stinging retorts—for even a stone thrown by a child was capable of inflict-ing pain—then seemed to think better of it.

"Lady Ariana says you are smitten with me," she said after a moment, taking him completely off-guard as she swept past him in a whisper of silk against flagstone, then turned to wait for him to follow her. "Do you know something, my lord? I believe she might just be correct. The only question remaining now is whether I choose to be flattered or appalled."

He had thought her barbs infantile compared to his practiced insults? He was being proved wrong over and over again this evening. Christian pushed open the glass-paned French door, elegantly gesturing for her to precede him into the ballroom. "And the answer to that question, Miss Laurence?" he prompted, wishing he had time to ferret out Ariana Tredway and stuff something large and constricting down that ambitious lady's lovely throat.

Gabrielle sighed theatrically. "Why, my lord, at

least for the moment I believe I shall settle for being vastly amused. As long as you never attempt to touch me again. Then, dear baron, I believe I should have to bring you down. And I can do it now—can't I?"

"Lord love you, do you think I could be destroyed because of a single kiss?" Christian inquired, his smile bright as he motioned for Lord Osgood to come and rescue him from the woman who had just thrown down the gauntlet to him when she should be cowering and whimpering and begging to be returned to her chaperone.

"It's hardly a mortal blow to have one of my manly accomplishments bruited about in Society, Miss Laurence," he continued to explain, "but clearly fatal to *your* aspirations, I fear. Contrary to your rosy description of the consequences, you would not be a beloved martyr but a fallen woman, gone quite beyond the pale. Would you risk social destruction in order to take some misguided revenge on the man who has lifted you to the pinnacle of Society? Besides, although I may be putting my neck on the block to say so, have you not yet realized that if you were to tell the world that I have compromised you I should, of course, play the gentleman—and wed you at once?"

Christian could barely keep his composure as Gabrielle squeaked: "Wed—*wed* me? *Marry* me?"

"Yes, Miss Laurence. Marry you." So much for any thoughts he might have harbored that she would fall, weeping on his neck with happiness at the prospect. She really must loathe him, even as her clinging lips had hinted otherwise. Why else wouldn't she be thrilled to make the match of the Season, even in this backhanded way? Certainly she wasn't so juvenile as to be holding out for both fortune *and* love? "You really should think before you speak. Why, one false word from you and the banns will be read in the morning. Now, are you still so ready to denounce me?"

"I don't know, my lord," Gabrielle answered, and he could hear the truth in her tone. "I know I must sound ungrateful, but I do not appreciate awaking each morning wondering if this will be the day the powerful St. Clair cuts me. And now—after tonight?"

Then she brightened, seeming to become more invigorated, more reckless, thanks to her burgeoning anger. "All right, St. Clair. It's agreed. We both know that a marriage between us is out of the question, for we would doubtless murder each other within a week. Therefore, *neither* of us will speak of your indiscretion this evening. But I am not without other options if you dare to assault me again. Therefore, I feel honor-bound to tell you that you have made discovering a way to eliminate you from my life a near mission from on high. If you possess a weakness, my lord, I shall discover it—and, if necessary, use it."

"Indeed? And how would you destroy me if I were to, as you say, assault you again? What weakness of mine would you exploit? Why, I don't even so much as chew with my mouth agape." Christian wished Lord Osgood would hurry, so that he could get away before Gabrielle said anything more. But she had the bit between her teeth now and would tell him everything, heedless of the way she was opening herself to counterattack.

Silly, headstrong, transparent child!

Didn't she realize she was warning him?

Didn't she realize that her belief in her feminine powers could be her undoing?

Didn't she realize that he could no more turn his back on her now than he could walk up to Lord

Sidmouth, introduce himself as the Peacock, and expect to be asked to dine?

Obviously not.

"Ah, so I do have your attention now? I wonder why. Very well, my lord. If you will play the gentleman, I will play the lady, and issue my warning plainly. Assault me again, or try to take back the social consequence you have given me, and I will not hesitate to act. How, you ask? I will share my thoughts with you."

"That should take somewhat less than five seconds, I imagine," Christian said, yawning to show his indifference to her threats.

"I could," she pressed on doggedly over his insult, "have it whispered about that you not only champion the Peacock, but that you *are* the Peacock!"

He giggled, his handkerchief to his mouth, but his laughter seemed to have no impact as she continued to speak.

"Even you could not survive such a rumor, for everyone is avid to discover the Peacock's true identity and will leap at any mildly credible suggestion. How's that for a perfect way to destroy you? It's not that far a distance from a crowing rooster to a strutting peacock, I'd say, although I should have to practice my denouncement in order that I, like you, don't burst into hysterical laughter at the thought that you could aspire to be anything even remotely heroic. But it is something for you to think about as you try to find sleep tonight, dear baron, isn't it?"

Christian put a hand to his forehead, wondering why he wasn't surprised to hear her threaten him with the truth. Then he recalled how astutely she had seen through his pretense not to remember Symington's name. That verbal slip had been enough for someone as intelligent as she to leap upon and eventually employ to her advantage. He had been right to enlist his friends' aid in running a rig on her. But he hadn't expected to be *this* right!

"La, dear lady, but I quiver in fear with your each new threat. The Peacock? Me? How very droll. I believe you will have some difficulty proving that, my dear. But I can't blame you, for everyone believes they will be the one to ferret out the rascal's identity. I have—privately, of course—placed my money on Lord Buxley. Have you ever noticed how vehemently he protests the Peacock's little adventures? What better way to divert any undue attention from himself, I ask you?"

"Lord Buxley?" Gabrielle raised a finger to her mouth, nibbling on the tip of her glove. "I thought— for a moment, I did consider . . ." She shook her head, seeming to have talked herself into a corner.

Having gotten the last word—at last!—Christian lifted his quizzing glass and waved his handkerchief in the direction of the dance floor. "I say, is that Lady Ariana over there—with his grace? Best be careful, Miss Laurence, as Lady A. is a determined and increasingly desperate miss, and you might yet need a friend to drive you back to Percy Street this night once old Harry defects. Are you quite sure you couldn't love me? I have a carriage, you know, and might be convinced to bear you home."

"Oh—shut up, you posturing fool!" Gabrielle exploded, proving at last to be susceptible to Baron Christian St. Clair's irreverent, reprehensible bantering. *Thank the Lord,* Christian thought, feeling as if he had just won a great victory in having pushed Gabrielle into resorting to childish insult.

Lord Osgood, having been detained by a determined matron shepherding her homely but eligible daughter, pulled up short in front of Christian and Gabrielle after trotting across the ballroom, nearly coming to grief as he weaved his way through dancers annoyed that he had dared to interrupt their enjoyment in a lively Scottish reel.

"Saw you wave to me, Kit, and I got here quick as I could. Didn't think I was plump enough in the pocket for her ladyship, but with a chick that spotty to pop off, I imagine she's out to nab whichever one of us she can. Good evening, Miss Laurence, and all that," he ended breathlessly, taking time to wink a hello to Gabrielle.

To Christian's secret delight, Gabrielle, obviously recovering some of her early spirit, winked back.

"I say," Lord Osgood exclaimed, looking from Gabrielle to Christian in confusion. "Did you see that? She *winked* at me! Why'd she wink at me, Kit?"

"I winked, my lord, because you winked first," Gabrielle told him, leaving go of Christian's sleeve and very accommodatingly taking hold of Lord Osgood's, for Christian always deposited her with one gentleman or another when his nightly harassing of her was completed. The fact that he had summoned Lord Osgood obviously concluded their association for this evening, and tonight there would be no waltz. "You do know that you wink at people, don't you, Lord Osgood?" she asked, smiling at the flustered man.

"I do?" Lord Osgood asked in apparent surprise. "Blister me, but that's dashed odd. Wink, you say? Kit—is it true? Do I wink?" he questioned his friend, winking at him.

Christian shook his head. "Not to my knowledge, Ozzie," he said, deliberately biting on the inside of his cheek to keep from laughing aloud at his friend's shock at Gabrielle's accusation. "Miss Laurence must have been mistaken. No gentleman would wink at a lady."

"There are a myriad of things no gentleman would do to or with a lady," Gabrielle said, her quick glare in his direction assuring him that the clouds had left her eyes and the sparkling jewels caused by her anger were back once more. "One of them, Lord Osgood, is to keep a lady standing when she is longing to dance. Do you waltz, my lord?"

Lord Osgood looked as if his eyes would pop from his head. "Waltz? With me? But you and Kit—that is, don't you two always—won't it seem odd if you and I—*Kit?*"

Gabrielle tugged on Lord Osgood's sleeve as she glared at Christian. "Please, my lord. I would perish of embarrassment if you were to turn me down now that I have been so forward as to ask you to dance with me. St. Clair, pity the man, please, and give your dear friend permission to dance before he expires in a dead faint for fear of taking a step wrong. Or do you enjoy seeing everyone, your friends included, cowering before the altar of your consequence?"

Striking yet another pose, and finding it deuced difficult to play the role of fop when he would like nothing better than to toss Gabrielle over his shoulder and drag her out into the night with him, to prove to her that he was more than she saw, more than she could believe him to be, Christian drawled, "La, such a to-do, Miss Laurence. Ozzie, be a dear, would you, and partner the lady whilst I circulate. I've still to see Lady Ariana and a few others before I can retire. You mustn't forget that I am promised to a private, very *select* party yet this evening."

"Private party?" Lord Osgood parroted. Then his brow cleared and he winked at the baron. "Oh, yes. A private party. A very select guest list. I remember now. Shouldn't do it, though, Kit. Grumble says—"

"Grumble is always saying something, Ozzie," Christian cut in when Gabrielle seemed to be listening too closely for his comfort. "That is why we call him 'Grumble,' if you'll only remember."

"It is? I thought it was because he's always such a doom-and-gloom merchant."

"Ozzie," Christian intoned, lifting his arms to waist level in order to adjust his cuffs one after the other, "I am leaving you now. Miss Laurence," he continued, bowing over her hand—a hand she had very ungenteelly balled into a tight fist—"I am, of course, devastated to desert you, but duty calls. If I were to cut Lady Ariana she would never forgive me."

"If you were to cut any of us, my lord, we would all find it impossible to forgive you," Gabrielle reminded him, smiling without mirth. "Why, some day a few brave ones among us might decide the only way to avoid worrying over your favor is to make you superfluous to Society. Good evening, my lord. Enjoy your private party—and sleep well. Lord Osgood? I believe the musicians are beginning the waltz."

Christian watched as Lord Osgood, with a last, questioning look to his friend, escorted Gabrielle onto the floor, then smiled broadly as he hailed Lord Undercliff, who appeared both pleased and embarrassed to see him.

Knowing he had to circulate, and to circulate the story that he was to be in attendance at a private party after leaving Lord Blakestone's, Christian deliberately turned his mind away from thoughts of Gabrielle.

Thoughts of her inviting mouth, whether kissing him or threatening him.

Thoughts of his heart-stirring reaction to having at last held her in his arms, having touched her firm breast through the yielding silk of her gown, having desire all but destroy his ability to remember the precariousness of his position or his value to people like the villagers of Little Pillington.

In less than an hour he would be riding through the night in his guise of the Peacock: the avenger, the savior, the nemesis of unfair laws and power-hungry men. He had no time for thoughts of Gabrielle Laurence.

Even if he could still taste her.

CHAPTER 7

～

*Faith! That man's a marvel.
His cheek is preposterous, I vow!
—and that's what carries him through.*

Baroness Orczy

Just a few miles outside London, in a tumbledown stable at the very end of a narrow dirt lane located close by a small village that boasted only one street and a curiously uninterested populace, preparations were under way for a rider intent on a midnight journey.

Hooded lamps hung from low rafters as a bandy-legged, bent-over former jockey teetered on an overturned pail near the line of stalls and threw a blanket, then a saddle, over the back of a coal-black, head-tossing, dancing stallion. "That's it, Zeddy, yer bloody, heathen beast," the man said encouragingly. "Chomp at the bit. Ye're in fer a long ride this night, jist the way yer loiks it."

"The name is Zedekiah, Lenny, remember? It's taken from the Greek, you understand, and means 'justice of the Lord.' "

Lenny pulled the cinch tight and hopped down from the pail. "And ain't that poet-ical, yer worship," he remarked as he grabbed at the simple leather bridle and motioned for Christian to open the double doors as he turned the stallion. "Wouldn't think this here beast had a jot of business with anythin' the Lord might have to mind. Yer gots yer barkin' irons?"

Christian held open his black, many-caped riding cloak, arms akimbo, to display the dull hilts of two pistols he'd stuck inside the waistband of his tight-fitting black trousers. The remainder of his costume was equally dark, with his shirt as black as his boots. The ebony silk mask that tied behind his head, covering his head and face down to just above his mouth, also hid his telltale shoulder-length blond hair.

He made an impressive dark angel, Baron Christian St. Clair did, all six feet three of him, comprised of long straight legs, powerful thighs, narrow waist, and broad shoulders.

Christian had felt the now familiar yet always exciting metamorphosis coming over him as he'd discarded his finery in the bedroom of the small cottage near the stable and once more taken on the persona of the avenger—that most beloved savior of the downtrodden, the Peacock.

All thoughts of his London successes, of the dizzying whirl and glitter of Society, even of the fiery-haired, fiery-tempered seductress who alternately intrigued and confused him, had melted away along with his fine satins and laces. They had been replaced by the thrill of the hunt, the giddy anticipation of his coming encounter with danger, with excitement, with the possibility of a hairbreadth escape from those who sought to bring him down.

It was heady, intoxicating, gut-stirring. Better than any drink, more invigorating than running his on-going rig on the members of the *ton,* more addicting than the opium that held such attraction for Byron and others who would seek adventure; the glory of riding through the night, toward danger, toward excitement, was worth any risk.

And there was all the good he was accomplishing, of course. The children he was feeding, the men he was giving hope to, the women he was rescuing from lives of ever-increasing despair and deprivation. Of course there was that. *That* was most important of all.

Of course.

"Has there been any more word from Sal, Lenny?" Christian asked, running a reassuring hand down the quivering flank of the brave steed that would carry him through the night, then return him just as dawn was breaking over the land and the rest of the world was either retiring to their beds after a night of parties or rising from their cots for another endless day of drudgery.

"Not a peep," Lenny said, as Christian slipped a foot into the stirrup and mounted in a single, smooth motion. Christian employed his spur-free heels and strong hands to remind Zedekiah that his master was atop him now, and that master would brook no nonsense of the sort the stallion attempted when Lenny was exercising him. Only last week Lenny had found himself flying over Zedekiah's pointed ears as the horse took exception to being held to a canter in an open field.

"I'll check the usual spot to see if there's a note," Christian said, turning Zedekiah toward the road. "Close up here, Lenny, and get some sleep. Tell

Perkins I'll need the coach ready again by dawn or soon after."

"Yer shouldn't be goin' alone, yer worship," Lenny warned, shaking his head, a head considerably too large for his small frame. "A wise'un don't take chances. Not iffen he wants ta live ta see his grand-kiddies."

Christian smiled down kindly at the man. "I'll remember that for the next time, Lenny," he said, then pressed his knees against Zedekiah's sides, signaling the eager stallion into an immediate, head-clearing gallop, leaving the former jockey behind to wave away the dust thrown up by the animal's hoofs.

Christian held the stallion to a steady but not punishing pace during the forty-minute ride across moonlit fields to Little Pillington, knowing he had to reserve most of the great horse's strength should a speedy exit from that village become necessary.

As he rode on—the nocturnal smells of freshly turned earth moist with dew mixing with the occasional stench of a polecat disturbed in its nightly hunt reaching his nostrils through the concealing mask—Christian thought ahead to his coming encounter with Herbert Symington.

The man would be armed, of course, and most probably surrounded by half a dozen well-paid bounders primed to fire their pistols at anyone or anything that moved. That's why Christian had insisted upon traveling alone. It was easier by half to slip a single person past guards than it was to mount a full assault.

Was Symington losing sleep, waiting for the Peacock to return? Or would Christian discover him in his nightcap, snoring nineteen to the dozen, stupidly secure in the knowledge that he had bought himself protection?

Christian decided to opt for his second notion, having already had the mixed pleasure of meeting the belligerent mill owner twice and therefore holding no high opinion of the man's ability to employ his brainpower for anything more than making money on the broken backs of those unable to stand up against him.

After stopping on the outskirts of Little Pillington to check the lightning-split oak for any sign of a note from Sal, he dismounted and secreted both Zedekiah and the black cloak among the tall bushes of an overgrown spinney.

Christian then alternately hugged the wood-and-wattle walls of the crooked, top-heavy houses lining the narrow streets of the village and ran, bent over, from alleyway to alleyway, lightly leaping over puddles and avoiding the yellow circles of light thrown by the occasional lamppost.

In less than ten minutes, and without even beginning to breathe hard, Christian was looking up appraisingly at the drainpipe that ran from shingles to gutter at the left rear corner of Herbert Symington's townhouse on the more affluent end of High Street. Reaching above him and grabbing the drainpipe with both hands, he braced one foot against the wall and tugged with all his might, testing the strength of the spikes that held the drainpipe in place.

"Good man, Symington," he whispered beneath his breath as he began to climb toward the third floor of the narrow house. "It's a prudent owner who doesn't stint on those essentials another man might slight in order to spend his blunt on more showy decorations."

Christian continued his climb past the ground floor to the next level. There a careful peek through the window and the sheer draperies Symington seemed to favor showed a small sitting room crowded with no less than five burly laborers armed with pikes, doubtless in order to keep their master safe from that dastardly Peacock.

He also noticed with a smile that the men seemed much more interested in the decanter of brandy they were sharing among themselves than in keeping a keen eye out for their employer's safety. By the look of them, they were all three-parts drunk—all of them save one, who was seated off in a corner, a partially clothed, giggling housemaid straddling his lap as he plundered beneath her skirts with both hands. In all, the scene reminded him of a Cruikshank etching of lower-class debauchery, but he felt no overwhelming desire to linger and commit the picture to memory.

Both his fine physical condition and the heady excitement of the moment lent strength to Christian's arms as he continued his climb, hand over hand, soundlessly scaling the Symington fortress.

Upon reaching the third floor, knowing from a prudent, earlier reconnoitering of the house that Symington's chamber was located there, he discovered that the nearest window was both closed and bolted against him. He had expected as much. Symington didn't appear to be the sort of fellow who delighted in fresh air any more than he would put all his eggs into one basket—meaning that he would leave his protection solely to hired protectors.

Finding purchase for his feet on the broad decorative wooden ledge two feet below the window, and keeping one hand firmly wrapped around the drainpipe, Christian reached inside his pocket and extracted the small glass-cutting tool he had seen fit to arm himself with earlier.

He drew a semicircle in the glass just at the lock, retracing it several times. Then—with the ease of long practice gained at the hands of a housebreaker he had saved from a trip to Newgate that past December—he carefully removed the glass and turned the lock. Moments later, he was standing safely inside Herbert Symington's dressing room, smelling stale air clogged with the odors of shaving soap and sweat.

He allowed a moment for his eyes to become accustomed to the dimness, then crossed soundlessly to the door that would most logically lead to the bedchamber, dropping to his knees to squint through the keyhole.

What he saw brought a smile to his lips, and he rose, drawing one of the pistols from his waistband as he depressed the latch and eased into the chamber. Not that there was any great need for quiet, as Symington was much too involved in self-abuse to take notice if an entire regiment had decided to camp at the foot of his enormous bed.

"Found something that couldn't turn you down, I see," Christian drawled, just as it appeared Symington was about to enjoy the fruits of his labor. "Rather a piddling handful, Herbert, isn't it?"

Symington all but leaped from the bed, his fingers still wrapped around their rapidly shrinking prize. "You!" he shouted, although his voice was no more than a frantic rasp as he stared, bug-eyed, at the intruder. "How'd you get past my men?"

"How, Herbert? What if I were to say that *my* men and I managed to take them by surprise, neatly slit all their throats, and then very unneatly left them to bleed all over your Aubusson carpet?" Christian responded, easing a hip against one of the bed's massive mahogany posts. He watched, only half in amusement, as Symington's usually ruddy complexion blanched. "God's teeth, man, don't swoon on me. Your henchmen are all right, just out of commission for the evening," he lied, confident that Symington wouldn't scream for help he believed lost to him.

"You're a vile man, Peacock."

"Ah, Herbert, how you do wound me. But I'm not vile, really. I'm just having a spot of fun with you. Not as much fun as *you've* been having with you, understand," he added consideringly, motioning with his pistol in the direction of Symington's exposed privates, "but enough to improve my mood. Now, if you would do me the supreme favor of hopping under the covers—ah, there's a good fellow—I believe we have matters to discuss."

"I have nothing to say to you," Symington declared, pulling his nightcap from his head and throwing it in the general direction of his intruder. "I'll not have truck with the likes of you—not when Lord Undercliff has agreed that it would be folly to bow to your demands."

"Lord Undercliff?" Christian deliberately feigned confusion, for it was possible the Peacock would not have heard of his lordship's involvement with the mills. "Would he be a particular friend of yours then, Herbert?"

"That's none of your business, you rotter," Symington exclaimed, seeming to have discovered his courage beneath the red satin bedspread. "I'm not afraid of you. Not at all. You've had your run, but it's over now. Any day now Lord Sidmouth will be sending real troops to guard this house, *and* my mills. We'll have you then, and pluck your feathers once and for all!"

Christian allowed the pistol to rest against his thigh as he perched himself on the edge of the bed. "Dear me, Herbert, you don't say? Perceive me before you, crushed. It is never pleasant, you understand, to have one's illusions dispelled. Finished, am I? About to be done in by Lord Sidmouth and—and *you,* Herbert?"

He lowered his voice rather menacingly as he ended, "And what, pray tell, is to be the means of my demise? Do you intend for me to *laugh* myself to death?"

Symington clutched the covers up to his chin protectively, although his tongue continued to wag even in the face of Christian's mounting anger. "You can't last much longer, hiding behind that thing," he said, staring at Christian as if he might be able to see past the mask and to the features hidden beneath it. "You've gone too far, dared too much. Undercliff isn't the only one who dabbles in trade. Sidmouth isn't alone anymore. They all know you're one of them, and they hate you for betraying them. It's just a matter of time until you're found out. You aren't amusing anymore, Peacock. You're too dangerous."

"How interesting. And you learned all this from Lord Undercliff? I suppose that would explain why you are not hastening to accede to my demands. I suppose that would also explain why I, this hapless wretch on the brink of defeat, am sitting here, in your private bedchamber, pointing a pistol at your ample stomach while you cower beneath your covers. I don't know, Herbert," he said, shaking his head. "Perhaps —just perhaps, mind you—you and I should rethink the matter."

"You won't make me change my mind," Symington declared, although his voice had begun to waver.

"You're the quality, and won't kill me. If only I can hold out, then your power over other mill owners will be broken. The rest of them collapsed at your feet, but I am not so easy to cow. Lord Sidmouth has promised me that no more of my properties will burn. He promised me protection!"

"Protection, is it, Herbert? My, my, my. You will keep harping on that subject, won't you?" Christian smiled behind the silk mask. "I wonder. Are you persisting in taking comfort in the notion that your precious protection has anything to do with the men my ineffectual cohorts and I interrupted as they enjoyed themselves in your private sitting room, drinking your brandy and diddling your housemaid? I had thought you'd hired them. But they're Sidmouth's men as well, the vanguard he has sent to protect you until troops arrive? My, what prime specimens. Herbert, I tell you, I am quaking in my boots at the thought of fellows of their dedication planning my demise."

"Bertha?" Symington levered himself up onto his elbows, his complexion ruddy once more. "They were after Bertha? *That's* why she's so late in coming to me? The bastards!" He threw back the covers and made to rise. "I'll take my whip to the lot of them!"

Christian raised the barrel of his pistol. "No, Herbert, in point of fact, you will not. I have other plans for the remainder of the evening, I fear. Or have you forgotten that I have promised a further punishment if you did not implement my demands? Yes, that's it—sit down, Herbert. Make yourself comfortable."

Christian stepped closer, suddenly struck with inspiration. He had come to Little Pillington with only a vague idea of what he would do to prod Symington into easing the plight of his workers. Now, seeing the man in his least prepossessing appearance, he knew just what form that punishment would take.

"You are comfortable, aren't you, Herbert?" Christian asked, smiling. "Good. But it occurs to me that it is a warm evening, and you might be even more comfortable if you removed that heavy nightshirt."

"Removed—*what?*" Symington clutched his nightshirt to himself with both hands, his eyes bulging as he stared at his nemesis.

Christian sighed, feeling rather full of himself as he savored his own genius. "Ah, Herbert. I have a long ride ahead of me and, much as I have enjoyed our intimate interlude, I must ask you to desist from any more questions and merely do as I say. Now, at the count of three—I'd have you count to ten if I thought you could follow along—remove your nightshirt."

Symington became most cooperative when he realized that Christian was in earnest, even tying his own gag once Christian had stuffed a handkerchief into the man's mouth. Within five minutes Symington, stark naked and with his hands bound securely behind his back, was tripping down the front stairs, which were located quite a distance from his private study.

It still lacked more than an hour until dawn when Symington, prodded by the pistol Christian pressed into his spine, stepped barefoot into the low fountain in the deserted village square and felt his arms and legs being firmly lashed to the center column of that fountain. He moaned low in his throat as Christian tucked a single peacock feather into the makeshift ropes fashioned from drapery ties banding his barrel chest, then began to cry, looking far less sure of his eventual victory than he had a half hour earlier.

"Now prepare yourself, Herbert," Christian said

bracingly as he backed out of the low fountain himself and stamped his boots in order to remove most of the water that beaded on the shiny leather.

"There will be vulgar people in this square not too very long from now," he told the weeping man. "Horrid people. Easily amused people. People who might even delight in the misfortune of such a fine, upstanding, beloved member of the community as yourself. I wonder. Is there usually a goodly supply of rotted vegetables in Little Pillington? But never fear, Herbert. You are covered by Lord Sidmouth's impressive protection. You do feel *covered,* don't you, Herbert? Safe? No, I suppose not. Forgive my ill-timed levity. Well, I must be going."

Christian turned to leave, then looked toward the frantically struggling Symington once more. "Will I be seeing you again, Herbert, or will you be cutting the laborers' hours, I wonder? Will you bow to the sweet reason that tells you that it is better to have the Peacock's neglect than the protection of those like lords Sidmouth and Undercliff, who promise much but personally sacrifice nothing? Ah, well, as you are not up to speaking at the moment, I shall simply have to continue my close watch on you until I can see for myself that you have recognized the error of your ways. Lord knows the whole village will be viewing the remainder of your *shortcomings* in a few hours. Ta-ta!"

A moment later Christian had melted away, slipping back into the darkness even as he could hear faint stirrings in one of the small houses that bordered the village square. If he was lucky—and he was most always lucky—he would have no difficulty in remounting Zedekiah and putting several miles between himself and Little Pillington before Symington could recover himself sufficiently to gather up his hired henchmen and instigate a pursuit.

He dawdled only a moment at the edge of the square, the same square where, in two days' time, Slow Dickie would be flogged, mentally picturing the scene and how he would rescue the unfortunate laborer from his punishment.

A slight breeze caught at a sign hanging over a small tobacco shop to his left, and Christian smiled as he looked up at it, the plan that had already been forming in his mind now complete. How easily he conjured up mischief. Was it a failing, or a talent?

"Love a duck, yer worship, what a sight! Ole Symington starkers. Makes me proud ta make yer acquaintance, yer worship. Only ye shoulda stuck that feather up his bloomin' arse, don't ye know. The blighter could do with some tailfeathers!"

As he looked down at the raggedly clad Irishman standing beside him, Christian cursed himself for being so caught up in the moment, in his own glory, that he had been unaware of the man's approach. The fellow was a friend—of that he was fairly certain—but he could just as easily have been one of Sidmouth's men, one of his "agents provocateurs." Wouldn't Grumble have been depressed to have himself proved right?

"And who might you be, good sir?" Christian asked quietly as he began to walk away from the square and toward the spinney that lay at the edge of the village, the little man falling into step beside him, uninvited.

"Me? Oi be O'Dell, yer worship," the Irishman whispered, beginning to skip a little to keep up with Christian's long strides. "No sense in tellin' me who ye are, don't ye know. Ye be the Peacock, sure as spit.

It's a fine thing ye done here the other night." He gave out a reedy chuckle. "And a right glorious thing ye done here this night! Cain't think o' anythin' that'll buck up the lads more than the sight of Symington come the dawn."

"Speaking of the dawn, Mr. O'Dell," Christian asked, never breaking stride, "isn't it a bit early for you to be up and about?"

"Not when we've been meetin' the whole fuckin' night long, it ain't," O'Dell countered. "Jackey—who thinks hisself smarter than the rest o' us—has us beatin' our heads ta figure out a way ta spring Slow Dickie away from the constable. Or ain't ye heard tell of that yet?"

"I've heard," Christian said, stopping at the end of the dark alleyway and looking at O'Dell again, this time taking more than a moment to wonder if the Irishman was what he appeared to be—or if he was one of Sidmouth's agents. It didn't pay to be careless. "Jackey is your leader, I presume? Who else is with you in this venture?"

O'Dell scratched at the side of his nose. "A whole clutch of run-at-the-mouth roosters. Ones what lost their holdin's, old soldiers, mill workers loik me, and a couple o' out-an'-outters willin' ta pledge theirselves ta anythin' iffen there's a goodly supply of cheap gin passed about whilst the speechin' is goin' on. We calls ourselves the Volunteers fer Justice, fer all that's worth ta us. Oi just come from the Bull and Cock, where we wuz talkin' about poor Slow Dickie. Didn't come up with anythin', though. We never does. We just talk."

The Irishman shook his head, then brightened. "There's still a coupla the blokes there, yer worship.

Would ye be willin' ta go there with me? Jackey'd never get over the shock o' seein' ye with the loiks o' me. Warm the cockles off me heart ta see his face, that it would. It's a bleedin' shame all m'kiddies are abed. Be like Father Christmas has come ta have them clap their daylights on ye."

Christian continued to smile as he mentally calculated how long it would take him to return Zedekiah and slip back into London. He had time, if he didn't tarry too long in this alleyway listening to the Irishman run his mouth.

"I would be honored to be your guest at the Bull and Cock, Mr. O'Dell—if you promise to make no mention of Mr. Symington's dilemma until I am gone. Is there any way to gain entry to the Bull and Cock without causing undue notice of our passing?"

O'Dell nodded vigorously. "Jist ye follow me, yer worship. There ain't a thing Oi doesn't know about Little Pillington. Oi can get ye from here to there and back again without so much as a wee mousie twitchin' his nose as ye pass by. And don't ye be worritin' yerself about me spillin' the news about Symington. Everyone'll tell ye how O'Dell keeps his potato trap shut!"

True to his word, O'Dell delivered Christian to the back door of the Bull and Cock after leading him on a twisting journey through narrow, garbage-strewn alleyways and sorry-looking vegetable patches, then slipped inside ahead of him to check out the lay of the land before giving the okay for Christian to follow after him.

Christian had to bend his head as he entered to allow for the low ceiling of the room, a hand on one of his pistols. He stopped just inside the doorway, his gaze skipping over the half dozen occupants. "Good evening, gentlemen," he said at last, when no one spoke. "Would there be a mug of ale for a weary traveler?"

Four of the six immediately sprang from their chairs in their fervor to serve him—only O'Dell, who was too busy puffing out his chest, and a man sunk into his collar in the corner of the room not joining in in what had all the earmarks of becoming a riot as everyone scrambled to secure the single clean mug left on the table.

The tallest of the men, and the one with the greatest look of intelligence in his narrow, close-set eyes, secured the prize and filled the mug to its brim before crossing the room to present it to Christian. "Oi'm Jackey," the man announced, then added, "sir," seemingly caught somewhere between reverence and bravado. "Oi'm the leader of this sorry lot. For them, and for me and the rest of Little Pillington, may Oi say, our thanks ta you, Mr. Peacock, sir."

"It has been my pleasure, Jackey," Christian told him, easing onto a rude bench that was representative of the seating in the room. "I understand you are convened here to devise a stratagem for extraditing one of your fellows from his current imprisonment?"

O'Dell elbowed one of the other men. "See, Petey? Didn't Oi always tells ye the Peacock wuz one o' the gentry? Didn't understand a word o' what he said, but he sure enough said it pretty, didn't he?"

"Stifle it, O'Dell," Jackey shot back over his shoulder. "We can listen ta yer flap yer jaws any time. We wants ta 'ear what his worship 'ere 'as ta say."

Christian dismissed Jackey as a candidate for agent provocateur, as he just as quickly discounted the other men in the room—except for the laborer slumbering in the corner, his hat pushed forward over his eyes. He seemed taller than the others, even as he slouched on the bench, and much better fed, even if his clothes were little more than rags. "Who's that?" he asked Jackey softly, inclining his head in the direction of the sleeping man.

"'Im?" Jackey responded. "Said 'e's a soldier. Served with Wellington 'imself at Waterloo. Says 'e's not seen a bent penny o' 'is pension, not that it keeps 'im from drinkin' like a fish. Don't say much else, come ta think on it. Only reason 'e comes 'ere a'tal is fer the drink, ta my mind. Ta drink and ta sleep."

"His name, Jackey," Christian prodded as he rose and began moving in the former soldier's direction, his hand on the hilt of his pistol. The men, awed by Christian's presence, had not been unduly loud, but they'd certainly made enough of a commotion to rouse the sleeping soldier unless the man was dead drunk.

Jackey shook his head, beginning to look worried only because Christian's movements were far from casual, and not because he understood the possible danger. "Bobbie? Robbie?" he whispered. "Cain't be sure, yer lordship. There's so many o' us, yer see. Wot's wrong?"

"Nothing, Jackey," Christian assured him, stepping back a pace and leaning a shoulder against the door, not wishing for the other men to take up the hint of trouble and turn into a noisy mob, thus risking Christian's exposure to anyone still lingering in the common room. But even as he spoke he kept his gaze riveted on the former soldier. "I just like to know who I'm drinking with, I suppose."

Jackey nodded. "'E's safe enough, yer worship. Been comin' 'ere off and on fer weeks now, and ain't never caused no trouble. Now, sir, 'bout Slow Dickie . . ."

Deliberately, and not without apprehension, Christian shifted his gaze away from the soldier and motioned for Jackey to lean closer. "My men and I plan an assault on the guardhouse here in Little Pillington tomorrow night," he said, not bothering to lower his voice. "The way we see it, the best time to break in would be sometime after midnight and before dawn, when there is only one constable within the guardhouse. Don't worry, Jackey. My men and I won't allow Slow Dickie to be flogged on my account."

"Ha! Oi knowed it all along. There wuz no way the Peacock would let Slow Dickie take a beatin' fer 'im—even if 'e was nicked in the nob to be runnin' about Symington's place, a bleedin' feather in his paw. 'Ere now, yer lordship, yer mug is empty. O'Dell— fetch us another pitcher of ale from the taproom, would ye?"

Just as O'Dell, who had been busily whispering to the other men, stood up to do Jackey's bidding, a commotion broke out in the common room beyond the door at the opposite end of the room. Seconds later, a barmaid poked her head in to announce: "Perk up yer ears, yer lazy dogs. The Peacock's bin agin, and 'e's gone and trussed up Symington and stuck 'im bare-rumped in the fountain!"

"The divil ye say! Did ye hear that? And ye all wuz sittin' 'ere callin' me a liar!" O'Dell exclaimed, slapping his palms on the rough tabletop as he stood up. "Come on, boyos. Oi'll leads the way!"

The hated Symington tied up naked in the fountain? Having the Peacock in their midst was exciting, but these simple men could barely understand him, they couldn't see much of him through his mask, and, once seen, there was nothing much else they could find to do with the man. But to clap their world-weary peepers on Symington in the fountain? Now there was a sight they could appreciate!

Within a heartbeat, Christian found himself alone in the room, even the formerly slumbering soldier having barreled out the doorway to the common room, leaving their unexpected guest behind.

Which was most likely for the best.

With the entire village of Little Pillington awake beforetimes and heading toward the square, it would be simple enough for Christian to make his way back to the spinney and get safely away. Not, he decided as he threw a half dozen gold coins on the table, that his detour to the back room of the Bull and Cock had been without profit.

He now knew the leader of the group of mill workers, a man he might find reason to appeal to for assistance in besting Symington if the mill owner stubbornly continued to oppose him.

He had gained the confidence of an Irishman named O'Dell, who knew the ins and outs of Little Pillington better than he ever could.

And, lastly, he had seen the agent provocateur Lord Buxley had spoken of so proudly. He could now go back to Grumble and the rest of them and relate that he was suspicious of the loyalty of one of the villagers, warning them to take special care, without having to disclose the fact that the earl had already admitted that Lord Sidmouth had made Little Pillington the focus of his search for the Peacock.

A single agent operating in their midst might be troubling, but Grumble would never countenance any further adventures in Little Pillington if he knew how dangerous the game was fast becoming.

Adventures? The game? The words echoed in Christian's ears as he untied Zedekiah and vaulted into the saddle. Those were the wrong words. He and his friends went out on *missions,* not adventures. Not games.

Didn't they?

Christian deliberately pushed the unsettling thought from his mind as he concentrated instead on the comforting notion of Lord Sidmouth's men passing what he sincerely hoped was a damp, rainy night hiding in the dark outside the Little Pillington guardhouse, waiting for the Peacock and his men to arrive.

The thought cheered Christian throughout his ride back to the small stable outside London and beyond, until Frapple had shut the front door of the mansion behind his master and ushered him upstairs, to strip him of his satin evening clothes and help him into a hot tub.

"Have you ever seen a fat man naked, Frapple?" Christian asked as he eased his weary body into the soothing, hip-deep water.

"If I say I haven't, my lord," Frapple answered, handing his master a sea sponge, "will you gift me with one for my birthday? I'd much rather some French brandy, you know."

Christian threw back his head and laughed aloud. "Ah, Frapple, what would I do without you?"

"Wither and die, my lord, as I always tell you," Frapple declared coolly, unceremoniously pouring a bucket of water over Christian's head in preparation of soaping his hair. "I cannot begin to tell you how powerful I feel whenever I think of it. Oh, and by the bye, Mr. Trumble will be calling at nine. I tried to put him off until later, but the only way I could extradite him from the drawing room at all was to agree to that early hour. He worries about you, you know, although I cannot for the life of me understand why."

"He loves me, of course." Christian took a deep breath and submerged himself in the tub, only to rise again and shake his head like a terrier exiting a pond. "Everyone loves me, Frapple," he said, grinning up at his trusted servant. "Absolutely everybody."

"Including Miss Laurence?" Frapple inquired, readying another bucket of rinse water. "Mr. Trumble, a talkative fellow once he unbends a bit, seems to believe she quite determinedly detests you. Ah, what a crushing blow that must be to your considerable St. Clair pride."

"Frapple, you're dismissed. Fired. And I'll be damned if I'll give you a reference."

"There's no need, my lord," the servant answered calmly, taking up a large white towel that had been warming by the fire and wrapping it around Christian's body as he exited the tub. "I have a half dozen references from you already tucked up in my portmanteau. None of them are dated this month, however, as you have not seen fit to dismiss me since February."

"I give up," Christian said, raising his hands in surrender. "I spent a long night slaying dragons in Little Pillington, only to return home to abuse. Frapple, are you going to feed me?"

Having, as usual, achieved an opening for the last word against the acknowledged master of the last word, Frapple smiled and said, "Feed you? Of course, my lord. To precisely what wild animal do you wish to be fed?"

While Christian was sitting down to an early breakfast of ham and biscuits and strong coffee, many blocks away, tucked up in a narrow house in Percy Street, Miss Gabrielle Laurence had at last found her rest after a night spent alternately congratulating herself on her courage and berating that same self for her gross stupidity.

As she slept, the covers twisted due to her restless slumber, dawn crept over Mayfair, a sliver of sunlight finding the scarred desktop in front of the window of her bedchamber. On that desktop, half hidden among some rather crushed yellow silk flowers and a necklace of very good false pearls, was a single sheet of paper that had been scribbled over and then discarded.

The sunlight slid across the paper, dancing over the damning evidence of Gabrielle's personal confusion, tracing along the lines that read: "Lady Gabrielle St. Clair . . . the Rt. Hon. Lady St. Clair . . . Lord and Lady St. Clair . . . Christian . . . Christian . . . Kit . . ."

CHAPTER 8

———————

The ass is still an ass,
e'en though he wears a lion's hide.
The chameleon may change its color,
but it is the chameleon still.

William Shakespeare

Why, good evening, Lord Buxley. How nice of you
to seek me out in this dark corner," Gabrielle said
with forced brightness as the earl presented himself in
front of her, looking impeccable, as always, in his
Brummell-styled evening clothes.

She and Elizabeth had been sitting together to one
side of Lady Cornwallis's drawing room, eager to
exchange a few private and not quite complimentary
comments about the poor quality of the amateur
performers partaking in this musical evening. However, Gabrielle knew it wouldn't do to shoo the wealthy,
handsome, but most depressingly boring man away
when he had purposely approached her. "I don't
remember seeing you last night at Lord Blakestone's,
my lord."

Lord Anthony Buxley released Gabrielle's hand,

having bowed over it without really kissing it, and looked at her solemnly. "Someone must be about the King's business, Miss Laurence, putting down malcontents like that reprehensible Peacock before the situation becomes dangerous," he said, barely sparing a nod for Elizabeth. "Have you read this morning's *Times?*"

Gabrielle gazed up at the earl in mild shock, for the Peacock's weekly letter had been particularly heart-wrenching, full of descriptions of stick-thin orphans covered with chilblains and fed thin gruel by harsh, unfeeling warders. "Please, my lord. You are surely not going to tell me you are about to take exception to the very necessary printing of that sad tale of work-house children. Did you read about how many of them perish before their third birthday? Or are you saying that the Peacock is lying, and that these sad conditions do not truly exist?"

Lord Buxley waved away her question. "Forgive me, Miss Laurence. No one can be guaranteed a perfect world. I was not in truth referring to the contents of that coward's hysterical letter, but to the fact that his evil missives are still being published in the metropolis at all. Even you ladies must understand that the Peacock is undermining the very structure of our government."

"And the children?" Elizabeth prodded, inserting herself into the conversation, even though for the most part she restrained herself to the role of silent companion when she and Gabrielle were in public. "How, my lord, does being made aware of their pitiful plight undermine our government? Truly, sir, I would greatly like to hear an explanation for such horrors as were depicted in the Peacock's latest letter."

Gabrielle turned to her friend in surprise, only to be

further shocked to see that Elizabeth was sitting extremely straight, her chin tilted pugnaciously, her hands drawn up into tight fists in her lap. "Elizabeth? My dear, are you all right?"

"I'm perfectly all right, Gaby," Elizabeth assured her in a whisper. "It's just that Roger and I had so wanted a child of our own to love. And when I think of all those unwanted children . . ." She shook her head and rose to her feet, motioning for Gabrielle to remain seated. "Lord Buxley, please accept my apologies for causing a scene. I would prefer to retire by myself for a nonce, to recover my composure, if I can rely upon you to be sure not to leave Miss Laurence unattended in my absence."

Always a stickler for the conventions, Lord Buxley inclined his head, saying, "It would be my extreme pleasure, Mrs. Fletcher," as Elizabeth brushed past him, holding a handkerchief to her mouth as she headed for the hallway and the small salon set aside for female guests.

"I've never seen her like this. She shouldn't be alone. Excuse me, my lord, but I have to go after her," Gabrielle said, wanting nothing more than to be shed of this obtuse, blockheaded man who had upset her friend. "Perhaps we might continue this conversation at some other time—although I must say I am finding this continual fascination our Society has with the Peacock to be most wearying. One would think there is no other subject of interest in all of England."

"If you insist, Miss Laurence," Lord Buxley agreed, offering Gabrielle his arm and assistance in exiting the drawing room. "However, as I had approached you this evening in the hope of gaining your assistance in a personal matter—a matter of the heart, actually—

well, I must admit to being disappointed that we will not be able to have a few minutes alone."

"A personal matter? Of the heart?" Gabrielle was confused. Lord Buxley had not yet shown her any real affection, although he had been kind enough to escort her down to dinner at a few balls, and he had never done anything to impede the popularity St. Clair's championing of her had brought. Surely the man wasn't about to propose to her? Even to save Rose Hill Farm, Gabrielle didn't believe she could contemplate such a boring marriage.

Besides, considering the way Elizabeth had glared at the man just moments before, Gabrielle knew she could never risk losing her friend in order to gain a fortune, no matter how large.

That thought brought her up short, nearly causing her to stumble as his lordship, obviously secure in the thought that any of his problems clearly outweighed those of a weeping, highly strung female, directed Gabrielle's steps toward the open doors leading to the balcony.

What *was* she willing to give up in trade for a fortune, to save Rose Hill Farm, to escape a precarious life of genteel poverty that, thanks to her father's free way with his purse, daily inched closer to very ungenteel penury?

Not Elizabeth. Certainly she wouldn't give up that sweet woman's friendship, her good opinion.

Gabrielle had already experienced Baron Christian St. Clair's clear disdain, his constant references to her money-mad pursuit of a wealthy husband. His opinion of her, much to her constant amazement, also mattered more than she could like.

There was good reason to rethink her motives.

When it came to putting her ideas to the sticking point, did she really have it in her to be a fortune hunter? It had all seemed so simple in theory, during those weeks of planning while still at Rose Hill Farm; but these past two weeks, her first in Society, had been growing daily more untenable. Everything was so superficial, so artificial.

And hardly worth the subterfuge, as a lifetime spent among petted and pampered creatures who cared more for appearances than they did for the people around them could be seen as no better than a dead loss.

After all, was it really so bad to lose a thing—something like her birthplace, a structure of unfeeling brick and mortar—when so many of her countrymen had lost everything? Perhaps the Peacock was right, Elizabeth was right. There were larger things in this world than the secure feeling to be found in a life of luxury. Things like a mind free of guilt at seeing beggars on the streets of London. Ah, the Peacock was doing his work well if others in Society were beginning to think as she was tonight.

"Miss Laurence?"

Gabrielle heard the earl as if from a distance and frowned, only becoming aware of her surroundings as a cool evening breeze skimmed across her bare shoulders.

How had they come to be outside? From behind her she could hear Miss Abigail Frawley launching herself into an Italian aria whose composer had done nothing to incur the young lady's vocal assault, and she knew that she could not reenter the drawing room now in order to seek out Elizabeth in the withdrawing room. There was nothing else for it than that she smile up at the earl, listen to his proposal, and then cudgel her brain into alighting upon some way to turn away his suit without insulting the man who was, after all, a Tory, and not accustomed to thinking kindly of anyone below the rank of Honorable.

"La, your lordship, forgive me, please," Gabrielle trilled, seating herself on the wrought-iron bench that had been provided for guests wishing a respite from the overheated drawing room. "I have been wool-gathering, haven't I? It's just that I have never before seen my dear companion so overset."

"Yes, and it's unforgivable that this Peacock, this revolutionist, should stoop to upsetting our fair ladies," Lord Buxley pronounced, splitting his finely fashioned midnight-blue coattails as he sat himself down beside Gabrielle. "And I agree that the subject of the seditious malcontent and his identity has become fatiguing in the extreme. Females most especially aren't to be concerned with such matters. It taxes their brains in ways no female is prepared to comprehend."

Gabrielle wished she had decided to carry a fan with her this evening so that she could, as Shakespeare had written, "brain" the earl with it. "Are you saying, my lord, that the female's intelligence is inferior to that of the male's? That we are gifted only with soft hearts to be easily stung by a sad tale, and ever softer heads, unable to recognize injustice when it is served up for us in the *Times?* If you are, my lord, then I feel it only fair to tell you that this particular soft-hearted, soft-headed female is shocked, sir—shocked."

"Such heat, Miss Laurence," Lord Buxley remarked soothingly, his smooth brow furrowing below his immaculately arranged black hair. "I suppose I should expect no less of such a fiery-headed miss. My apologies, I'm sure. After all, it wouldn't do to upset you, not when I have brought you out here to request a boon."

Was the man impervious to insult, those he inflicted upon others as well as those aimed in his direction? Wait! What was he speaking about now? A "boon"? He was asking a favor? He wasn't about to propose? She might not want him, but how dare *he* not want *her?* Gabrielle brought her wandering thoughts back from images of Lord Anthony Buxley in rags, holding out his bowl for a serving of watery gruel, and listened to what the man was now saying.

". . . And as Lady Ariana informed me just this afternoon that you and she have become fast friends, I thought I might apply to you as to where her heart lies. Surely not with St. Clair, I know that. But is she still dead-set on a duke? Even in her second Season?"

"Lord Buxley—" Gabrielle began, only to be cut off as he smiled benignly and requested she address him more informally, as "Anthony."

"Very well, your lordship—Anthony," she continued, relieved that she wouldn't have to fend off his proposal or, worse yet, his physical advances, while still feeling faintly put out that he would prefer Lady Ariana to her. It was going to take some time to realign her thinking, away from convenient matrimony and onto more serious paths. "Am I to understand that you are in love with Lady Ariana?"

The earl patted Gabrielle's hand as he would affectionately pat the uncomprehending head of an obtuse but pitifully earnest child. "Lady Ariana and I suit each other, Miss Laurence—Gabrielle. We are both handsome creatures, if I might be so bold as to refer to such things, well accepted in Society, equally well to go, and we are of like minds. Tory to the backbone.

She would make me a fine hostess, and exemplary sons."

How cold-blooded it all sounded. Gabrielle winced inwardly, knowing her own plans had not been so far removed from Lord Buxley's. A convenient marriage. A pleasant hostess and upper-class broodmare in exchange for a deep gravy boat of financial security and social position. Gabrielle suddenly longed to flee the balcony and hide herself away—preferably in a room without mirrors.

"I can see you have thought long and hard on this subject, Anthony," she heard herself saying as a slight buzzing began in her ears. "However, I'm afraid I can't help you, as Lady Ariana has not seen fit to confide in me. St. Clair, however, has hinted that she is still hoping for an alliance with the Duke of Glynnon."

"St. Clair?" Lord Buxley's handsome but usually expressionless face colored with indignation. "That prancing ninny? His opinion is worth nothing, Gabrielle. Less than nothing. Why, when I think how thoroughly I debased myself by going to him, imploring his assistance in unmasking the Peacock—" He broke off, abruptly turning away to look down at the dark gardens, clearly upset with himself for having said too much.

"You . . ." Gabrielle began, trying her best to assimilate what the man had let slip. "You believe St. Clair could lead you to the Peacock? How very strange."

"Really? In what way, Gabrielle?" the earl asked quickly, turning to her once more and looking at her carefully, making her wonder if the man's verbal faux pas had been as innocently stupid as he'd attempted it to be, making her wonder if his mention of Lady

Ariana had only been a ploy meant to draw her into some other, deeper discussion.

Lord Buxley might be single-minded, but he was not simple-minded. Yes, perhaps there was some darker purpose to this conversation. After all, the earl knew that she and St. Clair were seen together every evening, always disappearing for a few minutes onto any handy balcony or into a darkened garden. What did he think she knew about St. Clair's private life? What did he suppose about that life? Did he believe, as she was beginning to believe, that the baron had a few secrets of his own?

Things were moving too fast. First she had believed Lord Buxley was going to propose marriage to her. That notion had certainly put her off her stride. Then he had shifted the conversation to Lady Ariana, further weakening Gabrielle's defenses, as she was put into the position of either saying anything that came into her head so as to look as if she were indeed a bosom chum of that important lady, or admitting, as she had, that she knew nothing, less than nothing, about the woman's personal life, damning Gabrielle as no more than a casual acquaintance.

And now, now that she had exhibited her lack of knowledge on the matter of Lady Ariana's expectations, the subject had somehow shifted once more, to St. Clair—and the Peacock.

Why were those two names always mingled together in her mind? The two men were nothing alike, even if Gabrielle had threatened the baron with exposure as the masked avenger of downtrodden souls and general thorn in the side of the Tory government.

"Strange in what way?" Gabrielle repeated, wondering if Lord Buxley wouldn't have been a great success during the Spanish Inquisition, speaking calmly and confidently while applying the thumb-screws to his hapless victims. "Why, in no way at all, I'm sure. St. Clair. The Peacock. Two such disparate creatures. They could be no more different from each other than they are, don't you agree? Why, the last, the absolute *last* two people to have anything in common with each other would be our strutting baron and that courageous outlaw."

"Yes, Gabrielle, that's true, although I differ with your description of the Peacock as courageous," the earl said, picking up her hand and beginning to stroke it, causing Gabrielle to wish she had applied herself to mastering the genteel swoon, for she felt a great need to escape this wandering yet, she felt sure, dangerous conversation. "I have thought the same myself. Why, as a matter of fact, if I were to be forced to choose the least likely candidate for the role of Peacock, St. Clair's name would sit atop the list."

Gabrielle extracted her hand from the earl's grip and said, believing herself to have made a brilliant recovery from her verbal confusion, "But you said you have applied for the baron's assistance in discovering the Peacock."

"I did?" Lord Buxley smiled indulgently. "No, I'm sure you're mistaken. What I said, Gabrielle, was that I, acting on behalf of our government, had applied to St. Clair for his assistance in bringing the bounder down. St. Clair will persist in reciting the man's missives to the newspapers aloud whenever he is in public, inciting sentimental ladies to imagine that England is awash in starving infants and elevating that disruptive outlaw to the status of a Wellington, or higher. But my mission was in vain, for all St. Clair could do was to express a wish to capture the Peacock. *Capture* him? That shallow-pated popinjay? I'd as soon expect to see it raining cats and cabbages tomorrow morning when I look out my window."

Gabrielle laughed, amazed to learn that Lord Buxley wasn't entirely without humor, then quickly covered her mouth as she executed a polite cough when she realized that not only was his lordship not smiling, he was *lying* as well. "St. Clair is a Whig, then?" she asked, quickly trying to cover her lapse into levity when the earl persisted in being so depressingly sober.

"He is nothing more than you see, Gabrielle," Lord Buxley corrected her, his full lips—the ones that so incongruously never seemed to move when he spoke —drawn into a small sneer. "Vain, vacuous, and terminally useless. Never a soldier, never applying himself to anything more weighty than inventing a new sort of clearly Frenchie neckwear, never so much as taking up his inherited seat in government. His poor deceased father must have found his only son a dead loss, as do I."

For a reason she didn't at the moment care to explore, Gabrielle felt impelled to defend St. Clair. "But that's not true. Elizabeth tells me that the baron was once committed to equality such as the French peasantry strove for in that terrible Revolution. It's so strange that he seems uncaring now, Elizabeth says, and not—" She shut her mouth, biting down hard on her bottom lip, as Lord Buxley seemed to be listening to her with his full concentration, his handsome blue eyes narrowed, the strong planes of his cheeks rather pinched.

"Yes?" he prodded, as Gabrielle began fanning herself with one hand, for the cool evening had somehow turned unexpectedly warm. "You were saying?"

Gabrielle tapped her cheek lightly several times, as if punishing herself. "Oh, Lord Buxley—Anthony. Please excuse me. I have become confused. Elizabeth wasn't speaking of St. Clair. She had been telling me about *Roger,* her late husband. And, now that I recall correctly, Roger only expressed those views as a headstrong youth, long before he saw the error of the French and went off to fight so valiantly against Napoleon."

She searched in the pocket of her gown for a small, lace-edged handkerchief and lifted it to press at the corners of her eyes. "Roger Fletcher died a hero, you know," she said, sniffling. "And poor, poor Elizabeth. Not even so much as a body to bury, a grave to visit, bear-bearing flowers." She buried her head in her hands, forcing out a genteel sob. "Oh, Anthony, I am overcome!"

And you talk too much! she berated herself silently, remembering to shake her shoulders slightly, as if succumbing to maidenly grief, as was the custom of empty-headed, hysterical females.

Lord Buxley offered some "there, theres" as he patted her arm sympathetically, seemingly expecting no less than an emotional outburst from any female, then said bracingly, "I believe the entertainment for the evening has concluded, dear lady. Come, I'll deliver you back to Mrs. Fletcher."

Gabrielle looked up at the earl, dabbing at her dry eyes one last time. "But—but I thought you wished to speak to me about Lady Ariana. I agree that you two would make an unexceptional couple, and it would, of course, be the match of the Season. Are you truly going to propose to her?"

Lord Buxley rose, holding out his hand to assist Gabrielle to her feet. "I am a proud man, Gabrielle," he intoned solemnly, not gifting her with any new knowledge she hadn't already gained on her own. "I refuse to open myself to the possibility of rejection. I had planned to first approach her esteemed father and then press my suit with the lady, but you have done nothing to convince me that my offer would be accepted."

He straightened his already perfect posture. "But if I were to capture the Peacock, expose him for the rotter that he is . . ."

Did every conversation, every plan or hopeful scheme of everyone she knew, including herself, have to return to uncovering the identity of the Peacock? Gabrielle took Lord Buxley's arm as he led her into the drawing room. "It's a pity, Anthony," she suggested archly, "that *you* are not the Peacock, as I believe Lady Ariana, like all of us witless ladies, is already half in love with him."

"Me? The Peacock?" the earl exclaimed, looking down at her as if she had just blasphemed. "I believe I am insulted, for there is no one more different from that creature as I."

"Except for St. Clair," Gabrielle pressed on, wishing she could jam her fist into her mouth to stop herself, but nervously continuing to speak, "who has, if he can be believed, placed a private wager that *you*, Anthony, are the Peacock. And, employing St. Clair's reasonable logic of looking for the most unlikely suspect as best as any weak female mind can, I believe I now see the sense in his argument, which, surprisingly, much resembles your own."

And mine, she added mentally. *Is all of London about to come to the same conclusion?*

Lord Buxley smiled, making him even more spectacularly handsome than usual. If he rose as high in the Tory government as he clearly hoped to do, the statue commissioned in his honor would be breathtaking. Indeed, if his legs were as well formed as his stockings implied, he would be quite stirring immortalized in marble as a Greek god.

"I assure you, Gabrielle," he told her, sobering quickly, for he seemed uncomfortable when smiling, "I am *not* the Peacock. And if Lady Ariana is in any way infatuated with that low creature, I perhaps should rethink making an application for her hand. I shouldn't wish my sons to be encouraged to flights of fancy. The world is a deadly serious place, Gabrielle. Deadly serious."

And you're a deadly bore, Anthony, even when you are playing the role of intriguer, Gabrielle thought, nodding her head in agreement with his sentiments and hoping her own expression showed suitably solemn and impressed.

"Leading us back, I believe, Anthony, to the beginning of our conversation. I am sorry I couldn't be of any more assistance to you, but I must acknowledge that ours has been a most edifying interlude. I have gained a new friend, which is eminently more pleasant than knowing you as a mere acquaintance and sometimes dancing partner. And I have learned that you are a loyal servant of your government, doing your utmost to put a period to the Peacock's treasonous activities. I hadn't known you to be so personally involved with the man's possible capture. You have flattered me with your confidence in me. I am impressed, Anthony. Truly."

"Of course," Lord Buxley said evenly, accepting her praise as his due, which made Gabrielle long to box his ears almost as much as St. Clair's constant silly bantering and sly insults incited her to consider violence on his person. There really wasn't much to choose from between the righteous prig and the court clown, she decided, except for the fact that St. Clair had kissed her, and that kiss had served to turn her world upside down.

Gabrielle hailed Elizabeth when she saw her friend at the opposite side of the room, her companion already holding both their shawls in preparation of retiring to Percy Street for the night.

They both made their polite farewells to Lord Buxley, who had murmured something about having a few words with his host and hostess, Gabrielle wondering all the time if Elizabeth had been able to successfully filch a few of the iced cakes Lady Cornwallis had served. All this thinking and conjecturing had served to make her ravenous!

"Are you feeling better, Lizzie?" Gabrielle asked, as the two of them entered their hired coach, a near-crippling expense in her campaign to find a wealthy husband but one that couldn't be avoided. "I don't remember the last time I saw you so animated or so upset. No, that's not true. You are always on edge on the days the Peacock's communications are printed in the *Times*. Perhaps the earl has a point, and you shouldn't read them anymore."

"And will that change anything, Gaby?" Elizabeth asked, rounding on her, the woman's usually well-modulated voice trembling with emotion. "Oh, Lord Buxley made me so angry! I hadn't known how absolutely *livid* I could become when presented with the evidence of our government's failure to raise its own people out of poverty—or its willingness to divide us into a nation of haves and have-nots. Is this why Roger died? To perpetuate such injustice? There are soldiers sleeping on the streets, Gaby. Only think of the thousands and thousands of brave men who have given an arm or a leg or an eye to their government—men who have given their very lives to the Crown, only to have their widows and children thrown out of their homes and forced to labor in those terrible mills. Oh, if only I could be like the Peacock . . ."

Gabrielle pried Elizabeth's hands from their death grip around her reticule. "Here now, Lizzie, you're crushing the cakes," she said, trying to ease the tension in the coach. "And don't look at me as if I am some sort of heartless wretch. It may surprise you to learn that I agree with you. I didn't know it for certain until this evening, until Anthony—Lord Buxley— held up a looking glass to show me what I was in danger of becoming. His ambitions embarrassed me even more than St. Clair's constant badgering, his continual pointing out of my shallow nature. I have been selfish as well as self-deceiving, and I have done with both."

"What do you mean?" Elizabeth asked, peering at her friend intently. "Are you saying that we no longer have to keep up this pretense? That we can go home now? Truly, Gaby, I would very much like to go home. I don't believe I can continue to mingle in a Society so blind to the tragedy that our dear land has become. I still have Roger's small pension. There is an orphanage near Rose Hill Farm. I could go there, I thought, and possibly—" Her voice broke off as she began to cry.

"Ah, Lizzie," Gabrielle said soothingly, gathering

her friend to her, rocking her like a child. "You're such a saint, my dear, and I am honored to know you. However, I don't believe it is yet time to give up and go home. The Peacock needs my help, you see."

Elizabeth's tears gave way to shaky laughter before she composed herself, pushing out her clasped hands and then pulling them back, as if to apply a figurative brake to Gabrielle's speech as she said, "Forgive me, Gaby, but could I have heard you a-right? *You* are going to help the Peacock? How?"

Gabrielle sat back against the rather inadequate squabs, snuggling herself into the lumpy velvet. "Why, I should have thought that would be obvious." Then she frowned. "Oh, maybe not. I didn't tell you yet, did I? Well, you see, Lizzie, Anthony—Lord Buxley—told me just tonight that he is working to expose the Peacock's true identity. The earl is deadly dull, but he is determined, and not without his suspicions. I believe he is beginning to think—not entirely without my help, as my mouth is much too quick to speak—that Baron St. Clair might be his man."

Elizabeth shook her head as the coach lurched to a stop outside the narrow house in Percy Street. "No," she pronounced determinedly. "Not St. Clair. We've already discussed this, and the notion is ludicrous. But wait a moment. Gaby? *How* did you help Lord Buxley come to that conclusion?"

Gabrielle waited until they were inside the minuscule foyer before answering. "I'm already convinced that Anthony despises the baron and was harboring suspicions of his own before I said a word tonight. Why, he even *lied* to me, Lizzie, although that part is a little hazy in my mind right now. But do you remember my theory of looking for the least likely suspect? Well, it seems I'm not the only one to have taken that tack."

"So you're saying that Lord Buxley is also thinking along those lines," Elizabeth said, shaking her head. "Would that make you brilliant, or Lord Buxley simplistic?"

"It makes me brilliant, Lizzie, just as I've always told you. And don't interrupt, for I'm being deadly serious. You see, I may have slipped and mentioned that Roger told you about St. Clair's political vehemence during his youth," she added, avoiding Elizabeth's eyes as she turned to strip off her gloves. Really, she'd have to practice, if she was about to launch herself on a life of intrigue. "But," she continued brightly, "I'm convinced I recovered nicely, saying it was Roger, and not the baron, who had sympathized with the French revolutionaries."

"Oh, Gaby!" Elizabeth groaned, leading the way into the small drawing room, carrying with her the single candle they had agreed would be all the illumination they would allow themselves. "How could you? How could you have involved Roger?"

Considering the fact that Roger Fletcher was dead, and beyond taking umbrage at the insult, Gaby merely shrugged and curled herself up on the couch, leaning forward to ask, "Don't you wish to hear all of what Lord Buxley and I discussed this evening?"

Elizabeth sat herself primly in her usual chair, rubbing at her arms to ward off the chill caused by the lack of a fire this late on a damp evening. "Not if you're going to tell me that Lord Buxley now knows that Roger and I eloped. Or did you feel you needed to gift him with that knowledge in order to keep the conversation moving along? Honestly, Gaby, and you have the gall to tease me about my lists? I can't imagine why I tell you anything. You're worse than the town crier!"

"You and Roger eloped? To Gretna?" Gabrielle inquired eagerly, momentarily diverted. "How wonderfully romantic! You never told me that. Being younger, and not knowing you so well at the time, I have always thought you and Roger to have shared an independent streak, cutting yourselves off from your families. And I had also thought that we had no secrets between us. I'm disappointed in you, Lizzie, truly I am," she ended, wagging her finger at the woman.

"Oh, fiddle!" Elizabeth exclaimed, hopping to her feet. "I'm going to bed now, Gaby. I have to be up before dawn if I'm to visit the markets before any of the *ton* is up and about and liable to see me among the stalls, buying up our share of bruised fruit. Come along now, if you don't wish to be left in the dark. You can save the Peacock tomorrow."

"Yes, Lizzie, I can," Gabrielle agreed happily, following after the older woman as the two of them made their way up the narrow stairs, the candlelight throwing weird shadows on the wall as they went. "And do you want to know why?"

"I'd rather not, actually," Elizabeth answered, one hand already on her bedchamber door latch as she waited for Gabrielle to dip a rude kitchen candle into the flame of her own taper.

"I will be able to help the Peacock because we are going out driving with St. Clair tomorrow at eleven. He asked me earlier this evening, when we saw him at Lady Quigley's," she said proudly, although she had earlier been dreading the thought of spending a full afternoon with the man who had kissed her so thoroughly the other evening, touched her so intimately, then continued to infuriate her with his disdain for her aspirations to conquer Society.

"We'll stop somewhere while we're out, I'm sure," she continued, her excitement growing, "and while you excuse yourself for some reason or other, I'm going to warn him that Lord Buxley is after him. He should know that, you understand, so that he'll be especially careful whenever he's with the earl—even more careful because of my little slip this evening. And then I am going to offer the baron our services in his cause."

"Offer 'our services'?" Elizabeth repeated, putting a hand to her head. "I must be more tired than I thought. You didn't really say you were going to offer St. Clair our *services,* did you?"

"Yes, Lizzie, I did. And don't look so pained, for I didn't mean anything lascivious, for pity's sake. I always have thought St. Clair harbored a secret, and now I have discovered it. He's the Peacock. I'm convinced of it now. Wouldn't you like to be one of the Peacock's gang, if that is what his aides are called? It promises to be much more daring than simply conquering Society, and more rewarding too, if in a very different way. And it shouldn't be too taxing. After all, we are already quite adept at pulling the wool over the collective eyes of Mayfair. Why, I should say we are both admirably qualified for subterfuge."

"More fish," Elizabeth said, as if to herself. "That's what's wrong. The child isn't getting enough fish. Food for the brain, I've heard it called. And more vegetables. Perhaps that will help. Heaven knows it's eons too late to apply to her father to imbue her with some common sense, not that the flighty man possesses a jot of it himself."

Then she turned to Gabrielle and asked, "Weren't you going to expose St. Clair as the Peacock, even when you weren't thinking, as you are now, that the baron truly is the Peacock?—which he *isn't*. And didn't you already go so far as to personally threaten the man with exposure, all to advance your own standing in Society? What makes you think he would accept your offer of help now, only a few days after you vowed to destroy him?"

Elizabeth had made a valid point, not that Gabrielle was about to agree with the woman. Instead, she decided to confound her friend even more by saying, "I'm still not entirely convinced that St. Clair *is* the Peacock. I'm only going to hint at my eagerness to help the Peacock, and slip in that business about the earl being hot on his trail. Then I'll wait to see if he confides in me. After all, I am still not positive that Lord Buxley isn't the Peacock, even though he vehemently denies it. You do remember that business about people who doth protest too much?"

Elizabeth lifted a finger as if to make another point, then allowed her arm to drop to her side. "Never mind, Gaby. I'm not going to say another word. Good night. Perhaps—hopefully—in the morning you will have overcome this latest bout of silliness."

"One of them is the Peacock, Lizzie," Gabrielle called after her as the woman made to shut her bedchamber door behind her. "And now that I'm no longer interested in saving simply Rose Hill Farm but *all* of England, it is more important than ever that I discover which one of them is the real Peacock. I've had enough of playing the flighty debutante, which is crushingly boring, by the bye. So if we're destined to be poor, Lizzie, we might as well be poor *heroines!*"

Elizabeth's only answer was the swift, rather loud shutting of her door, and Gabrielle sighed as she headed for her own chilly chamber, muttering under her breath, "I'll show that miserable Christian St. Clair that I am not simply another useless female. And then, once he's apologized, I might just allow him to kiss me again."

Gaby looked about rather incuriously as she and Christian waited for their driver to return from his mission to a nearby shop to fetch some specially rolled tobacco for his master. Why the baron insisted upon dealing with a shop in this dreary village miles outside of London was beyond her, but then Christian St. Clair was the most deliberately confounding man she had ever met, so that she at last decided that searching for any sensible reason behind his choice could only end in disappointment.

For instance, why had he asked her to drive out with him when he had not said above five words to her since leaving Mayfair and was even now quite pointedly ignoring her? Why, he hadn't even complimented her on her walking dress when she had placed every stitch in it herself and knew it to be all the crack. Dreadful man. Anyone would think he had never held her, never kissed her. Would it really be possible to work with him once she had earned his trust by telling him about Lord Buxley's suspicions?

Suddenly something caused her to notice a commotion on the far side of the square. "St. Clair, wake up.

What's happening over there? There—across the square, on the other side of that ugly fountain."

St. Clair had been reclining at his ease against the velvet squabs of his elaborate, opened-top landau, his chin deep in his immaculately white lace neck gear, his hands crossed and resting atop the head of his ebony cane, as lace foamed from his jacket cuffs.

Upon hearing her question, he lifted his heavy-lidded eyes a fraction and slowly slid his indolent blue-green gaze toward the small knot of people just entering the village square.

"Why, my dear Miss Laurence," he drawled, once more dropping his chin and closing his eyes, "although I fail to fathom why you should apply to me for an explanation of something that has nothing to do with Mayfair, my particular area of expertise, I do believe the local constable is about to soundly flog the poor unfortunate you see being dragged between those two stout men. Turn away, do, else you might be terminally offended. I know I shall not look!"

"Flog him?" Gaby responded, leaning close to the side of the landau, her expression anguished. She had never seen anyone flogged, and she immediately decided that if that constituted a lapse in her education she was glad of it and had no great longing to correct the situation. "Whatever for?"

"Ah, dearest lady, how should I know? Probably the man stole a crust of bread or some such heinous crime." His sleepy eyes had opened wide as he spoke, and he sat up straight, momentarily animated, to wag a well-manicured index finger at her, the dull silver of his odd ring glinting in the sunlight.

Then he frowned. "No, no. Not bread. I believe the Peacock has written that we transport for bread. Yes, that's it, I'm sure, as I committed that particular missive to memory. So affecting with the ladies, you know. And we hang for any theft in excess of four shillings. Not always, you understand, for we are a civilized people, but just enough to keep the fear of God in our citizenry."

His recitation complete, he then began looking about him, appearing nervous. "Lud, where's Perkins with my cheroots? Don't fret, Miss Laurence, I beg you. We'll be shed of this place in a moment."

The small knot of people had come closer now, three weeping women following after the men, and Gaby believed she could smell the fear emanating from the ragged man being led to a stout wooden post near the fountain, surely the scene of his punishment. Her fear turned to righteous indignation. "St. Clair, I cannot believe that you of all people will allow this!"

"Tiens, would you listen to the girl! Believe or disbelieve what you will as is your wont, dear lady. Heaven knows it makes no nevermind to me," he answered, in that smooth, insufferable drawl she had grown to loathe, pushing his hat down over his eyes as he once more slouched against the squabs. "Excuse me now, as I plan to nap until Perkins returns and we can be off. If you desist in your screeching, that is."

This was the Peacock? Impossible! How could she have been so wrong? How had she ever taken such a maggoty idea into her head? Elizabeth would tease her forever for this terrible mistake in judgment!

Christian St. Clair was just as he presented himself and no more: an empty-skulled, foppish dandy intent merely on the cut of his coat and the latest silly gossip. Oh, he might parrot the Peacock's words in order to infuriate sober-minded people like Lord Buxley, but he would never move a finger to *emulate* the brave and daring Peacock.

She should have known no man who dared to take liberties with innocent maidens on darkened balconies could be anything nearly approaching noble. Thank heaven she hadn't yet embarrassed herself by offering to become one of his assistants. And thank heaven she hadn't *really* begun to fall in love with the creature because of one silly kiss!

Gaby sat forward, reaching for the door handle, surprising herself with her reaction to the pending punishment of a man she did not know. But this was the first time she had actually *seen* the administration of any of Lord Sidmouth's strictures firsthand.

How fortunate that Elizabeth had dutifully followed her instructions and alighted from the landau to poke around in the shops, and so would not be here to witness such an injustice. The tenderhearted woman would doubtless have become instantly hysterical.

But not Gabrielle Laurence! *She* wouldn't weep, or faint, or stand by, doing nothing. She would act!

"Very well, you cowardly dolt," she informed the ineffectual baron. "Sleep if you must—hide your eyes. But I cannot and will not stay here and watch such uncivilized torture. For pity's sake, St. Clair, there are little children with those women. They cannot be made to witness such barbarity against their father!"

But before she could exit the vehicle, a rumble like approaching thunder came from behind her—in actuality, the sound of rapid hoofbeats signaling the arrival of four horsemen. She turned on her seat, her heart pounding, as the mounted men, all of them dressed in severe black, with silken masks covering their faces, galloped into the square and rode straight up to the constable and his prisoner.

Gaby looked to the masked men, then to Christian St. Clair, the man she had believed to be the Peacock. Her mouth was gaping open, she realized after a moment, so that she quickly closed it and lent her full attention to the drama now taking place in the square.

"You, jailers! In the name of the Peacock—unhand that man at once!" one of the riders shouted imperiously as the two burly men who had been holding the prisoner took to their heels and the constable raised his arms in surrender—obviously understanding that he was no match against the heavily armed outlaws.

In a moment it was over: the prisoner pulled up behind one of the riders, the constable watching impotently, then ripping off his hat and throwing it to the ground in disgust as the four rescuers rode off. The cheers of the women and children could be heard above the curses of the frustrated constable.

Gaby looked at St. Clair, who was still reclining at his ease, the brim of his hat obscuring all but the faintly sensuous line of his lips and the clear definition of his jaw. "Christian!" she shouted, unknowingly addressing him informally in her excitement. "Did you see that? It was the Peacock! Look—over there on the ground. I can see the peacock feather he always leaves behind. Isn't he *magnificent?*"

"Dressed entirely in that depressing black?" Christian questioned her, pushing up the brim of his hat and looking at her in wide-eyed astonishment. *"Fort amusant!* I can hardly term the fellow magnificent, Miss Laurence. I should dress all in blues and greens if

I were the Peacock. Satins from head to toe. Yes, that's the ticket: satins! And a flowing cape, lined in white silk. Ah, here is Perkins, my resident Lazarus just lately risen. How wonderful! I shall be safely back in Town in time for the theater after all, if Mrs. Fletcher doesn't dawdle."

Elizabeth! Gabrielle looked down the street in the direction in which her friend had disappeared, hoping she had come out of the shop in time to witness the Peacock's daring rescue. All she saw was a woman who looked like Elizabeth, who dressed in her clothes and even walked like her, but who could not possibly be Elizabeth.

For this Elizabeth was holding the hand of a ragged girl-child looking no larger than four years old, who was limping along beside her, and she was smiling so broadly that she appeared nearly demented.

"Elizabeth!" Gabrielle called out anxiously, nearly tripping over Perkins as that man hastened to open the door of the landau and put down the steps. "Whatever are you doing? Did you see him? Did you see the Peacock?"

Gabrielle picked up her skirts, longing to run to Elizabeth and warn her that she had been wrong, dreadfully wrong. St. Clair wasn't the Peacock. He couldn't be the Peacock, not when she had seen that brave man ride out of the square just a few moments before. But then she stopped, after taking only a few steps, as the child stumbled and Elizabeth swept her up into her arms, carrying her the remainder of the way to the landau.

"Elizabeth?" Gabrielle's voice was hardly more than a whisper as she looked at the bundle of rags and spindly arms and legs that made up the small child, whose enormous blue eyes held all the worst knowledge of the world. "I don't understand."

Elizabeth was crying silently even as she smiled, large tears running down her cheeks behind her spectacles as she hugged the child to her. "This is Lily, Gaby," she announced quite calmly, lifting her chin. "I purchased her just now, for the grand sum of ten shillings. She's six years old, and quite bright, so that her mother believed she deserved a better price for her than she garnered for the two sons she sold to a chimney sweep last month. I would have introduced you to the lady, but I believe she has already departed for a local gin shop."

She lowered the child to the flagway, keeping a hand on the child's shoulder. "Lily, stand up straight and say good afternoon to Miss Laurence, if you please."

"Hullo, missus," Lily chirped, then hid her head against Elizabeth's skirts.

"You—you *bought* her?" Gabrielle shook her head in disbelief. It was true. Everything the Peacock had written about was true, and more. People were actually being reduced to selling their children. How had she lived to the age of eighteen and not known such a terrible world existed? And how could she have been so incredibly selfish?

"Oh, Lizzie," she said, unable to adequately express either her horror over the child's plight or her great love for her brave friend, who didn't merely speak of doing heroic deeds but acted.

"Don't even attempt to talk me out of this, Gaby," Elizabeth warned, looking past her and toward the landau. "And if St. Clair is the Peacock, as you say he is, I don't expect him to resist when I ask him to bear us all back to Percy Street."

"But—but that's just it! He *isn't* the Peacock," Gabrielle all but hissed, placing a hand on Elizabeth's arm as that woman made to approach the barouche. "The Peacock was here a few moments ago, effecting a rescue. Didn't you see him?"

"I was otherwise occupied, Gaby," Elizabeth returned, squaring her shoulders as she obviously prepared to do battle with the baron. "But I did tell you your notion was farfetched, didn't I? And I'm not surprised to hear that the Peacock is in the area. This village is Little Pillington, Gaby. Mr. Symington's Little Pillington. Now, my dear, are you going to prove to me that you meant what you said about leaving your hopes for a fortuitous marriage behind you and emulating the Peacock, or will you refuse to incur St. Clair's displeasure by demanding he bear Lily up with him?"

Gabrielle sighed, knowing the moment of truth—of *real* truth—had come for her, and much sooner than she ever could have expected. Had she meant it when she'd declared that she was giving up the notion of rescuing Rose Hill Farm—and herself—by marrying a fortune?

Had she been true to herself when she'd envisioned discovering the true identity of the Peacock, not to unmask him in order to boost her standing in Society to a level that would make her invulnerable to St. Clair's possible cutting of her, but to offer him her services in assisting the poor in their struggles?

And why—*why?*—was she so disappointed to learn that, if she remained wedded to her method of deduction, Lord Anthony Buxley, and not Christian St. Clair, was the Peacock?

Certainly it wasn't simply because asking him to

allow a street urchin to ride up beside him in his white-velvet-lined barouche would turn him against her utterly, so that her reputation would be destroyed at that instant, and it would no longer *matter* how much she might wish to remain this Season's sensation.

It was more than that. Much more than that. She wanted to see St. Clair accept what she was about to do, and even praise her. If only she knew why the ridiculous dandy's good opinion was still so important to her. . . .

At last, burning her carefully fabricated social bridges and all they meant behind her, Gabrielle held out her hand to the child, her decision made. "Come with me, Lily," she said, smiling reassuringly. "We're going for a lovely ride. Won't that be nice?"

Perkins stood back as the trio of females, one threatening to become pugnaciously belligerent, one looking fearful but adamant behind her gold-rimmed spectacles, and one small and dirty and wide-eyed, approached the open door of the landau.

"St. Clair," Gabrielle declared loudly, for the baron still appeared to be asleep beneath his curly-brimmed beaver, "we will have a guest for our return to London. Lily," she prompted more gently, pulling the child forward, "say good afternoon to his lordship."

"Coo," Lily piped up, leaning forward to peep into the vehicle, "ain't 'e the purty 'un? Mum ne'er bedded the loiks o' anythin' that fine."

Gabrielle felt her heart, and her courage, descend to her toes. "Thank you, Lily," she said, swallowing down hard to keep from groaning. "That was, um, that was *fine*. Just fine." She winced as she looked up at Christian. "St. Clair?" she squeaked pleadingly, longing to sink into the flagway.

The baron—who did indeed look rather splendid, sitting there in his colorful satins, his sleekly tied-back blond hair gleaming in the bright sunlight as he doffed his curly-brimmed beaver—returned Gabrielle's gaze, drawling, "Yes, Miss Laurence? Was there something else you wanted? You were, perhaps, awaiting applause, or even credit for Mrs. Fletcher's good deed?"

He turned to Perkins, who was still holding open the door. "Fetch a blanket from somewhere and spread it on the seat, my good man, for I have grown attached to the velvet, and should be greatly saddened by its loss. Oh, and Mrs. Fletcher," he added, as the three females clambered up into the vehicle, "I believe that if you remove the pebbles from the child's shoe her limp will be greatly improved. It's an old beggar's trick, but one we can dispense with, now that Miss Lily is about to enter upon a new life."

Elizabeth immediately bent to remove Lily's wooden clog, dumping a handful of small stones over the side of the landau and into the street. "What a vicious thing to do! How did you know, my lord?"

St. Clair smiled as he eased the curly-brimmed beaver back down over his eyes. "The Peacock wrote about it some weeks ago, most probably before you and Miss Laurence traveled to London. I am nothing if not retentive of useless information. Perkins? Please don't spare the horses as we make our way back to the city. The child is amusing, but she does not smell of fresh milk and clover."

Gabrielle sat collapsed against the squabs all the way back to London, staring at the sleeping baron, unable to understand him. He wasn't the Peacock, but he also wasn't what he presented himself to be—a vain, empty-headed dilettante. He was an incredibly handsome, immeasurably witty, endlessly intriguing enigma.

And he still seemed to good-naturedly despise her.

CHAPTER 9

A fly, sir, may sting a stately horse and make him wince; but one is but an insect, and the other is a horse still.

Samuel Johnson

Christian stepped out the door of his Hanover Square mansion at precisely eleven of the clock. He was, as usual and as expected, resplendent in his striped-green-on-green knee-length revised, re-invented frock coat with a stand-up rather than turn-down collar, skintight natural nankeen trousers, and, of course, his *de rigueur* soft, pristine white linen and foaming lace jabot.

He sported a fine curly-brimmed beaver placed on his blond head at a jaunty, the-devil-with-it-all tilt down toward his left eye. Two watches with satin fobs hung from his formfitting gold-on-white brocade waistcoat, and he carried with him a long, pointed walking stick decorated with tassels just below the knob.

He made his way across the cobblestones of the square to Bond Street, then along Piccadilly and past Devonshire House—an attractively blooming Green

Park eventually appearing to his left—at a brisk, "healthful" pace.

He doffed his hat to the ladies and greeted passing gentlemen with a nod and a smile but did not stop to linger with any one of them, all of whom knew it would be fruitless to attempt to intercept the great St. Clair when he was taking one of his famous constitutionals.

When he reached Bolton Street he turned to his right, making his way down the flagway with determination rather than haste, stopping outside Number 81 for a moment before allowing a liveried footman to usher him inside the confines of that once glorious but now faltering establishment known as Watier's.

Begun in 1805 at the instigation of the Prince of Wales himself, Watier's had been a favorite gaming haunt of Beau Brummell's and the remainder of the members of what Lord Byron had termed "the Dandy Club."

But after Brummell's disgrace and flight from London, even the macao tables could not continue to command the allure the club once held, and within a year or even less, Christian believed, the splendid gentlemen's establishment that had once been the great Watier's would cease to exist.

He might have brought the place back into fashion if he chose, but as he did not harbor any great affection for gaming, and as the food was no longer better than at most clubs, he had abstained from making the effort, preferring the rooms as they were: uncluttered by gentlemen at loose ends and craving conversation, and private enough for conversations of his own.

After being relieved of his hat, gloves, and stick, Christian wandered into the main rooms, quickly discovering his trio of closest friends already ensconced in a corner, sipping wine as a clearly bored waiter stood nearby in case any of them desired to order the boiled lunch.

"Gentlemen!" Christian exclaimed, threading his way toward them through the maze of empty tables. "Good gracious, what have you done to be shuttered off here in this corner? Ozzie, you haven't been throwing food again, have you? That would be too bad. Not everyone, you really must endeavor to perceive, has your same literal interpretation of the term 'Please pass the rolls.'"

"Heigh-o!" Sir Gladwin exclaimed, clapping his friend on the back. "Kit's in rare form today, Ozzie. If I were you, I'd not tell him what a jack pudding you were yesterday with our latest, temporary acquisition."

He turned to Christian, who had taken up a seat beside George Trumble, and added quietly, "Ozzie here inquired of the fellow if he came by his name of Slow Dickie because he wasn't too bright. The fellow took umbrage, I must tell you, Kit. I had to peel him off our good friend here before he could come to grief. Handy with his fives, Slow Dickie is."

"I thought you said I shouldn't tell him, Winnie," Lord Osgood grumbled, taking a generous sip of wine.

"That didn't mean *I* couldn't tell him," Sir Gladwin countered, his smile wider than Christian had seen it in some time.

Christian looked more closely at Lord Osgood, who hadn't winked once since he'd been at the table, and noticed that the man's left eye—his *winking* eye—had been touched up with powder, although a bruise could still be seen just below the eyebrow. "Planted you a facer, did he? That doesn't seem quite sporting of the fellow, considering the way you all rescued him from a beating. Winnie, maybe you'd best explain further. Oh, and I must congratulate you again, Grumble: You made a most impressive Peacock yesterday. Didn't he, gentlemen?"

George shook his head, his color a rather embarrassed rose, and he mumbled something incomprehensible beneath his breath while the suddenly eager-to-please waiter placed a new glass and Christian's usual bottle of iced champagne on the table with a flourish, then withdrew, the coin the baron had tossed to him already tucked up in his pocket.

"Enough of Grumble's debut at play-acting, or else his head will swell. Please, Kit, you must allow me to finish my tale." Sir Gladwin's smile widened into a broad grin. "It's a simple enough story, isn't it, Grumble?"

"Yes," George answered, winking at Christian. "Extremely simple."

"I agree," Sir Gladwin said, laughing. "Well, here goes, Kit. It seems Slow Dickie didn't appreciate what he felt was Ozzie's insult to his manhood. Slow Dickie, you see, is more a description than a name, to hear the man tell it. Something to do with his way with the ladies before he stumbled into a parson's mousetrap ten years and eight children ago. According to the man, his expertise was legendary in his home village of Frimley, which is, by the way, where our reformed Casanova and his brood are now heading, safe out of reach of the constable of Little Pillington."

Christian giggled inanely, then quickly raised his ever-present lace handkerchief to his mouth and coughed discreetly, for he never deviated from his role of fashionable but somewhat brain-to-let dandy when in public, not even at times such as now, when he longed for nothing more than to throw back his head and howl in delight.

But then he became serious, for he had kept his secret long enough and it wasn't fair to allow his friends to continue to participate in the Peacock's exploits unaware of the evidence he'd seen as to the very real possibility that Sidmouth's agents had installed themselves in Little Pillington.

"You saw him? You actually were in the same room with the spy?" George asked, once Christian had told them of his encounter in the low-ceilinged room in the Bull and Cock. "And did *nothing?*"

"There was no time, unfortunately, for Symington had been discovered taking his daily ablutions in the fountain, and everyone ran off to see the sight. It's enough that we're warned, Grumble," Christian pointed out, "and therefore fore-armed. Besides, I know now who can be counted upon if we should need assistance. Jackey and O'Dell. They're good men, and we might be able to use them if Symington persists in resisting our demands."

"Which he will," Sir Gladwin put in, downing the remainder of his wine as he stood. "Well, I must be off. M'mother demands my presence at dinner in Richmond. Something to do with a cousin of mine who's come to town. Ozzie? Drink up. You've been invited too, you know. I believe m'mother considers us a couple, which is passing strange, now that I think on it."

"A moment, Winnie," Christian said, and Sir Gladwin and Lord Osgood immediately sat once more. "I sent Perkins on a private mission yesterday while we all were in Little Pillington—in through the tobacco shop, out the rear door—and he checked our post. We have had another communication from Sal."

"And it's not good," George asked, frowning, "is it, Kit?"

Christian lifted his quizzing glass and tut-tutted as he surveyed his friend. "Always looking for any dark clouds hovering behind the sunshine, aren't you, Grumble? However, in this case, I believe you could be correct. It seems that the villagers of Little Pillington, buoyed by the Peacock's presence, have decided to boost dear Herbert toward reform in the mills by conducting a torchlight procession of protest on his townhouse a fortnight from now."

"Odds bobs, Kit, Grumble's right. That's not good!" Sir Gladwin remarked, beginning to gnaw on the knuckle of his right index finger. "Not good at all. Everyone knows no group of more than fifty is allowed to meet without being subject to arrest. With Sidmouth's troops about to descend on the place to protect Symington, and an agent provocateur already in place in order to report on the villagers' intentions before the fact, why, we could end up with a disaster."

"You mentioned this Jackey fellow," George cut in. "Couldn't we contact him and warn him off?"

"We could, I suppose," Christian said, looking to each of them in turn, his jaw firm as he willed them not to succumb to panic, to remember that they had not failed yet. "However, as any change in plans would be reported by the agent provocateurs—for surely there are more than the single man I saw—and if Symington still refuses to budge, we would only be delaying the inevitable. We always knew it could come to open rebellion, my friends, and perhaps it is time for the downtrodden to rise up and be heard."

"I see what you mean. They'll be heard, Kit," Sir Gladwin remarked dully. "Every condemned man gets to make a small speech before he's turned off at the gibbet. I don't like this, Kit. I don't like it above half. We don't have to keep on with this. We've been on a mission of sorts, but it isn't as if it was a call from God on high."

"Winnie's right, Kit," Ozzie added. "Those mill workers and their families would be like lambs gone to the slaughter if they marched bald-faced through Little Pillington. Orator Hunt is already courting trouble in the Midlands with his meetings. Can you imagine the carnage in a smaller place like Little Pillington if a troop of mounted troops were to appear in the square?"

"Winnie's right, Kit. We've been lucky so far," George commented. "Would you want us to have blood on our hands?"

Christian fingered his dull silver ring. What was the matter with his friends? Had they thought this past six months—indeed, this past nearly two years—had all been a lark, and easily walked away from if the danger accelerated from invigorating to intimidating? He felt his teeth beginning to clench and deliberately relaxed, smiling. "All right, ladies. You've all had your little bouts of hysterics. Now—let's hear some ideas."

Sir Gladwin stood up, shaking his head. "Not this time, Kit. You won't bully me, or tease me, or even embarrass me into joining with you this time. The game is over. It is time we retreated, went back to our original plan, without all this riding about the countryside, raking up trouble. Are you with me, Ozzie?"

Lord Osgood looked to George, then to Christian and, last, to his best friend, Sir Gladwin. "I—I need time, Winnie. I feel like a rotter, abandoning all those people who have grown to count on us. And it's jolly good fun racing around the countryside, remember, playing the savior and delivering bread to the children. But at the same time," he continued, turning to Christian, "I don't want blood on my hands. Oh— when did it all become so difficult?"

"Very well," Christian said, lounging back in his chair, his glass dangling from his fingertips. "If you will shy at the first hint of a real battle, I suppose I wouldn't wish you to be guarding my back anyway. You're both dismissed, gentlemen."

Lord Osgood leaned over and touched Christian's sleeve. "I say, Kit, don't cut up stiff. I didn't say I was abandoning you, just that I need time to think. We both do, don't we, Winnie?" he asked his friend.

"We need a plan," Sir Gladwin announced solemnly as Lord Osgood slowly stood up and went to stand beside him, wringing his hands together like an old woman. "Neither Ozzie nor I are much good at planning. You and Grumble here, you two work it out. If you can find a way to best Symington without bloodshed, to continue on as we were, we're with you. But we won't be a party to a riot, Kit. You can't ask that of us."

Christian, like all good leaders, knew when it was time for compromise. "Very well, Winnie. It's agreed. George and I will put our heads together and formulate a plan that will bring Symington around to our way of thinking and not place any of the villagers in danger. Only give me at least a week to conjure up this miracle, and then we'll meet again. I'll be going out of town for a space tonight. Buxley's getting too close, for one thing, demanding my assistance in unmasking the Peacock, and I need to think free of distractions."

"I get your meaning, Kit. Distractions like Miss

Gabrielle Laurence," Ozzie put in, winking, then wincing as his eye pained him.

Christian waited as Sir Gladwin frowned, obviously mulling over his friend's proposition, for Sir Gladwin was at heart a serious, thoughtful soul. "Agreed, Kit," he said at last, extending his hand to shake on the bargain. "You've taken us all on a lovely ride, and we've done our share of good. It wouldn't be right to balk at the first high jump. George, we're counting on you: Keep him within reason."

George lifted his glass to the two men, then drank deeply, avoiding Christian's eyes until Lord Osgood and Sir Gladwin had quit the room. Only then did he speak. "And when did Buxley approach you? A week ago? A month? And never a word to us. Ozzie and Winnie are well shed of this business, and I should have gone with them."

Christian felt his temper nearing the flashpoint. "Don't allow me to detain you, Grumble," he drawled smoothly. "I have no great need of faint-hearted friends."

"No, you don't, do you? What you need, my childhood chum, is a keeper. Unfortunately, fate seems to have decreed that I be given that dubious honor." George then gave a weak smile, and Christian knew he had got him. It would remain as it had always been. George wouldn't desert him. Not now. Not ever.

"And now that we have settled that," George went on, "perhaps you'll let me in on your plan. You do have one, don't you?"

"Not the ghost of one, Grumble," Christian admitted, leaning forward to pour himself another glass of champagne. "But we won't think of that now, for an idea will come to me. One always has," he said, wondering if he was indulging in a boastful form of whistling to keep himself from being afraid of the dark. "That's why I'm leaving the city, to go visit with the so-loyal Lenny for a space. I think I need to shed myself of these clothes and walk the countryside, get back in touch with the people I have sworn to help. Away from Society, away from women—from one particular woman. For only a week, Grumble, no more. Would you care to join me?"

George shook his head. "I'm in no mood to rusticate right now, Kit," he said, avoiding his friend's eyes. "I have taken it into my head to make the better acquaintance of Mrs. Elizabeth Fletcher."

It had taken more than two dozen years, but the always predictable George had finally surprised him. "Gabrielle's chaperone? Good God, Grumble, have you been sipping more of this stuff than I thought?" George was an avowed bachelor and had never been much in the petticoat line. Christian wouldn't have been more shocked if his friend had just announced he was leaving for America, to live amongst the wild Indians.

George pulled himself up straight in his chair, obviously taking offense at Christian's bantering. "Mrs. Fletcher is an outstanding woman. Widow of a fine soldier, totally unexceptionable in her demeanor, and of a like social station to mine. And then there is the matter of the child. I haven't been able to stop thinking about her heroic gesture since you told me of it last night. I would have approached her then if I had chanced to see her, but she was not present at any of the functions, as far as I could see. Did you speak with Miss Laurence? Perhaps Mrs. Fletcher is ill? Or the child!"

"They didn't appear in Society at all last night, Grumble," Christian told him, happy that George was letting him off so easily in this ticklish matter of discovering a brilliant, bloodless plan to save the villagers of Little Pillington.

"Gabrielle doubtless remained at home last night, assisting Mrs. Fletcher in scrubbing up their urchin," he went on. "They were like children with a new toy all the way back to Percy Street. I should like to think I'll have the opportunity to praise Gabrielle publicly for her good work when I return from my hiatus. Why, just think, Grumble, within a fortnight of St. Clair's lavish praise of her charitable works, every hopeful debutante will have adopted an orphan of their own. It could be a huge success, if I didn't believe three quarters of the children would be tossed back into the gutters within days of their rescue."

He sighed, hating himself for his low opinion of the woman he could love. "I only wonder how long Miss Laurence's attack of social conscience will last."

"You and I have become cynical, Kit," George accused, frowning. "I believe both ladies are very different than we have supposed them. You've allowed yourself to concentrate on Miss Laurence's beauty, while I must admit that I have overlooked Mrs. Fletcher merely due to the lack of hers. You have told me that Miss Laurence has the makings of intelligence, and in that I am convinced you have not erred. However, I think they're *both* deeper than either you or I have believed."

Christian smiled and shook his head. "Ah, you've been well and truly struck by Cupid's arrow, Grumble, if you believe that."

"Perhaps," George responded, and Christian looked at him intently, sensing that his old friend was about to trump whatever card he played in their verbal game of attempting to understand the female mind. "But other than to champion Miss Laurence and keep her under your socially powerful thumb because you have been chagrined to learn that she has a profound effect on you, what do you really know about her? About either of them? For instance, Kit, did you know that Miss Laurence was filching food from Lady Cornwallis's the other evening? You're getting sloppy, Kit, beginning to believe in your own consequence."

For the first time in his recent memory, Christian found himself, more than merely surprised, but at a total failure for words. No witty rejoinder sprang readily to his lips, and even waving his ridiculous lace handkerchief would prove nothing but a futile attempt to cover his loss of composure. "Repeat that, Grumble, if you please: She was doing *what?*"

"I saw her myself. Why, she must have slipped a half dozen shrimp in her reticule before I could blink. I had an aunt once, Kit, who nipped silverware and things whenever she came to dine, even though my uncle Francis was rich as Croesus. My father said she was dicked in the nob. But Aunt Rosemary never took shrimp. Only a hungry person steals food, Kit, to my way of thinking."

Christian puffed out his cheeks and blew several quick breaths out his pursed lips, cudgeling his brain for a reason behind Gabrielle's thievery. No ready answer came to him. However, an idea—a rather *wicked* idea—did.

"All right, Grumble," he said at last, trying to keep his expression blank. "I think we must get to the bottom of this. You're right, you know: I haven't really judged Gabrielle on more than her appearance and the pleasure I've garnered by baiting her."

He reached into his pocket and extracted his watch,

snapping open the gold cover to see that it had just gone noon. "If I am quick about it, I believe I can compose a suitable invitation to a small dinner party this evening before the theater. Miss Laurence might bridle at the lateness of the summons to Hanover Square, but she wouldn't dare deny me."

"Who else will make up the party, Kit?" George asked carefully, his furrowed brow telling Christian that his friend was worried that he had stirred up a hornets' nest best left alone. "Winnie? Ozzie?"

"No, no. Winnie and Ozzie have asked to be excused for a space, as you recall. It will be a most intimate dinner, with only my dear friend George Trumble, Miss Laurence, and, of course, her dear companion, Mrs. Fletcher, sitting down to table with me. After all, Grumble, if the girl is hungry enough to steal shrimp, the least—the very least—thing I can do is to feed her." He pushed back his chair and called for the waiter to bring him pen and paper.

"Smile, Grumble," he then admonished his friend bracingly, suddenly feeling back in control of himself. "We are in for a most interesting evening!"

"Does he think me a fool? Am I a child to be hoodwinked so easily? Well, let me tell you something, Lizzie Fletcher: He may think so, but I think *not!*"

Gabrielle was in the small kitchen of the house on Percy Street, supposedly doing her best to salvage some edible bits of lettuce from a wilted head Elizabeth had picked up in the Covent Garden markets for a half-penny. She was dressed in one of her older, plainer gowns, although nothing she wore could detract greatly from her startling good looks, an enormous apron tied around her narrow waist as she wielded the knife with more vengeance than prudence.

"Watch your fingers, Gaby, and pay attention to what you're doing," Elizabeth cautioned as she sat at the table, shelling peas. "You can't disguise a bandage beneath kid gloves, you know. And I don't believe a word you're saying, in case you were about to ask."

Gabrielle put down the knife and began pulling at the lettuce with her fingers. "But it only makes sense, Lizzie. Think about it for just a moment and you'll see the wisdom in what I'm saying."

"If you insist," Elizabeth agreed, sighing as she readjusted her spectacles so that they rested above the slight bump on her nose.

"I tell St. Clair that I think he might be the Peacock, and the next thing I know I'm sitting in a landau with the man, watching the Peacock come charging into the square. Isn't it stretching coincidence just a mite too far to believe that St. Clair happened to patronize a small tobacco shop—in Little Pillington, of all places—at the exact hour the Peacock was effecting his heroic rescue?"

"It could have happened that way," Elizabeth said, smiling as she looked down at Lily, who was sitting on the floor, all clean and smelling of lilac water, and wiggling her feet as she admired her new soft kid slippers. "Besides, Gaby, I cannot but be grateful to the man for allowing me to take Lily up with him for the ride back to London."

"I don't see that we gave him much choice, Lizzie," Gabrielle countered, going to the sink to pour some water into a bowl and begin rinsing the lettuce. "He could hardly leave two women on their own in the middle of the countryside, now could he? And how about the way he knew that Lily's"—she hesitated for a moment, looking down at the child, then went on, spelling out the words—"that Lily's *m-o-t-h-e-r* dropped those *p-e-b-b-l-e-s* into her *s-h-o-e* in order to send her out *b-e-g-g-i-n-g?*"

"Lord St. Clair knew because he isn't *s-t-u-p-i-d,* Gaby," Elizabeth responded sharply, "and neither is Lily, who is not so easily shocked and harbors no great illusions concerning her mother, I have already learned. So please stop spelling every second word whenever you're around her! Only this morning she asked me if you were 'a mite light in the brainbox.'"

Gabrielle smiled down at the child, who had shown to be surprisingly pretty beneath the grime accumulated in her life on the streets of Little Pillington, her hair so fair after several washings that it was nearly white. Once her bruises had mended—at least two of them earned in her wild struggles to get out of the hip bath—and she had a few good meals behind her, she would be an extremely pleasing sight. Of course, something would have to be done about her vocabulary, which, although limited, contained several words not usually expected to be heard issued from such childish lips.

Gabrielle was already quite fond of the child, and the overnight transformation of her friend Elizabeth from reluctant chaperone to doting mama seemed to have taken the nearly five years of pain since Waterloo off the gentle woman's face.

"But St. Clair *could* be the Peacock, Lizzie, couldn't he?" she persisted, as she placed lettuce on three plates and deftly arranged sliced fruit on the leaves. "It isn't outside the realm of possibility. Oh, face it, Lizzie, I'd still much rather it be St. Clair than Lord Buxley. There's not a jot of romance in that sobersides of a man, where at least St. Clair, if annoyingly irritating at times, can be amusing."

Elizabeth motioned for Lily to join them at table, then busied herself slicing peaches into child-size portions, not having much success before Lily began gobbling up the fruit with both hands. Elizabeth sighed but allowed the breach of good table manners, for Lily had years and years ahead of her to learn polite behavior.

"Frankly, Gaby," she commented reasonably, "I don't think you should limit yourself to just the earl and the baron when you are considering candidates for the role of Peacock. There are at least several hundred other peers who could be your man."

Gabrielle began nibbling on a piece of cheese, which made up the remainder of their meager luncheon. "No, Lizzie, there aren't. Think about it. We know that the Peacock is between the ages of twenty and thirty-five—or at least that's what we've heard. We know he is taller than the ordinary, slim but muscular, and extremely articulate. The consideration of intelligence alone eliminates more than half the male members of the *ton.*"

"Leaving the other half," Elizabeth pointed out in her maddeningly reasonable way, wiping peach juice from Lily's chin with a corner of her serviette.

"Yes, Lizzie," Gabrielle went on patiently, for she was confident in her conclusions. "And when we strike off those too old, or too timid, or too *married*— for the Peacock is most definitely a bachelor, as no man could keep such a secret from his wife—we are still left with only a half dozen or so candidates. When we consider that the most *unlikely* candidate would be the most *likely* candidate, we are then left with only two, Buxley and St. Clair. See?" she questioned her friend, grinning as she spread her hands in triumph. "It's really most elementary."

"And after a night believing that Buxley is our man, you are back to believing the baron to be the Peacock, even though you were sitting directly across from him when the Peacock appeared," Elizabeth said, watching as Lily hopped down from the chair and began playing with the kitchen cat, a wizened old tabby who more than earned her keep by putting down the mouse population on Percy Street. "This decision has nothing to do with the fact that you find St. Clair more attractive than you do the earl? After all, even without my list to guide me, I can remember that Lord Buxley never did make your roll call of Gaby's Glittering Grooms."

"He's a dead bore, Lizzie," Gabrielle protested. "But I never had St. Clair on the list either."

"An oversight, I'm sure," Elizabeth said, then cocked her head to one side, taking a single step toward the hallway that led to the front of the house. "Was that the knocker? Oh, I hope that wasn't the knocker."

Gabrielle gathered up the plates from their simple luncheon and placed them in the dry sink. "Don't worry about it, Lizzie," she said teasingly, *"Soames* will surely answer the knock." She giggled as Elizabeth pulled a face at the mention of their nonexistent butler and left the kitchen, only to return a few minutes later, bringing with her a folded sheet of paper.

"What is it?" Gabrielle asked, untying her apron and laying it across a nearby chair. "Another invitation? Goodness, I never knew there could be so many ways to spend an evening."

"And here is one more. It would seem that we have

been invited to the Baron St. Clair's Hanover Square mansion tonight at seven, for dinner," Elizabeth said, then sighed deeply. "The two of us."

"What! Tonight?"

The cheek of the man! It had already gone nearly one in the afternoon, and he was only now getting around to issuing her an invitation for that very same day? Did he think she had nothing better to do than to wait around each day, hoping he would rescue her from an empty evening? Why, she already had a dozen invitations sitting on her mantel, including at least three for tonight, the rest having been sent in ample time to respond to requests for her presence in the next week.

However, Gabrielle thought, considering the matter, none of those invitations included being fed at seven o'clock this evening. Having spent a good deal of the funds they had set aside for provisions on clothing for Lily, and with the earliest hint of victuals being the midnight supper they were sure to find at Lord Hertford's, the idea of dining earlier did hold some appeal.

That, and the fact that no one in their right mind would ever think to snub an invitation from the great St. Clair.

"Is there a boy outside, awaiting an answer?" Gabrielle asked when she completed her mental appraisal of the baron's invitation and her options, which numbered less than three: She could either attend, or she could leap feetfirst into the Thames, for if she refused, her social life in London would then be over.

"Yes, there is," Elizabeth answered, frowning.

It wasn't that she cared a snap for that social life anymore, Gabrielle reminded herself as she took the note from her friend. She had other plans now, plans to aid the Peacock, and to devote her life to saving children like little Lily.

It was just that she had decided to wean herself slowly, for the social whirl did still hold some appeal. Besides, until she located the Peacock and talked him round to allowing her to join him, she needed her social contacts. She also needed to eat. At the moment, almost all her money was tied up in homemade gowns and paste jewelry necessary to her debut. Until the arrival of her next quarter's allowance from her mother's estate—a mere pittance, actually—and Elizabeth's widow's pension, which was less than a pittance, she and her friend had planned to do most of their dining "out."

"I can't go, you know," Elizabeth said as Gabrielle made her way to the small drawing room, intent on sitting at her desk and composing a civil answer to St. Clair's invitation. "Which means that you can't either, for you'd have no chaperone. Unless one of the other female guests would agree to take you up in her carriage."

Gabrielle was confused for a moment, then understood. How could she have forgotten! *Lily.* They couldn't go off and leave her, with only the kitchen tabby to keep her company. As a matter of fact, unless they could afford to hire a maid of all work to stay with Lily at night, Gabrielle wouldn't be going out in public again!

She turned in her chair to look at Elizabeth, who had a mulish expression on her face—as if Gabrielle would be so attic-to-let as to insist her friend accompany her and leave a six-year-old child alone.

"Very well, Lizzie," she said, turning back to pick

216

up a quill as she mentally threw caution to the four winds. "There is nothing else for it than that I inform the baron that we ladies shall be delighted to accept his invitation. It says right here in his note that he is inviting 'the ladies of Percy Street' to dinner, and he knows perfectly well that Lily has come to live with us. There will simply be three of us responding in the affirmative, that's all."

"You can't do that!" Elizabeth exclaimed as Gabrielle dipped the quill into the dish of ink and began scribbling furiously. "It isn't *done!*"

"It is now," Gabrielle said, quickly sanding the note and then folding it. "We have to eat, we can't turn down any invitation from St. Clair, and besides, I need to talk to the man." She skipped past Elizabeth, who made a valiant stab at wresting the paper from her friend's hand, and presented it to the boy waiting in the small foyer, giving him a penny for his troubles while she was about it.

"There!" she pronounced, as Elizabeth stood behind her and the two women watched the boy run off down Percy Street in the direction of Hanover Square. "That will teach the baron to issue last-moment invitations. Tell me, Lizzie, do you believe we can encourage Lily to recite that little ditty again at table tonight? You know, the one she told us last evening? Something to do with the farmer from Whit who dabbled in—"

"Gaby!" Elizabeth exclaimed, her cheeks flaming. "I refuse to allow you to use Lily to get some of your own back on Christian St. Clair. Do you understand me? Now close this door and—oh my stars! What have I done to deserve this? It's Lady Ariana again!"

Gabrielle whirled about to see the Tredway crest on

the magnificent closed coach that was just then pulling up in front of the house. "Drat that pernicious woman," she groaned. "I told her I would be in contact with her. Can't she even follow simple instructions?"

"Apparently not," Elizabeth said under her breath, pushing Gabrielle behind the door and stepping forward to usher her ladyship into the house. "Good afternoon, my lady. How pleasant to see you again—and so soon after your last visit, too. We're still at sixes and sevens here, as you see, being reduced to answering our own door when the knocker goes. But come in, come in, please."

Gabrielle pulled a face behind Elizabeth's back, then pasted a welcoming smile on her face as she stepped forward and quickly seconded her friend's invitation to have Lady Ariana join them in the small drawing room. "Yes, please do come in, Ariana. I'm convinced your constitution is healthy enough so that you will not succumb to the illness ravaging this household. First Soames, then dear Mrs. Wilbert, and now the maids, Amy and Brigitte . . ." She sighed. "Why, both Elizabeth and I have remained prisoners in our own house rather than go out in Society and risk bringing illness to thousands! But if you're willing . . ."

"I haven't been ill in years. I don't allow it. Now, have you given any more thought to our problem, Gabrielle?" her ladyship asked without preamble as she sat herself in Elizabeth's chair, lifting that woman's knitting bag and laying it in her lap.

The woman was nothing if not direct, Gabrielle thought consideringly. And totally without compassion, not even mentioning their domestic staff problem but only doggedly going along, concentrating on her own agenda.

"No," Gabrielle answered, smiling apologetically, "to tell you the truth, I haven't really considered it. St. Clair, you see, has been much more amenable these past days. He took me out driving yesterday, and I am to be his guest this evening in Hanover Square. I believe you might have been correct, and the baron does hold me in some affection. So you see, I no longer have any real reason to wish him toppled from his pedestal—not so long as he is being so good to me. Why, just think if he were to apply for my hand. I would become his consort as ruler of the *ton.*"

Remembering how she had discommoded the woman on her last visit by asking if she was to make up one of the Duke of Glynnon's party for the theater, she asked—as if the question was an afterthought, which it wasn't, for she hoped with all her heart the lady had not been invited—"Are you to be one of the baron's party for this evening as well, Ariana?"

"This evening?" At last the beautiful Lady Ariana looked out of curl, her chin quivering slightly before, being the staunch little Tory she was, she rallied, declaring, "Oh, yes, I quite forgot about that. I have cried off, as a matter of fact. So tedious, St. Clair's dinners, you know, and *I* have enough consequence to refuse him and not fear reprisals. The duke and I—that would be the Duke of Glynnon, of course— have plans to attend the theater after a dinner at *his* mansion in Grosvenor Square."

"Which proves my point, Ariana, doesn't it? You have no real reason to fear that St. Clair could depress your consequence, isn't that so?" Gabrielle asked, trying for a blighting smile and knowing she had succeeded when Lady Ariana shifted her gaze to Elizabeth to inquire if that lady was possibly as ill as the servants, for she looked rather pale.

"Ariana?" Gabrielle prompted, as Elizabeth glared at her ladyship without saying a word.

"Oh, all right, Gabrielle," Lady Ariana said, smiling. "I said you were a bright one, and I shouldn't be surprised that you have seen through my little deception."

"I'll see if the water is hot enough for tea," Elizabeth broke in quietly, then quickly left the room, for she was an intelligent woman and wasn't about to wait for Lady Ariana to dismiss her, as she had on her first visit.

"'Deception,' Ariana? I don't understand." Gabrielle was beginning to feel a prickling at the back of her neck that told her that, somehow, she wasn't going to be overjoyed by whatever her ladyship said next. It was true. She remained nearly as green as grass, for all her recent successes, and these queens and kings of Society could still confound her with relative ease.

Lady Ariana put down Elizabeth's knitting bag and stood up, walking over to the window to look out on Percy Street. "It's simple enough, Gabrielle. My papa—" she began, then turned to face Gabrielle. "Well, Papa is most closely aligned with Lord Sidmouth. He meets with him *all* the time, even in our home, which is where they were discussing the fact that St. Clair is being most uncooperative in his refusal to desist in his public championing of the Peacock's malicious missives to the London newspapers. I've even overheard Lord Buxley speaking to Papa in the library about how the baron has actually been so blockheaded as to turn aside a direct request from the earl."

"Listen at keyholes a lot, do you, Ariana?" Gabrielle asked, beginning to understand that she had been used—or had been singled out to be used—by Lady Ariana in some wild attempt to please her "papa."

Lady Ariana returned to the chair and sat down once more. "It doesn't matter a jot how I stumbled upon the information, but it is my responsibility as a loving daughter to assist my father in any way I can."

She lowered her gaze, which Gabrielle could only consider to be a good thing, as her ladyship was beginning to look rather feral. "It's the baron's own fault that he is about to topple from power. If he won't cooperate with Papa, he must be driven from Society so that he cannot do any more harm. And I am becoming heartily sick of St. Clair, if the truth be told," she added, her nose wrinkled in distaste, "for he *will* persist in teasing me unmercifully about my lack of an offer from the duke."

Gabrielle nodded. "He can be irritating. But why involve me? Why not approach Lord Buxley for assistance in silencing St. Clair? He certainly is not lacking in consequence in the *ton,* and you already know where his sympathies lie on the subject of the letters. Why, for all you know, I might be a staunch supporter of this Peacock fellow and not at all eager to bring down any of his enthusiasts, even someone so shallow and useless as Christian St. Clair."

Now Lady Ariana smiled, and Gabrielle blinked, having never before realized how much the lady resembled a well-groomed cat just licking up the last of a pot of fresh cream. "True enough, Gabrielle," she almost purred. "My first visit was more the inspiration of the moment, and not well thought out, but that visit was not without its benefits. It no longer matters whether or not you wish to assist me in helping my father. You cannot refuse me—unless you are eager to have a certain list made public?"

"Gaby's Glorious Grooms," Gabrielle muttered, knowing she had just been repositioned beneath a figurative Sword of Damocles.

"Glittering Grooms, to be exactly correct, my dear friend," Lady Ariana said, openly preening now. "That, and the quaint notion I have in these past days taken into my head that you are not only an unusually eager debutante but a conniving fortune hunter into the bargain. I mean, *all* of your servants ill? How long did you really think to maintain this ridiculous farce? After all, you've been residing in Mayfair for just over a fortnight, and already I have found you out."

She's got to go, Gabrielle thought to herself, not contemplating actual physical assault on her ladyship's person, but knowing that the woman had to be taken out of the game in some way before she could flap her tongue all over Mayfair. Why had she teased Lord Buxley that Lady Ariana might have dreamt about the Peacock with some affection? She had failed to use a golden opportunity to throw the two of them at each other's head, as she had considered doing when her plan was in its early stages. And now it might be too late, for the earl probably wasn't interested in matrimony anymore, even to align himself with Lady Ariana's powerful father. *Stupid. Stupid. Stupid!*

"Nothing to say, Gabrielle?" Lady Ariana persisted after an uncomfortable silence. "Oh, don't frown so, for I shan't tell anyone. Not so long as you continue to help me in spiking Christian's social guns, that is. I believe I shall have a plan formulated within the next week." She sat back against the cushions, smiling. "It will be above all things wonderful to succeed where Lord Buxley has failed. Papa will be so proud of me!"

"How lovely for you and your papa, Ariana," Gabrielle said dully, beginning to wonder if helping St. Clair, assisting the Peacock, was really worth the trouble. "Just let me know what I can do."

CHAPTER 10

~~~~~~

We should often be ashamed of our very best actions, if the world only saw the motives which caused them.

Duc de La Rochefoucauld-Liancourt

The immense St. Clair mansion in Hanover Square, inhabited only during the Season, had been only a very small part of Christian's vast inheritance from his late father, who had received it from his, the pattern repeating itself back to the 1720s, when the sublease for building rights was granted by the Whig magnate Lieutenant-General the Earl of Scarbrough.

The square was the first and the most impressive of three Mayfair squares, and if for the most part the inhabitants were stuffy as closed closets and ancient as the Old Testament, Christian considered his address to be, plain and simply, his home away from home.

George Trumble, however, was sitting stiffly on the edge of his chair in the ornately formal drawing room, his lips pursed disapprovingly, and acting for all the world as if the stately mansion were momentarily to become the scene from a play he'd titled *Innocence Debauched*.

"Grumble, it would please me immensely if you would stop looking as if the world were about to come to an end at any moment," Christian implored as he posed at the mantelpiece, a glass of his favorite chilled champagne in his hand. "After all, we are not doing anything so terribly out of the ordinary. We're having a small dinner party. It is only a slice more intimate than most. Ah, Frapple, here you are. You look quite imposing in the role of majordomo and chaperone of sweet young things brought into a bachelor household. Odds fish, I've just had a thought: Does this mean you will no longer dress me? I'll tell you what you must do: You must give me lessons in how it is done."

Frapple, used to being commandeered into playing various roles for his friend and employer, and more than accustomed to that same employer's teasing, calmly continued about the business of filling a silver receptacle with fresh ice.

"I imagine I could teach you how to do the thing yourself, my lord," he answered smoothly as he worked. "Dress yourself, navigate your way across a room without prancing, dazzle your audience with your clever speech—even how to make love to a woman. But I won't. You don't deserve my faultless tutoring."

"Ha! Frapple got you that time, Kit," George exclaimed, smiling for the first time since the two had departed Watier's. "It's a shame you aren't king, Kit, and could knight the fellow. He's more the gentleman than most anyone I know."

"Thanks to the long-ago temporary mental aberration of my salad days that prompted me to have him educated alongside me, just to have the ungrateful fellow turn on me. By rights, he should be a perfect specimen of politeness and such. Isn't that right,

Frapple?" Christian drawled, taking a sip of his champagne.

"Someone had to mediate between you and that long list of tutors appointed to ride herd on you, my lord," Frapple said, looking about the drawing room as if to give it one final inspection before their guests arrived. "It was almost criminal, the way the lad was forever courting a caning. Why, between us, Master George, I would imagine the fact that the baron survived to reach his majority is totally to our credit."

"You mean it's our fault, Frapple," George countered, throwing a dagger glance at Christian.

Christian sighed dramatically, flourishing his handkerchief. "I believe, dear gentlemen, that I am commencing to feel most shockingly abused."

"As well you should be. And stop waving that damned scrap of lace about as if you enjoy looking like a bloody fop! I still cannot believe either of us has allowed ourselves to become a party to this latest insane travesty. Sending all the other servants save the cook to their rooms, having Frapple here acting as man-of-all-work, serving us a cold collation here in the drawing room, hoodwinking two entirely innocent women into—"

"Hold there, Grumble," Christian cut in, delighting in taking his friend to task, so that he decided to tease him even more. "I believe I must object to the word 'innocent' when coupled with Miss Gabrielle Laurence. The girl actually dared to accuse me of being the Peacock. And she's a thief as well—and that information came to me out of your own mouth, Grumble. Why, her name might not even be Laurence —only daughter of the fairly pockets-to-let but socially unexceptional Reginald Laurence. Gadzooks, Grumble! Only think! She may have made me a party to foisting an actress or some such tawdry creature on the *ton*. My consequence is at stake here! What I don't understand is why you two refuse to take me seriously. I am nothing if not responsible."

"Perhaps, my lord, it has something to do with trussing up a naked man in his village square," Frapple put in reasonably as he moved about, lighting a few more candles. "Such actions are not conducive to being thought a solemn, sober sort."

"Grumble? Do you agree?" Christian asked, just as the knocker sounded.

George refused to answer, choosing instead to drop his chin into his neckcloth, avoiding everyone's eyes, as Frapple left the room at a suitably stately pace to perform the services of St. Clair butler.

The valet-cum-butler-cum-coconspirator returned a few moments later, his grin so wide his seldom-seen teeth were clearly visible beneath his mustache. He stopped just inside the doorway, drew himself up straight, and announced, "Mrs. Elizabeth Fletcher, Miss Gabrielle Laurence—and Miss Lily to see you, my lord."

"She brought the child?" George exclaimed, hopping to his feet. "How deuced odd—but wonderful all the same. Don't you think so, Kit?"

Christian remained silent, for he knew George would not appreciate his opinion on the matter. After all, he hadn't sent all the servants packing for the evening just to have been presented with a chaperone in the form of a near infant. Not when he had carefully planned out a minor seduction, followed upon closely by a major *abduction*. What was Gabrielle up to, that she would so flaunt convention as to bring a child—and an untutored and most probably uncouth one as well—to a dinner party?

"Good evening, my lord, Mr. Trumble," Gabrielle trilled a moment later, sweeping into the drawing room, her chin held high, her expression daring—just daring—anyone to say a word against the small towheaded child she held by the hand. "My goodness, there is no one else here. Are we unfashionably early—rather than late, as was your kind invitation? Forgive us, please, as we were hoping for a swift beginning to the evening, as Lily should not be kept abroad too much past her bedtime. Lily, you do remember the baron, don't you? You had the unfortunate experience of retching in his lovely landau yesterday."

The little minx! Out to get a little of her own back because his invitation was so presumptive, was she? Well, Christian thought, he was nothing if not swift to recover after being presented with an unusual occurrence.

"Never mention it, sweet Lily! It was solely the fault of the springs, *ma petite,* I am sure," he said, sweeping the child, and the two women as well, an elegant leg before allowing one of his trademark inane giggles to escape his lips. "We will not give it another thought. Mrs. Fletcher! So good to see you again. I vow, you grow more beautiful with every day that passes. George! Come, come. I will introduce you!"

"I already know Mr. Trumble," Elizabeth said shyly, smiling at George, who raced to bow over her hand, causing her to look at Gabrielle in easily read amazement. "How—how nice to see you again, I'm sure."

George, Christian noted with secret amusement, had turned beet-red and seemed to have lost control over his tongue, so that Christian quickly suggested that the ladies be seated while Frapple served sherry —and lemonade for Lily, of course. While the child let go of Gabrielle's hand, to press herself against Elizabeth's skirts, George rapidly retraced his steps, picking up the candy dish in which he had been grazing for the past quarter hour.

"Here you go, Lily—sugarplums," George offered encouragingly, and the child quickly deserted Elizabeth, smiling widely at George as she dipped both hands into the dish. "Now, now," he warned, pulling Lily onto his lap as the two of them sat beside Elizabeth on one of the couches, "one at a time. Nobody is going to take them away."

"She reminds me of a squirrel at times," Elizabeth said fondly, stroking the child's white-blond hair, "stuffing her cheeks full and then running off to eat where she feels no fear of anyone appearing to take her food away." She sighed, looking at George from behind her spectacles, her eyes soft with love for the child. "One can only wonder at the troubles she has seen, the trials she has witnessed."

"But you have rescued her from her cruel existence, Mrs. Fletcher," George told her, his own gaze warm as he looked deeply into her eyes. "When Christian told me of your heroic action, I knew I had been remiss in not having sought out your company long ago, when first you and Miss Laurence came to London."

Elizabeth smiled sweetly, watching as George hand-fed Lily from the dish. "We have only been in Society for a fortnight, Mr. Trumble. You cannot be held guilty for your lapse."

She then turned to look at Christian, her host, her smile now more nervous than sweet.

Christian had taken up position standing behind

the chair of the uncharacteristically quiet Gabrielle, wondering if he had ever seen such sweet treacle performed on the stage and deciding that he had not.

"Mrs. Fletcher?" he asked, raising his quizzing glass to his eye and peering at her genially. "You wish to say something to me? I would appreciate being spoken to, as Miss Laurence here, although looking as lovely as ever in that particular gown—it has always pleased my eye—appears to have been struck momentarily dumb."

"Yes. Yes, I do have something to say. My lord, please forgive me for insisting that Lily be a part of our party. I could not bear to leave her with a maid so soon after coming to us. I merely wished to assure myself that Miss Laurence would have female companionship this evening, and that one of your guests would be willing to transport her back to Percy Street after the theater. Once your other guests arrive, I assure you, Lily and I will be going. In the meantime, perhaps there is a conservatory in which we two may wait?"

"Lizzie, hold a moment, please. Something's strange here. I don't think we should be—" Gabrielle began hurriedly, only to have Christian cut her off.

"What a lovely idea, Mrs. Fletcher. Truly sterling, and how motherlike. I'm quite convinced the child would be greatly entertained to see oranges still on their trees. Grumble, be a dear and play the guide for Mrs. Fletcher. And show her the music room while you are about it. Perhaps the dear Miss Lily will show a talent for the harp. Why, I'll even see that Frapple serves you. There's a lovely table in the music room—a Sheraton piece, I believe—that folds out, and which would suit perfectly for an intimate dinner.

I am not, you see, the sort that cannot adjust my plans, accelerate them, as it were."

"Kit, I—"

"Tiens, Grumble, don't frown so. You'll frighten the child," Christian persisted, busying himself by adjusting the lace of his cuffs. Leave it to the prudish George to prove sticky at the last moment! "Now go—shoo!" he commanded, motioning them out of the room. "I assure you, Miss Laurence is in no danger from me. Why, to hear her tell it, I would be the last—the very last—man on earth with whom she would wish a clandestine assignation. We will just sit here and await our other guests, speaking of nonsense of little consequence, as we most often do. Isn't that correct, Miss Laurence?" he asked, moving around to the front of the chair to smile down at her as she twisted her hands in her lap.

"Oh, go on, Lizzie," she said at last, her lovely smile only slightly apprehensive. "I'm used to the baron's ridiculous bantering, and if I should become too fatigued by it, I shall simply smile politely as you've taught me and patiently await the remaining guests."

"Kit, I know what you've said, but . . . ."

Christian spread his arms wide. "Grumble, Grumble, Grumble. Have a look to the child, if you will. She is anxious to be off on a little adventure. Surely you aren't going to disappoint her? Or yourself?"

George looked at Lily, who was holding up a sugarplum, aiming it toward his mouth as if to share the confection with him, and he was lost. "Oh, very well, Kit," he said, lifting Lily high against his shoulder as he stood, holding out an arm to assist Elizabeth in rising. "I don't know why I argue with the man, truly I don't, Mrs. Fletcher. He always wins out in the end."

"Conk 'im a good 'un in 'is brainbox, guv'nor," Lily piped up in her slightly lisping voice, which was impeded by the fact that her top-front milk teeth were missing, helpfully offering George the solution of the streets. "That'll fix 'im right 'n' tight!"

"Lily!" Elizabeth exclaimed in motherly embarrassment as George laughed out loud at the child's remark. "You promised not to speak, remember?"

"Oh, don't shush her, Eliz—that is, Mrs. Fletcher," George begged, leading the way out of the drawing room. "Knocking a bit of the arrogance out of the man might be considered a gift to mankind in general, and to me in particular."

"Zounds!" Christian exclaimed, knowing he had won the battle for George Trumble's conscience. "Grumble, that was a near-mortal blow, I vow!"

The three walked past Frapple, whose expression remained noncommittal as he wheeled about smartly with his tray holding a single glass of lemonade to follow after the trio, leaving Christian exactly where he wanted to be: alone with the noticeably apprehensive Gabrielle Laurence.

He pulled up a small satin-covered stool and sat down directly in front of her, his smile wide as he waited for her to speak.

"When will your other guests be arriving, my lord?" she asked after a moment, during which she raised a hand to pat her hair, as if Christian's amusement came from some lapse in her appearance. "We were somewhat early, I agree, but surely someone else should have arrived by now."

"Feeling peckish, are you, Miss Laurence?" he countered, going immediately on the attack, as he was one who knew the power of having the upper hand in any conversation. "Perhaps I should ring for Frapple to fetch you some shrimp. Grumble tells me you're inordinately fond of the delicacy, although it must play the devil with reticules."

Gabrielle lowered her eyelids and looked at him as if measuring him for the depth of his malice. "You—you know about that?" she asked, tight-lipped.

"I know many things," Christian responded, placing a hand over his heart as he recited, quoting the bard, "'I could a tale unfold, whose lightest word would harrow up thy soul; freeze thy young blood; make thy two eyes, like stars, start from their spheres; thy knotted and combined locks to part, and each particular hair to stand on end, like quills upon the fretful porcupine.'"

His recitation complete, he lifted his lace handkerchief to his lips and giggled.

Which, it immediately appeared, did not impress Gabrielle as to his want of seriousness. "'The fellow is wise enough to play the fool,'" she quoted, also employing Shakespeare for her purpose, "'and, to do that well, craves a kind of wit.'"

As he had been previously over the past two weeks, Christian was struck both with Gabrielle's varied knowledge and her sterling use of it to attack him. "La!" he exclaimed, grinning. "The child has wounded me!"

"Not wounded you, St. Clair, but found you out," she shot back, rising from her chair and brushing past him, nearly knocking him from the stool.

She moved a good three feet away from him, then turned, saying accusingly, "There is no dinner party, is there? No, don't bother to lie, for I can see the truth in your eyes. Oh, you're such a sneak, St. Clair! You

233

thought to trick me with that little scene you had enacted for my benefit yesterday, but I'm not so easily gulled. Admit it, St. Clair: *You* are the Peacock!"

"Moi?" Christian exclaimed, pressing his spread fingers to his chest, not nearly as surprised by her insight as he appeared to be. "Perhaps," he suggested with a giggle, "the poor girl is light-headed with hunger?" His expression hardened. "You *are* going to tell me why you were seen stealing food, aren't you, Miss Laurence?"

"Of course. As soon as you tell *me* why you invited me here tonight when obviously there is not going to be any dinner party," Gabrielle shot back, pressing her fists against her waist, her arms akimbo, as she went on the attack. "Or are you planning to maul me again, as you did the other night?"

Christian was entranced by her fire, her spirit— even her acuity as to his intentions—and deliberately goaded her on. "How silly of me! I didn't realize a mauling could be *mutual,* my dear."

"Oh, how I loathe what you believe to be your great wit! Don't say another word on the subject, as I don't care a fig what you know or what you might want. You're the Peacock, and you're desperate to keep me from telling the world what I know. Aren't you, St. Clair? Is that why I'm here? Do you plan to kidnap me, or are you merely going to strangle us and throw our bodies in the Thames? Please, my lord, only spare the child," she ended, her voice dripping with sarcasm.

"The Peacock does not do murder, Gabrielle," Christian replied quietly, rising and kicking the stool to one side as he stepped forward to place his hands on her forearms, a move that would prevent her from "conkin' 'im a good 'un in 'is brainbox," which he thought she just might do.

Gabrielle seemed to sag slightly as she turned her head away from his. "I know that, St. Clair," she said. "Just as I want so desperately for you to know that I would never expose you."

She looked up at him, her green eyes glittering with determination. "I've learned something these past two weeks, St. Clair. I learned that I want *more* than to simply cut a swatch in Society. And I don't particularly want a wealthy husband. Oh, I thought I did, because I put it before myself to save Rose Hill Farm, but I can't continue dancing the night away with rich, vacuous twits when so many brave Englishmen are struggling for their very survival. I want to *help* you, Christian. Your ploy of playing the fop was brilliant and may have served you for a while, but you are under suspicion now. I know who's after you, and I could act the spy around both of them, gaining information as to how close they are to ferreting you out once and for all. I—I could even ride with you on occasion as well, for I am an accomplished horse-woman, and Lizzie says she would help too, taking care of the orphans and—"

"I'm not the Peacock, Gabrielle," Christian interrupted her, longing to tell her the truth but not so addled by desire that he would jeopardize his mission for a pair of melting green eyes. Not when only days before she had promised to expose the Peacock and bring him down in order to build herself up. Was she being honest with him now, or was she merely indulging in another round of romantic nonsense, aided in no small part by the kiss he'd stolen from her the other evening?

He repeated himself, just so that he could be sure he'd broken through her excitement. "I'm sorry to disappoint you, truly I am, but I am *not* the Peacock."

She stared at him, clearly incredulous, and still mildly stubborn. "But—but I was so *sure*. I mean, it only made sense. It was simple deduction. It had to be either you or Lord Buxley—"

"Buxley?" Christian threw back his head and laughed, knowing he'd be interested in hearing how she had come to that ridiculous conclusion. "That solemn-faced stickler for propriety? Why, the fellow virtually lives in Sidmouth's pocket. I'd take you more seriously if you said Prinny himself was the Peacock."

"Don't try to make a May game of this, St. Clair!" Gabrielle tore free of Christian's loose embrace and crossed to the far side of the large room. "*You* are the Peacock. I just *know* it! As I said, I—I . . ." Her voice trailed away to an awkward silence. She had her back to him now and she was quiet for some moments, her entire body still, as if listening to something, seeing something she had not before seen.

He took a single step toward her before stopping as she spoke again, her speech rapid, her tone now self-accusing. "I—I feel like such a fool!" she said, as he tipped his head and looked at her rigidly held back. "I've come here tonight, bared my soul to you, allowed myself to be exposed as a penniless fortune hunter trying to save my home from my father's wastrel ways—and all for nothing!"

She turned to him, her emerald eyes awash in maidenly tears. "Oh, St. Clair—*why* couldn't you be more than you seem to be?"

No. He was hunting mares' nests if he thought she still was out to best him. He had trumped her ace, and the game was his. But in the process, he had lost her admiration. And that hurt. It hurt more than he had believed possible.

"Forgive me, St. Clair. Please," she uttered plaintively, turning her face from him once more as her lovely features began to crumple—into tears, he was sure.

Oh, yes. The game was his. She was clearly overset, her back still to him as she seemed to stare at the draperies hung beside the door to the dining room as if mesmerized. Even more clearly, she was a woman with a deeply emotional nature and had obviously been building romantic castles in the air, installing him as her resident Romeo. Christian had her now, he knew it. Her disappointment could change to admiration again in a heartbeat. Only a few well-chosen words, and . . . But no. Only a complete cad would take advantage of her vulnerability at a moment like this to . . . hold her in his arms . . . to kiss her . . . to love her.

He thought on the possibilities for a moment, remembering how Frapple and George had earlier revealed their opinions on his arrogance and his lack of seriousness. He thought about his plans for this evening—and his secret hopes for the next week—and how difficult it had been to gain their cooperation, convincing them at last only because he'd made them believe that Gabrielle's continued presence in London presented a danger to them, to their mission to prevent bloodshed in Little Pillington. That, and the irresistible added fillip of gifting George with the chance to be a supporting prop to a worried Elizabeth Fletcher for a full seven days.

And now, now that Gabrielle had so conveniently

told him "all," as she doubtless thought of her confession, she was even more dangerous than before. Why were all women's tongues hinged at both ends?

"Oh, what the devil!" he exclaimed beneath his breath, deciding that he might as well be hung for a sheep as a lamb. He approached Gabrielle again and, placing his hands on her bare shoulders, turned her about to face him. "Gabrielle," he intoned earnestly, if not quite truthfully, "I am not the Peacock. But you are not entirely wrong. I am playing a role when I move in Society. You see, I am honored to be one of that fine fellow's loyal followers, with my main mission to remain prominent in Society so that I can bring others around to his way of thinking on the matter of Corn Laws and other inequities."

"Truly, Christian?" Gabrielle gushed, quickly placing her hands on his forearms as she addressed him informally in her new excitement, her eyes bright, almost feverish. She was such a child. Such an innocent, seductive child. "Then I wasn't being silly and stupid?"

"No gentleman would dare to so insult a lady as to prove her wrong when she is convinced she is right," Christian said most seriously, stepping closer, so that he could breathe in the sweet rose scent of her fiery hair. He was a cad. He was the lowest of the low. He was wondering how long it would take him to bed the enchanting beauty once he'd whisked her away from London.

"Then I can tell you the rest," she whispered fiercely, squeezing his arms. "Lord Buxley is out to expose the Peacock, Christian—and I think he believes you are his man! He's doing it because he's Sidmouth's agent or something, and because he wants to wed Lady Ariana because of her social station, and capturing the Peacock will stand him in good stead with her Tory papa—although now he may not want her anymore because I told him she is half in love with the Peacock, which she isn't. She dislikes the Peacock intensely."

"She does?" Christian broke in, wondering how Gabrielle had come to be the confidante of these two powerful people. "How disappointed he'll be to hear that news. Please, go on."

"I will, although the story doesn't get any better as it goes along. Lady Ariana is out to bring *you* low, St. Clair, but not because she thinks you're the Peacock, but only to please her papa, whom you refused to help by condemning the Peacock. It's confusing, I know, but I'm telling the truth—honestly I am!"

"Perhaps I should be writing all of this down," Christian said flippantly. "Otherwise I don't know if I will be able to understand any of it."

Gabrielle rolled her eyes. "It's not that difficult. Although Lady Ariana is blackmailing me into helping her—sort of. But that's another story entirely. As to Lord Buxley's mission to unmask the Peacock, well, I hadn't worried too much about that, considering that his lordship might have been the Peacock, and only running a very clever rig on Lord Sidmouth, but now it is imperative that the Peacock know of the earl's mission."

"I see," Christian said, slipping his hands around Gabrielle's waist while she was too distracted to notice. "Is that all? Or, heaven forbid, is there more the Peacock and I should know?"

"Oh, there's more," Gabrielle said, sighing soulfully. "And it's the worst of all, now that I know you are so valuable to the Peacock," she went on quickly, as if she had something terrible to say and wanted to have it over with quickly. "I—I may have said something that helped to raise Lord Buxley's suspicions that *you,* St. Clair, are the Peacock. I was so singularly stupid, so caught up in trying to best you that I didn't think. Oh, I'm so sorry! And so completely *useless!"*

A tongue hinged at both ends? Hah! This woman's tongue ran on wheels! Perhaps having an intelligent woman about wasn't quite so wonderful as he had thought it would be, for her convoluted curiosity, her very *public* curiosity, was beginning to prove wearing.

He'd have her weeping out her guilt into his jabot in a moment, and although Christian longed to have Gabrielle pressed tight against him, he'd rather it be in passion, and not despair.

It was time to call a halt to this disjointed discussion and implement the latter half of his plan—now, before Gabrielle called for Elizabeth and raced from Hanover Square, from London itself, to hide her embarrassment at Rose Hill Farm or whatever name she'd given to her beloved, endangered family home. Any further seduction of the fiery-haired female could wait until he had her safely ensconced in the country.

Putting a finger beneath her chin and lifting up her face so that he could look searchingly, seriously, into her eyes, Christian took a deep breath and asked, "Would you like me to take you to the Peacock so that you might make your apologies in person? He has, in fact, asked to meet with you. I have told him, you understand, of your great interest in learning his identity."

Gabrielle moistened her lips with the tip of her tongue, nearly driving Christian to distraction, although he was sure she wasn't aware of the pain she was causing to both his body and his usually convenient conscience. He wished he could see her expressive eyes, but she kept them averted. Poor thing. She was doubtless embarrassed by her confession. "He wants to see me? He *really* wants to see me? And you're to take me to him? Why? When?"

"Because the Peacock is always on the lookout for recruits to his mission," Christian fibbed with the ease of long practice. "And as to the when of it, I believe now is as good a time as any. Truthfully, it was what I had planned for the evening, even before your so startling revelations. If what you say is true, and you are agreeable to acting the spy when around Buxley and Lady Ariana, you could be most useful to him."

He allowed his voice to drop menacingly. "Unless, of course, you are lying to me, Gabrielle, and still out for your own gain? If that proves to be the case, I suppose I should take you to the Peacock so that he can decide what to do with you."

"Oh, no—no!" she protested, shaking her head so vehemently that her carefully arranged hair began to loosen from its pins. "I wouldn't do that. Surely, after seeing how Elizabeth and I have taken Lily as our own, you would never believe such a thing. And you already planned this for tonight? How clever! How spur of the moment—but so prodigiously clever all the same. Oh, my stars—Lizzie! She'd love to accompany me, but with Lily here and all . . ."

She frowned, biting her bottom lip, clearly cudgeling her brain as to how her chaperone would react to hearing that her charge was about to go off on an adventure without her. "We'd have to leave London, I suppose, if we're to see the Peacock. He is outside the city, isn't he? And tonight would be for the best, for I must tell him how I may have raised Lord Buxley's suspicions concerning you, St. Clair. He may ask me to replace you as his agent here in London for a space in order to allay the earl's suspicions. I feel confident you'll have me back in Percy Street by morning, but what will I tell Lizzie?"

"You will tell Mrs. Fletcher nothing," Christian said, allowing her notion of being returned to London by dawn to stand even as he was feeling amazed at how quickly she was picking up on the idea of leaving the city with him. She was clearly eager for the adventure. He felt vaguely insulted. Didn't she think he was in the least dangerous to her maidenly virtue? It was rather depressing, actually.

Frapple, never one to shrink from listening at doorways, then appeared as if on cue with Gabrielle's light evening cloak, his smile showing his amusement at her notion that one frail female could replace the indispensable St. Clair as the Peacock's chief operator in London. "As I have already told George that something of this sort might happen this evening, he will know just what to do when Frapple apprises him of our departure."

"Then Mr. Trumble is one of you as well?" Gabrielle asked, her eyes wide, and innocent, and so very ready to receive any lie he might tell her, any truth he might reveal. "And I suppose Lord Osgood and Sir Gladwin are also the Peacock's men. How above everything wonderful!"

Gabrielle allowed Frapple to drape her cloak around her shoulders, never breaking eye contact with Christian. "I like you so much better when you throw off the role of fop, St. Clair." Then she shivered, probably as she realized just what sort of adventure she was about to embark upon, and just who would be her companion on that adventure. "I must be mad to even consider going off with you like this," she added, her smile tremulous, as she cast a quick look toward

Frapple. "You will remain the gentleman, won't you, St. Clair, even if you have most thankfully ceased to giggle and posture like some performing ape?"

"Odds fish, Frapple!" Christian exclaimed, flourishing his handkerchief as that man arranged a peach silk-lined traveling cloak around his employer's shoulders. "Did you hear this gel's nonsense? I ask you, Frapple: Me—not act the gentleman?"

"I shall just place this basket of victuals in the coach, as I early on deduced you'd be leaving in some haste, my lord," Frapple said, obviously declining from gifting Christian with an answer to his question. "Perkins is already on the box, ready to spring the horses."

Gabrielle eyed the basket as if it might be stuffed with snakes. "This is all happening so quickly. Perhaps I should rethink the matter . . . consult with Lizzie . . ." she said, her words trailing off as she seemed to hesitate once more as they neared the now-open door to the street.

In a moment Christian was going to toss the infuriating female over his shoulder and single-handedly launch her into the coach! Not that he'd let her see, or allow Frapple to see, how very much his continued happiness appeared to depend on having this woman-child to himself for a space, learning all about her without having to play the role of Society fop, either driving her witchery from his system forever or allowing himself to love her completely.

He stepped out onto the portico, then shook his head. "So faint-hearted? Very well. I'll have Frapple summon Mrs. Fletcher and you two and the child can return home. I should have realized that you were only indulging in some female wishful thinking. The Peacock has great faith in you, but I always believed you were only willing to talk about helping our cause as long as you could consider it an adventure that had little chance of coming to fruition. I should have known you wouldn't give so much as a single evening of your life to such a serious pursuit as a private meeting with the Peacock."

"Oh? Is that what you thought, St. Clair? Well, I'll just show you how very wrong you are!" Gabrielle protested, walking, chin held high, past Christian as Frapple opened the door to the coach and let down the stairs. She climbed into the coach, then leaned her head out the doorway for a moment, baiting him with her smile and the taunt "Coming, my lord? Or are *you* having second thoughts?" before disappearing into the darkness of the interior of the coach.

"Frapple," Christian whispered as the servant stood by stoically, "you may live to see me rue this day. And it will probably soothe you no end to watch me brought to my knees, now that I think on it."

"Yes, my lord," Frapple drawled, smiling. "Just as you say, my lord. *Godspeed,* my lord."

And then the coach door slammed shut behind Christian, and Frapple motioned for the coachie to give the horses their office to start.

Gabrielle was going straightways to Hades in a handbasket—which was the same as to say she was riding into the dark countryside with Christian St. Clair—and she had never been so excited, so over-whelmed, so in love, or so completely furious in all her eighteen years.

How dare he try to trick her when she had found him out? The least he could have done was be gracious when she had confronted him with her evidence, her suppositions, her careful deductions. But no, not Christian St. Clair. Not the great Peacock.

And she had almost believed his denials. Almost fallen neatly into his trap, unawares. Almost. As a matter of fact, she had been about to call for Lizzie and slink away to Rose Hill Farm in defeat, to nurse her wounds of unrequited love, when she had caught sight of Frapple hiding behind the draperies covering the door to the dining room.

What a dear man, and so clever! He had held a finger to his lips to warn her to silence, then showed her a single peacock feather and surreptitiously pointed in St. Clair's direction. The addition of a smile, a wink, and the reassuring gesture of a ring being slipped onto his finger were more than enough to make her see the light—and to see red at the same time.

That was when she had finally understood, the moment when the last of the veils St. Clair had deliberately hung between them had dropped from her eyes.

Christian had to be allowed to keep on with his games, his secrets, his barely veiled desire to gain her agreement to go with him and toss away any notion she might have of retaining her place in Society, her chances for an advantageous marriage with some rich, insipid member of the *ton,* her very reputation.

He had to prove to himself, and most especially to her, that *he* was the attraction, and not the Peacock. He had to know that she wanted *him,* would risk everything for *him.* And he would use his other identity, that of the Peacock, to get her alone so that she could discover that love for herself.

Such a vain man, so easily read once she could see

straight to his heart, his mind, and so very, very sweet. How could she refuse him anything—which wasn't the same as to say she would make his eventual victory easy for him.

For from the moment she had seen Frapple, understood what he was silently trying to tell her, the tune had become hers to call, although St. Clair couldn't know it. Her sudden gushing confession, her tearful pleas—how difficult it had been not to laugh in his face, even slap his handsome, lying countenance as she deliberately prattled on like some brainless ninny.

And that near balk at the last minute, once he had maneuvered her into the hallway, had been pure genius. He was at her mercy now, dancing to her tune, and she would put him through his paces for as long as it suited her, playing the innocent, the dupe, the brainless chit who believed herself in love with the Peacock—and never letting on that she knew the Peacock and Christian St. Clair were the same infuriating, mysterious, complex, thoroughly intriguing man.

Would you like me to take you to the Peacock? How dare St. Clair say such a thing to her? And without a blink? Oh, he was a good liar. A prodigiously talented liar.

Luckily, Gabrielle thought, snuggling into her corner of the coach, so was she.

"Miss Laurence—Gabrielle?" St. Clair drawled from his darkened corner as the coach turned onto a deeply rutted dirt road and began to slow down.

She grabbed onto the strap to keep from flying from the seat as the off wheel hit a particularly deep rut. "So, you've decided to wake up, have you, St. Clair? It has been nearly an hour. We must be nearing our destination, I suppose?"

"All in good time, Gabrielle. And please, as we are quite unaccompanied in this coach and therefore beyond the strictures of polite Society, I imagine you might address me as 'Christian,' or even 'Kit.' Why, we might yet end this nocturnal adventure as close, *close* friends."

"That eventuality is scarcely likely, my lord," Gabrielle shot back, bridling at his suggestion, knowing that he was inferring that she was now thoroughly compromised. Did he think she didn't know that if he chose, he now had all the ammunition he needed to destroy her? Did he have to harp on the subject until she was forced to tell him that *she* knew he would do no such thing—which would be the most foolhardy thing she'd ever done, for then, surely, he would have the coach turned about at once, ruining everything!

"I have only come with you to meet the Peacock," she declared flatly, with what she believed to be inspiration meant to confound any suspicions he might harbor, "and will then return to London as soon as the horses are rested. So if you think that I shall end this evening by sharing a bed with you—"

"Good God, but the girl harbors lofty aspirations!" St. Clair exclaimed, bolting upright in his seat. "That will teach me not to kiss willing lips, now won't it? But not to worry your impressionable head, Gabrielle, my dear girl. You will doubtless forget your foolish infatuation with me once you have met the Peacock."

"I am *not* infatuated with you," Gabrielle shot back at him, lifting the leather curtain to peer out into the darkness so that he could not see her betraying eyes. "And I am not such a looby as to be one of those foolish females who dreams nightly of being swept up on the Peacock's black stallion and being carried away to be ravished. That's nonsense!"

"Is it?" St. Clair countered, as the coach turned one last time, then drew to a halt. "Ah, here we are," he said, peering out the window. "Oh, dear me. The coach is already gone. I was afraid of that, but you would dawdle, wouldn't you? We will not meet with the Peacock anymore this evening, I fear, as he is already out and about, performing heroic deeds meant to set maidenly hearts aflutter, and all that sort of rot. Ah, well, we're here now, and the horses wouldn't be ready to depart before dawn at any rate. We might as well stay. Tomorrow night will be soon enough for introductions."

How deflating. He can't do any better than that cock-and-bull story? Very well. Let him think he has surprised me, she thought, slowly counting to ten. The silence within the coach grew to be deafening before Gabrielle said another word. "Tomorrow night? But —but I have nothing to wear!" She then wailed, neatly taking refuge in what he seemed convinced was her hysterical feminine logic.

"Tiens! Such faint-hearted words. Well, there is nothing else for it, then, but that we should return to London at once. Lord knows a suitable wardrobe to be more important than offering your services—and your apologies—to the Peacock."

A neat turnabout, sir, getting me to agree to spending the night and washing your hands of any hint of abduction. How simple it is to read you now—now that I know your greatest secret. "La, sir, do not fret. I suppose I shall manage, as it is in a good cause," Gabrielle groused quickly as she allowed a small, bandy-legged, rather dirty man to assist her from the coach and onto a packed-dirt stable yard.

She looked around curiously, seeing a tumbledown stable, a small thatched cottage, and not much of anything else, partly because, except for the light from a few torches, it was impossible to see anything, and partly because there really wasn't all that much to see.

"I'll just settle the lady now that she has refused my offer to return her to her own home, Lenny," St. Clair said from just behind her, "and then help you put away the horses. Hide the coach in the usual spot. Perkins will stay with you, as the lady will require one of the cots in the cottage."

"As yer says, sir," the man addressed as Lenny responded sprightly, moving off with the coachie, who had climbed down from his perch. "Pretty thing, she is," Lenny added not very quietly. "Time yer took a space fer some slap and tickle, Oi says. Oi'll see me and Perkins stay least in sight."

Not wishing to argue with the man, for the softly laughing baron would surely enjoy to no end listening to her try to defend her honor—something it was clear *he* had no intention of doing—Gabrielle lifted her skirts above the packed mud and stomped off toward the cottage in a fine imitation of high dudgeon, wondering if her nurse had perhaps dropped her on her head a time or two, that she actually was enjoying herself.

BOOK THREE

A MASTER STROKE

~~~

Whatever natural right men have to freedom and independence, it is manifest that some men have a natural ascendancy over others.

Fulke Greville, Lord Brooke

CHAPTER 11

From pros and cons they fell into a warmer way of disputing.

Cervantes

Ah, there she is. The acknowledged queen of Society, rising from her slumber before seven and come to mingle with the little people. I am in awe, truly. I trust you slept well. Was your straw pallet to your liking, ma'am?"

"Don't you dare talk to me, St. Clair. Don't say another word. Not one single, solitary word."

"I wouldn't dream of it, Gabrielle," Christian answered, as she walked completely into the small kitchen and went about the business of pouring herself a cup of coffee from the heavy pot sitting on a ledge to one side of the rude fireplace. "Especially after the way you threatened mayhem on me last night before bolting for what I had considered to be *my* bedchamber. Although, if I might be so bold as to mention it before I lapse into obedient silence, I thought we had agreed that you would address me as 'Kit.'"

She shot him a look over her shoulder which warned that "mayhem" might still be an option if she were to take up the huge knife sitting on the wooden table behind her, then surveyed the room, as if mentally inventorying its meager contents.

He sat back and watched her efficient movements, surprised to see how confidently she attacked the mundane chores associated with getting oneself one's own morning meal—almost as if she was no stranger to the kitchens. He would be interested in hearing how she had come by her expertise.

She looked little the worse for wear, having been forced to sleep in her shift and then dress once more in the gown she had worn to Hanover Square, and if her fiery hair seemed more wild than domesticated this morning, he could only consider it an improvement. Yes, all in all, Christian believed himself to be rather pleased with the way this abduction was tripping along.

After plunking the earthenware mug on the tabletop with enough force to send some of the coffee sloshing over the rim, she picked up the knife and hacked a hunk of brown bread from the loaf Christian had earlier discovered in the room's single cabinet.

"Much as it pains me to disobey your excruciatingly clear orders to hold my tongue," he drawled as she lifted the slice toward her mouth, "I fear it is my duty to tell you that those small, darling holes in the crust of that loaf were undoubtedly caused by nibbling rodents."

Gabrielle's mouth snapped closed as she peered at the slice for a moment, then flung both it and the loaf straight at Christian, who swiftly ducked in reaction, nearly tumbling from his tipped-back chair. "Here, here!" he exclaimed, righting himself. "I could have kept silent, you know. You ought to be thanking me, not doing your utmost to take the top of my head off."

Her sneer was a picture, Christian decided, chuckling softly as Gabrielle slammed her fists onto her hips. "You think you're so droll, don't you, St. Clair? You think you've brought me out here to the back of beyond to teach me a lesson, to show me rather than tell me that my ability to help with the Peacock's work to aid the poor and oppressed could be measured on the tip of one of Lily's small fingers. Well, far be it from me to burst your little bubble of amusement. I'll leave a note for the Peacock, and *he* can decide if he wishes to contact *me.* You can just tell Lenny, or Perkins, or whoever was outside my window a few minutes ago, making all that racket, that they can drive me back to London this minute!"

Christian decided to allow her to continue in her ignorance of his real reason for bringing her to the cottage, believing that explanation would best be kept for later, when her mood had improved, then stood up, looking out the opened door and into the stable yard.

"I would tread hot coals for you, dear lady, climb the highest mountain. But, alas, it is impossible for me to obey that particular order," he said, turning to look at Gabrielle. "That *racket* you spoke of was Perkins hitching the team to the coach. They're gone now, with my blessing, and shan't return for a week. I had so hoped you would be pleased, as I have given you the opportunity to spend seven full days of uninterrupted time in which to indulge your passion for helping the Peacock in his work. And you did still wish to meet him, didn't you, to commune with the great man?" His grin, he knew, had to be enough to send any female into strong hysterics.

"A week!" Gabrielle's green eyes grew as large as saucers, then squinched themselves down into narrow emerald slits. "You are such a bastard, St. Clair," she gritted out from between clenched teeth, then turned her back on him, probably to hide her angry tears.

"Gabrielle! Such language! Clearly no one put pepper on your tongue when you were a naughty child."

He shouldn't be enjoying himself so much, Christian knew, but he believed he had earned himself a little recreation after so many long months leading a dual life, exposing himself to danger and—just lately —finding himself daily bedeviled by one particular female with a lush, too-talkative mouth, an overly inquisitive mind, and a haunting beauty that had made pudding of his brains.

"Yes, well," he said, admiring the stiff set of Gabrielle's shoulders, "now that everything is settled, I believe I shall throw off these London clothes and immerse myself in bucolic pleasures—taking a stroll into the village that lies no more than a stone's toss away, for instance. I cannot wear my satins there, you understand, for fear I might arouse suspicions as to my reasons for being in the area. The Filthy Duck serves a tolerable breakfast, as I recall, and I may even stop in the single shop the village boasts of, and pick up a few of the necessities for meals here in the cottage. Lenny will serve as chef, if I can convince him to wash the manure from beneath his fingernails."

He got halfway to the ladder leading to the loft, and his bedchamber for the week—less, if he was lucky— when Gabrielle spoke. "I'm going with you, St. Clair," she announced flatly, so that he kept his back turned lest she should see his triumphant smile. "That is," she added, "if you'll allow your prisoner such freedom?"

He eased himself about and swept her an elegant leg. "My prisoner, Gabrielle? What a quaint notion, I'm sure. You are free to leave at any time, I assure you." He tapped a finger against his lips, as if in thought, then pointed to his left. "I believe you head *that* way. Of course, you'll miss your chance to meet with the Peacock, but—"

"Oh, cut line, you prancing ninny!" Gabrielle exploded. "I told you I liked you better when you didn't play the fool, but now I am beginning to believe that you can't help yourself—for you *are* a fool. Why the Peacock puts up with you I'll never comprehend, but I will find out, tonight. In the meantime, I refuse to stay here, starving, and without so much as anything with which to clean my teeth!"

"Very well, Gabrielle, if you insist," Christian told her, bowing once more. "However, as lovely silk gowns are as conspicuous in the Filthy Duck as dearest Lenny would be in Carleton House, I believe I won't be the only one donning a disguise this morning. But never fear. Thankfully, you're somewhat tall—your height and that flaming hair making my transformation of you from country miss to social sensation such a delicious challenge—so that it shouldn't present too much of a problem to turn you into a tolerable boy."

Gabrielle's mouth dropped to half-cock. "You expect me to wear *breeches?*"

Christian's answering smile was meant to inflame, and he knew he had succeeded when Gabrielle's cheeks flushed nearly as fiery as her hair. "Wellington trousers, actually. And you'll flatter them no end, I'm sure. You'll also find shirts, hose, a rude jacket, and a toque—that would be a full, soft cap much favored by fishermen, in case you're wondering—in the cabinet in your boudoir. Stuff your hair up into the toque, if you please. That done, you should discover several new pairs of clogs in the corner behind the door— leftovers from a recent mission that your hero, the most illustrious Peacock, ordered stored here. You would please me immensely if you were to be ready to leave for the Filthy Duck in twenty minutes."

"I loathe you," Gabrielle stated firmly, continuing to glare at him.

"Yes, yes, of course," Christian answered, turning once more for the ladder. "How you wound me with your repetitive, cutting declarations. I should have known you'd soon run dry of amusing repartee, not that you haven't given me an inspiration. I believe I shall introduce you at the Filthy Duck as my slow-witted cousin Edgar from Chipwick. That will keep you from having to say anything, although if you could produce a measure of drool it might help allay suspicions further," he ended, wondering if he had gone too far, pushed too hard.

When the earthen mug shattered against the ladder just inches above his head, he knew he had. Yet when he returned to the kitchen after changing into his favored buckskins, a comfortable pair of boots, a simple, collarless, flowing white shirt, and a natural leather vest, it was to see Gabrielle dressed as he had ordered, all her luscious mane of hair tucked up inside the toque.

Not that he spent much time inspecting that area of her tall, slim body. He was much too occupied in his appreciation of the way her breasts pushed against the fine lawn of one of his best shirts, the flare of her hips below her slim waist, the length of her long, straight legs. Only a blind man could ever believe Gabrielle Laurence to be a boy of fifteen, and then only if she didn't come close enough for him to smell the roses in her hair, the sweet, lingering aura of soap that clung, overnight, to her fair skin.

He walked over to the fireplace, wiping a hand on the soot-black inner wall, then smeared his palm against her cheeks, first one side, then the other. As she stood there, seething silently, he stepped back to admire his work, then frowned. Even dressed as a lad, and with smuts on her cheeks, she was the most feminine female he had ever seen.

"This isn't going to work," he told her matter-of-factly as he wiped his hands on the damp rag he had used earlier to wash himself. Then he sighed. "Ah, well, it's only the Filthy Duck. No one asks too many questions there. Come along, Cousin Edgar. I feel the need for some country ham and eggs."

"At times I almost hope Lord Buxley finds you out," Gabrielle said as she raced to keep up with him, for he felt the sudden need to indulge in some form of physical exertion—most probably in order to keep himself from flinging his unwilling companion to the floor of the cottage and having his "wicked way with her," as the Pennypress novels invariably and depressingly described unbridled lovemaking.

"That was your original intention, as I recall," Christian responded, waving Lenny away as that man motioned to the stable, silently asking if his lordship required that Zedekiah be brought out to him. "I still am not quite clear as to what changed your mind on that head."

Gabrielle was breathing heavily almost immediately as she skipped to keep up with Christian's lengthy strides. "That doesn't surprise me," she said between breaths. "I wouldn't suppose you to understand anything remotely involved. It's enough that you reported my intentions to the Peacock and he asked to see me. He will be back this evening, won't he? Or aren't you in on his plans all that much, so that you simply brought me here to await his pleasure?"

Christian could feel a tic beginning to work in his left cheek as he felt a frisson of jealousy running down his spine at Gabrielle's complete trust of the Peacock, while she seemed to have relegated him to the role of lackey and errand boy to the great man. He pushed a hand through his unbound hair, the near shoulder-length blond locks swinging back against his cheeks in the slight breeze.

"He'll be here tonight," he answered sharply, then grabbed her arm as he turned to his left, taking the narrow path that led through the trees and ended directly in front of the inn known as the Filthy Duck. He pulled up short just at the tree line. "A word in your ear before we proceed, if I might, Miss Laurence."

She peered past him at the inn, and toward the half-dozen larger buildings that made up the small enclave. "Why, this isn't a village at all. It's nothing more than a few tumbledown buildings, and that one small shop I can see just down there." She looked up at him curiously. "What is this place, anyway?"

"This place, as you term it, is without name, unless you wish to refer to it, as do its sometimes visitors, who call it the devil's ken. If that rather truncated explanation is not sufficiently intelligible, I shall attempt to be more explicit."

"I'm afraid you're going to have to be, St. Clair," Gabrielle told him, tilting her head to one side as she watched a small dark man sidle nervously toward the door of the Filthy Duck, a most lovely candlestick clutched in his mitted paws.

As she would never find her way to this place on her own, and as he couldn't be convinced she would hold her tongue unless he somehow managed to frighten her, Christian decided upon complete truthfulness. "This lovely collection of buildings, dear lady, serves as a safe haven for a variety of housebreakers, highwaymen, murderers who'd put a knife in your throat for a penny, and a varied assortment of lesser felons such as pickpockets, cutpurses, and even the occasional forger. And their women, of course."

"Fiddlesticks, St. Clair! You're just saying that to frighten me," Gabrielle said belligerently, although she looked rather pale beneath her chimney black. "I don't believe a word of it."

"While I confess to being malicious enough to wish you cowed, at least while we are here," Christian admitted wryly, "I must disabuse you of any notion you might have that the Peacock would set up his headquarters no more than a stone's throw from a law-abiding village complete with a lovely, grassy square, scrubbed-cheek children, and plump nosy housewives. Here, you see, everyone tends to their own business, releasing the rest of us from the necessity of explaining ours. Do you understand now?"

Gabrielle remained silent for several moments as Christian waited, wondering what she was thinking, then said, "Real murderers, Kit? Truly? I've never seen a real murderer. Will you point one of them out to me while we're having something to eat?"

"Point one out to you? God's teeth!" Christian exclaimed, but quietly, for it didn't pay to raise one's voice in this particular village unless willing to explain why one didn't have the good sense to keep his mummer shut. "Have you no conception of the danger you're in, Gabrielle?"

"The danger *you've* put me in, you mean," Gabrielle countered brightly, pushing past him and heading for the door to the Filthy Duck. "Now come along, my lord, if you will. As Lily would say, my stomach's been thinking my throat's been cut."

"A laudable idea," Christian whispered to himself as he followed close on her heels, wondering just precisely when he had lost control over this particular expedition. "And for the love of heaven, don't refer to me as 'your lordship' once we're inside. I'm 'Kit' here, and nothing more."

Gabrielle gave the broom one last, satisfying push, launching the remainder of the dust past the threshold of the cottage door, then leaned against the doorjamb, admiring the setting sun.

It had been a lengthy, often trying day, but she had come to the end of it without much trouble from one Baron Christian St. Clair—not once she had put him in his place, that is.

Their meal at the Filthy Duck had proved an education to Gabrielle, who had seen her share of poverty-stricken Englishmen but had never before listened as a one-eyed former soldier cried into his mug of ale while explaining to an unsympathetic barmaid by the name of Ripe Betts how he had come to his life of crime after returning home from Waterloo to find his wife and infant daughter dying in the local workhouse.

"'eard it all an' more afore, bucko. Wot yer needs is a bit o' work ta set ye right," Ripe Betts had told the man, pulling away the empty mug when the soldier could not produce money for another drink. "Clem!" she'd called out. "Oi gots a cove 'ere who'll join yer

crew an' 'oist the glim whilst yer charm the locks o'
that there ken yer wuz thinkin' ta crack. Says 'e's a
sol-jer, but 'e looks a fine prigger ta me, an' up fer a
rig."

"A 'ken'? That's what Lily called our establishment
in Percy Street. Good gracious! Are they actually
planning to rob a house?" Gabrielle had asked Christian, careful to keep her voice low.

"They aren't proposing a meeting for tea and cakes,
Gabrielle," Christian had answered just as quietly,
then had drawn his index finger across his bare throat,
clearly signaling her to be quiet or he—or perhaps
Clem and some of his cronies—would find a way to
keep her quiet.

After that, Gabrielle had lost some of her enthusiasm for dining with thieves and was more than happy
to adjourn to the small shop to purchase the stores
necessary for a week spent "rusticating" in the small
cottage.

Not that Christian had been best pleased by the
amount of her purchases, which included a dusty
bottle of rosewater, two rather fashionable gowns that
most likely had lately resided in some London lady's
clothes cabinet, a pair of flat black slippers that had
appeared to be her size, an apron, a comb, tooth
powder and other necessary items of any lady's toi-
lette, and even a small, silver-backed looking glass
bearing the engraved initials "RHJ."

He had stumbled back to the cottage, muttering all
the way, lugging several heavy sacks of flour, smoked
bacon, and other foodstuffs, with Gabrielle at his
heels—and twirling the pink grosgrain beribboned
parasol she had begged him to purchase—asking him
if he thought the looking glass had once belonged to

Regina June Habrisher, one of the debutantes she had met during her first two weeks in Mayfair.

Poor, poor, befuddled Baron Christian St. Clair.

If he had wanted to frighten her, he had failed, and failed badly.

If he had planned for her to see the folly of wishing to be one of the Peacock's loyal followers, he had missed his mark by a long chalk.

And if he had whisked her off into the countryside in order to prove to her once and for all that he, Baron Christian St. Clair, was not the Peacock, well, he had failed at that too.

A whole new world had opened up to Gabrielle today, and she wouldn't have changed a single thing that had happened for the relative comfort of Percy Street. She would, perhaps, have found time to pack a small satchel with her personal items, but other than that, basically she was a happy young woman.

At least the baron had allowed her to pen a note to Elizabeth, telling her friend that she was "safe as houses with the Peacock" and suggesting that she take the knocker from the door so that no one would call for the week of Gabrielle's absence from Society.

Upon her return, Gabrielle had also written, they would both either reenter Society under St. Clair's umbrella of social protection in order to do the Peacock's work, or lease out the Percy Street house again and retire to Rose Hill Farm, which was where Elizabeth wanted to be anyway. Holding out that second possibility had seemed only fair, for Elizabeth had to be worried half out of her mind about her missing friend. The fact that she was lying to dearest Lizzie had only stilled her hand for a moment, before she'd signed her name with her usual flourish.

St. Clair had ridden out to post the letter in a nearby "real" village and attend, in his words, to "the Peacock's business." Yes, he had *ridden* out, astride a fine black stallion; he, the man who had made such a point of abhorring riding, leaving Gabrielle behind to amuse herself for the remainder of the afternoon.

Kit was extremely put out with her for insisting upon penning the note when he had promised that George Trumble would explain everything to Elizabeth, another thought that had served to make Gabrielle's day pleasant. She rather liked him when he was angry with her, as he had been on that memorable evening on Lady Blakestone's balcony, when he had kissed her . . . when she had allowed that kiss to deepen . . . given his hands the freedom to rove . . .

Besides, she still had to make him pay for those horrible moments in his mansion the night before, when he had all but undermined her suppositions about him, when he had played the game so well that she had doubted him, doubted herself—if only up to the point where she had seen Frapple wink at her from behind the draperies, reassuring her that everything would be all right.

Ah, Kit, if you only knew what I now feel sure I know, what lengths I would dare, am daring, so that you will see me for who I am—as I see you for who you are!

Gabrielle turned and went back inside the cottage, propping the broom in a corner as she looked to the fireplace and the bubbling pot of rabbit stew that needed stirring. The cottage smelled of fresh-baked bread, loaves she had mixed and kneaded herself. The wooden table was scrubbed clean, a mug filled with wildflowers she had picked behind the cottage sitting in the middle of the table, with two place settings ready for when St. Clair deigned to return from his so-private business concerning the Peacock.

Gabrielle had changed out of her mannish clothes, washing at a basin she'd carried into her room and then donning one of the two gowns she'd purchased earlier—a rather lovely yellow-sprigged muslin creation that fit her almost perfectly. With her hair tied back in a sunshine-colored velvet ribbon and left to hang down her back nearly to her waist, she knew she looked young and guileless—the sort to believe in fairies, and good witches . . . and a conveniently appearing and disappearing Peacock.

"Odds fish! Am I in the right place?"

Gabrielle wheeled about in surprise, nearly tipping over the stewing pot as the ladle scraped along its edge. She must have been deeper into her private musings than she had believed, if she hadn't heard the baron ride into the stable yard.

"Good afternoon, my lord," she said as evenly as she could, laying the ladle on an earthenware plate on the hearth. "Or should I say, good *evening?*"

Christian, who had been hanging in the threshold, half in and half out of the doorway, strolled into the kitchen area, stripping off his riding gloves. "I'd rather by far you said goodbye, Gabrielle," he drawled, kicking one of the rough chairs back at an angle from the table and seating himself wearily. "But then, we can't always have what we want in this world, now can we?" He tipped back his head and looked up toward the loft. "Spent the day playing, I see. May I assume that your housekeeping talents extended to my quarters?"

The man had elevated the art of insult to spectacular levels, and when she wasn't being thrilled by him she could really detest him for his wickedly amusing banter. Many were the moments in London when she had wished to bash him into flinders, even as she had felt herself being spun closer and closer inside the fascinating web of silky contradictions that had first drawn her to him.

Gabrielle longed to fling the ladle at him now, except that he'd most probably duck, and she'd miss, and he'd make some horrid comment about her aim being off once again. "If I am going to be held prisoner here, I see no reason to live in filth. However, I also see no need to make my jailer's life more comfortable."

"Tut-tut, Gabrielle," Christian reminded her, pointing an index finger in her direction and wagging it the way a parent might in correcting a child. "You are *not* my prisoner. As I informed you this morning, you have merely to take yourself outside—"

"And turn left," Gabrielle cut in. "I remember. Did you post my letter to Elizabeth while you were taking care of the Peacock's business?"

"Against my better instincts, yes, I did," Christian told her, rising from the chair to go over to the sink and pour water into a low basin from the jug Gabrielle had filled at the pump just outside the cottage door. He then bent over the basin, sluicing water over his face, hands, and neck, even into his hair, before drying himself and turning back to her, his smile broad and only faintly mocking.

"Do I dare allow any of that stew to pass my lips, or are you adept at more things than I could ever have dreamed—including the correct preparation of a lethal dose of nightshade?"

Gabrielle picked up two wooden bowls and began ladling out portions of the stew. "Lenny already ate an hour ago, St. Clair. Why don't you toddle on out to the stable to see if he's stretched out in one of the stalls, his tongue all purple and swollen half out of his mouth. If it isn't, perhaps you'll join me at the table?"

"Ah, a temperamental cook. All the best chefs are, I understand," Christian responded, taking his seat once more and pulling the bread basket toward him, lifting the cloth Gabrielle had wrapped around the bread and sniffing appreciatively. "Ambrosia of the gods, I'm sure. Very well. You may serve me."

"Serve yourself, you arrogant popinjay!" Gabrielle exploded, dumping the contents of one of the bowls back into the pot. She pulled one of the small loaves from the basket, took up her spoon and her own steaming bowl, and headed for her room. "And clean up after yourself when you're done, if you know how!" she ordered, before kicking the door closed behind her.

She heard the knock on her door a few minutes later and ignored it. She might love him, but she couldn't vouch for his safety if he entered her orbit before she had time to remember that fact. He could pound on her door until his knuckles bled. He could stand there until his boots stuck to the floor. She was not about to answer him.

"Gabrielle? Miss Laurence? It's senseless not to answer me. We both know you're in there, now don't we, Gabrielle? So why don't you stop being such a stubborn child and come out here with the grownups. I'll apologize, really."

"Go away!" she called out, shifting her body so that she was facing the wall rather than the door.

"The stew was excellent, Gabrielle," Christian called through the door, a door he could easily have opened, for there was no such thing as a lock in this rude cottage.

"I don't care!" she shouted back to him. Why couldn't he be a gentleman and just *go away*?

"The bread was a tad chewy, though," he added, then stepped back, out of harm's way, as Gabrielle flung open the door to glare at him.

"Chewy!" she exclaimed, more than ready to commit mayhem on his ungrateful person, so that it could be considered only a blessing that she had put down the bowl before confronting her critic. "I already have it on Lenny's authority that those loaves were as light and airy as fairycakes! Chewy? Never. Why, I'll have you know that everyone at Rose Hill Farm goes into positive *raptures* over my bread!"

"And I'd give a great deal to know why *everyone* is already familiar with your culinary talents, Gabrielle, when debutantes who can do more than embroider the occasional slipper are as scarce as hen's teeth," Christian answered with maddening calm, taking hold of her arm. "However, we have other things to discuss at the moment. For instance—the Peacock sends his regrets and hopes you will be at home to his call two nights hence."

"At—at home to his call? You mean, back in Percy Street?" Stupid fool! Had he brought her to the back of beyond and then lost his nerve? What was she going to have to do to prove to him that they were meant for each other? Hold him at knifepoint as she kissed him?

"Hardly, Gabrielle," Christian said, pulling her along after him until he could seat her in one of the chairs in front of the softly glowing fireplace, then pull another one up directly in front of her and sit down himself. "He will be coming here. He's still engaged in business in Little Pillington, which is where I traveled to today, although he had hoped for a quiet week."

Gabrielle smiled in what she hoped appeared to be sympathetic understanding. "He must be exhausted, poor darling, riding about the countryside, performing his good deeds. I must tell you, I'm very much in awe of the man. So much the opposite of yourself, isn't he? Although I must remember that you do serve him, in a very small, personally safe way."

"Yes, well," he continued after a moment, during which she delighted in watching a tic appear in his left cheek, "the Peacock's fatigue and my pitiful contribution to the cause to one side, it would appear that a small problem has developed with one of his loyal contacts in Little Pillington. Perhaps not such a small problem. One of his agents has been apprehended and will be transported to London in two days' time, to be questioned by Lord Sidmouth himself. Therefore, the Peacock needs must ride again tomorrow night."

Gabrielle swallowed down hard on the thought of being dragged off in chains to face the Tory leader and being asked questions that could end with her person either being shipped off to New South Wales or turned off a gibbet outside the Old Bailey. Men were not the only ones to face such fates. The law allowed for the hanging of women, the transportation of women. Suddenly Gabrielle didn't feel quite so brave, and her plans not nearly so romantic. "What happened?"

"Does it matter? It was my fault, and that's enough for me to live with at the moment," Christian answered dully, and she looked at him closely for the first time since he had come back to the cottage. He was hardly the giggling dandy she was used to seeing as he glittered in the ballrooms of Mayfair. He looked tired, and drawn—and all she was doing was giving him more to worry about.

Poor St. Clair, he was so dedicated, so noble. Playing the fop in London, while secretly . . . She sighed. Yes, he definitely needed a few days of rest, a few days devoid of problems.

Only Christian couldn't rest, because *she* was here with him in this cottage: a thorn in his side, a threat to his exposure, a hindrance to his work. She was nothing but one more problem to Christian, who seemed to have the problems of the world hanging from his shoulders. Perhaps it was time for the complete truth, and the devil with waiting for him to see the obvious.

"I'm sorry, Kit," she said quietly, reaching out a hand to touch his arm. "So very sorry. I—" Her confession caught in her throat. No. She wouldn't say anything. If she did, he'd return her to London at once. She had to stay here. She had to help.

His smile was delightfully crooked, not the practiced half smile, half sneer he employed in Society, and she watched, her stomach feeling strangely tight, as the skin around the corners of his eyes crinkled in a most appealing way. His blond hair framed his handsome face in an equally appealing way. His open-collared white shirt, devoid of lace, fit his broad shoulders in an appealing way, and tucked into his slim waist in an appealing way. That was Christian St. Clair, she decided—*appealing.*

But appealing to what part of her? To her mind? Her heart? Her strangely treacherous body? Was she truly in love, as she believed, or had she allowed her fanciful dreams and her nearly obsessive quest to learn all his secrets to muddle her thinking? Gabrielle

271

didn't know. She knew only that if Christian, her dear, dear Kit, dared now to giggle in the affected high-pitched way he employed in London, or broke into one of his ridiculous, French-littered speeches, she would most surely burst into tears.

She had to get through to him somehow, without telling him what she knew. She had to earn his complete trust, no matter how devious the means.

"Christian?" she asked, as his smile faded and he looked once more a man suffering under a considerable strain. "Why did you bring me here?"

He patted her hand as it lay on his arm, then shook his head. "Not now, Gaby," he said, giving her back her hand. "I've got to decide what to do about Sal."

"Sal?" Gabrielle frowned at the unusual name. "Is he the man who was captured?"

"Not the man, Gabrielle," Christian answered dully, running a hand through his hair, mussing it so that she longed more than anything in creation to smooth it for him. "Sal is a woman. My contact in Little Pillington, as she was elsewhere. Damn and blast, Gaby! This is my fault. I knew they were getting close. I should have told her to leave the village. The only reason Sidmouth is waiting two days to transport her to London is so that the Peacock will hear of it and attempt to rescue her. That way the man thinks he can put an end to us once and for all. He'd be clever, if he weren't so obvious."

"*Your* contact?" Gabrielle was stung by what she knew to be an unreasonable jealousy, so that she had stopped listening to his words long before Christian had finished speaking. "You know her that well? She reports to you personally?"

Christian rubbed at his forehead as she strained to see his eyes, for the light from the fire had died to a soft glow, and it was difficult to make out his features, even more difficult to read his expression.

"No, no. Sal's the Peacock's personal contact. But I recruited her to our cause. She has been invaluable to us, as no one looks twice at a new prostitute come to town. You'd be surprised what a man like Symington will tell a willing female. Symington, and others."

Gabrielle's jaw dropped. "You—you're telling me that you—that the Peacock works with—with ladies of ill repute?"

St. Clair's head snapped up, and she could tell that he was angry. "Much as it may pain you to hear it, we have precious few of the clergy clamoring to do our work, Miss Laurence. Sal lost her husband to an accident in a mill in the Midlands. He was mangled so badly, I'm told, he was buried in the carpet he was crawling over to check the knots when the smoothing machine came down and crushed him. Sal was denied his last wages, to help defray the cost of the carpet. So yes, the Peacock works with prostitutes. Prostitutes, and poachers, and even murderers. Even," he said, sighing, "with empty-headed debutantes who think it would be endlessly titillating to ride with the mysterious, romantic Peacock."

"There's no need to be crude, Christian," Gabrielle told him, stung by his candor. "Will—will you be riding with the Peacock tomorrow night, Kit?" she asked, wetting her suddenly dry lips with the tip of her tongue. "Forgive me. That was a silly question. I suppose you and Mr. Trumble, and Lord Osgood, and Sir Gladwin Penley will all be involved in the rescue of this woman."

Christian shook his head. "There isn't time for a gathering of all the members. I'll just have to make do with those I can most easily summon," he said, adding, almost as if to himself, "and those who haven't turned into old women."

"May—may I go along?"

Christian sat back in the chair, his legs spread wide, his hands on his knees. "You? Now there's a thought to send a shiver down my spine. Such an eager soldier, full of fire and resolve! Why, if you were to go I shouldn't imagine that I would be needed at all."

"Yes, *me,*" Gabrielle countered, doing her best to keep her voice determined, and not verging on hysterical pleading, the sort of feminine outburst Kit was most likely prepared to hear. "And don't be so insulting. I already told you that I am a very good horsewoman—and I don't need a sidesaddle, if you were going to throw that up to me as a reason to leave me behind. And I'm tall enough to pass for a man. Besides, I'm here, which is more than you can say for your friends, who are in London. It's just obvious that I should go."

"Obvious," Christian repeated, pulling his chair closer to hers, as if he wished to see her more clearly in the light from the dying fire. "I will need a distraction if I hope to get past the guards, and God knows you'd be a fine candidate for playing such a role. I don't know, Gaby. I suppose, if I were to dress you for the part, teach you a few words of cant and such, you could be of—*no!* Absolutely not! It's out of the question!"

Gabrielle reached forward impulsively and laid her hands on St. Clair's shoulders. "No, no," she protested, ignoring the way her palms tingled as she touched him so boldly, so intimately. "Tell me your idea. I know you have been struck by some sort of inspiration, Kit. I could see it in your eyes before you remembered that I am not Sal but only a green girl. You want me to distract the guards, isn't that it? You want me to play the strumpet for you, don't you? Sal has played that part in the past, I just know it. If she could do it, so can I! Please, let me help you!"

He shook his head. "It's too dangerous. God's teeth, Gaby, do you have any idea what those soldiers might say to you? What they might try to *do* to you before I could intervene?"

Gabrielle nervously wet her lips, searching deep inside herself for the courage to pretend she wasn't afraid. "Test me, Kit," she implored him. "See if I will pass muster." Taking a deep breath, she pulled the ribbon from her hair and shook her head, allowing the flaming curls to cascade around her shoulders.

"There," she said, trying for an arch, sophisticated smile as she dredged her memory for the words Lenny had used last night upon seeing her. "Love a duck, mister," she crooned, pushing one shoulder free of her gown, "would you be caring for a little slap and tickle?"

"*Sweet Jesus,*" Christian hissed from between clenched teeth. "You're Eve's daughter, Gaby, and, God help me, I'm no saint," he whispered hoarsely, moving forward so that his knee slipped between her thighs for the length of at least six inches, her gown scarcely impeding this probing, never before experienced intimacy.

She fought to keep her enticing smile from wavering, to keep her eyes open and boldly, deliberately staring into his. He was trying to frighten her, that was obvious, but she would show him that she was no faint-hearted, die-away miss. Even if her bones were slowly turning to water and her heart was pounding violently enough for her to feel it throbbing inside her ears as she sat there, her hands folded in her lap . . . squeezing into tight fists in her lap.

St. Clair inched closer, his overwhelming presence seeming to suck all the air from the small room, so that she found it difficult to breathe. And when he slowly—oh, so slowly—reached out a hand and captured her breast, she ceased to breathe at all.

"Such a pretty round-heeled piece," Christian crooned quietly, the pad of his thumb tracing circles around her nipple through the fabric of her gown as he played the part of crude customer to her willing prostitute. His second hand came up to capture her other breast, squeezing it, almost hurting her, molding her softness to fit his palm. "So perfect, the little whore is. Custom-made for touching. Feel her pert nipples reaching out to me, begging for my caress—my kiss."

"Please," Gabrielle whispered, her eyes closing as sensations she had never felt, never even knew existed, coursed through her body, heating her, frightening her with the urges his touch provoked. "Please, Kit."

"Please, Kit?" her brain screamed at her. *Is that all you can say? "Please, Kit?" Not "Please, Kit, stop?" Why? Why don't you tell him to stop? Does love totally destroy shame?*

He had pushed her bodice down—although she couldn't remember him doing it, for his knee had advanced another few inches, and the sensations centering between her thighs had taken her attention away from his hands.

And then she felt it: his mouth—warm and wet—pressing between her breasts.

Gabrielle's eyes flew open and she looked down to

see Christian's head, his upper body, pressed close against her. She felt his blond hair warm and silky against her skin . . . his hands cupping her . . . his lips, his tongue, touching her, finding her, loving her . . . his knee advancing, spreading her thighs . . . causing her to long for something she shouldn't want at this time, in this place, yet longed to have.

This went beyond any "test" of her aptness as a pupil in the school of willing harlots. This was no assault. Kit was worshiping her body, and she was glorying in that carnal adoration.

Please. Please. Please.

And then he was gone, gone from her body, gone from his chair, standing with his face turned to the dying fire.

"All right," he said almost conversationally as Gabrielle quickly straightened her bodice, "I suppose you could play the doxy with some credibility. If you promise to obey my every order—without question, Gaby—I'll take you along tomorrow night."

Then he turned to face her, his eyes glowing with a heat she could not interpret. "But for now, Miss Strumpet, I suggest you take yourself off to your maidenly bower—before I begin to believe it is me you are striving to please, and not the Peacock."

Her eyes wide, and her hands pressed to her mouth, Gabrielle prudently did as Kit asked, slamming the door behind her and then leaning against it, trembling so convulsively she had to wait some moments before she could summon the strength to throw herself upon the bed and weep in frustration and fear.

Frustration, because she hadn't wanted to leave him, hadn't wanted him to stop his assault, hadn't wanted to be treated like a lady but as the whore he had pretended her to be.

And fear, because even as she was closing the door she could see Christian raising one of the wooden chairs above his head, and the slamming of her door did not block out either Christian's abrupt curse or the sound of that chair smashing against the stone wall of the fireplace.

CHAPTER 12

~

In fact, at this moment, [he] might have been on his way to a garden-party . . . instead of deliberately, cold-bloodedly running his head in a trap, set for him by his deadliest enemy.

Baroness Orczy

Lady Ariana Tredway expertly tooled her yellow-wheeled curricle—a gift from her doting mama on her precious daughter's last birthday—into the park for the promenade, ordering her maid to keep a sharp lookout for Lord Buxley, who was almost always to be found exercising his favorite mount at this time of day. He had to appear soon, or else she would be forced to seek him out at his townhouse, a breach of acceptable behavior she loathed to perform but one that might become necessary.

"Yoo-hoo!" she called out in relief a few moments later, already reining her showy white horses to a stop on the rim of the drive, as the earl, looking splendid in his buff riding clothes, rode toward her across the grass.

"Good day to you, Lady Ariana," Lord Buxley said, tipping his curly-brimmed beaver to her even as his gelding danced in a near circle, eager to be off once more. "How may I be of service to you?"

"I believe, my lord, that it is I who might be of some service to *you,*" Lady Ariana responded archly, giving a quick motion of her head so that her hapless companion, used to such silent directions, clumsily clambered down from the plank seat and walked off to admire the spring flowers that grew near a small stand of trees. "However, as I do not wish to shout, and we are perfectly well chaperoned by this crush of people taking the air, may I suggest you join me?"

"With the greatest pleasure, my lady." Lord Buxley promptly dismounted from his horse and tied the reins to the rear of the curricle before lightly springing up onto the seat beside her ladyship. "I will, of course, take the reins if you wish to continue around the circuit."

"No, Anthony, you will not," Lady Ariana answered, releasing the brake and flicking the reins, setting the curricle into motion.

They drove on in silence for some moments, both of these London luminaries bowing their heads to passersby and generally acting out the parts that their birth, breeding, and inclination had led them to perform so well. It was only as they reached a less crowded portion of the park that Lady Ariana spoke once more.

"You've captured one of the Peacock's followers in Little Pillington and plan to transport her here to London tomorrow," she announced without preamble.

"Ariana!" Lord Buxley exclaimed, clearly horrified.

"There is no possible way you could know such a thing! Unless—"

"Unless I have taken to listening at keyholes when you visit Papa, yes, I know," she cut in, waving to Lady Cornwallis as the woman was driven by in an open landau, her daughters sitting on the facing seat, their plain-as-pudding faces shielded by parasols.

"However, that is beside the point, Anthony, for I have much more important matters on my mind at the moment than any lengths I might find myself forced to go to in order to satisfy my daughterly concern for my father's happiness—matters, as it happens, that concern Miss Gabrielle Laurence and Lord Christian St. Clair."

"St. Clair?" Lord Buxley repeated, his handsome face drawn up into an unflattering sneer. "Ariana, my dear girl, there is nothing—absolutely *nothing*—you might say about that lace-bedecked, prancing ninny that could interest me in the slightest."

"Not even if you could bring him down?" Lady Ariana challenged. "Destroy him? Send him off to languish in a filthy prison, so that he could never again regale his fawning audience with recitations of the Peacock's missives to the newspapers?"

"You know about that as well?" Lord Buxley, who had been looking straight ahead, concentrating on the horizon, turned to peer curiously at his now openly preening companion. "You know we've asked the baron to cease his championing of the Peacock?"

Lady Ariana lifted a lace-edged handkerchief to her upper lip, for the late-afternoon sun was proving warm and the heat, added to her excitement, was causing her to—horror of horrors—perspire! "You men," she said, sighing. "Why do you all persist in believing we females care for nothing save the latest fashions? Now, do you wish to be rid of St. Clair or not? My horses are becoming restless, and Papa has lectured me that I should not keep them standing."

She waited impatiently while the earl seemed to mentally cudgel himself for an answer before asking at last, "St. Clair has become a thorn in your side this Season, hasn't he, Ariana? Miss Laurence as well, I might suppose, as she is St. Clair's latest protégée. You did mention her name earlier, as I remember. And I had thought you two had become fast friends, giggling together, as you females will, about the romantic Peacock."

The cheek of the man! She had summoned him to her in order to help her papa, help her King and country—and he dared to insult her! Giggling? She *never* giggled! The earl might be gloriously handsome, but handsome was as handsome did, and his manners were atrocious. To dare put forth the notion that she had ulterior motives for daring to put a spoke in St. Clair's social wheel! To intimate that she had befriended Gabrielle Laurence only in order to find a way to dull the sheen on her unexpected popularity within the *ton!* Why, it was the height of effrontery! It was insulting, debasing, vile . . .

She rolled her lovely china-blue eyes and gave in to the truth.

"All right, Anthony," she said coldly. "I admit it. I want them gone. I want them both gone. I already have Gabrielle Laurence's reputation dangling by a thread thanks to information I have tucked up in my jewelry box—but it has just this morning come to my attention that I might gain victory without so much as having to lift a finger, for she has compromised herself. Now, if you are through insulting me, perhaps you will listen to what I have learned, for what I know goes well beyond our usual social intrigue."

"By all means, Ariana," the earl said, inclining his head. "It matters not the motive, as long as we obtain our objective. And, by way of apology, allow me to say that I am convinced it is your great loyalty to the Tory cause that has brought you to me. I cannot tell you how flattered I am that you should trust me with your confidence."

Lady Ariana smiled, believing it was incumbent upon her to be forgiving of his earlier insult. "It is imperative that the Peacock be stopped, Anthony," she told him, her tone growing passionate as she warmed to her subject. "It is likewise imperative that St. Clair be destroyed. And I now know just how to accomplish both objectives. It is really quite delicious, Anthony."

"As you say, Ariana," Lord Buxley responded, sounding slightly bored. "But how do you propose to bring the baron down? He is firmly entrenched in the affections of the ladies, and an idol to most of the younger gentlemen who ascribe to his outrageous fashions."

"Are you afraid of the baron, Anthony?" Lady Ariana teased, delighting in the way the cords in the earl's strong throat became prominent as he did his best not to react. She hadn't thought of it before with any sympathy, but Lord Buxley must be as put out by the baron's popularity as she was with Miss Laurence's social success. They had both been usurped—but not for much longer! "No," she went on hurriedly, "of course you are not. But you will agree that he is offensive to people of our bent—those who know the true meaning of nobility."

She placed a hand on his arm. "I went to see

Gabrielle Laurence this morning, Anthony," she went on in a near whisper. "I have dropped in at the Percy Street address often in the past days, and I must say, it is a most peculiar household. Why, if one did not choose to believe the explanations Miss Laurence and her mousy companion have given, one might think both women were no more than shabby, down-at-the-heels country gentry, conspirators of only slightly noble lineage who were foisting themselves upon the *ton* in order to elevate their financial status through an advantageous marriage."

"Ariana," Lord Buxley said with a sigh, "if we are to get on with this any time before the dinner hour, I suggest we speak with the gloves off. Are you saying that Miss Laurence is a fortune hunter?"

"Worse!" She leaned closer to the earl. "She is no better than a whore!"

"Lady Ariana! I must protest!" his lordship exclaimed, carefully removing her kid-encased paw from his sleeve as if he elsewise might somehow acquire her taint of vulgarity. "I said we should speak with the gloves off. I did not give you office to descend into obscenities."

"There is no way to wrap this thing up in clean linen, Anthony," she explained, taking a moment to wave to Lord Blakestone as that man cantered by on his famous gray mare. "Now listen to me: I went to Percy Street this morning after not seeing Miss Laurence in public these past two evenings—or St. Clair, either, which is something I wish for you to remember —only to have Mrs. Fletcher tell me that Gabrielle is indisposed and cannot receive visitors. They've been trying to fob me off for days with tales of an illness in the house, but it won't fadge. They have no one to so much as answer the knocker, Anthony!"

She took a deep breath, doing her best to arrange her thoughts in order so that she could present them in a reasonable, convincing manner, thus enlisting the skeptical Lord Buxley in her cause.

"While I was there," she continued, "I asked Mrs. Fletcher to fetch me a glass of water, knowing full well she would have to do the chore herself, and leaving me to examine a certain knitting basket that has been a source of interesting information to me in the past."

"A knitting bag," Lord Buxley said, his smile so patently patronizing that Lady Ariana longed to cuff his perfectly sculpted ears. "How deep you are, Ariana."

"Yes, Anthony," she replied, pulling a face at him, "I am. And do you know what I found? I found a letter from Gabrielle directed to Mrs. Fletcher. And St. Clair had franked it, for I recognized his scrawl! I couldn't take the letter with me, as it would be above everything silly to have the woman learn that I had read it—but I can tell you what it contained."

"Go on," Lord Buxley said, not bothering to tip his hat as Lady Hertford's carriage drove by. She had his interest now, and it soothed her jangled nerves no end to bask in the power of her superior knowledge.

"It said," Lady Ariana intoned importantly, "that the Baron St. Clair had taken her into the countryside to meet with the Peacock. St. Clair doesn't just parrot the Peacock's words—he's *in league* with the man. And now he has compromised Miss Laurence, who is doubtless one of those brainless chits who believes herself in love with the Peacock. They are both done—destroyed—if only you, Anthony, can succeed in discovering them together in their country hide-away. Why, you might even find the Peacock with them, so that they can all be locked up in prison together. There!" she concluded, wriggling slightly on the bench seat in her elation. "Now, aren't you happy I thought to share this information with you?"

Lord Buxley was quiet for several moments, a small crease appearing between his brows as he considered what Lady Ariana had said. "You couldn't take the note?"

"I already told you why I couldn't, Anthony," she said in growing exasperation. Honestly, you'd think the man would be crowing in glee, not just sitting there, stone-faced, asking her why she hadn't done the impossible. "Mrs. Fletcher would know that it was gone. Isn't it enough that I read it, then came to you?"

"And you're not telling me this simply because you are jealous of Miss Laurence's adventure? Riding off to see the Peacock?"

"Jealous! Anthony, do you think I am a child? This is so much more important than romantic notions. The Peacock threatens to destroy England with his treasonous letters, his illegal acts against the Crown. Papa has explained it thoroughly to me. England needs a wealthy upper class such as ours, for we are the ones who know how to spend money. It is by our spending that the lower classes can find work: building our carriages and yachts, spinning cloth for our gowns, forming brick for our country houses, growing food for our dinner parties. Why, without a rich upper class, the poor would all starve. I only think it terribly ungrateful of them to complain."

"You're a good daughter, Ariana," Lord Buxley said, patting her hand, "and a loyal subject of your King."

"Yes, I am, aren't I, Anthony? But I must tell you, I am appalled at everything I saw in Percy Street this morning. You see, after I left, I ordered my coachman to halt at the end of the street, just to watch for a while, curious as I was to see if Miss Laurence might return, which would be too bad, for then we couldn't prove anything, could we?"

"And?"

"I'm getting to it, Anthony," she said, removing her hand from beneath his, as the duke of Glynnon might drive by at any time and she didn't wish for his grace to see her appearing intimate with another man. "After a bit, St. Clair's coach drove up and George Trumble appeared from inside. He went into the house, where he remained for no more than a quarter hour, then emerged once more with Mrs. Fletcher and a child, all of them carrying baggage. St. Clair's coachman then removed the knocker from the door and they all drove off. They went to Hanover Square, Anthony. What do you suppose that means?"

"Unless St. Clair is setting up a whorehouse— excuse *my* blunt speech, Ariana—I would say that Miss Laurence is well and truly in the company of the baron, and they indeed did travel into the country to meet with the Peacock. It also must mean that Trumble, Sir Gladwin, and Lord Osgood are also in league with the Peacock, for everyone knows the three of them are close as sticking plaster to the baron. I knew I never liked them, especially that fellow Trumble, who is not really one of the nobility but simply a hanger-on. I'll have men put to following all three of those bounders at once."

"Then you are thinking as I am, Anthony? You expect the Peacock to attempt a rescue of the woman you are holding in Little Pillington? They will strike after dark, I am convinced of that. That's why the Peacock wears black, so that he won't be seen as he goes about his seditious assaults."

"You amaze me, Ariana," Lord Buxley said, stepping down from the curricle as her ladyship's maid, appearing flustered and out of breath, came up to them. "But yes, that is precisely what we are hoping. By tomorrow morning the Peacock will be in my hands. The Peacock, and even St. Clair and the rest of them, if we're lucky. It's as Miss Laurence has said to me: St. Clair is the least likely person to be the Peacock or in league with the man. She must have acted on her suspicions and somehow convinced the baron to take her to the Peacock. I wonder why St. Clair agreed."

"He is smitten with her," Lady Ariana answered without much interest, eager now to be on her way, as she really should attempt to catch up with the Duke of Glynnon if he had joined in the promenade, just so that he didn't forget her existence. "I've seen it clearly since the first evening that redheaded horror entered Society. Love can be so debilitating, can't it, Anthony? I feel blessed that I have no capacity for such a destructive emotion."

"A failing usually limited to the lower classes, I agree," Lord Buxley said, then went to the rear of the curricle to retrieve his horse. "My dear lady," he told her, as he walked his mount forward and tipped his hat to her ladyship, "come tomorrow you will reign supreme in Society once more, but none but I will know that you have single-handedly *saved* that Society from the possibility of revolution. I am humbled to be in your presence!"

"Of course," Lady Ariana said, frowning as the plump-kneed maid lifted her skirts indelicately in order to mount the seat. "I wish you Godspeed, my lord. Please do not leave me in suspense over the success of your mission. I will be at Lady Hertford's ball tomorrow evening, breathlessly awaiting your good news."

"Not Lady Hertford's, Ariana, as I will be otherwise occupied for a few days, dealing with the Peacock, interrogating him and such, and will not be in London," his lordship corrected her. "But as you may recall, I have planned a small dinner party to take place three days hence, before the Countess of Royston's ball. St. Clair and Miss Laurence have been issued invitations, as it was impossible not to include two such luminaries, but we will have to struggle through without their presence, I suppose," he said, his features almost forming themselves into a smile. "Your esteemed father is to accompany you, I believe? I can relay the success of my mission to you then, and—if I may be so bold—I can also have a private conversation with him on another matter, a highly personal matter."

"Really, Anthony?" Lady Ariana said, not so silly that she didn't know she should appear flattered at this hint of a proposal—as if she would ever agree to such a suit when she had always aimed considerably higher than the earl. "I vow, your lordship," she added without a hint of emotion, "you put me to the blush." And then she drove off, on the hunt for the Duke of Glynnon.

Christian had avoided Gabrielle all day, spending his time in the stable with Lenny, exercising his horse, sending off a note to be hand-delivered to his mansion in Hanover Square.

Spending his time hiding, knowing himself to be a coward of the first water, a thorough-paced rotter, a monster he barely recognized, pushing forward in a mission he barely recognized.

When had he taken this dangerous turn, embarked on this well-intentioned but clearly self-serving path on which he now trod—exchanging his high ideals in order to play the daring avenger, the fire-starter, the rabble-rousing instigator of revolt?

Grumble saw it coming, Christian thought as he rode the fields on Zedekiah's back. *Grumble, and Winnie, and even Ozzie. Everyone save me. The risk has become the game, a game played with no rules, no safe harbors, no concern for the powerless pawns caught up in the game, caught up in the retribution of an angry, frightened government. Slow Dickie. Sal. Gabrielle. Who else will I ask to pay for my folly, my reckless desire to win at all costs?*

This is the last time, I swear it, Christian had bargained as he dressed for the part he would play this night. *Give me one last success—let me save Sal—and it will be over. I'll go back to the original plan, and no more. I'll stop the march on Symington's house. Somehow. Some way. I promise. I've already set one possible plan in motion. But everything hinges on tonight, this one dangerous night. Otherwise I would never risk such danger for Gabrielle, no matter how willing she is to be my helpmate.*

Don't laugh at me, God! Like all sinners, I'm desperate for Your help. I'll promise anything if only You'll help me. Let me save Sal, protect Gabrielle, keep the villagers of Little Pillington safe. I am the sinner. I am the one who deserves punishment. Not them. Dear God, not them!

He had thought no more of the interlude he and Gabrielle had shared before the dying fire, for any vile name he hadn't called himself as he spent a sleepless night in the loft, listening to her soft sobs, Lenny had called him during the day, for the former jockey had taken an immediate liking to Gabrielle and her way with a crusty loaf.

"Bringin' 'er with us? That dear little darlin'? Are ye daft, yer worship?" Lenny had asked, shaking his large head as he worked over some tack he was polishing.

"I don't want to, Lenny," Christian had explained, wishing he could sound more positive. "But I have no choice, and she'll barely be in danger. We need someone to play Sal's role."

"Christ on a crutch! Puttin' 'er ta do Sal's work? That sweet angel? Don't go tellin' me why she's willin', or why ye're so mean as ta let 'er. 'Tis a'cause o' the way she's soft on the Peacock, ain't it, which is 'alf agin as silly as anythin' Oi've 'eard, seein' as 'ow that means yer 'atin' 'er fer goin' soft on ye when it's plain as a pikestaff that ye're soft on 'er? Ta love the lass and put 'er in danger? Tis a black, twisted 'eart ye 'ave, yer worship, a black, twisted 'eart."

And Lenny was right, on all counts. Christian knew he must have a "black heart" to hold Gabrielle's fascination with the Peacock against her. Especially when he considered that *he* himself was the Peacock. How Frapple would laugh, to see his old friend so twisted up in knots, so irrationally jealous of himself!

And Christian knew he also had been black-hearted to have pushed Gabrielle last night, daring her to undergo the humiliation of his assault so that she could prove to him that she was capable of helping in tonight's rescue. She'd do anything, dare anything, in order to help the cause, even put up with his crude advances that had somehow turned into a passionate if one-sided interlude, when it was clear she detested him.

Detested him . . . while he loved her with all his black heart.

Oh, what a tangled web we weave . . . Christian thought, remembering the overworked saying as he pulled a shaggy gray wig over his blond head and turned to the small mirror to take one last look at his disguise.

The skin on his face, neck, and hands had been darkened with a solution of tree bark and egg whites, and when the mixture dried, the stiffness of the egg whites had created new wrinkles beside his mouth and around his eyes, while etching an aging landscape of lines on his smooth throat.

He owed the weeping sore on the back of his left hand and the mole on his nose to the talents of a beggar he had met in Spitalfields, a man who was a master in the art of manufacturing sympathetic maladies meant to elicit a penny or two from passersby.

The small bag of rags he'd tied around his body—providing a disfiguring hump on his left shoulder—would not interfere with his movement, he already knew, although he would have to remember to walk bent-legged in order to disguise his unusual height.

He needed only three last touches: some greenish brown paste rubbed over his straight white teeth; the rag that would serve as an eye patch to cover one of his blue-green eyes; and the single peacock feather he tucked up behind his back, in the waistband of his breeches and beneath his ragged, stiff-with-sweat jacket.

At last, just for an added fillip, he popped a garlic clove into his mouth and chewed it a few moments before shoving the odoriferous mass to one side in his cheek, then climbed down the ladder to see if Gabrielle was ready to leave.

"You're looking particularly evil tonight, Kit. You seem oddly well suited to the role of ruffian," he heard her say coolly as he was descending the last rung. "Lenny told me I wouldn't recognize you, and he was correct. You're, um—I imagine I should say *magnificent*. Not nearly as magnificent as the Peacock was the other day in Little Pillington, of course, but I know I would be hard-pressed to convince myself I would wish to do battle with anyone so menacing. I wonder, would all the dandies hop to emulate this new fashion if the great St. Clair were to debut it in Mayfair?"

Christian turned slowly, almost reluctantly, prepared to see Gabrielle looking like a child dressed in a costume ill suited to her innocence, prepared to tell her that it wouldn't work, that she was no longer a part of his plan. It took only one quick look for a dagger-sharp shaft of agony to twist in his gut. This was no child, no Society miss who would give the game away within a heartbeat.

No indeed. She was a magnificent whore, a queen among whores! The once white peasant blouse, now gray with age, one elbow-length sleeve torn, rode low on her breasts, exposing her creamy shoulders and the enticing curves and hollows he had kissed the night before. A full gypsy skirt patterned in red, blue, and green left her shapely bare ankles exposed above skimpy black slippers, the half-dozen petticoats dragging bits of lace.

She had tied a bright green sash around her narrow waist and lifted one corner of the skirt through it, so that the topmost petticoat was visible nearly to the apex of her thighs—an advertisement of her availability as well as an inducement to rent her "merchandise."

But it was the riotous tumble of her glorious copper curls that nearly did him in, for she looked wild, abandoned, and so very, very lush. Her vibrant hair, and that enticing mole—that beautiful, mesmerizing, sanity-destroying mole beside her mouth. God's teeth! Was there ever such temptation put before man? And he had been worried about *her?* It was the men she was setting out to dupe who needed his compassion, for they would be defeated in a heartbeat.

Even beneath the layer of chimney dust she had applied to her face and arms—for Little Pillington was not the sort of village that had ever boasted a clean whore—Gabrielle remained beautiful, vibrant, *seductive.*

"So? Do I pass muster, Kit?" Gabrielle asked, her tone nervous. "Lizzie would faint dead away if she could see me now, but I must say it: I feel wonderful, and rather daring!"

Christian gave silent thanks for his own disguise, hoping the growing dusk also shadowed the hunger, the agony, in his single, admiring eye. *Mad. Mad. This whole idea is mad. I must stop it now, call it off, find another way. But there is no other way. Sal, Sal. How long before you are forced to talk? How long before Grumble falls, Winnie falls—we all fall? How can I take that chance, Sal? How do I turn my back on you? How could I have allowed you to be caught! Please, God. Just this one time. Just this one last time . . .*

Assuming the bent-over, shuffling walk of an out-at-the-elbows beggar, Christian advanced toward Gabrielle, awkwardly swinging his left arm as if to keep his balance, which was hampered by his hump. "Ripe, ain't ye? Where's your crib, ducks?" he cackled in a rough, Cockney voice, sweeping up a bottle from the table and seeking salvation in a long pull of wine.

"My—my *crib?*"

Christian stood up straight as he shoved the rag

covering his eye up onto his forehead, the better to glare at her. He changed his mind yet again, for the hundredth time in a minute. This wasn't going to work. He should have known it wouldn't work. She was too young, too green. "Yes, Gabrielle—your crib. It's where cheap whores sleep, when they're not spreading their legs for any man jack with the price of a tumble."

"Oh," she said, wincing. "Lenny didn't mention the word during our lessons this afternoon. And, I must say, I was rather put off by your appearance. You're frightening, Kit, even when I know who you are. Do you know that you smell? And your teeth—they're positively *green!* But I suppose someone would notice if they weren't. Please, can we try again?"

Christian spread his arms wide, inclining his head graciously, sure this second time even she would realize that she would be more of a hindrance to the Peacock than she could ever be a help to him. "By all means, Gabrielle." He once again assumed the bent-over position of a beggar. "Now, ye prime piece," he growled, grabbing her wrist with his left hand, the hand displaying the oozing sore. "Where's your crib?"

"Ain't gots one, boyo—and m' name ain't 'Ducks.' It's 'Peg,' on account as 'ow Oi'm always 'anging m'self on one," Gabrielle answered belligerently as she roughly flung off his hand and struck a pose, her hands on her hips as she shifted her shoulders suggestively. Clearly she had taken Lenny's afternoon lessons to heart, for she was better now, more convincing by half.

"'ad me a flash cove onct," she boasted, giving her curls a toss, "but 'e threw me over years back, when Oi snaggled m' first dose o' the clap. Bin workin' the cobbles in Jack Ketch's Warren, goin' ta the wall fer a penny a poke, but Oi wuz pinin' fer a spot o' fresh air. Yer wants ta beat yer gums or fuck, ducks? Oi ain't gots time ta chat."

"Sweet Jesus! I ought to throttle that sawed-off manure raker," Christian muttered beneath his breath, taking another long swallow of wine. "Memorized every word he said, didn't you? Gabrielle—do you have any idea of what you're saying? Even the foggiest notion?"

She tugged the wide neck of the blouse up and over her shoulders, concealing two areas of creamy skin only to have the bodice gape, exposing more of her magnificent breasts. Untying the lace, she pulled it tighter and tied it again, all the while glaring at Christian as if he should know any *real* gentleman would turn his back while a lady rearranged her attire.

In short, she was the most appealing mixture of innocent youth and sexual profanity he had ever seen. The jailers in Little Pillington would knife their own brothers to be the first to ride her. Not that they'd get that chance.

"No, Kit, I most definitely do not understand what I'm saying, and I'd appreciate it greatly if you allowed me to continue in my ignorance. Now, if you'll help me with my cloak, I believe it is dark enough for us to be on our way. Or," she added, eyeing him carefully, "are we waiting for the Peacock to arrive?"

"He'll join us at the split oak just outside Little Pillington," Christian informed her tightly as she turned her back, allowing him to drape a rough woolen cape around her shoulders and pull its hood up to cover her flaming hair.

And then he hesitated.

This was his very last chance to abandon their mission—or at least remove Gabrielle from it—by stoutly tying her to a bedpost if necessary. But hesitation was useless, second-guessing his scheme was useless, for he already knew he wouldn't change his plans now. He couldn't. Not when Sal needed him. Not when Sal could otherwise end on the gallows. When all his friends could end on that same gallows. As for himself? Hah! Maybe what he needed was hanging. Lord knew he deserved it!

"Lenny rides with us, Gabrielle," he further explained, "and we'll be meeting two men—Jackey and O'Dell—who'll be with the Peacock. It has all been arranged."

"Really?" She smiled at him over her shoulder, the hood falling from her hair, and his spirits sank even lower as she asked, "Then I will meet the Peacock tonight, Kit? That will be most amazing."

Christian found it difficult to speak, as his jaws seemed prone to lock in his sudden, intense anger. "No, Gabrielle. You will not be meeting the Peacock tonight. You may see him, but you will in no way attempt to attract his attention. You will be quiet, and as near to invisible as it is possible for you to be until I send you off to complete your portion of our plans. If we're lucky, and all goes as I hope, you will then return here to the cottage with me. Is that clear?"

"Lenny was right, Kit," Gabrielle said as she brushed past him and out the doorway. "You're like a bear with a sore paw whenever anyone mentions the Peacock. Why, if I didn't know how loyal you are, I would think you don't much care for the man. Oh, yes, by the way," she added, turning to face him as Lenny, dressed all in black, in the way of the riders she'd seen in Little Pillington the day of Slow Dickie's rescue, brought three horses from the stables, "I would like to strike a bargain with you."

Her hair glowed a deep, molten red in the light from Lenny's lantern, and Christian reached out to lift her hood, once more concealing her glory and, hopefully, dousing his treacherous thoughts as well. "What is it?" he asked tersely, wondering what else this woman would ask of him, wishing he held the power to deny her anything.

"If you promise not to touch me again, Christian St. Clair, I will not inform the Peacock of your assault on me last night," she said, avoiding his eyes.

"Assault?" Christian would have laughed if he could believe she was joking. "You damn near ordered me to touch you," he said feelingly.

"Lenny didn't touch me when he was giving me my lessons," Gabrielle pointed out, her bottom lip thrusting forward mulishly.

Now Christian did laugh, for the whole thing was ludicrous. "True enough, love, but then Lenny only taught you the words. You need more than the right words to play the part. I'm the one who let you know what it feels like to be a whore."

"Yes, Kit," she answered dully, turning away. "You most certainly did."

"Ready ta go fetch Sal, yer worship?" Lenny asked, winking at Gabrielle.

"Yes, Lenny," Christian answered, taking Zedekiah's reins and preparing to mount as the former jockey steadied a dun-colored mare beside the mounting block for Gabrielle. "Let's get this over with before I have a belated attack of common sense."

* * *

Look at him, Gabrielle ordered herself sourly as she rode behind Christian, dutifully following his lead just as it had seemed natural to follow that lead since the night they first met.

Anyone would think he was on his way to another ball where he will be welcomed with open arms and fêted for having the condescension to grace the event. He rides so upright, so much at his ease, not bothering to look left or right, showing no concern for the very real possibility that he might be discovered and captured at any moment. Is he so very brave? Or is he the most smug, overbearing, and arrogant creature in nature? And if, with all that is crowding my mind at the moment, I could explain to myself why I love him so very much when he refuses to tell me all of the truth, I certainly would welcome the explanation!

"Quiet now, Gabrielle," Christian called softly as they left the open field and neared what looked, in the darkness, to be an overgrown spinney. "Not a word from this point on, you understand."

Christian's instructions brought Gabrielle back from her musings. Oh, how she sometimes longed to box his ears. Of course, she understood she had to be quiet. Did he think she was a simpleton?

But Gabrielle only nodded as Lenny spurred his own horse forward and relieved her of her reins, guiding her mount toward a thicket where, she could see, three men were waiting. Two were on foot, two men dressed much as Christian but holding large wooden, evil-looking clubs, and resembling common laborers.

The third—ah, the third—was mounted on horseback, his flowing black cloak enveloping his body and sweeping behind him to cover his mount's rump.

Gabrielle squinted through the darkness, doing her utmost to make out the horseman's features, but it was impossible, for the man was masked in black silk from his chin to his pate.

A neat trick, she silently congratulated Christian, her hero of the ever-so-unromantic wart and hump, *but then I've seen it before, haven't I?* She then dutifully opened her mouth and gushed inanely, "Oh, Mr. Peacock, sir—I am so very honored!"

CHAPTER 13

They loved each other beyond belief—
She was a strumpet, he was a thief.

Heinrich Heine

I have a word to say to you," the Peacock grumbled through his silken mask as he reached out and took hold of Christian's arm.

"Say as many words as you like, my dear man, only not just now, if you please," Christian answered smoothly as he pointedly removed the black-gloved hand from his ragged sleeve and dismounted, tossing the reins to one of the two peasants who were standing, open-mouthed, observing the scene. "In something less than an hour, I should imagine we'll have ample time for a comfortable coze. Not that I'll listen, in any case. Besides, it isn't prudent to speak too much at this time."

"Love a duck," Lenny whispered close to Gabrielle's ear. "This ain't good. They'll be tuggin' caps in 'alf a 'eartbeat."

Gabrielle tried to shrink into her saddle, sure that the masked man, the man whose voice she had instantly recognized, was angry because Christian had brought her along on this hastily arranged rescue. And then she felt herself growing rather angry. Did no one think she was capable of one small deception? Little they knew. Why, she was already juggling any number of secrets!

"Very well," the Peacock said after a moment, making a great business of rearranging his cloak around his shoulders. "It was a rather slight matter to elicit so much displeasure as for me to presume you needed to hear it at once. I shall wait the hour, and whisper my chagrin into your ear as you lay at death's door."

"I have no intention of dying this night, my friend," Christian responded lightly, the night-dark green of his teeth turning his grin into a hollow of blackness in his hideously disguised face. "After all, I ride with the Peacock, who is well known for his brilliant plans. O'Dell," he called out, barely raising his voice, "help our brave warrior in descending from his horse."

Help the Peacock to dismount? Gabrielle watched, her admittedly inappropriate amusement growing, as the man named O'Dell stepped forward and all but tumbled to the ground as the Peacock awkwardly slid from the saddle and into his thin arms. Not much of a bruising rider, this tall, mysterious Peacock. The other one had been much better, that day in Little Pillington. Such a pity that she had yet to see the real man in such romantic garb.

She hastened to dismount from her own horse, eager to inquire if the Peacock needed her assistance —and to whisper a quiet word or two of assurance to him if she got the chance.

"Peg!" Christian ordered, halting her in her tracks by the quiet vehemence of his tone. "Stay where you are. Blister it, woman—if you can't obey orders I shall have Lenny return you to the cottage."

"Yes, Kit," Gabrielle said, wondering how she could love a man and wish to see him throttled at the same time. "I'm sorry."

"No, no, my dear," the Peacock drawled, extending a hand to her, bidding she come closer. "Never be sorry. Please, it is with the greatest pleasure in life that I dare to kiss your brave little hand. Truly, I am forever in your debt."

She put out her hand to allow the romantic gesture, giggling, and hoping Kit was slowly roasting to a turn beneath his hump.

"Sir!" Christian bit out as the Peacock made an elegant leg, then pressed his silk-clad lips to the back of Gabrielle's hand. "I believe we are about to undertake a rescue?"

"Oh, that," the Peacock said, sighing. "We are to storm the jail, as I recall. Such a tame undertaking, or so I shall consider it, if we all do not die in the attempt. Very well. Shall we get on with it?"

"Unless you wish to stand here all night, prosing on about our chances of meeting our Maker," Christian grumbled, grabbing Gabrielle by the elbow and motioning for everyone to gather close for instructions.

Instructions which he, rather than the Peacock, gave. Didn't he realize how strange that might seem to her, to the men he had gathered to undertake Sal's rescue? But yet, Gabrielle thought consideringly, how easily explained if anyone should ask. The Peacock was the acknowledged leader, but he was not the sort to trouble himself in explaining ideas and stratagems he had undoubtedly formulated, then turned over to his lesser officers—much in the way the great Wellington planned attacks but did not ride out with each of his captains.

Yet Kit's instructions, although fairly clear, fell short of completeness, as they held no mention of the

Peacock. So what, if anything, would that man be doing this night? Hopefully nothing to do with cutting a dash on horseback.

"O'Dell," Christian said, the serious tone of his voice calling Gabrielle back to attention, "you will lead Peg to the square, point her in the right direction, and then work your way around the square to meet with me behind the jail. Jackey, have you got everything ready?"

"Aye, that Oi does," the man answered, nodding his head vigorously. "Oi'm ta get m'self ta the High Street, then count ta ten onct fer each o' me dabblers, and onct ta ten fer each o' me toes, then strike the flints an' hie m' dewbeaters 'ome ta tuck m'self inta bed."

"You know, if friend Jackey here has less than ten fingers and ten toes, it could set our timing off badly," the Peacock remarked conversationally, causing Gabrielle to giggle nervously, for she knew it would soon be time for her to make good on her promise to help free Sal.

"Good man," Christian congratulated Jackey, then turned to the Peacock. "If there is something else you'd like to say," he drawled in a quiet voice strangely tight and tense, "I shouldn't think to hinder you. Please, Master Peacock, regale us with anything that comes to mind. We are all breathless to hear your pearls of wisdom."

"No," the Peacock answered calmly, dramatically flinging one side of his black cloak up and over his shoulder in the way of Drury Lane heroes—and villains. "I believe I'm finished—for now."

"Kin we be gettin' on wit' this?" Lenny asked, looking about him as if certain a troop of the King's men would be marching into the small clearing at any moment. "Ye're loik two old biddies scratchin' at each an' other, an' it's beginnin' ta wear on me sumthin' terrible."

Christian looked at each one of them in turn, his gaze lingering longest on the Peacock, whom Lenny was helping back into the saddle. "All right," he said at last, sounding so reluctant that Gabrielle wondered wildly if Elizabeth would be kind enough to pay to have her friend's body driven home to Rose Hill Farm and buried in her best gown, and not these colorful rags. "We're off!"

The next thing Gabrielle knew, she was being dragged through a small stand of prickly bushes and into a dark alleyway smelling of urine and rotting garbage. From there, O'Dell pulled her through miniature yards composed of packed dirt and the occasional weed, turning this way and that until she was certain they were traveling in circles.

She snagged her sleeve on a drainpipe, her arm stinging from the resulting cut, as the Irishman squeezed her hand, warning her to be silent as they skirted one ramshackle hovel after another until, more breathless than frightened, she was standing at the side of one of the houses, looking out into the square.

"There's the guardhouse, an' don't ye know," O'Dell whispered in her ear as she bent to hear him, the smell of his breath making her believe that Christian's breath, when he had spoken to her back at the cottage, had been that of a bouquet of spring lilacs. "There be a pair of buggers at the front, whilst two more are coolin' their 'eels 'round back. Ain't much of a jail, ye ken, an' nobody's inside save Sal. The others are 'angin' 'round somewheres, peekin' out from behind windows an' the loik, watchin' fer ta snaggle the Peacock, an' them's the ones we're worrit about. Yer ta be takin' care o' the ones in front. Iffen we doesn't gets that there door open, or gets the keys, the jig'll be up fer sure."

Gabrielle nodded. "I know what I have to do, Mr. O'Dell. I simply have to entice them," she said, wishing her voice wouldn't quaver so. Her mission was quite cut and dried, actually. How difficult could it be? After all, she had stared down Lady Ariana Tredway and run a rig on the entire *ton*. Anything less should be mere child's play.

"Don't know 'bout no 'ticing, luv," O'Dell answered. "They'll be on the lookout fer trouble, so ye'll most likely 'ave ta show 'em yer wares ta get 'em waggin' after ye."

"Show them my wares?"

O'Dell roughly grabbed at her bodice, pulling down until Gabrielle's breasts nearly came free. "Yer wares, luv. Yer apple dumplin' shop. Christ on a crutch, Oi shulda 'ad m' missus run the rig, loik Kit asked me to, 'ceptin' she's fat as a vicar, an' ain't gots but two teeth. Now git on wit ye. Oi gots ta make m' way 'round back afore Jackey's done countin'.'"

So saying, O'Dell gave Gabrielle a mighty shove in the small of her back, catapulting her out into the torch-lit square. She staggered to a stop, squared her shoulders, silently reminded herself that she had asked—begged—for this assignment, and began to walk.

Her steps were slow at first, and reminiscent of a young debutante carefully threading her way past the assessing gazes of the patronesses at Almacks, but she soon realized her mistake. Taking a deep breath, she placed one hand on her hip and used the other to hold onto her skirt, waving its fullness back and forth as she began to saunter, head up, hips loose, toward the small brick guardhouse and the two guards that stood at the front door.

"Coo! Would ye look at that, Willy? Ain't she a rare treat!" one of the pair of guards said, poking his mate with one elbow. "'ow'd ye loik a piece o' that? M' breeches are gettin' tight, no mistake!"

"Shut up, Hackett, an' stick yer poppin' daylights back in yer head," Willy admonished, although he did lower his rifle so that the butt was on the ground as he looked at Gabrielle. "It'd be more 'an our hides be worth ta e'en think 'bout it."

Lord, but these men were ugly. And big. And dirty. *But definitely interested,* Gabrielle decided, smiling. She'd have to examine her feelings once this was over and decide if she really did harbor the makings of a loose woman. She didn't think so, but she did rather enjoy play-acting.

"Evenin', lads," she called out as she drew closer, winking in the way of Lord Osgood and hoping she looked more intriguing than he did when he indulged in the exercise. "Oi 'ears ye gots m' sister Sal locked up in 'ere. Lugged m'self all the way from East Chippwick, so worrited Oi wuz. All but raised me, Sal did, an' Oi loves 'er dearly. Taught me all Oi knows, iffen ye take m' drift. Now why'd ye go an' do such a sorry thing?"

"Yer sister, is it? That old bawd?" Willy asked, while running his eyes over Gabrielle's body in an openly assessing way. "Then ye should know her's bin runnin' loose with the Peacock. She'll be goin' to Lunnon when the cock crows, ta be hanged, no doubt."

"Speakin' o' cocks, Willy—an' 'angin'," Hackett slid in, rubbing at his crotch, "wot say we . . ."

Gabrielle felt herself blanching at the guard's crude gesture. But, as she had left it rather late to rethink her impetuous adventure into the seamier side of life, she only stepped forward another pace and pushed her shoulders together, knowing that the movement exposed more of her breasts—or her "apple dumpling shop," as O'Dell had so rudely put it. *Not too close, Gaby,* she warned herself silently. *Remember what Lenny said: Close enough to see, not close enough to touch.*

"Primed fer a tumble, are ye, ducks?" she questioned him, her smile hurting her cheeks. "'ow long ye bin standin' 'ere, guardin' sich a terrifyin' blackguard as m' sweet sister? Could ye be needin' a little rest," she went on, raising her spread hands to cup her breasts, "mayhap a little lie-down on a soft cushion?"

Willy and Hackett exchanged looks, Willy wetting his lips with a lascivious swipe of his fat tongue, Hackett rubbing at the back of his neck and grimacing, before the latter said, "We could take turns, Oi suppose. Tain't loik Sal'll be goin' anywheres."

Now was her chance to recite her carefully learned lines! "Turns, is it?" Gabrielle sniped, turning her back. "Loik Oi'd turn a tumble with both o' ye. One's enuf fer lettin' me take a peek at dear Sal. Oi come ta see m' lovin' sister, an' not ta spend all m' time with m' back pressed agin' the cobbles."

She wheeled about, sliding her tongue around the circle of her opened, lewdly smiling lips the way Lenny had taught her, deliberately concentrating her gaze on Willy, who had the key to the door hanging from a string tied around his thick waist. "Now 'ere's a thought, mates. Wot say we goes inside? Oi'll gets ta see Sal, and we all kin 'ave us a rare time?"

"We cain't do that," Willy protested, looking to Hackett as if begging for his agreement, as Gabrielle gave a silent sigh of relief. "'e told us not ta open the door fer any save 'im."

"'im?" Hackett shot back, the pair of them still

eyeing Gabrielle, who kept smiling as she rolled her bare shoulders invitingly a time or two, then trailed the middle finger of her left hand slowly down her throat and lower, until it pulled against the bodice of her blouse. "Christ on a crutch, did ye see that? An' yer wants me to be worrit about 'im? That crab lantern? An' where would 'im be, Willy? Apposed ta be inside, ain't 'e? But 'e's not. Oh, no. Whilst we're out 'ere coolin' our 'eels, 'e's with that puff guts, Symington, eatin' offa gold plates an' drinkin' Frenchie wine."

Sure that Hackett was referring to the leader of whatever men Sidmouth had sent to Little Pillington to capture the Peacock, and equally sure Willy and Hackett held no great love for the man, Gabrielle took a deep breath, mentally voiced a quick, silent prayer, and went to their second plan—and the one she secretly preferred—saying, "Well, iffen ye cain't, ye cain't. Poor old Sal will jist 'ave ta pine fer me, I suppose. Pity, ducks. Oi wuz so hopin' we could 'ave ourselves a spot of fun. Especially ye an' me, Willy," she said, winking once again. "Oi've taken a rare likin' ta yer, an' would do yer fer free, an' that's no lie."

So saying, she turned away once more and slowly— oh so slowly—began to walk toward the side of the guardhouse, knowing that somewhere in the dark, Sidmouth's men were watching.

Now, she thought as she turned the corner, her knees rapidly turning to jelly as she prayed Willy would soon follow after her. *Now it's Kit's turn. If I've done my job right, that is.*

She had taken no more than a dozen steps into the shadows beside the jail when a rough, hurtful hand came down on her shoulder and she suddenly felt as if her stomach would turn on her. Plan two had worked.

"'old it 'ere now a minute," she heard Willy say as he pulled her about roughly, agitatedly wrestling to free himself from his ragged pants even as he was shoving her up against the slimy brick wall. "Oi'll be takin' wot yer offered, luv, an' a bit more. No two-penny whore walks away from Willy Burns."

"No, but I'll wager they run fast enough," Christian drawled silkily as he pressed the business end of a pistol against the guard's neck. "That's a good lad, you keep those two hands just where they are, holding tight to the one thing you understand and would dearly hate to lose, while I relieve you of this," Christian continued just as pleasantly as he yanked the key free and tossed it over his shoulder to O'Dell, who caught it neatly.

"You—you're going to kill him?" Gabrielle asked as she slid her back down the brick wall and pushed herself sideways, removing her trembling body from Willy's proximity, and from his hateful stare.

"Only if he has touched you," Christian responded quietly, pushing the pistol so hard against Willy's neck that the guard began to whimper. "Has he touched you?"

Gabrielle began rapidly shaking her head. "N-no. No, he didn't," she said nervously, wondering if she lacked the blood lust all good avengers must have in good supply. "Please—don't kill him."

"Your smallest wish is my command, good lady," Christian replied, then placed his free hand on the back of the guard's head and neatly forced it into a quick, hard acquaintance with the brick wall. A moment later, an unconscious Willy Burns slid bonelessly to the ground. "Rest well, my friend," Christian said tightly. "You're a very lucky man.

O'Dell, drag him around back and lay him with his similarly sleeping comrades."

"And would ye be mindin' if Oi wuz ta gift 'im with jist a little kick first?" O'Dell asked as he handed Christian the key to the guardhouse. "Seein' as 'ow our Willy 'ere be one of Symington's rum coves, 'e oughta be used ta it."

"There's no time for personal pleasures, O'Dell," Christian cautioned, barely sparing a moment to look at Gabrielle, just as if he didn't care a fig for her, which she, feeling rather smug, knew not to be true. "Now," she heard him say as he barked out instructions to the Irishman, "you just take Peg back to the horses and wait for me there."

"Back to the horses?" Gabrielle was immediately incensed, forgetting that Kit had been ready to do murder for her. "Oh no you don't! You can't fob me off like that. I didn't come all this way to miss the fun."

Christian roughly grabbed her arm, treating her no more gently than he had Willy a few moments earlier. "I also don't have time for one of your tantrums now, Gaby," he warned her, forgetting to address her as "Peg." "I have to get out front and engage the remaining guard in conversation before he decides to come looking for his friend and Sidmouth's men become suspicious. Our alternate plan worked well, but the door isn't open yet, remember? Jackey's little diversion will be ready in about two minutes, and I want you completely clear of the area before—"

A loud explosion shook the ground beneath their feet, effectively cutting off Christian's arguments, and they turned as one to see flames shooting into the air about three hundred yards away along the High Street.

"Shoulda checked Jackey's toes, Oi expects," O'Dell remarked, scratching his head. "Coo!" he exclaimed, watching the fire grow toward the rooftop of the largest house bordering a lane just to the right of the High Street. "Ye wuz right, guv'nor. That there stuff ye gave Jackey sure 'nough makes a grand mess o' noise and fire!"

Gabrielle, whose gaze was likewise glued to the gigantic blaze, felt herself being rudely pushed into the Irishman's arms as Christian grabbed the key and bolted for the front of the guardhouse. He was not the lone running man, however, for bodies seemed to pour by the dozens out from dark doorways and rapidly opened windows, everyone racing toward the burning building.

"Sidmouth's men," O'Dell told her, pushing her flat against the wall and standing beside her, his own body flattened against the bricks. "Runnin' loik rabbits, ain't they, ta save that bugger, Symington. Shall we stay a bit an' watch?"

Gabrielle nodded furiously, her breath coming so fast she couldn't trust her voice. She had never been so close to danger before this night, and while she knew herself to be frightened almost beyond measure, she would rather have died than turn away.

By now Christian had taken Hackett out of the game and used the keys to slip inside the guardhouse to retrieve Sal. And then what? Getting Sal freed was all she knew of the project, and what would come next was as much a mystery to her as it must be to the multitude of Sidmouth's men and ordinary villagers racing to quell the blaze that was once Herbert Symington's impressive townhouse.

All was madness, the night filled with shouts and running feet and the crackle and roar of ever-building flames. And then, swimming against the rising tide of humanity, there appeared a tall, dark man: a man supporting his one arm with the other as he threaded his way through the crowd, shouting orders to the air—for no one was listening.

"Go back! Go back, you fools!" he shouted as he attempted to use his body to block any more of his men from deserting their posts. "It's a ruse! It's nothing but a ruse!"

Lord Buxley. Gabrielle would have recognized his voice anywhere, even though his handsome features showed black with soot and his fine London clothes were hanging from his tall body in tatters.

"'e's with that puff guts, Symington, eatin' offa gold plates an' drinkin' Frenchie wine." That's what Hackett had said. Good lord! She'd known Jackey had been sent to blow up Herbert Symington's house— but with Symington and Lord Buxley still inside? This *was* a serious business!

She continued to watch as Lord Buxley pushed and shoved his way through the growing confusion, doggedly moving toward the guardhouse, a pistol now in his right hand, his left hanging useless by his side.

But even one pistol was enough to destroy Gabrielle's world.

Where was Christian? He should have been back by now, Sal in tow. Was he having trouble with the key? Had Sal been tied up inside her cell? Damn the man for a lollygagging idiot! What was taking him so long?

"I've got to help Kit!" Gabrielle shouted above the din, pushing herself away from the wall before O'Dell could stop her. Picking up her skirts, she ran out into the square as fast as she could, deliberately aiming herself at the injured side of Lord Buxley's staggering body.

The collision was horrific, sending both Gabrielle and Lord Buxley sprawling to the ground.

And then, as more and more of the rushing throng moved out of the square and toward Symington's burning house . . . as the earl sat on his rump and held his arm while he cursed . . . and as Gabrielle did her best to crawl away, hiding her face behind the curtain of her hair . . . two black-clad horsemen rode into the square.

Everything that had already happened had happened quickly, but now time stood still as Christian emerged from the guardhouse, a mousy-looking woman of indeterminate years in tow. Lifting her high against his chest, he ran toward the horsemen and hefted Sal up and over the saddle of the second horse, where she lay head-down, legs dangling, as Christian gave a hard slap to the horse's rump.

"It's the Peacock! It's the Peacock!" someone began yelling, and the few people who still had not followed the crowd to view the fire began raising a cheer as the pair of horsemen turned about and dashed off the way they had come—one carrying his precious bundle, the other holding onto the reins with both hands as he bounced and swayed in the saddle.

Gabrielle shook her head as she raised herself fully to her knees, marveling at the sight of England's supposed hero even as she was disappointed at this particular Peacock's lack of horsemanship, then felt herself being unceremoniously hauled to her feet.

"Obstinate woman!" Christian exploded, his grotesquely disguised features drawn into an evil sneer as he delivered a sharp kick to Lord Buxley's shoulder, sending the earl onto his back on the cobblestones. He reached behind his back and drew out a single peacock feather, which he held with two fingers, then allowed to float down onto Lord Buxley's inert form before he employed those same fingers to give Gabrielle's arm a rough tug. "Come on!"

They ran back into the darkness beyond the almost day-bright light from the fire, joining with O'Dell and following him back through the maze of houses and to the spinney. By the time Christian let go of her hand, Gabrielle was totally out of breath, her sides stabbed with knives of pain, her poor feet bruised from the cobblestones and the rough terrain they had covered.

"I—I need to—to rest," she gasped out, leaning against her horse. Her arm was stinging from her cut, she had nearly been mauled by a filthy brute, she had been running for what seemed like days, she hurt in places she hadn't known she possessed, and even the thought of riding another hour through the night was totally beyond her. She needed to sit down, to rest herself, just for a few moments. Was that too much to ask?

Apparently it was.

"Later, Gaby," Christian bit out testily, showing her no pity—and no thanks for most probably saving his miserable life, now that she had a moment to think about it. "Now get up on that saddle before I toss you over it."

"How I loathe you," she whispered, not caring that she couldn't find the eloquence to be more original in her declaration as she glared up at him through the tangle of her hair.

"Yes, I know," he answered, making a foothold of his cupped hands so that she could mount her horse. "We'll discuss your penchant for redundancy later as well. O'Dell, hie yourself home or, better yet, find

Jackey and join the brigade trying to put out the fire. And remember: Not a word of this night's work to anyone."

"Nary a peep will they 'ear from me," O'Dell said firmly as Christian mounted his stallion. "Godspeed ta yer, sir, and thankee—Oi 'ad me a right fine time this night. A right fine time!"

They had traveled back to the cottage in silence, Christian leading the way but turning often to check on Gabrielle, fearful she might tumble from her saddle in fatigue.

She had been magnificent tonight, and they could not have succeeded half so easily without her assistance in getting the key to the guardhouse before the explosion—and the very real possibility that the guard would run off to see the fire, taking the key with him. But Christian was still berating himself for having agreed to take her along.

Especially now, now that he could not be sure that Buxley hadn't seen her, hadn't recognized her beneath her disguise as she had knocked him down. A person, Christian knew, saw what he expected to see, and the earl certainly could not have been expecting to see London's newest and most beautiful Society sensation in Little Pillington—but he could not be sure.

He had been right to determine that the game must end now. He had taken his last chance with fate, played his last hand at the table of adventure and derring-do. Seeing Gabrielle in the clutches of that brutish guard, watching as she daringly hurled her body at Buxley in a stupid but brave attempt to save him—it aged a man.

Maybe even matured him.

There had been no deaths yet, but tonight's adventure had once and for all time proved to Christian the very real possibility that there could be, and soon. He could no longer ignore the warnings of his friends or allow himself to believe that he could accept the deaths of Sal, or O'Dell, or even Lord Buxley as no more than a means to an end. Violence came too easily once allowed the opportunity to enter one's life. It had taken everything in Christian, every scrap of humanity he still retained, to ease his finger away from the trigger as he'd held his pistol to the guard's throat.

He had taken the precaution of buying off Symington's servants so that they left his house a good ten minutes before Jackey lit the fuses outside the kitchen door, but he had turned a blind eye to the possibility that Symington, sure to be snug in his drawing room at the front of the house, might have died in the explosion. Symington and, it would appear, Lord Anthony Buxley himself, who must have set out his guards and then retired to the mill owner's townhouse for a convivial evening while brutes like Willy did the real work for him.

No deaths, yet. All successes, so far.

But now it was over. There would be no march on Symington's townhouse now. There *was* no townhouse now, in point of fact, a thought that had tickled Christian when he had first considered his plan for this evening. Besides, it was more than likely Symington had been injured along with Buxley, and he would be in no condition to meet with any marchers come to give him a list of their grievances.

Unless he was dead. No, Christian decided as he rode into the stable yard and dismounted, men like Symington don't die so easily. Like maggots, like cockroaches, they always find a way to survive, all their ugliness of mind and spirit still intact. What a pity that the Peacock, retired as of this moment, would not be able to personally show Herbert the way to real salvation.

"Let me help you," Christian said, approaching Gabrielle, who was still sitting atop her horse, her head dropped forward onto her chest in exhaustion.

She handed over the reins and reached out her arms to him, sliding out of the saddle, her knees buckling as her feet found the ground. "I want a bath," she whispered as she lay her head against his chest, probably too tired to remember how much she hated him. "Please, Kit. I feel so dirty."

He rubbed his cheek against the tangle of her hair, molding her close to him as he massaged her slim back, trying to ease some of her fatigue. "There's no tub in the cottage," he told her as he picked her up and walked across the stable yard, sure the tired horses would wander no farther than the water trough or the hay feeder. "We do, however, have a small, fairly deep pond nearby."

"Anything. A pot, a bowl, a pond," Gabrielle breathed against his chest. "If I can't wash I'd rather die now than sleep."

Gabrielle in the pond? He and Gabrielle *alone* in the night, naked in that night?

Lenny still had to return Frapple to his coach and safely deliver Sal to a posting inn for her journey north tomorrow morning before he could return to the cottage and see to the horses. Then the former jockey would go straight to his room at the rear of the stables, for the last thing Lenny would have on his mind tonight, as it would be any other night, was personal cleanliness. No one would disturb Gabrielle and himself at the pond. No one would come looking for them.

Oh, he was going to hell when he died, Christian knew—straight to a blistering-hot hell.

He gently deposited Gabrielle on the wooden bench just outside the cottage door, tersely ordering, "Stay here," before he raced inside to quickly gather up a collection of toiletries, towels, and fresh clothing for them both before he could change his mind. Before he could remember that he was a gentleman, and above such tawdry things as the seduction of innocents.

"Come with me," he said, holding out a hand to Gabrielle in order to help her rise, then he carefully picked his way through a darkness broken only by the stars and a helpful full moon, locating and following the narrow dirt path that led to the pond.

It was the ideal setting for a seduction, although Christian had been bathing there for months without ever seeing the possibilities for romance in the shadows of nearby willows that darkened the water, or the croaking of frogs and the chirping of crickets that lent an air of fantasy to the place.

He opened the blanket he had used to bundle up the clothing and spread it on the grassy ground, motioning for Gabrielle to sit down, which she did.

He then lifted her left foot into his hand, gently removed her battered slipper, and motioned for her to raise her right foot so that he could perform a similar service for it, which she did.

Swallowing down hard on his rising excitement— born partly from the heady adventure he had just engaged in, but mostly coming to life through his proximity to the woman he loved, wanted, desired above all things—he stripped off his eye patch and wig and slid out of his ragged cloak and peasant shirt before motioning for Gabrielle to stand up once more, which she did.

He reached out slowly, careful not to startle her, and untied the bright green sash that accentuated her slim waist, slipping it from her body and slinging it around his bare throat.

He raised a hand to the bodice of her peasant blouse and tugged on one end of the string holding it closed, easing it loose inch by tantalizing inch, until the bow she had tied there came free.

And that's when Gabrielle's fatigue-engendered compliance with what Christian had in mind disappeared in the flash of light bursting behind his eyes that accompanied her hard slap to the side of his blond head.

"I said I wanted to bathe, my lord," she bit out angrily, clutching her gaping bodice over her nearly bare breasts. "I did not say I wished to *be* bathed! Thank heaven the smell of garlic roused me, or heaven only knows what other liberties you might have taken."

Her words, as well as her slap, brought Christian momentarily back to his senses, and he remembered that he was still the possessor of darkened skin, a few warts, green teeth, and the remnants of garlic that remained tucked between cheek and gums.

"My apologies, Gabrielle," he said, stepping away from her and removing the garlic, throwing it into the bushes before searching through the mound of clothes to find the tooth powder and a piece of soap. "I'll take my offensive self off to the other side of this willow tree. Its branches reach all the way into the water and will serve as an effective curtain, I imagine."

Gabrielle looked past him, obviously gauging the thickness of the branches and the amount of concealment their leaves might lend her, before nodding and saying, "Oh, very well, Kit. And only because I want so much to be clean. I only wish there were not a full moon. Just don't come back until I tell you. *Promise* me, Kit."

Christian made a small ceremony of crossing his heart with his right hand. "Upon my honor, madam," he said, bowing. "And now, with your kind permission—"

"Oh, go away!" Gabrielle ordered, already searching for a piece of soap in the small pile. "I'm beginning to think Willy had fleas and some of them hopped from him to me, seeking a fresher meal."

Five minutes later, having carefully removed his warts and the running sore that had been on his left hand, then cleaned his teeth and face, Christian was just about to ease his naked body into the pond—praying it would be cold enough to soothe his burning body—when he heard Gabrielle call out his name.

"Yes, my dear?" he called back hopefully, knowing himself to be a pitiful specimen, ready to beg for any crumbs of her attention.

"Stay where you are. I have a question. How deep is this pond?" she asked him from beyond the curtain of willow leaves.

"Do you swim?" Christian asked her in turn, beginning to smile. The number of females who when immersed into deep water would not sink like stones was very few.

"*No,* I do not swim," Gabrielle replied testily from the dark. "Oh, Kit, this is entirely stupid!" she wailed. "And I wanted so to bathe!"

The gods were smiling down on Christian, he was certain of it. "I have an idea, Gabrielle, if you're interested," he put out helpfully.

"Go on," her voice came back to him, sounding reluctant but resigned.

"Look out over the pond, Gaby," he told her as he took up his soap and eased into the water soundlessly, "to where the moonlight seems to raise up in a bump on top of the water. That's a rock, a very large rock. When you first step into the pond, the water will be as high as your knees—if I might be so personal. But there is a sort of shelf not five feet from the bank. From that point to the rock, which is a bare twenty feet away from the shore, the water will be deeper than either you or I are tall. But this is the only area of the pond not clogged with water lilies that could tangle around your legs and pull you down."

"Then I can't go in," she told him. "What if I slipped? I haven't lived through this night only to drown, Kit."

"Indeed, no," Christian replied, wetting, then lathering his body as rapidly as possible. "But if you were to walk into the water very slowly, very carefully, you could then sink to your shoulders nearer the shore, and I could enter the water without, um, without your modesty being offended. That way, we could both bathe, and I could swim close enough to offer you assistance if you were to slip."

"Oh, no. Oh no, oh no-no-*no*. I think not, Baron St. Clair."

Christian counted slowly to ten as he rubbed the soap across his bare chest and lower, only the croaking frogs and chirping crickets breaking the tense silence, before he smiled in the darkness and asked plaintively, "Don't you trust me, Gaby?"

"To indulge my failing for redundancy—in a word, no. In two words—definitely not," she answered, but her voice lacked conviction. "I don't need any further lessons in playing the fallen woman, Kit," she reminded him after a moment. "Tomorrow I meet with the Peacock, and then I return to London."

"Still intent upon being one of his assistants, I see," Christian said, slipping fully into the pond and pushing himself out into deeper water in order to rinse himself clean. "I commend you on your courage."

"Well, don't," she answered sadly. "I have done some silly things in my life, Kit, including trying to foist my near penniless self on the *ton,* but this latest adventure bears off the palm. I am retiring from intrigue as of this moment, and I can't say I'm sorry. I think I'll return to Rose Hill Farm with Lizzie and knit socks for the local orphans. It might make only a small difference, but at least I will be helping, and not indulging my own girlish fantasies of adventure. And something else, Kit: I don't believe I like the Peacock half so much now that I've seen him up close and heard him speak. He takes all the glory while you do all the work. It doesn't seem fair, does it? Now, tell me again how I can bathe in private with you sharing the pond?"

So much for his jealousy of the Peacock—or Frapple, who, in Christian's opinion, had made a passable if not particularly graceful Peacock.

Christian smiled in the darkness, submerging himself and his soaped head, only to come back to the surface a moment later, refreshed, renewed, and grateful that it had not taken his beloved as long as it had taken himself to learn that rash acts of revolution were no real answer to their country's problems.

"You know what you have to do, Gaby," he said,

speaking quietly so that she could not know that he was near the rock now, and could clearly see her standing at the edge of the pond, her hair hanging darkly past her shoulders to hide her breasts, a towel protecting her nakedness but not covering one delicious sweep of hip, nor concealing the glory of her long, straight legs.

"Yes. Yes, Kit, I do know what I have to do," she said after another short silence. "But don't come into the water yourself until I say that you might."

Still, Gabrielle continued to linger between commitment and commission for long moments more before slowly dropping the towel, exposing her body to his grateful gaze.

Christian nearly slipped beneath the water as his knees buckled in reaction to the sight of her naked body glowing in the moonlight, the sweet perfection of her breasts, the narrow span of her waist, the bewitching shadow at the apex of her thighs.

His breathing became labored as she stepped slowly into the water, easing her way into its coolness until it reached just past her knees, bending to splash water onto her arms, her shoulders. And when she began to soap herself, spread smooth white lather onto her graceful throat, over those perfect breasts, and lower, Christian knew he was on the verge of most happily, willingly, losing what was left of his mind.

Gabrielle stepped deeper into the pond, lowering herself until she could, by dint of tipping her head from side to side, wet her hair.

Watching her work the soap into that hair, looking on hungrily while she lifted her arms to wash away the memory of her sojourn into the world Sal and her sisters of the night regularly inhabited, Christian could see Gabrielle beginning to relax, to regain her youth, her innocence, her energies that had been so taxed these past days.

He would be a cad to approach her now, kiss her now, hold her now. Take her now.

And then, just as he was about to turn away, to swim to the middle of the pond and do his best to drown himself, Gabrielle raised her hands high above her head, palms together, and threw herself face-forward into the deep water, submerging out of sight!

"Gaby!" he called out frantically, pushing away from the rock and swimming furiously to the place where he had last seen her, only to feel something tug at his ankle before he was pulled under the water.

Both broke the surface at the same time, Christian angry and sputtering, Gabrielle laughing and looking extraordinarily pleased with herself. "Did you think I didn't know you were out there, Kit? As if I was such a simpleton as not to notice that your voice was coming from near the rock. Did you enjoy yourself, *watching?*"

"I don't believe it!"

"And so easily hoodwinked, dear baron," she continued in easily recognized glee not at all tinged with shyness. "I've been swimming for years. It serves you right, you know, telling me to *trust* you! Oh, and by the bye, I think I'd like to be married from St. George's, my sweet darling lech. You'll be a vision in your groom's clothes, although I shall find a way to outshine you, I'm sure."

"You thorough minx! I ought to strangle you," Christian gritted out from between clenched teeth as he lay his hands on her shoulders, then pushed her under the water once more.

She resurfaced some yards away from him, her laughter mingling with the chirping of the crickets.

How he loved her! How he had always loved her, from the first moment he had seen her. She was his soulmate, his other half—the two of them so alike that they'd had no other choice than to take an instant, if temporary, dislike to each other.

While he'd played at fop, she had played at debutante, when they were both, in reality, scoundrels of the highest calling—living their lives as they wished, flouting convention, daring everything for adventure, seeing life as it should be, and not as it was.

No wonder she had intrigued him, no wonder she had angered him.

No question that he had frustrated her, no question that she had wished to see him as she imagined him, wished him, to be.

Christian struck out after her as she swam away, his strong arms and kicking legs cutting swiftly through the water until he could capture her calf and pull her back to him, pull her tight to him, hold her slippery body close against his. He drank in the sight of her heavy wet hair sleekly shaping her skull, the way the moonlight kissed her glistening features, the sight of her moisture-heavy eyelashes spiking thickly around her emerald-green eyes.

"Kiss me, St. Clair," she ordered breathlessly, keeping herself above the water by entwining her arms and legs around his long body. "Kiss me . . . and hold me . . . and teach me. But first, please, my darling Kit—tell me how much you love me."

His longer legs soon helped him find purchase on the pond's muddy bottom, and he held her tightly as he began making his way toward the shore, only slightly hampered by her insistence upon alternately stroking his bare shoulders and running her fingers through his wet hair.

"I love you, Miss Gabrielle Laurence," he told her seriously, wondrously, gratefully. "I love you beyond words, my darling Gaby, beyond actions, beyond my own comprehension. You're my life, my love, and the most beautiful woman in the entire world."

Then he grinned and drawled in his best London accents, "But, blister me, madam, I can't see as how you'll ever outshine me."

"Beast!" Gabrielle exclaimed, laughing as Christian lowered her onto the spread blanket, quickly following her down, unwilling to leave her for even a moment. "But I suppose it's true. Even without your satins and lace, you are the most beautiful creature on earth. *Especially* without your satins and lace."

"Hardly, my love," Christian responded, beginning to nibble her ear as he gently stroked her flaring hip with one hand.

He wanted to go slowly, rouse Gabrielle gradually, without frightening her, without hurting her more than he had to. With nothing between them but the water that still clung to their bodies, and with none save the frogs and the crickets to disturb them, he knew he had all night to introduce Gabrielle to the wonders of lovemaking.

There was no reason for haste, no impediment to a leisurely loving.

Save one.

"Kit, please!" she cajoled him, shifting her body so that it lay partly beneath him as he balanced himself on his side, doing his best to play the gentleman. "I'm shameless, I know it. But I have already done everything but give myself to you. Please. Please—take me. Take me now, so that I can know what you know."

The last vestiges of gentlemanly behavior deserted Christian at that moment, any remaining scruples concerning innocent misses and their sensibilities flying to the four winds as he swooped down on Gabrielle, capturing her mouth with his own.

Their arms tangled as their hands roved, their legs intertwined as Gabrielle raised herself to his touch and Christian lowered himself between her thighs, holding back only at the final moment, that last threshold he must cross before the girl he held could become the woman he would make her.

And then all the barriers were gone.

All their protective social façades were down, washed away on the waves of passion.

All their hungers leaped to the front of their combined consciousness, and they melded together, moved together, flew to the stars together.

His tongue dueling with hers . . .

His fingers at her nipple, hers tangling into his long hair . . .

Her heels digging into the small of his back . . .

His manhood pushing against the gateway of her womb, filling her, heating her, spilling life to beget life, to complete the bond their love had forged.

Taking . . . giving . . . loving.

She was a strumpet, he was a thief.

CHAPTER 14

Odd's fish! you are a bloodthirsty young ruffian.
Do you want me to make a hole in a law-biding man?

Baroness Orczy

She was at the pond again, sitting on the mossy bank with her breeches rolled past her knees and her bare toes dangling in the water, clearly not eager to return to her confining gowns and the social strictures incumbent upon her gentler sex.

She had taken to shirts and breeches with the same ease she had taken to the water. With the same ease she had taken to Society, to intrigue, to play-acting, and even to making love.

Gabrielle Laurence. His sweet, sharp Gaby. She was a puzzle never to be solved, the sum of her parts never to be cataloged and counted, never to be fully understood. Haughty one moment, playfully, exotically seductive the next, Christian never knew which Gabrielle Laurence he would find when next they met.

He knew only that he loved all the Gabrielles there were, and that the love he carried in his heart for her would never grow old.

" 'When I approach her loveliness, so absolute she seems, and in herself complete, so well to know her own, that what she wills to do or say seems wisest, virtuousest, discretest, best; all higher knowledge in her presence falls degraded. Wisdom in discourse with her loses, discount'nanc'd, and like folly shows,' " he quoted softly as he stood behind her, watching the dappled sunlight plant fiery kisses in her unbound hair.

Gabrielle leaned her weight back on her outstretched arms and tilted her head to look up at him. "And don't you ever forget it, dear baron," she teased, then sat forward and patted the ground beside her, wordlessly commanding that he sit down. "John Milton, if I remember rightly. Are you practicing your foppish Society manners in preparation for our return to London?"

Christian reclined on his side, his head propped on one hand. No, she didn't wish to go back, to end this wonderful idyll. But, then, neither did he.

"Do we have to go back, Gaby?" he asked, intrigued by the way his white shirt became a thing of beauty when Gabrielle wore it, the discreet slit caused by the two opened buttons at the neck showing him a hint of creamy cleavage, a tantalizing promise of hidden fruit that tied a delicious knot of hunger deep in his gut. "Faith, woman, but I'd just as lief remain here in the country, indulging in simple pleasures."

"Indeed?" Gabrielle turned on her side to face him, reaching out a hand to push his blond hair behind his ear, then trace the line of his jaw before pressing her fingertips to his lips for his kiss. "And you don't miss your satins and lace, your ranking as premier dandy of all Mayfair? You aren't longing to create a new fashion or flatter another hostess with your exalted presence?"

"Not in the slightest, my love," Christian told her sincerely, then took hold of her wrist so that he could keep her close, beginning to suckle lightly on each of her fingertips in turn as he gazed deeply into her eyes. His adoration of her slim fingers complete, he smiled at her, adding, "I much prefer playing at Adam and Eve in our bucolic paradise, although I believe both of us are wearing entirely too many clothes."

"True," Gabrielle countered, withdrawing her hand. "But I don't believe Adam and Eve had to deal with a chaperone like Lenny. He told me just this morning that he'd blacken both your devil eyes if you didn't soon get me to the nearest autem bawler and make me your whither-go-ye. An 'autem bawler's' a minister, Kit, and the latter is a rather poetic way of saying 'wife,' in case you aren't familiar with the terms. Terribly possessive, Lenny is, now that he's decided I'm a prime one. How I do love thieves' cant—it's so extraordinarily colorful!"

Christian shook his head, wondering what sort of punishment his Maker had planned for him for his corruption of this particular Innocent. "It's no wonder he and Grumble rub along together so famously. Two very disparate backgrounds, but the both of them no better than nervous old women, finding new ways to condemn me. Of course we're going to be married, Gaby. That's already settled."

"Yes, and it's almost a pity, for these last days have been the happiest in my life," she countered, levering herself into a sitting position. "Why, I believe I enjoy being a fallen woman."

Christian knelt behind her, tickling the side of her slim throat with a long blade of grass. "And you succeed very well in the role, my love," he teased her. "However, if you promise to forget everything your mother ever taught you about being a dutiful, dull-as-ditch-water wife, I believe we shall not notice any great change in our union once it has been blessed by Society."

"But the breeches still will have to go, won't they?" she questioned him, pouting—the sight of her full bottom lip thrust out in mock despair bending his thoughts away from the necessity for their return to Mayfair before Lord Buxley's dinner party and toward indulging his inclination to invite her to another swim in the pond.

"As wife to the illustrious Baron St. Clair, you will of course be a trend-setter, but I do believe bringing ladies' breeches into fashion might be beyond even our combined consequence. Besides, dear heart, could you really wish to see Lady Cornwallis going down the dance in the clingy things?"

Gabrielle's giggle answered his question, but then she turned suddenly solemn, moving away from him yet again. "I know we haven't discussed it, but as we'll be returning to London as soon as I can say goodbye to our pond, I have to ask you something. I keep thinking about the dinner party planned for this evening. Do you think Lord Buxley recognized me the other night?"

It was out now, the question he'd been dreading. Christian reached up to pull off a slender length of willow branch and slowly began stripping it of leaves. "It was fairly dark, with only the light from the fire and a few torches to illuminate the square. The entire area was a near riot scene. Buxley was injured and looking toward the jail. . . ." He sighed. "I don't know, Gaby. I just don't know."

"But if he did?" Gabrielle asked, as she dried her feet with her stockings.

Christian could feel the cords in his neck tightening. "We can't be sure. Grumble hasn't come racing to the cottage to wring his hands, telling me that Buxley is raising a hue and cry in London for your arrest. But I know I wouldn't wished it bruited about that I had let an attack by a mere girl cause me to let the Peacock slip through my fingers, so I imagine the earl is keeping anything he knows very close to his vest."

"He must be hating himself for going to dine at Mr. Symington's and leaving others to follow his orders. I imagine he is not being congratulated by Lord Sidmouth for allowing Sal and the Peacock to escape. Will the person who captures the Peacock really be treated as a hero, as the earl believes? I know I had thought so when I planned to take much that same course myself, but now I'm not so sure. He is greatly admired, you know."

"So was Byron, my love. So was Brummell." Christian stripped off the last fragile leaf and flung the branch into the pond. "If the Peacock's pretty tail feathers were clipped, he wouldn't seem nearly so lovely a bird."

Gabrielle nodded her agreement, then ran a hand through her unbound hair. "I think Lord Buxley has to go, Kit. Lord Buxley, and Lady Ariana as well, while we're about it. They're too close, even though you've said the Peacock is to ride no more."

He pulled her close. "Feeling bloodthirsty, are you? How do you propose we dispense with them? Knives? Pistols? Fire and pestilence?"

She wrinkled her nose at his nonsense. "The Peacock does not kill—remember? And neither should his loyal followers." She raised her hand, measuring the space of a mere inch between her thumb and index finger. "But if we were to injure them in some way—only this much . . ."

"Sorry, Gaby," Christian told her, taking her hand in his. "They must be destroyed. Completely removed from the scene. Even though the Peacock will ride no more, Buxley and Ariana must be eliminated, simply because they're too suspicious and much too ambitious. Besides," he ended, pulling her down on top of him as he collapsed once more against the grass, "I don't like either one of them."

"You don't like them?" Gabrielle put her hands on either side of Christian's head, smoothing his blond hair close against his temples. "Well then, dear baron, our problem is solved! You will simply have to deal them both the cut direct, refusing to attend the earl's dinner party, then subjecting Lady Ariana to one of your withering stares through your quizzing glass before turning from her without so much as a nod. After all, if the great St. Clair refuses to acknowledge them, they might as well not exist."

"You over-rate my powers, darling," Christian said, busying himself in opening the remaining buttons on Gabrielle's borrowed shirt and slipping his hands inside to cup her breasts. "But don't worry. I already have a plan well in train. If Grumble and the others followed my instructions to the letter—you would be dazzled, no doubt, to know the entirety of my rather uniquely talented acquaintance—this evening should prove most interesting, whether Buxley dares to accuse you of treachery tonight or not."

"You already have a plan? And you're not going to tell me about it?" Gabrielle gave his hair a quick, painful tug. "I call that very poor sporting of you, Kit. Especially when it is I who could end up being dragged off to prison, and not you."

He lifted his head and pressed a quick kiss on her chin. "Ah, yes, my love, but then it is also you who is always on the lookout for new adventures. Just think: appearing in the dock, playing the role of tragedy queen as you are dragged, weeping copiously, to a dank cell deep in the bowels of—"

"Oh, do be quiet!" Gabrielle exploded, reaching between them to slap at his roving hands. *"Ouch!"* she exclaimed, rolling off him and quickly shaking her fingers before raising them to her mouth, to suck on one of her knuckles. "I hit my fingers against that dratted ring! It's so huge, and not even passably pretty. I've always wondered why you wear it."

Christian took off the ring and handed it to her, watching as she turned the dull silver this way and that, investigating the design impressed into it.

"Why, it's a spur, isn't it?" she asked, alternately inspecting the ring and frowning at him. "The design is rather crude, but I'm sure it's meant to be a spur. And there are two *R*s beneath it, twined together— and a date, 1685." She slipped the ring onto her thumb where it hung loosely, for it was indeed a large ring, and her fingers were long and slim. "This is very special to you, isn't it, Kit? Precious. I don't know why, but I can just feel it."

Sensing that any romantic interlude he might have been seeking was impossible at the moment, but grateful that she had turned away from the subject of Lord Buxley's necessary downfall, Christian propped himself up on his elbows and explained, "The initials stand for Richard Rumbold."

"Who?"

"I'm not sure exactly who he was or the precise nature of his crime," Christian explained, looking out over the still water of the pond, "but he was hanged in

1685. Before he died he was allowed a final statement. He said, 'I never could believe that Providence had sent a few men into the world, ready booted and spurred to ride, and millions ready saddled and bridled to be ridden.' "

He felt Gabrielle's eyes on him and turned to look at her. "I was born ready booted and spurred to ride, Gaby. Me, and the other chosen few whose birth and fortune set them above ordinary men. I made that ring myself when I was no more than sixteen, fashioning it out of a piece of one of the spurs my father gave me for my birthday, and I wear it to remember Richard Rumbold and the millions who had never asked to be saddled and ridden."

Gabrielle was quiet for some moments, so that Christian found himself embarrassed, feeling as if he were nothing more than a silly, romantic fool.

But then she took the ring from her thumb and reverently returned it to his finger. "I was wrong. It's a beautiful ring. The most beautiful ring I've ever seen. You make me feel so humble, Kit," she said quietly, tears beginning to well in her green eyes as she reached for the buttons of his shirt. "Oh, you darling, darling man—how I love you."

Another man might protest that he would be taking unfair advantage of a vulnerable, romantically inclined young lady in making love to her now.

But another man wasn't lying on this mossy bank, with Gabrielle's brilliant red curls cascading down onto his bare chest, or looking up into her shining eyes, witnessing her sweet smile turn bewitching as he concentrated his gaze on the delicious beauty mark beside her delectable mouth.

Another man couldn't feel her full, unbound breasts

pressing against his heated skin, or experience the grateful rapture he did as her clever hands made short work of the buttons of his breeches.

And another man never would.

"Gaby!" Christian exclaimed as her fingers closed around him, as her smile grew even more bewitching, more sensual and inviting.

"Yes, my love?" she asked, moving her body against him invitingly.

"Lenny's already getting the coach prepared," he reminded her, pulling her shirt free of her breeches as he turned her over onto her back, those breeches soon dangling from a single slim ankle. "We must leave for London within the hour if we're to attend the earl's dinner party."

Gabrielle was nibbling at Christian's throat as the fury of all the earth's oceans roared in his ears, and in moments he was sliding between her creamy thighs.

"Then I can only suggest you make haste, my lord," she whispered breathlessly between love bites. "I've heard it . . . on the highest authority . . . that one shouldn't . . . shouldn't keep one's horses standing. Oh, Kit. Oh, yes. Kit! *Ah, yes!*"

Gabrielle was once more where she had been only a few nights ago—a lifetime ago. Standing in the magnificent drawing room of Baron Christian St. Clair's Hanover Square mansion.

However, this time her gown was a Bond Street marvel of expensive ivory gauze over only barely blue silk—the soft clear color named "water of the Nile," or so Gabrielle had been told.

The bodice of the creation Christian had personally designed and commissioned without her knowledge had been cut in a wide scoop baring her shoulders above full, transparent gauze sleeves that nipped tightly around her wrists. The lightly flounced, bell-shaped skirt that dropped below her trim waist was slightly stiffened with buckram beneath the silk and cleared the ground by a good two inches, to reveal tiny heel-less slippers held in place by thin satin ribbons that laced around her shapely, daringly exposed ankles.

She wore a triple strand of pearls that clung snugly to her throat, a true Capri cameo nestled in sapphires sitting at its center. Long strands of matching pearls threaded through her fiery hair that had been heaped high on her head in curls, while a few thick ringlets also tumbled artfully down past her left ear and onto her shoulder. Small pearl drops banded in diamonds and sapphires were in her ears.

A fan fashioned of transparent ivory sticks strung with finest lace and her small reticule, a perfect match to the fan, hung from her wrists.

Gabrielle had spent the last two hours being bathed, powdered, perfumed, and dressed—and the results of all that labor by the St. Clair maids had been worth every minute of that time.

She looked beautiful, and she knew it.

She oozed confidence, from her lovely new silken undergarments to the tips of her slippers.

She was a creation of wealth, magnificent taste, and a man's love—the jewels shining in her eyes more brilliant than any mere precious stones, the glow of her love for Christian transcending the magnificence of the gown she wore.

So why was she standing here in this lovely drawing room, looking as if she could conquer any world, be mistress of any situation—and shivering inside with dread and the nearly overpowering inclination to run away to some place safe, and hide?

"Gaby! You look wonderful!" Elizabeth exclaimed as she entered the room. "I vow, George and I had our misgivings when the gown arrived this morning, but now I see there was no cause for worry. Those sleeves—so very original! St. Clair is a genius of invention. Thank the dear Lord you're home safely. Do you have a moment to talk before we must leave for Lord Buxley's, do you think? I am very much in need of reading you a stern lecture. I have, in point of fact, written out a long list of grievances, which is upstairs in my knitting basket, but I believe I have committed most of them to memory."

Gabrielle had already turned toward her friend, who was trailed closely by Lily. The little girl was so rounded and rosy-cheeked as to be almost unrecognizable. As Gabrielle had been hustled into the mansion by way of the kitchens, and then raced upstairs by a pair of giggling maids, she had not yet laid eyes on Elizabeth's small charge or her dear friend herself. "What a pleasant greeting, Lizzie. *'George,'* is it? Not 'Mr. Trumble'? Kit calls him 'Grumble,' by the way, which I believe to be an affectionate criticism. How have you two been rubbing along together? Rather well, I would suppose, if you are addressing him so informally. Hello, Lily. Aren't you looking fine as ninepence."

"Yes, ma'am, that I am, ma'am," the child chirped, dropping into a curtsy. "Thank you, ma'am." Lily then turned to Elizabeth. "Can I 'ave a sugarplum now, Mama? I did the pretty, just the way you told-ded me."

Elizabeth's sigh was more indulgent than long-suffering. "Of course you may, my darling. But remember, only one. Then you must go find Meg. She has promised to take you upstairs for your evening tea."

"Yes, Mama," Lily responded, dutifully lifting a single sugary confection from a crystal dish, then lightly skipping out of the drawing room as Elizabeth looked after her, an almost beatific smile lighting her increasingly pleasing face.

"It will take some time to break her of all her bad habits, but we are progressing," Elizabeth said, turning back to Gabrielle.

"She's wonderful, Lizzie," Gabrielle said, smiling, "and you're a grand teacher. To date, I would suppose I remain your single failure."

Elizabeth opened her mouth to answer, then seemed to think better of it, only sighing deeply and shaking her head before saying, "It's useless to point out how badly you frightened me, or to tell you that your actions were not those of a gently bred young lady. A midnight flit, indeed, and without so much as a note of explanation left behind for your dearest friend! And when that odious Lady Ariana came sniffing about and I was forced to invent yet another story, I thought—oh, fiddlesticks! As you seem to have landed on your feet—as you so often do—I don't suppose you'd listen to me anyway."

Gabrielle went over to her friend and kissed her cheek. "Ah, but I always listen to you, Lizzie," she said, laughing. "I simply don't do what you say. There is a difference."

"You also fib most outrageously," Elizabeth countered, wagging a finger at Gabrielle. "Penning me that ridiculous letter saying St. Clair took you to see the Peacock! You have come to believe your own vivid imaginings, Gaby. George and I laughed mightily at that, once I recovered from my shock at learning you and the baron had gone off alone and George brought Lily and me here to Hanover Square. Why, as I said to George, I could just as easily believe that he, or Lord Osgood, or even Sir Gladwin were in league with the Peacock as I could suppose that the baron knew the brave fellow. It is still difficult to believe that you once thought the baron *was* the Peacock! Were you very disappointed when you learned St. Clair had only been leading you on in order to get you away from Mayfair and declare his love?"

Clearly Elizabeth had not been let in on Christian's little secret, not if she could ask such questions. But then, Gabrielle supposed, deciding not to undeceive her, the less people who knew about St. Clair's secret, the better. Besides, Elizabeth seemed happy in her ignorance—and her romantic notions of a near elopement—and that was enough for now.

"I was devastated at first," Gabrielle said, inventing lies as she went along, "but then I realized Christian had only my best interests at heart. He wished me out of Society long enough to disabuse me of my fanciful notions, so that I would not end by making a cake of myself or—or some such thing. We, er, we spent a few perfectly wonderful days at his estate just outside the city, and I finally came to understand my conclusions had all been in error. Christian in league with the Peacock! And to wish to become one of the Peacock's band of followers? As if I could be of any help to the man! How could I have been so silly?"

Elizabeth frowned. "George said you were driven to Dover, to stay on the baron's yacht. He said there were chaperones in the form of servants and the like, although no one but I would believe you had not been compromised. As if even you would be so paper-skulled as to allow a man liberties before he has taken you to wife!"

Gabrielle's smile was blightingly bright as she mentally stripped Christian of several layers of skin for not having prepared her with the story he had concocted for Elizabeth's benefit. Why, he had probably only posted her letter to Elizabeth in order to demonstrate how necessary it was to remove the hysterical female from London before she publicly proclaimed herself an ally of the Peacock's!

"Yes, yes, that too, Lizzie. The yacht! We were almost constantly on the go. Here—there—*everywhere!* But enough of me." She took Elizabeth's hands and pulled her over to the couch. "Now tell me: Sits it serious between you and Mr. Trumble?"

Elizabeth's blush was a treat to see, flushing her usually pale skin a rosy red from her lace-trimmed throat to beyond the tops of her gold-rimmed spectacles. "George is a lovely man, Gaby. Oh, he is not nearly so handsome as the baron, I'll admit—with his nose too large by half, and his ongoing but losing battle with his love of sugarplums—but he is vastly appealing to me. His body, well, it looks lived in—comfortable. He makes me comfortable."

Gabrielle nodded as if she understood what her friend was saying, but she admitted to herself that she didn't feel in the least comfortable when she was with Christian. Excited. Alive. Adventurous. Wonderfully aware of her body, dangerously aware of his. But not comfortable. Perhaps after a few years . . . several decades . . .

"Will you marry?" Gabrielle asked, already sure of Elizabeth's answer.

"Yes," her friend answered simply, then looked to the doorway as if to be certain no one was about to enter. "Can you keep a secret, Gaby? Oh, never mind. Who would you tell?"

She took a deep breath, then rushed on, saying, "George and the baron have just successfully concluded a business arrangement, a most glorious plan the baron concocted the day you disappeared—which is probably why George agreed to go along with the baron's scheme of all but kidnapping you, for he did have the welfare of many hundreds of people in the forefront of his mind. George says it will prevent needless bloodshed and go a long way in keeping intact friendships of a dozen years or more that have fallen into jeopardy, not that I pressed him for an explanation, poor dear. He is such a caring creature, and Lily all but worships him, and—"

Gabrielle was near to bursting with curiosity. "Lizzie, for the love of heaven, will you get on with it!"

"No need to badger me, Gaby. As I was about to explain, St. Clair is advancing George the funds necessary to purchase three mills in Little Pillington —the very village where we discovered Lily. George will run the mills as they should be run, instituting all sorts of wonderful reforms, and he—*we*—will repay the baron from our profits until we are completely independent."

"Three mills?" Gabrielle sat back against the cushions, forgetful of her lovely gown as she silently admired her beloved's genius. "These wouldn't happen to be Herbert Symington's mills, would they?"

Elizabeth nodded in excitement. "The very same! Lord Undercliff has already sold his shares to George. George told me he began thinking about approaching his lordship the same night Mr. Symington embarrassed his lordship by telling the world he was dabbling in trade. But it was the baron who brought his dreams to fruition, for which we are both eternally grateful."

"Yes," Gabrielle commented dryly, "Christian is a busy little bee, isn't he, flying here, there, and everywhere, performing good deeds."

Elizabeth looked at her quizzically. "But he is, Gaby, he is. And George is ecstatic! Not being of the gentry—or at least not having a title or caring one whit about Society—George says he has no scruples against earning his daily bread. He thought if he could buy Lord Undercliff's shares he might be able to ease the hardship of the workers."

"Not just a good man," Gabrielle said, patting Elizabeth's hand. "Your George is a near saint."

"Yes, isn't he? So it happened that it was only Mr. Symington that had to agree to sell his shares in order for George to own everything outright, which Mr. Symington did just today—and without taking a penny of profit, if you can believe that. It would seem Mr. Symington has wearied of life in Little Pillington and wishes to move on. Not that I can blame him. The Peacock blew him up the other night—he and his house both. I believe George told me Mr. Symington is thinking of emigrating to Jamaica, and good riddance to him, I say!"

"Blew him up, you say?" Gabrielle repeated, doing her best not to giggle. "I see the Peacock has been busy in my absence. I'll bet that was a sight to see."

"I suppose," Elizabeth answered, "and although it is naughty of me to say so, I do believe the man deserved blowing up. Oh, Gaby!" she exclaimed, hugging Gabrielle. "Just think of all the *good* George and I will be able to do. George even promised me we will look for Lily's brothers and sisters, in the hopes we can bring them all into our new home. I'm so in alt I fear I can't stop smiling! And it's not as if I am deserting you, for George has promised me that he has insisted that the baron marry you within the month."

"*Tiens!* 'Insist,' is it?" Christian said from the doorway, and Gabrielle turned to see him standing in his usual studied pose, one hand clasping a lace handkerchief, the other holding up a stemmed quizzing glass just in front of his right eye.

"I believe that was the word Lizzie used, my lord," Gabrielle said, marveling at the transition from carefree country gentleman to polished diamond of Society. His blond hair, sleekly tied at his nape, was so startlingly in contrast to the near shoulder-length locks she had so lately plunged her fingers through while they both were caught up in the throes of passion. And his evening clothes, a stunningly fashioned satin creation in just the same shade of blue as her new gown, were enough to make any young aspiring dandy weep with chagrin.

He gave out a short, high-pitched giggle. "Blister me, madam," he drawled, approaching Gabrielle and dropping a brief kiss on her outstretched hand, "I thought we had agreed to fib and say our nuptials to be *my* idea, as I wished to protect your reputation by keeping secret your insistence upon running off with me. Grumble deals me so little credit but, alas, I am accustomed to such abuse."

"Oh, cut line, Kit," Gabrielle replied, pulling her hand away as she stood up, for now George Trumble was in the drawing room as well, and it was time they were on their way to Lord Buxley's. "If we four were to spend the next fortnight trying to sort through all the lies and half-truths that have been told these last days, we would end with nothing but headaches. You look very handsome, by the way. Or do you already know that?"

"Upon my soul, Grumble," Christian exclaimed, a hand to his chest, "but the woman is forward! Have I got myself a marvel, or not?"

"More a tiger by the tail than a marvel, Kit," George answered, assisting Elizabeth to her feet, "but then you deserve to spend the rest of your life in a perpetual whirl—begging your pardon, Miss Laurence. I imagine you'll both even enjoy it. As for me, I could not be more content with my Elizabeth."

"Oh, George," Elizabeth gushed, which surprised Gabrielle, for she had never supposed her friend capable of gushing.

They adjourned to the entrance hall to find Frapple and three footmen waiting with their evening cloaks. "Frapple, we shan't be long," Christian said as he turned his back to the servant and allowed him to drape a shimmering blue cloak over his broad shoulders. "You are up to having the kitchen staff produce a celebratory meal for six within two hours, I imagine."

"I am, my lord," Frapple answered, bowing stiffly. "What frightens me is that I am becoming accustomed to this sort of thing—my lord."

"A meal—in two hours?" Elizabeth questioned George, relieving Gabrielle of the need to ask much the same question. "I—I don't understand. Aren't we going to Lord Buxley's for a dinner party? George—"

George led his protesting fiancée out the door ahead of Gabrielle and Christian, so that Gabrielle had time to say without fear of being overheard, "I take it we don't plan to stay long at his lordship's, Kit. But are you convinced we won't be dining in prison, rather than back here in Hanover Square?"

"Frapple!" Christian exclaimed in mock horror.

"Did you hear that? I frankly despair of ever being appreciated within my own household."

"Just bring this off, my lord," Frapple answered him seriously, "and I may live to be proud of you yet."

And with those encouraging words echoing in her ears, Gabrielle found herself being whisked into St. Clair's crested carriage and off on her way to Portman Square.

CHAPTER 15

A fool, indeed, has great need of a title,
It teaches men to call him count and duke,
And to forget his proper name of fool.

John Crowne

Gabrielle loved Christian. She trusted him. She believed in him. And yet, and yet . . .

"Lord Buxley!" Christian called out brightly as, with Gabrielle clinging to his arm and George Trumble and Elizabeth following along behind, he strolled into the richly decorated yet sedate drawing room in Portman Square. "Conceive my dismay! Is that a sling I espy on your arm? Have you consulted with a physician? I can have my own quack sent round in the morning, for he is quite accomplished. Better yet—I shall have him summoned here at once. Can't be too careful, now can we, dear Buxley?"

Did Christian have to mention the earl's injury at once, Gabrielle wondered, doing her best to pretend joy in seeing Lady Ariana, who was sitting on a small brocade chair and looking unusually smug.

"Nonsense. It was only a small accident, baron.

Nothing to cause concern," Lord Buxley answered tightly, bowing greetings to the remainder of Christian's party and paying particular attention, Gabrielle felt, to her. It was the gown—that was all. The man was intrigued by the unusual sleeves on her gown. "Excuse me for staring, Miss Laurence," he said after a moment. "It's just that I never before realized quite how distinctive red hair can be."

"Thank you, my lord," Gabrielle replied, settling on the mundane for lack of anything more original popping into her mind. *They know, they know!* she thought hysterically. *And now Kit has blissfully strolled us all straight into the lion's mouth. I should have said yes when he asked if I should have liked to see Buxley and Ariana go down to fire and pestilence.*

She then seated herself on one of the couches, Elizabeth beside her, and said hello to the other members of the dinner party. Lord Tredway, standing behind his daughter, Lady Ariana. Lord and Lady Undercliff, tripping over themselves to greet Christian, who was in the process of showering her ladyship with compliments. The duke of Glynnon, leaning forward in his chair, the better to hear what was going on. Sir Gladwin Penley and Lord Osgood, seemingly doing their best to fade into the woodwork just inside the drawing room, although the latter did spare a moment to wink in Gabrielle's direction.

Quite an impressive coterie of guests, if Gabrielle didn't believe they were all here for a reason she was reluctant to discover. As witnesses, most likely. It was a sobering thought.

"Is your dear mother unwell, that she is not here?" Gabrielle asked Lady Ariana, then quickly cleared her throat as her voice caught on a plaguey lump of nervousness.

"La, yes," Lady Ariana answered, opening her fan and beginning to beat the air beneath her chin with it. "But it is nothing so serious, I'm sure, as the affliction that so lately laid your entire household low. She has the headache, you know. It's this beastly heat, so early in the year. However do you manage in those sleeves? They *are* sleeves, aren't they?" She smiled indulgently. "And quite lovely too, I suppose. Mrs. Fletcher, so nice to see you. Wouldn't you be more comfortable over there," she asked, pointing to a distant chair, "out of the way?"

Drinks were passed around as Gabrielle's anger simmered, displacing her earlier apprehension, and the conversation ranged from the boring to the stultifyingly boring for some minutes until Christian, walking to the very center of the room, struck a pose and announced: "I do abhor ruining everyone's evening before it is quite begun, and I am convinced our dear friend the earl has his own entertainment planned, but I fear I have something to say. Something quite distressing."

Lord Buxley was on his feet in an instant. "You are going to save me a good deal of trouble then, St. Clair, and confess?"

"Confess?" Lord Undercliff echoed, looking to his wife. "Confess to what? What does he have to confess to? Besides the crime of rigging himself out like some tricked-up mummer? Have I missed something?"

"Oh, do be quiet, Charles," Lady Undercliff warned, digging her elbow into her husband's side. "I *told* you something was up, didn't I? Why else would we have been invited only this morning? Only thank the Lord I convinced you to sell those horrid mills."

"Address?" the duke of Glynnon ventured gruffly,

cupping a hand to his ear. "Buxley, you say he's going to give an *address*? Stap me, I ain't sitting here listenin' to that dandy prose on about his usual nonsense as to flowers and any such drivel. Never liked the fellow above half, and I'm proud to say it! Buxley—have your man fetch me my cloak and hat. I'm off to my club, by damn!"

Lady Ariana rose to go to the duke, quickly explaining his error and begging him to stay, even as Lord Osgood and Sir Gladwin closed the double doors leading to the entrance hall and Elizabeth looked to George, her eyes frightened behind her spectacles.

There was a tension in the room that Gabrielle could feel invading her every pore, and she sat completely still, watching Christian, praying he hadn't just made an enormous mistake. No one knew for certain that Lord Buxley had recognized her the other night. All right, he had made mention of her hair as she came in tonight, but he could only have been being kind, couldn't he? Perhaps this was all for nothing. But *what* was for nothing? She shook her head, realizing that she still did not know what Christian was doing. Really, she'd soon have to have a long talk with him about his penchant for secrecy.

Christian lifted his handkerchief to dab at the corners of his mouth one after the other, then gave the lacy creation a slight flourish. "This may come as a small surprise to some of you—most particularly to our dear duke, here, I imagine—but I am not quite the frippery fellow I would have you all believe." He giggled. "Well, perhaps I am. But I do have my serious moments."

He turned to Lord Tredway. "Although our politics may differ, my lord, I have of late indulged myself in the latest *ton* amusement, that of ferreting out the identity of the Peacock. It wouldn't do, you understand, to have anyone but myself able to claim the honor of unmasking the man who threatens to usurp my position as the acknowledged leader of Society. I do have my reputation to consider, don't I?" he asked, looking at Lady Undercliff, who, open-mouthed, nodded her agreement.

"Eh? Speak up, boy," the duke called out. "I'm listening now. Have you found our man?"

"Found him?" Lord Buxley countered, using his uninjured arm to grab Christian's sleeve and give it a yank. "You've more than found him. You've ridden with him. You—and that red-haired minx. Now tell us. Tell us the name of the Peacock!"

"Have a care, dear Anthony," Christian warned quietly. "I should not use Miss Laurence in order to insult me, were I you."

"Zounds!" Lord Undercliff exclaimed, his elbow finding his wife's side as he winked at her, obviously delighted to be privy to such delicious goings-on. "Too bad they can't fight, what with Buxley's wing in a sling and St. Clair probably not knowing how to make a fist. But the gel? Now that's interesting!"

All eyes turned toward Gabrielle as she fought to prop up Elizabeth's swooning form. So much for thinking she could keep her friend in ignorance of her activities while in the countryside with Christian. "Kit?" she choked out, looking up at her beloved, caught between wishing to run into his arms for protection and a longing to murder him. "Now might be a good time to tell us all what you have discovered?"

"All in good time, my love," Christian said soothingly as he disengaged his sleeve from the earl's clutches. "Oh, by the bye, ladies and gentlemen, are you aware that Miss Laurence has agreed to become my affianced wife? You might be especially interested in knowing that, Ariana, as you have made it a particular point to concern yourself with Gabrielle's matrimonial prospects. But even your concern does not quite allow for stealing, does it? Or, and I shudder to say the word—blackmail?"

"You—you know about the list?" Gabrielle asked, shaking her head. "Lizzie told Grumble, I suppose, and then he told you. Honestly, Kit, it was all in fun, and I never even mentioned you, not that you aren't entirely wonderful, and—"

"Tut-tut, my dear," Christian said, cutting her off, and none too soon, for her tongue had been in the process of rapidly tying itself into knots. "Let us return to the matter at hand, shall we? Lord Buxley— dear, dear Lord Buxley—is it not true that you approached me in the not too distant past, begging my assistance in discovering the Peacock's identity?"

"You know it is," the earl responded warily, watching Christian closely, as if the baron were about to produce a rabbit out of his pristine white waistcoat. "Just as you know it was a complete waste of my time."

"*Au contraire,* my friend," Christian corrected him. "Your entreaty ignited in me a fire of curiosity, and I devoted myself forthwith to learning all I could about the Peacock, his motives, and his reason for being. It has something to do with people such as that man, Simons, who so rudely interrupted Lord Undercliff's little gathering the other night, I decided."

"St. Clair!" Lord Undercliff broke in. "I thought

you promised not to mention that again if I told you everything I knew about—"

"So true, my lord, so true," Christian said quickly, bowing to the clearly flustered man. "But it was all of a piece, I realized. This dabbling in trade." He wheeled about sharply, to point his quizzing glass at Lord Tredway. "Imagine my shock, dear sir, my utter surprise, when I learned—how, shall remain my secret, as no one can accuse *me* of loose lips—that you have interests in several mills in the Midlands. Ah, I fear I have shocked you, dearest Anthony," he added, solicitously turning back to Lord Buxley, who didn't look quite so handsome with his complexion drained to a sudden, pasty white.

"That's not true!" Lady Ariana protested, leaping to her feet. "Papa—tell them that's not true!" Lord Tredway looked away, clearly mortified. "No! We can't be in trade! Oh, I am so ashamed of you, Papa!"

Gabrielle was beginning to feel so very much better. "That's shockingly ungrateful of you, Ariana," she pointed out quietly. "And after all your dear papa has done for you. Perhaps it was the expense of a second Season that led him down this tortured path?"

Lady Ariana rounded on Gabrielle, looking ready to pounce on her. "Oh, be quiet, you traitoress—you scheming slut! Anthony has already told me what you've done, you and St. Clair. You're both in league with the Peacock! Anthony, don't just stand there as if you've been stuffed! *Say* something!"

"Death and fiends," the Duke of Glynnon, who had no difficulty in hearing conversations held at a near bellow, remarked to no one in particular, lifting his wineglass. "Stap me, if this ain't better than the opera!"

Lord Buxley pulled himself up to his full height, which may have been difficult, as he was still laboring under the crushing knowledge that he had nearly asked for Lady Ariana's hand in marriage—to be bracketed to a mill owner's brat!—and declared, "Christian St. Clair, I charge you with aiding and abetting the man known as the Peacock. You, and her!" he ended, wheeling about to point an accusing finger at Gabrielle.

Christian raised his hand to stifle a yawn. "Yes, I do believe we've already heard that absurd accusation. You know, I have half a mind to cut you when next we meet, except that I do not believe we will meet after tonight. Winnie! Ozzie! Up the stairs with you both, if you please. And don't brook any argument from his lordship's servants. You are on a mission!"

"Right away, Kit," Lord Osgood said, sparing a moment to wink at Gabrielle before pulling open the doors and bowing Sir Gladwin out ahead of him.

Lord Buxley looked completely at sea, and not a little angry. "What is going on here? What are they doing, running through my house? St. Clair, I'll have your heart's blood for this!"

"*Sacré tonnerre!* Such violent speech, dear Anthony," Christian responded, prudently removing himself from the earl's proximity by adjourning to the fireplace, leaning his shoulder against the mantelpiece while he crossed one elegant leg over the other. "Allow me, ladies and gentlemen, to tell you a little story."

"Gad, yes," Lord Undercliff said brightly. "If I'm going to dine out on my tales of this evening, at least let me make sure I've got the straight of what's going on. Let's see. You're getting bracketed to the red-haired chit, Tredway's in trade 'cause his daughter can't catch a duke—I think I win a monkey at my club for that one, as we've all been betting on the thing—and then there's this business about the Peacock—"

"Shut up, Charles," Lady Undercliff said automatically as she raised her glass of sherry to her lips.

Gabrielle quietly thanked George Trumble for relieving her of Elizabeth's unconscious form—she had roused once, only to faint again at Lord Buxley's repeated accusation—and went to join Christian, slipping her hand into his and squeezing it, for his comfort or her own she was not sure.

"Once upon a time," Christian then began, smiling down at Gabrielle, "there was a man who made it clear he detested the Peacock. This man—for the sake of making it easy for everyone to follow along, we shall refer to him as 'Anthony'—would be the last, the very last, person anyone could expect to be in sympathy with the more disadvantaged of our society. A loyal Tory, a supporter of Lord Sidmouth, this man, this Anthony—and his good friend, whom, again for simplicity, we shall call 'Ariana'—in point of fact, were leading double lives."

"Ariana?" Lord Tredway grabbed at his daughter's shoulder, shaking her. "What is this idiot prosing on about? You and Buxley? What were you two doing?"

"I don't know, Papa," Lady Ariana protested, pressing her cheek against her father's hand. "Truly, I don't know what St. Clair's saying. I lead no double life."

"Ah, but you do," Christian corrected her. "Lord Undercliff," he said, pausing to make sure he had his lordship's attention, "is it true the Peacock struck at Mr. Simons again just the other night? After you had prudently sold your shares in the mills to Mr. Trumble here?"

Lord Undercliff's head bobbed in agreement even as he smiled. "Heard there was a rare dust-up, what with Symington's house blowing up and the Peacock rescuing some drab from the guardhouse. Why do you ask?"

Christian's smile was terrifying in its sweetness. "Because I was there, your lordship."

"You see? You see?" Lord Buxley shouted, pointing a trembling finger at Christian. "He's admitted his guilt out of his own mouth! He's one of them, and so is Miss Laurence. I saw her. She knocked me down and I saw her—her and her red hair!"

Christian's sigh was eloquent. "Give it up, Anthony. You and Ariana both. Yes, you were there the other night. But you were there as the Peacock, for *I* saw you, dear fellow. I had been roaming that dreary countryside for days, searching out the Peacock, and just happened to be in Little Pillington the night your cohorts performed their raid on the guardhouse."

"Go on, St. Clair," Lord Tredway said. "You've got my interest."

"Thank you, your lordship. Anthony, you pretended to be there in the King's name, but you were really there to make sure your prisoner got away. No one could be so incompetent except on purpose, don't you agree, Lord Tredway? I never saw such shoddy work, or a more unconvincing Peacock. Why, the poor fellow could barely stay upright in the saddle. You had someone imitate you that evening, didn't you, so that you could be with that man, Simons, and above suspicion?"

"You're twisting everything. Making it all sound

wrong," Lord Buxley protested. "He's twisting everything!" he cried out, looking to Lord Tredway.

"If I might press on with this distasteful business?" Christian asked, waiting for Lord Tredway's nod of agreement. "As for the red-haired beauty traveling with the Peacock's men whom you spoke of in an attempt to sully the name of my soon-to-be bride? If Ozzie and Winnie have been as successful on their little hunt as I expect them to be . . ."

"Here you go, Kit!" Sir Gladwin exclaimed from the doorway, and everyone turned to see him holding up a large cloth sack. "It was all there, just as you thought, though I wouldn't have believed it. Ozzie neither, come to think of it."

"You found that in his lordship's dressing room, I would suppose?" Christian asked on a sigh, squeezing Gabrielle's hand to keep her silent as Lord Buxley loudly proclaimed that he had never before in his life laid eyes on that sack.

"Yes, Kit, and a pretty end to the evening it'll make when we dump it out," Lord Osgood said, winking at Sir Gladwin, who immediately did just that.

First to hit the floor was a black cloak, followed by equally black breeches, shirt—all of a size that could be worn only by a tall man—and a small scrap of silk Lord Osgood lifted to his face in order to demonstrate that it was a mask. Sir Gladwin gave the sack another shake and a bright green sash, a colorful skirt, a tattered white peasant blouse, and a garish, long red wig appeared.

"My proof, ladies and gentlemen," Christian said, taking Gabrielle with him as he walked across the room to stand before the pile of clothing. He picked up the wig and tossed it to Lady Ariana, who caught it in reaction. "Have you ever wondered, dear ladies and gentlemen, how the Peacock found it so elementary to outwit Lord Sidmouth's men? Why, one would suppose the Peacock was privy to every move the government might make, and therefore able to elude capture. Wouldn't one, Lord Tredway?"

"I told him everything," Lord Tredway said quietly, almost as if to himself. "Everything."

"And what you didn't tell Anthony," Christian informed him, "your dear daughter learned by listening at keyholes. A terrible curiosity dear Ariana has, I have learned, a terrible curiosity. But then, she was only relaying information to her lover in order to please him, weren't you, Ariana? And that's why you have been visiting Miss Laurence, and why Anthony has made it a point to seek her out also. Poor Miss Laurence, to have been so sadly used. You were jealous of her growing popularity which had nearly eclipsed yours, and wished to bring her down."

He looked to Lord and Lady Undercliff, his expression a picture of dismay. "The two of them have been planning for weeks, I would imagine, to throw suspicion away from themselves by foisting it on my betrothed—and on me as well, I have just realized. Now there's a shocker! A member of the Peacock's band of cutthroats? *Moi?* It is, as they say, to laugh."

"No," Lady Ariana mumbled, looking to her father, the damning wig clutched in her lap. "This isn't true. None of it is true. It sounds true, I'll grant you that, and it even looks true, but then St. Clair has always been clever. Papa, think on this for a moment: You know I have set my cap at Glynnon."

"Eh? What's that?" his grace asked, rising and aiming himself at the doorway as if he had been shot out of a cannon. "Set a trap for me? Females! Give me a good mare any day, that's what I say. Buried two wives, and would have taken a third long ago if I'd wanted one, which I don't. Buxley, you're a rotter, but she deserves you—and you can have her with my compliments."

"Me?" Lord Buxley exclaimed. "I don't want her."

Christian tsk-tsked, then remarked, "Take her, use her, and then toss her away. Who would have thought it? *Tiens,* you're a cold man at the bottom of it, aren't you, Anthony?"

"And what are you, St. Clair?" Lord Buxley countered angrily. "You're the one who is single-handedly destroying her."

"Me? Oh no, that can't be true." Christian looked to George Trumble as if for assistance. "I'm quite sure I like Lady Ariana vastly. Grumble? Don't I like Lady Ariana vastly?"

"So you've said, Kit," George answered calmly, busy waving Gabrielle's fan beneath his beloved's nose as she slept on, oblivious to her surroundings.

"Allow me, your grace." Sir Gladwin kicked the Peacock's costume and the gypsy skirt to one side in order to clear a path for the duke, who called for his carriage to take him to his club.

"They can stand there and shout at each other the whole night long for all I care," he said as he left. "I'm off to tell everyone that Buxley's the Peacock. About time somebody listened to me, and they will tonight, by God."

"Wait! This is insane!" Lord Buxley protested as

Lord and Lady Undercliff, doubtlessly spurred on by the duke of Glynnon's remarks, hastened to follow after him, cutting a wide berth around the earl as they headed for the door, eager to spread the news at Lord Royston's ball. "I am not the Peacock. Ariana—you know how we have been trying to unmask the rotter—tell them!"

And then Lady Ariana surprised Gabrielle, for she only said quietly, "It's finished, Anthony. Of course you're not the Peacock. Just as I am not the sort to run about the countryside in something as vile as *this,*" she added, flinging the wig onto the floor. "But no one will believe us now. St. Clair has bested us. Learn to accept your losses."

"True enough," Christian agreed. "The town criers are already out and about. By the morning there will be a dozen people who will swear to having seen the two of you together in Little Pillington, setting fires and breaking into the guardhouse."

"I knew you loved her. I recognized it almost at once. That should have warned me away from her. Your revenge is terrifying. But I never really supposed that *you* were the—oh, what does it matter now? It's too late for—" Lady Ariana broke off and rose to her feet, her slim shoulders slumped, and looked levelly at Christian. "What now, St. Clair? Do we have to hang in order for you to be satisfied, or will you be content with our disgrace?"

"You know something, Anthony?" Christian asked, raising his quizzing glass to peer at the earl. "I believe dearest Ariana has proved herself the better man between the pair of you." Christian's high-pitched giggle forced Gabrielle to cover her own mouth for fear she might break into laughter herself, which she shouldn't, for she was feeling almost sorry for Lady Ariana.

Christian gave out a slight cough and Lord Osgood hastened to pour him a glass of champagne. "Thank you, Ozzie. This has been thirsty work, hasn't it?"

"Huzza, Kit," Lord Osgood answered quietly, winking, then returned to the doorway.

"Now, where was I?" Christian asked, after taking a sip from his glass. "Oh, yes. We were about to discuss the future." He knitted his brow for a moment, then began ticking off conditions on his fingertips. "One, dear Lord Tredway has been exposed as a mill owner, which will not put him in good odor with his Tory friends, I fear, so that he and his lady wife shall undoubtedly find it convenient to rusticate for several months—or years. You will also be resigning from the government, I would imagine? Two, Lord Buxley is not in good odor with anyone, as he has been accused of being the dastardly Peacock. That cannot be considered a good thing.

"Unless, dear Anthony, you are hoping for the adoration of dozens of senseless females who believe themselves in love with our black-clad adventurer? They are certain to be on hand to support you, weeping copiously into their little handkerchiefs as you are turned off outside Newgate, or wherever it is they hang seditious traitors," he continued, peering questioningly at Lord Buxley, who was not looking at all well.

"The prospect doesn't appeal?" Christian sighed. "Pity. In that case, dear Anthony, I suggest a rapid exit from our fair isle. On the morning tide might be best. I'm confident you and Ariana will enjoy America, or wherever you might end up."

"Go with him?" Lady Ariana looked desperate. "Christian, surely you aren't suggesting that *I*—"

"Tut-tut, my dear," Christian interrupted, flourishing his handkerchief. "Don't thank me for my brilliant solution. Of course you must travel with your beloved. I, for one, would not dream to offer a bar to your happiness."

"My *happiness?*"

"Indeed," Christian said as Sir Gladwin motioned for them to adjourn to the entrance hall, which they could do now that Elizabeth had finally wakened from her swoon. "There must exist a myriad of worthy causes for you and the dear earl to champion in America. I only envy you your fire, your zeal to help your fellow man. Gabrielle, dear love, kiss your friend goodbye."

"Don't come near me, you traitor!" Lady Ariana exploded, finally succumbing to tears.

Gabrielle kissed her anyway, whispering into her ear before sprightly stepping back to safety, "You may think me a traitor, dear Ariana, but at least *I* have an apple dumpling shop!"

"Buxley," Christian said as he adjusted his cloak around his shoulders, "I bid you goodbye. You've been an interesting adversary, but disappointingly easy to outwit. But then I've always thought you devoid of imagination. Only consider your clothes. Scarcely a touch of lace, and those colors! Gad, sir, but you are a damned dull dog!"

And then they were all in Christian's coach, six good friends tumbled in together for the drive back to Hanover Square, five of them laughing quietly until Elizabeth asked politely if she might have missed something.

No one answered her, for they had all broken into gales of laughter at her question.

"Oh, fiddlesticks!" she exclaimed, burying her head against George's shoulder, which was probably a good thing, as she then did not see Gabrielle very deliberately reach up and kiss Christian square on the mouth.

WINNERS TAKE ALL

Not a bad day's work on the whole.
Not a bad day's work.

Baroness Orczy

He casts a sheep's eye at the wench.

Cervantes

They adjourned to the drawing room together after dinner, the gentlemen not lingering behind over brandy and cigars, for they were still happily discussing their recent victory.

All except for Christian, that is, who was cudgeling his tortured brain for some way to get Gabrielle off to himself, and if she didn't keep smiling at him in that blatant, come-hither, lady-of-the-evening way when no one else was looking, he was soon going to have done with politeness, toss her over his shoulder, and carry her off willy-nilly up the stairs!

"I have resigned myself to the fact that none of you will ever reveal the identity of the *true* Peacock, but tell me again," Elizabeth implored, looking to George. "How did Christian know that Ozzie and Winnie would find that sack?"

Gabrielle gave Elizabeth a hug. "Still having difficulty in accepting Kit's varied acquaintance, aren't you, Lizzie? Housebreakers don't always steal when they crack a ken. Sometimes, if they are doing a favor for a particular friend, they *deposit* things."

"Oh, Gaby," Elizabeth protested, looking pained. "I dearly wish you wouldn't keep delighting yourself by dropping thieves' cant into your conversations."

"Yes, well, she has been in Kit's company, my dear, so you can't really lay all the blame at her door. I still can't believe Buxley didn't put up more of a fight," George said then, not for the first time.

Christian sat himself down beside Gabrielle, taking up her hand and kissing it. "It's simple enough, Grumble, if you know your man. Buxley took it into his head that I worked with the Peacock, his second in command, as it were. That we all worked with him. But he could not make himself believe that anyone as patently foppish and dedicated to fashion as myself could ever best him. A mind that resists seeing anything in less than the starkest black and white is exceptionally vulnerable."

"Isn't he wonderful, my friends?" Gabrielle said, winking at Lord Osgood. "And so modest with it all, as well. But that doesn't mean that Lord Buxley won't return one day to cut out your liver and lights, dear Kit."

Christian shook his head. "No, my love. He wouldn't dare. In the morning he will be very publicly branded the Peacock by the one man who has the most to lose if his declaration is proved wrong: Lord Tredway. That poor fellow's only hope of salvation with his Tory friends is to claim that he unmasked the Peacock, even going so far as to banish his own traitorous daughter when he discovered her role in the plot—although I have requested he continue her allowance and turn over her dowry to the earl, for I am not entirely heartless. I have already sent a missive round to Grosvenor Square apprising his lordship of the fact that I shall deny all credit in the matter, leaving him to salvage what he can of his reputation. No, we have seen the last of Buxley and the lovely Ariana."

"He's so smug when he's being clever, isn't he, Gabrielle?" George asked, smiling to show he was tolerably pleased with the way things had worked out.

"Thank you, Grumble," Christian said, reaching up to release his hair from its queue and remove the jabot that he had no intention of wearing ever again. "And as the Peacock's raids have ceased, and there will be no more missives to the newspapers, it will be simple for Society to accept that the absent Buxley was truly the Peacock. I had rather wished for the letters to continue but, as it has fallen out, this is impossible."

Lord Osgood looked up sharply. "No more letters, Kit? So the Peacock is truly retired?"

"So he has informed me," Christian answered, sighing as Gabrielle began surreptitiously stroking his palm with her teasing fingertips. "I suppose there is nothing else for it than that I take up my seat in Parliament once more and return to bashing my head against the wall of indifference our government feels for its less advantaged citizens."

Sir Gladwin laughed in easily recognized glee. "A crusader in your lace and satins, Kit? And will you freeze Sidmouth to his bench as you glare down at him through your quizzing glass? I'd pay down half my quarterly allowance to see that!"

"You would have to, Winnie," Christian countered easily, tossing his jabot onto the low table in front of him. "You see, I have decided to bring an entirely new sort of ensemble into fashion. Picture it, if you will. The cloth frock coat—done in forest colors of green, or bark brown, or even pond blue. Fawn stockinette breeches that strap tightly beneath the instep. The shirt and waistcoat, white. Ah, but the cravat? Therein lies the genius. It shall be black, my friends, black as the Peacock's cloak, and wrapped tightly around the neck with only the shirt-points visible above it. Is that not genius?"

"Sounds as if you've traveled round the bend this time, Kit," Sir Gladwin groused. "I'll stick with m' yellow waistcoat, if you don't mind."

"Have I ever minded, Winnie?" Christian asked, winking at Lord Osgood before he rose, still holding Gabrielle's hand. "And that, I think, is all that I have to say. Dear friends, I do believe my lovely bride-to-be is weary after her long and varied day. If you will excuse us?"

"He's a cool one, ain't he?" Lord Osgood asked as Christian and Gabrielle exited the room.

"Yes, he is," George could be heard to answer. "And they need keepers—the pair of them!"

"Frapple?" Christian said, inclining his head to his highest servant and most loyal friend once in the hallway. "My congratulations on the meal we have all just recently enjoyed. You are, as always, a marvel."

"Yes, Kit, he most certainly is," Gabrielle said, smiling up at the man. "And as a reward for being such a loyal and agreeable man, I have asked that a liniment much favored by my father be sent to your room, Frapple. I am convinced it will ease your discomfort. It's never easy, is it, spending long hours on horseback when one is unaccustomed to such exertion?"

"Well, I'm damned!" Christian exclaimed as Frapple, for once at a loss for words, quickly bowed himself toward the rear of the entrance hall. "You knew, Gaby? You knew it was Frapple playing the Peacock?"

Her smile was a marvel of love liberally mixed with sweet pity. "Did you really think I could be so easily hoodwinked, my love? Lizzie might not see what is before her nose, but I most certainly do, and did. I only wish I could have seen you as the real Peacock once before your retirement. I'm convinced you were even more glorious than Frapple."

"Well, I'm damned," Christian repeated as he guided her toward the stairs. "How long, Gaby? How long have you known that I was the Peacock? Did you know that night at the pond?"

"Did I know you were the Peacock when I first made love with you, isn't that what you're asking? Really, Kit, must you know all my secrets, when I have been so good as to honor yours?" she teased, pressing her fiery head against his sleeve. "Isn't it enough that I love you?"

He stopped in front of her door, wondering how long it would be until the household was asleep, and he could go to her—love her. *"Tiens,"* he quipped, striking a dandified pose, "I should suppose it is, come to think on it."

"Idiot!" Gabrielle exclaimed, reaching up on tiptoe to kiss him. "Now," she said, turning him around and giving him a push toward his own bedchamber, "be a good little Peacock and go practice your speech."

"I can see who's going to be master of this house, my darling," he said fatalistically, silently wondering how Frapple was going to feel, handing over the mantle of authority. Then he began walking down the hallway, his step light, his heart even lighter, saying, "My lords, I rise today to speak on the question of equality in our Society—"

He broke off, wheeling about to see Gabrielle still standing in the hallway, smiling at him, her naughty tongue making even naughtier circles as it skimmed over her full, moist lips.

The devil with conventions anyway! Wait until everyone was asleep and then skulk about his own house like some criminal?

Not him.

Not Baron Christian St. Clair.

Not the Peacock!

"The pond blue, dearest Gaby," he drawled softly, smiling as he advanced toward her and she opened her arms to him. "For my first speech, you understand. I think I shall wear the pond blue. . . ."

Intriguing, sensual, witty,
and challenging defines
the novels of

KASEY MICHAELS

☐ **THE BRIDE OF THE UNICORN**
. . . . 73181-5/$5.50US

☐ **THE LEGACY OF THE ROSE**
. . . . 73180-7/$5.50US

☐ **A MASQUERADE IN THE MOONLIGHT**
. . . . 79339-X/$5.50US

☐ **THE SECRETS OF THE HEART**
. . . . 79341-1/$5.99US

Look for
THE PASSION OF AN ANGEL
(coming Fall 1995)

POCKET
BOOKS

The Captivating New Novel from the
New York Times Bestselling Author of
GRAND PASSION

Jayne Ann Krentz

TRUST
ME

Available in Hardcover

from

POCKET
B O O K S

Pocket Star Books
Proudly Announces

THE PASSION OF AN ANGEL

Kasey Michaels

Coming from
Pocket Star Books
Fall 1995

The following is a preview of
The Passion of an Angel. . . .

Banning Talbot, marquess of Daventry, is attending the Duchess of Richmond's ball on what would later be known as the Eve of the Battle of Waterloo. Daventry is on Wellington's staff, as is Colonel Henry MacAfee, who is feeling particularly morose this evening.

MacAfee, sliding slowly into his cups, spends his time talking about his young sister, his "angel," and Daventry nods and murmurs at the appropriate times, not really listening, while devoting most of his attention to watching as the lovely, desirable Miss Althea Broughton goes down the dance with a succession of eager partners.

It is only when Wellington summons the pair to his side, telling them of the coming battle, that MacAfee, shocked sober, pens a quick note turning custody of his sister over to Daventry "if the worst should happen, for I can't let her stay with that old fool, my grandfather. She deserves more, deserves a Season when the time is right. You will rescue my little angel, won't you, my good friend?"

With Wellington himself serving as witness, Daventry is agreed, trying only to humor his casual but affable friend, who has stubbornly sworn that the coming engagement will prove the end of him. . . .

"Prudence MacAfee, Prudence MacAfee," Banning grumbled beneath his breath as he reined his mount to a halt on the crest of a small hill overlooking the MacAfee farm. "Was there ever a more *pru*-dish, missish name?"

He lifted his curly brimmed beaver to swipe at the sweat caused by the noon heat of this early April day, exposing his silvered black hair to the sun, then turned in the saddle to squint back down the roadway. His traveling coach, containing both his valet, Rexford, and his sister's borrowed companion, the redoubtable Miss Honoria Prentice, was still not in sight, and he debated whether he should await their arrival or proceed on his own.

Not that either person would be of much use to

him. Rexford was an old woman at thirty, too concerned with the condition of his lily-white rump as it was bounced over the spring-rain-rutted roads to be a supporting prop to his reluctant-guardian employer. And Miss Prentice, whose pinched-lips countenance could send a delicate child like Prudence MacAfee into a spasm, was probably best not seen until arrangements to transport the young female to London had been settled.

Damn Henry for being right! And damn him for coercing his only cursory friend into this ridiculous guardianship! If Banning could have found Henry MacAfee's body among the heaps of nameless, faceless dead, he would have slapped the man back to life. Anything to be shed of this unwanted responsibility.

What was he, Banning Talbot, four and thirty years of age and firmly committed to bachelorhood, going to do with an innocent young female? He had asked precisely that question of his sister, Frederica, who had nearly choked on her sherry before imploring her brother to never, *never* repeat any such volatile, provocative question in public.

It wasn't as if he hadn't already lived up to most of his commitment. Having been wounded himself at Waterloo, which delayed his return to London only in time to discover that Frederica, his sole relative, was gravely ill, Banning had still met with his solicitor to arrange for a generous allowance to be paid quarterly to one Miss Prudence MacAfee of

MacAfee Farm. He had directed his solicitor to explain the impossibility of Banning's presence at the Sussex holding for some time, and had then dragged out that time, beyond his own recovery, beyond any hint of danger remaining in his sister's condition. Past the Christmas holidays, and beyond.

He would still be in London, enjoying his first Season in many years, if it weren't that Frederica, who had always been able to wrap her older brother firmly around her thumb, had not put forth the notion that she would "above all things" adore having a young female in the house whom she could "educate in the ways of Society and pamper and dress in pretty clothes."

Why, Frederica would even pop the girl off, when the time came to put up the child's hair and push her out into the marriage mart. Banning, Frederica had promised, would have to do nothing more than host a single ball, present his ward at court and, of course, foot the bills, which "will probably be prodigious, dearest, for I do so adore fripperies."

It all seemed most logical, and personally untaxing, but Banning still was the one left to beg Grandfather MacAfee to release his granddaughter, and he was the one who would have to face this young girl and explain why he had left this "rescue" of her so late if the grandfather was really the dead loss Henry MacAfee had described to him.

Banning jammed his hat back down onto his head, cursed a single time, and urged his mount forward and down the winding path to the rundown-looking holding, wondering why he could not quite fight the feeling that he was riding into the jaws of, if not death, great personal danger.

No one came out into the stable yard after he had passed through the broken gate, or even after he had dismounted and led his horse to a nearby water trough, giving him time to look more closely at his surroundings, which were depressing as the tepid lemonade at Almacks.

Banning already knew that Henry, born of good lineage, had not been all that deep in the pocket, but he had envisioned a small country holding: neat, clean, and genteelly shabby. This place, however, was a shambles, a mess, a totally inappropriate place for any gentle soul who could earn the affectionate name of "Angel."

Beginning to feel better about his enforced good deed—rather like a heavenly benefactor about to do a favor for a grateful cherub—the marquess raised a hand to his mouth and called out, "Hello! Anybody about?"

Several moments later he saw a head pop out from behind the stable door—a door hanging by only two of its three great hinges. The head, that of a remarkably dirty looking urchin, was rapidly followed by a slight body clad in what looked to be bloody rags. As a matter of fact, the urchin's arms were bloodred to the elbows, as if he had been interrupted while slaughtering a hog.

"I suppose I should be grateful to learn this place

is not deserted. I am Daventry," Banning said, wondering why he was bothering to introduce himself.

"Daventry, huh?" the youth repeated flatly, obviously not impressed. "And you're jolly pleased to be him, no doubt. Now get shed of that fancy jacket, roll up your sleeves, and follow me. Unless you'd rather stand put there, posing in the dirt, while Molly dies?"

The first shock to hit Banning was the bitingly superior tone of the urchin's voice. The next was its pitch—which was obviously female. Lastly, he was startled to hear the anguished cry of an animal.

He knew in an instant exactly what was afoot.

Leaving sorting out the identity of the rude, inappropriately clad female to later—and while lifting a silent prayer that she couldn't possibly be who he was beginning to believe she might be, or as old as she looked to be—the marquess stripped off his riding jacket and threw it over his saddle. "What is it—a breech?" he asked as he tossed his hat away, rolled up his sleeves, and began trotting toward the stable door.

Banning bred horses at Daventry Court, his seat near Leamington, and had long been a hands-on owner, raising the animals as much for his love of them as for any profit involved. The sound of the mare in pain was enough to turn a figurative knife in his gut.

"I've been trying to turn the foal," the female he hoped was not Prudence MacAfee told him as, together, they entered the dark stable and headed for the last stall on the right. "Molly's already down, and has been for hours—too many hours—but if I hold her head, and talk to her, you should be able to do the trick. I'm Angel, by the way," she added, sticking out one blood-slick hand as if to give him a formal greeting, then quickly seeming to think better of it. "You took a damned long time getting your miserable hide here, Daventry, but at least now you might be of some use to me. Let's move!"

Silently cursing Henry MacAfee, who had already gone to his heavenly reward and was probably perched on some silver-lined cloud right now, laughing at him, Banning pushed his murderous thoughts to one side as he entered the stall and took in the sight of the obviously frightened, tortured mare. Molly's great brown eyes were rolling in her head, her belly distorted almost beyond belief, her razor-sharp hooves a danger to both Prudence and himself.

"She's beginning to give up. We don't have much time," he said tersely as he tore off his signet ring and threw it into a mound of straw. "Hold her head tight, or we'll both be kicked to death."

"I know what to do," Prudence snapped back as she dropped to her knees beside the mare's head. "I'm just not strong enough to do it, damn it all to blazes!"

And then her tone changed, and her small features softened, as she leaned close to Molly's head, crooning to the mare in a low, sing-song voice that had an instant calming effect. She had the touch of a natural horsewoman, and Banning took a moment to be impressed before he, too, went to his knees, taking up his position directly behind those dangerous rear hooves.

Banning had no time to wash off his road dirt, and he didn't need to worry about greasing his arms to make for an easier entry, for there was more than enough blood to make his skin slick. He took a steadying breath and plunged both hands deep inside the mare, almost immediately coming in contact with precisely the wrong end of the foal.

"Sweet Christ!" he exclaimed, pressing one side of his head against the mare's rump, every muscle in his body straining as he struggled to turn the foal. His heart pounded, and his breathing grew short and ragged as the heat of the day and the sickening sweet smell of Molly's blood combined to make him nearly giddy. He could hear Prudence MacAfee crooning to the mare, promising that everything was going to be all right, her voice seemingly coming to him from somewhere far away.

But it wasn't going to be all right.

Too much blood.

Too little time.

It wasn't going to work. It simply wasn't going to work. Not for the mare, who was already too weak to help herself. And if he didn't get the foal turned quickly, he would have been too late all-round.

The thought of failure galvanized Banning, who had never been the sort to show grace in defeat. Redoubling his efforts, and nearly coming to grief when Molly gave out with a half-hearted kick of her left rear leg, he whispered a quick prayer and plunged his arms deeper inside the mare's twitching body.

"I've got him!" he shouted a moment later, relief singing through his body as he gave a mighty pull and watched as his arms reappeared, followed closely by the thin, wet face of the foal he held by its front legs. Molly's body gave a long, shuddering heave, and the foal slipped completely free of her, landing on Banning's chest as he fell back against the dirt floor of the stall.

He pushed the foal gently to one side and rose to his knees once more, stripping off his shirt so that he could wipe at the animal's wet face, urging it to breathe. Swiftly, expertly, he did for the foal what Molly could not do, concentrating his efforts on the animal that could still be saved. Endless, heart-clutching moments later, as the foal pushed itself erect on its spindly legs, he found himself nose to nose with the new creature and looking into two big, unblinking brown eyes that were seeing the world for the first time.

Banning heard a sound, then realized it was himself he heard, laughing. He reached forward to give the red foal a smacking great kiss squarely on the white blaze that tore a streak of lightning down its narrow face.

"Oh, Molly, you did it! You did it!" Prudence exclaimed, and Banning looked up to see her, still kneeling beside the mare's head, tears streaming down her dirty cheeks as she smiled widely enough that he believed he could see her perfect molars. "Daventry, you aren't such a pig after all! Henry wrote that you were the best of his chums, and now I believe him again."

As praise, it was fairly backhanded, but Banning decided to accept it in the manner it was given, for he was feeling rather good about himself at the moment. It was a sensation that lasted only until he took a good look at Molly, who seemed to be mutely asking his assistance even as Prudence continued to croon in her ear.

I know. I know. But, damn it, Molly, his brain begged silently, *don't look at me that way. Don't make me believe that you know, too.*

"Step away from her, Miss MacAfee," Banning intoned quietly as the foal, standing more firmly on his feet with every passing moment, nudged at his mother's flank with his velvety nose. "She has to get up. She has to get up now, or it will be too late."

Prudence pressed the back of one bloody hand to her mouth, her golden eyes wide in her grimy face. "No," she said softly, shaking her head with such vehemence that the cloth she had wrapped around her head came free, exposing a long tumble of thick, honey-gold hair. "No! She'll get up. You'll see. She'll get up. Oh, please, Molly, please get up!"

Banning understood Prudence's pain, but he also knew that the mare was already past saving, what was left of her life oozing from her, turning the sweet golden hay she lay in a sticky red. He couldn't let Prudence, his new charge, fall into pieces now, not when she had been so brave until this point.

Molly wouldn't have wanted that.

"Please leave the stall, Miss MacAfee," he ordered her quietly but sternly, already retracing his steps to fetch the pistol from his saddle.

She chased after Banning, pounding his back with her small fists, screaming invectives at him that would have done a foot soldier proud, her blows and her words having no impact other than to make him feel more weary, more heartsick than he had when Molly had looked up at him with a single, pleading eye.

He took the long pistol from its specially made holster strapped to his saddle and turned to face his young ward. He didn't like losing the mare any more than she did, but he had to make her see reason. To do that, he went on the attack.

"How old are you?" he asked sharply.

She paused in the act of delivering yet another punch.

"Eighteen!" she exclaimed, her expression challenging him to treat her as a hysterical child. "Old enough to run this farm, old enough to live on my own, and old enough to decide what to do with my own mare!"

He held out the pistol, which she stared at as if he might shoot her with it. Yet she stood her ground. He admired her for her courage, but he had to do something that would make her leave. When he spoke again, it was with the conviction that what he said would serve to make her run away.

"All right, Miss MacAfee. Prove it. The mare must be put down. She's hurting, and she's bleeding to death, and she shouldn't be made to suffer any more than she already has. Show me the adult you claim to be. Put Molly out of her pain."

He didn't know anyone could cry such great, glistening tears as the ones now running down Prudence's cheeks. He hadn't known that the sight of a small, quivering chin could make his knees turn to mush even as his heart died inside him. He found himself caught between wanting to push her to one side and go to the mare and pulling Prudence MacAfee hard against his chest and holding her while she sobbed.

"I'll do it," he said at last, just as she surprised him by raising a shaky hand and trying to grab the pistol. The sight of their two hands, stained with the blood of the dying mare, each of them clasping the pistol, brought him back to his senses. "I never meant for you to do it. And I'm sorry it has to be done at all. I'm truly, truly sorry."

"Go to blazes, Daventry," she shot back, sniffling, then grabbed the pistol from his hand and began slowly walking toward the stable, her shoulders squared, her chin high. Dressed in her stained breeches, and without the evidence of her long hair to prove the image wrong, she could have been a young man going off to his first battle, terrified that he might show his fear.

"Prudence," he called after her. "Angel," he said when she failed to heed him, "you don't have to do this."

She kept walking, and Banning wondered why he

didn't chase after her, wrest the pistol from her hand, and have done with it. But he couldn't move. He had put down his own horse when he was twelve, a mare he had raised from a foal, and he knew the pain, was familiar with the anguish of doing what was for the best and then living with the result of that fatal mercy. Molly was Prudence's horse. She was Prudence's pain.

The stable yard was silent for several minutes, so that when the report of the pistol blasted that silence, Banning flinched in the act of sluicing cold water from the pump over his face and head. His hands stilled as his head remained bowed, and then he went on with his rudimentary ablutions, keeping his head averted as Prudence MacAfee exited the stable, the pistol still in her hand. She returned the spent weapon, then placed his signet ring in his hand.

"If you'll assist me with settling the foal in a clean stall, I would appreciate it, as I can't seem to get it to move away from . . . from the body," she said stonily, and he noticed that her cheeks, although smudged, were now dry, and sadly pale. "And then, my lord Daventry, I would appreciate it even more if you would remount your horse and take yourself the bloody hell out of my life."

But Banning Talbot, marquess of Daventry, could not agree to Miss Prudence MacAfee's request. He had promised her brother that he would care for his "Angel." He had promised his sister he would fetch that same unwanted ward to Mayfair, where she could mold her into a simpering, giggling, die-away debutante.

He had promised a multitude of things to people he could neither contact nor refuse.

But the real trick of the thing, the promise he would find most difficult to keep, was the one he had made to himself—to stay as removed from the life of Prudence MacAfee as possible. To banish the image of this obstinate, headstrong, willful, profane, smudged-face "angel" from his mind and, eventually, his heart. . . .

Look for
The Passion of an Angel

Wherever Paperback Books Are Sold
Fall 1995